The Educated Ape and other Wonders of the Worlds

The Educated Ape and other Wonders of the Worlds

Robert Rankin

with illustrations by the author

GOLLANCZ

London

Copyright © Robert Rankin 2012
All rights reserved

The right of Robert Rankin to be identified as the author
of this work has been asserted by him in accordance with the
Copyright, Designs and Patents Act 1988.

First published in Great Britain in 2012 by Gollancz
An imprint of the Orion Publishing Group
Orion House, 5 Upper St Martin's Lane, London WC2H 9EA
An Hachette UK Company

A CIP catalogue record for this book is available
from the British Library

ISBN (Cased) 978 0 575 08641 8
ISBN (Export Trade Paperback) 978 0 575 08642 5

1 3 5 7 9 10 8 6 4 2

Typeset at The Spartan Press Ltd,
Lymington, Hants

Printed and bound by CPI Group (UK) Ltd,
Croydon, CR0 4YY

www.thegoldensprout.com

www.orionbooks.co.uk

THIS BOOK IS DEDICATED TO

FIELD COURT ACADEMY

YEAR FIVE

2010–2011

YOU WERE SO MUCH FUN TO BE WITH

'So little of what could happen, does happen.'

Salvador Dali

'History is not quite the way it was.'

Humphrey Banana

'Joy, joy moves the wheels
In the universal time machine.'

Friedrich Schiller
'Ode to Joy', 1785

1899

1

he Bananary at Syon House raised many a manicured eyebrow.

Although it was in its way the very acme of *fin de siècle* modernity, it so forcefully scorned the conventions of how a glass-house, intended for the cultivation of tropical fruit, *should* look as to cause tender ladies to reach for the smelling-salts.

Syon House itself was an ancient pile, the work of Robert Adam, embodying those classical features and delicate touches that define the English country house to create a dwelling both noble and stately. A venerable residence all can admire.

The Bananary, however, was something completely different. It boldly bulged from the rear of Syon House in an alarming fashion that troubled the hearts of those who dared to venture within, or viewed it from what was considered to be a safe distance.

The geometry was deeply wrong, the shape beyond grotesque. For although wrought from the traditional mediums of ironwork and glass, these materials had been tortured into such weird and outré shapes and forms as beggared a sane description. This was clearly not the work of Sir Joseph

Paxton, whose genius conceived the Crystal Palace. Nor was it that of Señor Voice, the London tram conductor turned architect whose radical confections were currently making him the toast of the town, and whose bagnio in Baker Street had been showered with awards by the Royal Institute of British Architects. The Bananary at Syon House left most folk lost for words.

One gentleman who was rarely lost for words was the Society Columnist of *The Times* newspaper. He had recently visited Syon House to conduct an interview with its owner Lord Brentford. His lordship had, four years earlier, been pronounced 'lost, believed dead', having gone down, as it were, on the *Empress of Mars* when she crashed into a distant ocean upon her maiden voyage. His apparent return from the dead had caused quite a sensation in the British Empire's capital. His horror at the Bananary, built in his absence and adjoined to the great house that was his by noble birth, had been – and still was – profound.

The Society Columnist of *The Times* had made a note of his lordship's quotable quotes.

'If this abomination is to be likened unto anything,' Lord Brentford had fumed, 'it is a brazen blousy harlot who has unwelcomely attached herself to the well-tailored coat of a distinguished elderly gentleman!'

'What manner of man,' Lord Brentford further fumed, 'could bring this blasphemy into being?'

'It is –' and here he employed a phrase that would be re-employed many years later by a prince amongst men '– a monstrous carbuncle upon the face of a much-loved friend.'

It would soon be torn down, Lord Brentford assured the Society Columnist, and he, Lord Brentford, would dance upon the scattered ruins as one would upon the grave of a conquered foe.

Strong words!

Exactly what the designer of the Bananary had to say about this was anybody's guess. But then he was *not* a reader of *The Times*, nor was he even a man.

He had, however, been born upon Earth, unlike many who, upon this warm summer's evening, gaped open-jawed at the Bananary and thronged the electrically illuminated gardens of Syon Park.

Fine and well-laid gardens, these, if perhaps overly planted with tall banana trees.

The moneyed and titled elite had come at Lord Brentford's request to celebrate his safe return and see him unveil his plans for a Grand Exposition: The Wonders of the Worlds. His lordship had spent his years in forced exile planning this extravaganza, and all, it was hoped, would soon be explained and revealed.

The great and the good were gathered here.

The rajahs and mandarins, princes and paladins,
Bankers and barons and Lairds of Dunoon,
The priest-kings and potentates, moguls of member states,
Even the first man who walked on the Moon.

As the Poetry Columnist of *The Times* so pleasantly put it.

Before going on to put it some more for another twenty-seven verses.

Here strolled emissaries and ecclesiastics from the planet Venus. Tall, imposing creatures these, gaunt, high-cheekboned and elegant, with golden eyes and elaborate coiffures. They gloried in robes of lustrous Venusian silks that swam with spectrums whose colours had no names on Earth.

The ecclesiastics were exotic beings of ethereal beauty

3

who had about them a quality of such erotic fascination that they all but mesmerised those men of Earth with whom they deigned to speak. Although their femininity appeared unquestionable, the nature of their sexuality had become the subject of both public debate and private fantasy. It was popularly rumoured that they were tri-maphrodite, being male and female and 'of the spirit', all in a single body. Nobody on Earth, however, knew for certain.

The ecclesiastics wore diaphanous gowns that afforded tantalising glimpses of ambiguous *somethings* beneath. From their delicate fingers they swung brazen censers upon long gilded chains, censers which this evening breathed queer and haunting perfumes into an air already overburdened by the heady fragrance of bananas.

The Ambassador of Jupiter was also present. Typical of his race, he was a fellow both hearty and rotund, given to immoderate laughter, extravagant gestures and a carefree disposition that most who met him found appealing. His skin, naturally grey as an elephant's hide, was this evening toned a light pink in a respectful mimicry of Englishness. His deep-throated chucklings rattled the upper panes of the Bananary, eliciting fears of imminent collapse from the faint-hearted but further mirth from himself and his Jovian entourage.

It was difficult not to like the Jovians. For although tensions between the three inhabited planets of this solar system – Venus, Jupiter and Earth – were oft-times somewhat strained, the jovial Jovians found greater favour amongst Londoners than the aloof and mysterious visitors from Venus.

Although there was that certain *something* about the ecclesiastics . . .

There were, of course, no Martians present at this glamorous soirée, for the Martian race was happily extinct!

The story of how this came about was known, in part, to almost every child in England, told as a bedtime tale to put them soundly asleep.

'Once upon a time,' so they were told, 'in the year eighteen eighty-five, Phnaarg, the evil King of Mars, declared war upon Earth and sent a mighty fleet of spaceships to attack the British Empire. These fearsome warships landed in Surrey and from them came terrible three-legged engines of death. The soldiers of the Crown fought bravely but could not best the Martians, who employed most wicked and ungentlemanly weapons against them. All would have been lost if not for patriotic bacteria in the service of Her Majesty the Queen, God bless her, which bravely killed the horrid invaders, and everyone lived happily ever after. Now go to sleep or I will give you a smack.'

Which was all well and good.

There was, however, a second half to this tale, but few were the children who ever heard it.

'To avoid the risk of further Martian attacks,' so the unheard half goes, 'Mr Winston Churchill took control of the situation and formulated a top-secret plan. With the aid of senior boffins Lord Charles Babbage and Lord Nikola Tesla, several of the abandoned Martian spaceships were converted for human piloting. They were then passengered by the incurables from the isolation hospitals of the Home Counties and dispatched to the Red Planet. It was effectively the birth of germ warfare, and it put paid to all the Martians of Mars.

'Thus the British Empire encompassed another world and Queen Victoria became Empress of both India and Mars. With the evil Martians now defeated, other inhabitants of the solar system came forward to establish friendly relations with Earth, which then joined Jupiter and Venus to form a family of planets.

'British engineering combined with captured Martian technology allowed Mr Babbage and Mr Tesla to take giant steps forwards in the field of science and by eighteen ninety-nine, the British Empire had reached the very height of its glory.

'The End.'

It was all in all an inspiring tale with a happy-ever-after, but not one that the British Government sought to publicise. The British Government felt that the British public would not take kindly to the business of the incurables from the isolation hospitals being sent off on their one-way trips to Mars.

The British 'public' were tonight notable only for their non-presence at Syon Park. The British Government, on the other hand, were most well represented.

The young and dashing Mr Winston Churchill was here, discussing the merits of Jovian cigars with the young and equally dashing Mr Septimus Grey, Governor of the Martian Territories. Sir Peter Harrow, a gentleman generally described on the charge-sheets as being the Member for North Brentford, conversed with the playwright Oscar Wilde regarding the conspicuousness of prostitution in the Chiswick area. 'Conspicuous by its absence,' was Sir Peter's considered opinion.

The controversial cleric Cardinal Cox shared a joke about beards and baldness with his cousin Kit, the celebrated monster-hunter and first man on the Moon. The Society Columnist from *The Times* had quite given up on writing down names from a guest list that read like a precis of

Debrett's and had taken instead to ogling the ladies and tasting the champagne and crisps.

Hired minions of the foreign persuasion moved amongst the exalted congress bearing trays of sweetmeats, petits fours and canapés. Champagne danced into cut-crystal glasses and ladies brought loveliness to a pretty perfection while Mazael's Clockwork Quartet did battle with the unearthly acoustics of the Bananary. The Moon shone down from a star-strewn sky and a distant church bell chimed the hour of nine.

All seemed right with the Empire upon this magical evening, all at peace and the way that all should be.

With such champagne and such nibbles and amidst such glittering company, the more charitable present could almost forgive the Bananary.

Almost.

But not quite.

But almost.

And as Lord Brentford strolled amidst the assembled multitude, bound for the flag-decked rostrum from which he would deliver a speech that had been four years in the preparation, it did not cross his mind that anything untoward might possibly occur to confound his schemes and spoil this grand occasion.

But sadly there can sometimes be a fly within the ointment, no matter how clean one has kept the pot or tightly screwed on the lid. For even as Lord Brentford strolled, his mind engaged in worthy thoughts, something that could truly be described as 'untoward' was rushing backwards through the aether, bound for Syon House.

No fly was this, although it flew.

For it was indeed a monkey.

A monkey that through its actions would come to change not only the present, but the past and the future, too.

Onwards rushed this anomalous ape.

As onwards strolled the oblivious Lord Brentford.

2

oth bearded and bald was Lord Brentford, yet oddly birdlike, too. His eyes were as dark as a raven's wing, his nose as hooked as a seagull's bill. His suit was cut from kiwi pelts and his burnished and buckled big black boots had trodden moors on pheasant shoots. His hands flapped somewhat as he spoke and he liked poached eggs for breakfast.

As he made his way to the flag-hung rostrum, as unaware as ever he had been of impending monkey mayhem, the crowd politely parted, polite converse ceased, polite applause rippled and the members of his household staff bowed their heads with politeness.

Upon his unexpected return to Syon House, the noble lord had been appalled not only by the beastly Bananary but also by the extraordinary number of servants the present incumbent had in his employ. There were pages and parlour maids, chore-boys and chambermaids, gentlemen's gentlemen, lackeys and laundrymen, kitchen boys, coachmen, porters and porch-men, bed-makers, tea-makers, chaplains and cheese-makers, carers and sweepers, cooks and housekeepers and even a eunuch who tended a parrot named Peter. Not to mention a veritable garrison of gardeners (all highly skilled in the arts of tropical horticulture, Lord Brentford noted).

To say that this multitude swarmed the great house and gardens like so many two-legged bees would be to paint an inaccurate picture of the situation. The majority of the minions draped themselves over settles and settees reading newspapers or playing games of Snap. To the now fiercely flapping Lord Brentford, it appeared that the present incumbent had, for reasons known only to himself, chosen to employ this substantial staff as little more than adornments to Syon House.

His lordship noted ruefully that the exception lay with the gardeners, whom he found to be hard at work cheerfully uprooting the century-old knot garden preparatory to the planting in of further banana trees.

Lord Brentford sacked each and every one upon the instant, then took down his now dust-cloaked double-action twelve-bore fowling piece from above the marble fireplace and went in search of the present incumbent.

The present incumbent, however, was not to be found. The staff, now packing their bags and cheerfully helping themselves to portions of his lordship's family silver, had little to offer regarding the present incumbent or his whereabouts.

During his search of the premises, Lord Brentford came upon a wardrobe containing a selection of the mystery fellow's clothes. Fine hand-tailored clothes were these, bearing the label of his lordship's Piccadilly tailor. This discovery now added mystery to mystery, for the missing person, this despoiler of English country houses, was clearly not as other men. The clothes had been tailored for a being who was positively dwarf-like, possessed of arms of a prodigious length and some kind of extra appendage that sprouted from his backside – for each pair of trousers bore a curious snood affair affixed to its rear parts.

Lord Brentford strutted, stormed and flapped from room to room, discharging his fowling piece into the frescoed ceilings, which helped to prompt a rapid departure by the servants he had so recently and unceremoniously dismissed.

At length, and with the aid of brandy from a bottle laid down fifty years before that had happily remained untouched in his cellar, he finally calmed himself to a state resembling that of reason and produced from his pocket a copy of *The Times*.*

Having located the section dedicated to *Domestics, for the hiring of*, he applied himself to the telephonic communication device that he of the freakish trousers had taken the liberty of having installed and demanded the operator connect him to Miss Dolly Rokitt, the proprietress of a Mayfair-based domestics agency.

Lord Brentford's requirements were swiftly made clear. He wished to employ the following.

A chef. 'And not a damned Johnny Frenchman.'

An upstairs maid. 'And make her a pretty 'un, not some frumpish strumpet.'

A monkey butler. 'Cos a gentleman ain't a gentleman without an ape to serve him.'

And a bootboy and general factotum. 'And get me one by the name of Jack, for such is the noble tradition. Or old charter. Or something.'

Miss Dolly Rokitt was politeness personified and replied with eagerness that just such a four-person staff had lately

* *For a gentleman would not conceive of journeying any distance at all without a copy of* The Times *to engage his intellect while travelling.*

been signed to her books and were even now crated up in her cellar awaiting a call such as his lordship was now making. So to speak.

'Then bung the boxes on a four-wheeled growler and dispatch them here post-haste,' was what his lordship had to say about that.

Miss Rokitt complied with these instructions and then returned to that dearest indulgence of feminine fingers, embroidery.

Lord Brentford poured himself another brandy and lazed in his family seat.

In truth, the concept of 'crating up' servants was a new one to him. But he had been away for a very long time and consequently was presently out of touch with many of the latest innovations, fashions and whatnots.*

His lordship shrugged his shoulders, rose to his feet and with all the grace of gait normally attributed to a Devonshire dancing duck set off in search of a crowbar.

Presently a four-wheeled growler crackled the gravel before Syon House and a cockney coachman, cheerful and chipper as any of his caste, stilled the horses, stepped from his conveyance, raised an unwashed hand and knocked with the unpolished knocker.

Presently the door swung open to reveal Lord Brentford, now somewhat far gone with the drink.

'Have at you, blackguard!' the inebriated nobleman declared, fumbling at the place where the hilt of his sword, had he been wearing one, would have been.

'No blackguard I, sir, guv'nor,' replied the cockney character, a-hitching up of his trousers and tipping his cap

---

* *The five-tier whatnot having lately superseded the four-tier version for reasons which, if not immediately obvious, probably had no bearing on anything at all.*

as a fellow must do when addressing himself to the gentry. 'But 'umble 'erbert is me name. Come as to deliver your staff.' And he gestured with a grubby mitt towards the four large packing crates that rested on his growler.

'Rumpty-tumpty,' said his lordship. 'Had you down as some Romany rogue, come to strip the lead off me roof. Sorry pardon and all the rest of it. Get 'em down from your wagon and hump 'em around to the servants' quarters.'

'That would be a two-man job,' observed the chirpy chappie.

'That would be a kick up your ragged arse,' Lord Brentford observed, 'if you don't do what you're told.'

'Right as ten-pence, guv'nor.'

Lord Brentford slammed shut the door.

The cockney coachman muttered certain words beneath his breath. Paeans in praise of the landed gentry, in all probability. Then he drove his growler around to the servants' quarters, shivering slightly at the sight of the Bananary, drew his horses to a halt and with the aid of his hobnailed boots relieved himself of his cargo. The job now done to his satisfaction, he stirred up the horses and left at a goodly pace.

Lord Brentford was forced to do his own unpacking. But he was pleased at least with what he had received: an upstairs maid who was spare and well kempt; a portly chef both bearded and bald; a monkey butler in waistcoat and fez; and a bootboy by the name of Jack.

A month had passed since this day and Lord Brentford had, during this time, managed to restore a degree of order to the chaos that had reigned in Syon House. Whether word of his return had reached he of the freakish trousers was unknown, but he had not returned and so had not been shot at.

★

Tonight, upon this special night, his lordship's new staff stood with heads bowed in politeness as Lord Brentford mounted the flag-bedecked rostrum and smiled upon all and sundry.

The all and sundry whose heads were not bowed returned smiles to the noble lord. The Jovian ambassador raised a thumb the size of a savoury sausage and offered words of well wishing.

'Cheers be unto thou, bonny lad,' he said.

Lord Brentford did that little cough which in the right kind of society indicates that silence is required, then formally greeted his guests.

'My lords, ladies and gentlemen,' he said. He would dearly have loved to have prefaced this with, 'Your Majesty,' but Queen Victoria had been unable to attend, having a previous engagement at a charity Wiff-Waff competition in which she was now through to the semi-finals.

'My lords, ladies and gentlemen. Emissaries and ecclesiastics of Venus. His Magnificence the Ambassador of Jupiter.' The ambassador broke wind, which caused some chucklings, but only amongst his entourage. 'I am honoured tonight by all your exalted presences. As you will know, I set off four years ago upon the maiden voyage of this world's greatest airship, the *Empress of Mars*, on a journey that was intended to girdle the globe in less than eighty days. That magnificent vessel of the sky came to a terrible end with many fine lives lost – a sad conclusion to what would have been a marvellous achievement. I was pitched into the sea and later found myself washed up on the beach of a cannibal isle. Alone was I and subject to the untender mercies of the savages. And well they might have dined upon me had not their instincts, base as they were, revealed to them that as an Englishman I was their natural superior. Within a month they had crowned me their King. Within two, I had taught them not only the Queen's English, but also the correct manner in which to lay out the knives and forks for a fish supper.'

There was hearty applause at this, for which his lordship politely paused.

Lord Brentford continued, 'The island was many miles from the nearest shipping lanes and if I was to return safely to England, it became apparent that a seagoing craft would need to be constructed. Under my direction the savages built such a craft. With only the most primitive of tools at my disposal and a willing though unskilled workforce, this task took more than three years to complete.

'My ship, the *Pride of Syon*, is now berthed at Greenwich.'

Considerable applause followed this disclosure. Although one or two folk appeared to be finding interest in the Heavens.

Lord Brentford continued once more. 'During my time upon the island, when not educating the natives or super-vising their shipbuilding, I had pause to think long and hard of our Queen and our Empire.'

There was some applause at this but more folk now appeared concerned with the dark sky above.

'We stand now upon the pinnacle of history, on the threshold of the twentieth century. Great achievements have been attained, but greater still are yet to come. It is my firm conviction that at this special time a Grand Exposition should be held, to exhibit the Wonders of the Worlds. Just as the Great Exhibition of eighteen fifty-one displayed the marvels of art and of industry of this world, so, then, the Grand Exposition will showcase the skills and sciences of the three worlds – Venus, Jupiter and Earth.'

The Venusians displayed enigmatic expressions. The Jovians applauded with vigour.

'More than this, I contend—' But here Lord Brentford

paused, for more and more folk were now gazing skywards. Gazing and pointing and shifting about in unease.

'What of this?' The noble lord surveyed the crowd, then turned and raised his eyes towards the sky. 'Oh goodness me!'

Lord Brentford fled. He took to his heels with hands a-flapping and his legs goose-stepping, too. Not alone in this was he, for now the crowd was all in a panic, making to escape as best they could according to their capabilities, running, screaming, tripping and falling, spreading as some human tsunami across the lawns and gardens. Away, away to escape what was to come.

And what was to come was tumbling down from above. It was a dark and terrible something, as would strike much fear in all who saw it coming. Down and down it tumbled, end over end, falling, falling, down and down.

Those who saw it knew it for the awful thing it was.

A battered Martian man-o'-war, such as was last seen during the Martian invasion.

Down it came, this horrible ship of space, this ugly vessel built only for war, moving now, it appeared, in slow motion, but moving ever down.

Until finally it struck planet Earth with a mighty explosion, a rending and mashing of metal and glass, of blood and bones and who knew what else. It rolled, it skewed, it swerved, it crashed, and finally it came to rest its terrible self upon the Bananary.

3

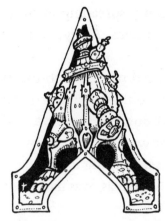

n unholy silence prevailed in the gardens of Syon.

A silence broken periodically by the occasional tinkling of glass, the settling of stonework and the woebegone grindings of clockwork. For Mr Mazael's Clockwork Quartet now had a spaceship upon it.

Gone, all gone, were the glitterati who had adorned the gardens with their fragrant presences. Now but four folk stood amongst the ruin and the mess, four folk who would probably be expected to play a major part in tidying it up: a portly chef, an upstairs maid, a monkey butler in a fez and a bootboy factotum named Jack. As Lord Brentford had neglected to issue them with instructions to run for their lives, these obedient servitors to the noble one remained standing where they had been told to stand, with heads politely bowed.

In truth not all of them were standing, and those who were, were not quite as clean and tidy as they had previously been. The spacecraft's concussion had blown off the upstairs maid's bonnet, the portly chef's bald head was smutted and the monkey butler had been toppled from his feet. He lay now with his legs in the air, but his head was still bowed in politeness. And he still had on his fez.

The portly chef spoke first. He cleared his throat and said, 'This is a pretty pickle, to be sure.'

The upstairs maid, both spare and kempt, said nothing.

The bootboy, being cockney, tried to see the brighter side. 'Well, if that ain't saved 'is lordship the price of a gang of navvies to knock down that there Bananary, you can poach my Percy in paraffin and use me for a teapot.' Stealing a glance at the ruination, he added, 'Strike me pink.'

The portly chef sighed deeply.

'If it's Martians,' the bootboy piped up, 'I'll go and cough on 'em – I've a touch of consumption on me. That'll teach the blighters to come back.'

'It is not Martians,' said the portly chef. 'I perceive this to be a Martian craft converted for use as a pleasure vessel. There will be men aboard this craft, not Martians.'

'Men, is it, guv'nor?' the bootboy chirped. 'And perceiving it that you're a-doing? What's all that about, then?'

'There is something familiar about that spaceship,' said the chef, helping the monkey butler to his feet and dusting him down around and about. 'Are you uninjured?' he asked of the ape.

The monkey butler looked somewhat startled, but as he *was* a monkey, he had nothing to say.

'I suggest we enter the spaceship and tend to any survivors,' said the chef.

'You might be wrong with your perceiving there, guv'nor,' the bootboy had to say. 'Best we all just 'ave a good old cough then 'ave it away on our toes.'

'Follow me,' ordered the chef and, turning to the upstairs maid, he said, 'You should wait here, my dear.'

The upstairs maid remained silent and the chef took the

monkey's hand. If the monkey harboured any doubts, none were apparent from his expression. He ran his long and pointy tongue around his lips. There now were a very large number of squashed bananas in the wreckage of the Bananary.

'Follow me,' said the portly chef. The monkey butler and the bootboy followed.

The Martian hulk was a sturdy affair, and the collision with a glass-house had barely dented it. Some of the paint-work looked a bit scratched here and there, but the enam-elled Union Jack and the nameplate were intact. The chef read from the nameplate. 'The *Marie Lloyd*,' he read. 'That rings a bell with me somewhere.'

The bootboy slipped on a banana skin and fell upon his bottom. The monkey butler laughed at this, for the classic humour of a man slipping upon a banana skin transcends all barriers of race and species.

'Ain't funny,' said the bootboy, struggling up.

The chef placed a plump palm upon the spaceship's hull. 'Hardly warm,' said he. 'It has therefore not plunged down from outer space.'

The bootboy tapped the hull. 'Anyone 'ome?' he called.

'Best display a modicum of caution,' said the chef. 'Stand back, if you will.'

The chef threw the emergency release bolts of the space-ship's entry port with a degree of expertise that surprised even himself. There was a hiss as atmospheres within and without equalised, then the port dropped down to form an entry ramp.

'Perhaps both of you should remain here,' the chef told the boy and the monkey. 'If folk are injured, their injuries may not be pleasing to behold.'

The monkey butler munched a banana.

The bootboy said, 'I ain't never been upon no spaceship. I'll come in there with you, if you please.'

'And you?' the man asked the monkey.

The monkey made a puzzled face, then twitched his sensitive nostrils.

'Ah,' said the chef. 'You smell something, do you?'

The monkey glanced up and a strange look came into his eyes.

'We had better make haste,' said the chef. 'Come on.'

Many of the Martian spaceships, abandoned by their occupants when they were struck dead by Earthly bacteria, had been re-engineered for human piloting. The British Government had taken control of all these spaceships and as they had only landed in England, this meant that the British Government now had effective control over *all* human space travel. This caused considerable complaints from other countries, notably the United States of America, who insisted that they should have a share of the captured technology.

Knowing what was best for all, Queen Victoria decreed that space travel and the exploration of other worlds would remain the preserve of the British Empire. And also decreed that the one and only spaceport on Earth would be constructed in Sydenham on lands beneath the Crystal Palace. The Royal London Spaceport.

A number engraved beneath the name the *Marie Lloyd* indicated that the crashed spaceship was registered there, rather than at one of the many spaceports on Venus or Jupiter.

The chef stepped up the entry ramp and entered the fallen ship. The bootboy followed him then whistled, for just as most boys of the Empire had been told the bedtime story of the Martian invasion, so too had most boys read comics that displayed cut-away diagrams of spaceships' interiors.

'This ain't right,' said the bootboy. 'What's all this 'ow's-yer-father?'

For how's-your-father there was a-plenty. The interior of the *Marie Lloyd* had been stripped bare of all its fixtures and fittings, along with the dividing walls between cabins, saloons and 'excuse-me's', and within was crammed a vast array of complicated electrical gubbinry. Tall glass tubes that flashed with miniature lightning storms. Cables and copper coils. Intricate panels sewn with valves that pulsated as if in time to a human heartbeat. Many and various wonders and weirderies of the modern persuasion. Bits and bobs were sparking and smoking and there was a definite sense that the whole damn kit and caboodle was likely at any moment to erupt in a devastating explosion.

'No sign of any passengers or crew,' said the portly chef, fanning at the air. 'Best have a look in the cockpit.'

He edged warily towards the prow of the crashed vessel. The monkey butler followed and Jack the bootboy tinkered away with things he should not be touching.

'Don't do that,' the chef called over his shoulder. 'And be prepared to run if the need arises.'

The door to the cockpit was jammed, so the chef put his shoulder to it. For a portly fellow the chef was surprisingly strong. The door, a panelled-oak affair, gave up an unequal struggle and toppled from its hinges into the cockpit beyond. The chef then entered the cockpit, dusting himself down as he did so.

Then he came to a halt.

'Oh my,' said he. 'Oh my.'

'Dead 'un, is it?' called the bootboy. ' 'Ead knocked orf or somethin'?'

'Wait where you are,' the chef called back and took another step forwards.

Within the cockpit was a pair of seats, one apiece for pilot and co-pilot. Only one of these was occupied and this by a curious being slumped over the controls spread out before him. He was small and slight and wore a one-piece silver suit with a modern zip-fastener running up the front. A single glance told the portly chef that this being was not human. The chef stepped forwards and lifted him carefully, setting him back in his seat. A face looked up, a hairy face, small eyes blinked and a broad mouth opened and closed.

'A monkey,' whispered the portly chef. 'A monkey pilots this craft.'

The monkey butler took a step forward. Then took another one back.

'There is nothing to be afraid of,' said the chef, and he stroked the pilot's head. This remark might well have been addressed to both monkeys. The one in the seat made coughing sounds, while the other looked somewhat upset.

The monkey pilot gazed up at the portly chef. The monkey pilot was old, his hair grey, the skin of his face and his hands lined with age. He opened his mouth and raised a withered palm.

'You are thirsty,' said the chef. 'Jack, fetch water, if you will.'

'I'm not your servant,' said the bootboy.

'Then let me put it another way. Fetch water now or I will box you brutally about the ears.'

'Your word is my command, guv'nor,' said the willing lad. 'Though if you'll take my advice when it's offered, you'd best 'ave it out of 'ere afore the 'ole thing goes up in a ruddy big bang.'

'Water!' ordered the portly chef.

22

The bootboy left at the trot.

'I think there is truth in his words, though,' said the chef to the monkey pilot. 'We'd best get you out of here. Have no fear, for I will carry you.'

The aged monkey shook his aged head and coughed a little, and then, 'I cannot leave the ship,' he said.

The chef jumped back a pace in amazement.

'There is something you must have,' croaked the monkey.

'You speak.' The chef's befuddled head was fiercely shaking now.

'No time to explain. You must take the letter.'

'The letter?' The chef stilled his shaking head and gaped at the monkey pilot.

'It will explain everything. You must not open it. Just take it to the address written upon it.'

'Where is this letter?' asked the chef.

'Here.' And the monkey pilot gestured to his heart.

The chef leaned down, unzipped the silver suit and drew out an envelope. He glanced at the name upon it. That name was Ernest Rutherford. The monkey butler peered towards the pilot.

The pilot glimpsed the butler. And the pilot smiled.

'So young,' he whispered. 'Ah, so long ago.'

'What was that?' asked the chef. But now a noisy kerfuffle was to be heard.

'Out of my way, you foolish boy,' called the voice of Lord Brentford.

'Hide the envelope,' whispered the pilot. But the portly chef was already doing so. 'Now go, my friend, just go.'

'Your friend?'

Lord Brentford burst into the cockpit. He clutched his double-action twelve-bore fowling piece and this he waved about in a furious fashion.

'What the devil?' cried his lordship. 'I gave you no permission to—'

'The pilot is injured,' said the chef. 'He needs medical assistance.'

'*Medical assistance?*' His lordship was fuming once more. 'Crashes a damned spaceship into me ancient pile. Ruins me party—'

'He needs our help,' said the chef.

'Get out!' roared his lordship. 'I shall deal with this.'

'Treat him gently—'

'Will you get *out*! Do something useful – fetch me a brandy. Out now, you, and take me butler, too.'

The chef took the monkey butler by a hairy hand. The monkey butler gazed towards the simian space pilot and his other hand reached out to touch the ancient ape.

'Best not,' said the chef. And, 'You will be all right,' he told the pilot. 'Farewell for now.'

'Farewell for now?' roared and fumed Lord Brentford. '*Out!*'

The chef led the monkey butler from the spaceship. The party folk were creeping back, peeping from behind trees, whispering to one another.

The monkey butler tugged at the hand of the chef.

'What is it?' the chef asked. 'You want to go back?'

A look of alarm was on the face of the monkey. And before the chef could say another word there came a terrible sound from within the spaceship.

The sound of his lordship's fowling piece.

Both barrels fired and then silence.

4

rnest Rutherford, First Baron Rutherford of Nelson, was a man of his Age. He was also a man who was truly ahead of his time. The Victorian period cast before the world a plethora of notable geniuses: Charles Babbage, Albert Einstein, Nikola Tesla and Mr Rutherford. Men who helped to shape their own Age and future Ages, too.

Mr Rutherford was a chemist, New Zealand born, who had come to settle in London. Early on in his career he had discovered the concept of the radioactive half-life. He differentiated and named both alpha and beta radiation and it was for work within this field that he would later go on to win a Nobel Prize.

The year of eighteen ninety-nine found him inhabiting a large Georgian house in South Kensington, within which he conducted a number of groundbreaking experiments, most of which involved a lot of electricity and a great deal of noise. He was not a man popular with his neighbours.

Upon a summer's morning of that year, with a nearby church clock chiming the hour of ten, there came a knocking upon Mr Rutherford's front door. On his doorstep stood two figures. One was a bald and bearded chef, the other a monkey butler. Mr Rutherford's front door swung open and something-or-other peeped out.

'Good morning,' said the chef in a cheerful fashion. 'We wish to speak with your master.'

'Go away, you beastly things.' The something put his shoulder to the door.

'I believe it to be most important.' The chef put his foot in the door, as might a travelling salesman.

'Remove your foot,' cried the something, 'or I will fetch a carving knife and slice it off at the ankle.'

'Enough of that, Jones.' A sound was heard as of hand striking a head and then the door swung wide. 'My apologies,' said a tall, distinguished personage with a luxuriant moustache and piercing grey eyes. He wore a white work apron over a well-cut morning suit and a pair of rubber gauntlets, the right one of which he was struggling to remove. 'May I help you, sir?' he asked. 'I regret that if you are of the religious persuasion and here to solicit funds, I must disappoint you. My earnings are insufficient to permit largesse, but I offer you my warmest wishes. Which in their way, I feel you will agree, are quite beyond price.'

He paused to let his words sink in.

The portly chef just shook his head and the monkey butler gawped.

'Sir,' said the chef, producing the envelope. 'I was given this to hand to you. I was instructed not to open it. I believe, although I cannot be certain as to the source of my belief, that it contains something *most* important.'

Mr Rutherford, for it was indeed he, gazed at the man who stood upon his doorstep. 'I know you, sir,' said he. 'We have met before. I never forget a face, but—'

The chef shook his head once more.

'The beard is strange to me,' said Mr Rutherford, and with that said he took the envelope. The man and the monkey watched him as he tore it open, removed its contents and gave these contents perusal.

Then Mr Rutherford gasped and said, 'Surely this cannot be!' He then stared hard at his visitors. 'What is your name, sir?' he asked.

'My name?' said the chef, and he thought about this. 'My name is Chef,' he said.

'Chef? Just Chef? Are you sure?'

'I am confused,' said the chef, and he was. 'My name is "Chef",' he said once more.

'Come in quickly, now,' said Mr Rutherford. 'We must speak of this in private. No one else must know of the matters we are about to discuss.'

The chemist ushered his visitors within and closed the door behind them. 'Jones,' he called, 'come here.'

They were standing in an elegant hallway, its walls made pleasant with framed watercolours depicting the landscapes that their owner had known in his childhood. A stuffed kiwi bird stared sightlessly from a showcase and a similarly stuffed Maori warrior served as a decorative hatstand. The chef raised his eyes to the Maori.

Mr Rutherford sighed. 'Rather tasteless, I agree,' he said, 'but a present from my mother to remind me of home. Jones – where are you, Jones?' he called.

The something-or-other poked its head through a banister of a broad staircase that swept up from the hall to numerous bedrooms above. 'I'm in charge here now,' it said.

'Yes,' said Mr Rutherford with a smile, 'of course you are. But please, employ the innate dignity and humility of the superior being you are and indulge this gross creature by bringing himself and his guests a pot of tea and some biscuits.'

The something named Jones made a face of perplexity, then sloped off to the kitchen.

'What exactly *is* that?' asked the chef. 'I do not believe I have ever seen anything quite like it before.'

'Except perhaps within the pages of fairy-tale books,' replied Mr Rutherford. 'It is indeed a troll.'

'A troll?' asked the chef. 'As in a goblin or a bugaboo?'

'They are all very much of a muchness, although they would have you believe otherwise. Each specimen has an inflated opinion of its own importance. One has to step warily when dealing with trolls.'

'So how did you come by it?' asked the chef. 'Another gift from your mother?'

Mr Rutherford laughed. 'Not a bit of it,' he said. 'Jones, how shall I put this, "came through" during the course of an experiment.'

'I have no idea as to what you might mean by *that*,' said the chef.

'And nor should you. But all will shortly be revealed, and not, I fear, in a manner entirely to your liking.'

The chef looked queerly at the chemist. 'Strange as it may sound,' he said, 'I do have the odd feeling that our paths have crossed before.'

'Oh, indeed they have,' said Mr Rutherford. 'And you, young sir,' he said to the ape, 'do you recall our meetings?'

The ape looked blankly at the man.

'He cannot speak,' said the chef. 'Although—'

'Although you recently encountered one who could? Which means that the experiment was a success. Where is the pilot now?'

'The pilot?' said the chef. 'Why, he is . . .' And he lowered his eyes. 'A terrible business,' he whispered.

'Oh, I am so very sorry. But come along now, do. The two of you must be "de-programmed", as it were. Then you will understand everything. Well, not everything, but a great deal more than you do right now, which is better than knowing only a small part, or no part at all, is it not? Yes, indeed it is.'

Mr Rutherford led the man and the monkey to a large metal-bound door adorned with many padlocks and with the words DANGER KEEP OUT posted upon it in letters large and red.

'I have misinformed Jones that a dragon dwells within,' said Mr Rutherford, 'and although he can get quite worked up thinking about dragons, he happily lacks the courage actually to confront one.'

The portly chef just shook his head, for he was most confused.

Mr Rutherford produced a ring of keys, selected one and turned it in the keyhole of the door. 'Done,' he said, swinging open the door. 'The padlocks are just for show. Inside, please, if you will.'

The chef and the monkey entered, then Mr Rutherford entered, too, locking the door behind him when he had done so.

The chef threw up his hands and said, 'How will your troll present us with the tea?'

'He won't,' said Mr Rutherford. 'He will do what he always does − go to the kitchen, think about things, then decide that he is being hard done by and that the making of tea is beneath his dignity. Then he will sit and have a good sulk. He will do that for an hour.'

'So we won't get our tea?' asked the chef.

'Nor will we be bothered by *him*,' said the chemist. 'But tea, I think, is hardly the thing. We must toast the success of the project with champagne.'

They stood now in a cosy sitting room upon a delicately patterned Persian carpet woven from wood fibre laid over a floor of varnished beech. The walls were panelled with pitch pine and the furniture was of mahogany. A fireplace was fashioned from gopher wood and fragrant logs burned in the fireplace.

The chef gazed about and so did the monkey.

So, too, did the chemist. 'I know what you are thinking,' he said. 'It's all a bit "woody", but that's a necessity with so much electricity bouncing about the place at times. Dry wood is a poor conductor, you see. The chances of you receiving a fatal voltage when you sit down are meagre.' The chemist smiled. Encouragingly.

The chef sighed and the monkey shrugged and then the two of them sat down upon an oak settle. It was not particularly comfortable, but as it lowered the chances of a fatal voltage to meagreness, it would do for now.

Mr Rutherford took himself over to a rosewood cabinet and drew from it a Gladstone bag. 'I will have to know how it was done so that I can undo it,' he said.

'I would really appreciate an explanation,' said the chef. 'And if it is not being too nosy of me, might I know what the envelope I brought you contains?'

'The latter is simple,' said Mr Rutherford. 'Well, to a degree. It is a letter. The latter is a letter,' said he, and smiled once more.

'Written by whom?' asked the chef.

'By me,' said Mr Rutherford.

'Ah,' said the chef. 'That does not lessen my confusion.'

'Nor will me telling you that the letter was written – or

rather *will* be written – six months from now. It is a letter from the future. The first of its kind, I do believe. But not, I trust, the last.'

'Ah,' said the chef once more. 'I think my companion and I should now take our leave.'

'Do you know your companion's name?' asked Mr Rutherford.

The chef gave his bald head a scratch. 'I know him only as "monkey",' he said.

'Indeed.' Mr Rutherford nodded. 'And again I say that in order to undo what has been done to you, I must first know how it was done.' He removed a stethoscope from the Gladstone bag and approached the chef with it. 'You see, my friend,' he said, 'and you *are* my friend, as we know each other quite well – you have been mesmerised, or otherwise put into a state of unknowing by a person or persons unknown. Your name is *not* "Chef", and your partner's name is *not* "monkey". Your name is Cameron Bell and you are the Empire's foremost consulting detective. This fellow here is your partner. His real name is Darwin, although for professional purposes he prefers to call himself Humphrey Banana. He holds the distinction of being the world's first and only talking ape.'

The chef, whose name might possibly be Bell, gawped at the chemist. 'This is madness,' was what he had to say.

'Madness?' said Mr Rutherford. 'Then you just wait until I free your memory and you recall the rest.'

'I am a chef,' said the portly fellow. 'I am a chef and my duty is to serve.'

'Hold hard,' said Mr Rutherford, and he hung his stethoscope about his neck, returned once more to his rosewood cabinet and plucked from it a newspaper. 'I kept this,' he said. 'I did not know why, but now perhaps I do. Here – see for yourself.'

And with this said he handed the newspaper to the now thoroughly befuddled chef. The newspaper was a copy of *The Times* dated one year previously.

ANOTHER VANISHMENT

ran the headline. Beneath this was a photograph of a gentleman who bore an uncanny resemblance to the illustrator Boz's representations of Mr Pickwick.

THE EMPIRE'S FOREMOST
CONSULTING DETECTIVE MISSING
POLICE BAFFLED

ran the copy beneath.

'I have a beard,' said the bald and bearded chef. 'Although the resemblance is—'

'Uncanny?' said the chemist. 'And so it should be, for the picture is of *you*.'

'And I am in partnership with . . . ?'

'Darwin,' said Mr Rutherford, 'or Humphrey Banana, as he prefers to be known.'

'For professional purposes?'

'Precisely.'

'And he is the world's one and only talking ape?'

Mr Rutherford nodded his head.

'But I've met another.'

Mr Rutherford shook his head.

'I did,' said the man who might be Cameron Bell.

'You did *not*,' said Mr Rutherford. 'The pilot was the same ape.'

'The *same* ape?' The now somewhat bewildered man stared down at the monkey butler.

'The self-same talking ape,' said the chemist. 'The pilot of the world's first time machine.'

5

t is always for the best if things are explained precisely. Clearly, unambiguously, with clarity. With perspicuity. Then there cannot be the slightest fear of confusion.

'I *am* confused,' said the man who might be Cameron Bell. 'I am *very* confused.'

'All right,' said Mr Rutherford. 'Then let us take this one step at a time. I feel confident that I can restore you both to your previous selves and return to you your memories. But first let me explain to you about the time-ship.'

'This would be your time machine, would it?' The chef-or-not did rollings of the eyes.

'Such a reaction is to be expected.' Mr Rutherford returned once more to his rosewood cabinet and this time drew from it a bottle of vintage champagne and three fluted glasses.

'Château Doveston,' said the possible-detective. 'I recognise the label.'

'Some things stay forever in the memory,' said Mr Rutherford, 'the fragrance of a well-loved wife and the taste of a fine champagne being two of them.' The chemist uncorked the bottle and poured the golden sparkly stuff into the three fluted glasses. He handed one to the bearded man, another to the monkey.

'Let me tell you a little story,' said Mr Rutherford, taking up his own glass. 'It is all about theory and putting theory into practice.'

The bearded man sipped his champagne and considered that there were probably worse ways than this of spending a morning. 'Go ahead, sir,' said he.

'Have you ever heard of the Large Hadron Collider?' asked the chemist.

A bald head took to shaking.

'It is a highly technical piece of scientific equipment and I have supervised the building of one right here beneath the capital.'

The bald head nodded thoughtfully. The monkey sneezed due to bubbles up the nose.

'A hadron,' said the chemist, 'is, simply put, a composite particle composed of quarks held together by something called "strong force". Which is to say one of the four basic interactions of nature, the others being electromagnetism, weak interaction – which is responsible for the radioactive decay of subatomic particles – and gravitation, of course.'

'Of course,' said he of the beard.

'You understand such matters?' queried the chemist.

'Not in the slightest, no.'

'Hmm.' Mr Rutherford sipped champagne. 'The Large Hadron Collider is a particle accelerator designed to enhance our understanding of some of the deepest laws of nature. Well, *my* understanding, at least. Imagine if you will a tunnel, fashioned into a loop. Particles are accelerated around it via a process known as the transperambulation of pseudo-cosmic anti-matter which results in a cross-polarisation of the beta particles and a—'

'I will have to stop you there,' said the bald and bearded fellow. 'Your words are as of a foreign language to me. I understand only that you have supervised the construction of something called a Large Hadron Collider beneath the streets of London. Might I enquire as to whether it is safe?'

'As far as we can tell,' said the chemist, finishing his champagne and recharging his glass with more. 'After all, people use it every day.'

'The technicians who work upon it?'

'The travellers who travel through it.'

'Excuse me, sir?' said the man of beard and baldness, holding out his glass to be refilled.

'Londoners call it the Circle Line,' said Mr Rutherford. 'They do not know it for the thing it truly is. Our experiments are run at night, when the trains are safely in their engine sheds.'

'Remarkable,' said the bald bearder. 'And thank you for the champagne.'

The chemist nodded. 'There sometimes needs to be a degree of, how shall I put this . . . *disinformation* is probably the best word. The Government and the scientific bodies involved in the funding of the project have not been informed as to the true nature of its purpose. It appears to be a tool to further our understanding of the universe, but it is of course nothing of the kind.'

'Of course.' The baldy bearded one downed more champagne.

'It is all to do with time and the speed of light. It is believed that if one could travel faster than light, then one would travel faster than time. Depending on how you chose to apply this, one could travel either into the past or into the future.'

'So the Large Hadron Collider is really a time machine?'

'*Part* of a time machine. The motive power. You encountered the travelling element when the actual time-ship crashed in Syon Park.'

'I did not tell you *that*,' said the champagne-supper, who could at least remember *that* with precision.

'It is in the letter you delivered to me. The time-ship was aimed there because you and I, and indeed Darwin, too—' he gestured to the ape, who had finished his champagne and was now wearing a foolish face '—knew that last night you and Darwin would be at Syon House.'

'I am not sure that your explanations are actually explaining anything.' The man who owned to a beard and baldness held out his glass for a further topping-up and received same.

'Then I will do my best to keep it as simple as I can. Regarding the time-ship, know this. The speed of light is presently calculated to be one hundred and eighty-six thousand, two hundred and eighty-two miles per second – a goodly speed by anybody's reckoning and one it would be difficult to best. The true purpose of this Large Hadron Collider is to slow the speed of light down to a velocity at which a conveyance designed for the purpose might outpace it in relative safety.'

'A fanciful notion, but one of extreme cleverness.' Podgy fingers toasted with the champagne glass.

'I pride myself on my ability to look at things from a different perspective.' The chemist located further champagne and took to its uncorking.

'Might I ask a question?' Podgy fingers held out the champagne glass for further refilling. 'If what crashed into the Bananary at Syon House was a ship of time rather than a ship of space, why was it piloted by a monkey? And if it is one and the same monkey as the monkey here—' the monkey here held out his champagne glass '—why was the monkey in the time-ship old? For he was an aged ape.'

'Old?' said Mr Rutherford. 'Indeed?' said Mr Rutherford. 'I regret that I cannot answer questions which refer to things that will happen in the future,' said Mr Rutherford. 'I think the thing would be for me to examine the time-ship with great care. You must understand that at present it is only in the first stages of construction. If I was to see what the finished article looks like, it might speed up the construction process considerably.'

The man with bald and beardness made a certain kind of a face and knocked back more champagne.

'You believe I might encounter a temporal anomaly by so doing? Affect a singularity that might destabilise the atoms of the universe?'

'Not as such.'

'Then what?'

'You have not, I trust, read the morning papers?'

Further champagne was danced around. The chemist shook his head.

'Then you will not know that the time-ship no longer exists. Lord Brentford entered it and shot the pilot. The cockpit of that craft was perhaps not the best place to discharge a firearm.'

'Some damage was done?'

'Some damage, yes. The time-ship exploded. It was utterly destroyed. The main reason I came here today, aside from delivering your envelope unopened – a tribute, may I say, to my honesty and steadfastness – was to enquire whether you might offer myself and monkey here positions in your household. With Lord Brentford lying upon what might well be his death-bed in hospital, we are presently unemployed.'

Ernest Rutherford, First Baron Rutherford of Nelson, dropped down upon a three-legged milking stool that lacked for comfortable cushioning and made a face of complete and utter despair. 'The time-ship gone, lost,' he said, and his chin sank onto his chest. 'And a noble lord mortally injured. Calamity.'

'Don't forget the monkey,' said the unemployed fellow.

'Naturally not.' Mr Rutherford sought to affect a brave face. 'But now we know that the theory is sound. That the time-ship will function. That it *has* in fact functioned. And when you are returned to the soundness of your mind, perhaps together we can mould the future in such a way that these tragic events do not occur. What say you to this?'

'I fear that I am somewhat drunk,' came a slurred reply.

'Myself, too, as it happens,' admitted Mr Rutherford. 'But no matter.' Champagne was sloshed into glasses and the chemist returned once more to his rosewood cabinet. 'We will start with the less toxic and dangerous memory restoratives,' he said, 'and if these prove ineffective we will raise the bar, as it were, and move on to the downright lethal.'

'Your words are pure confusion,' said the man without the hair. 'But I would like to recommend myself for the position of chef. I have extensive knowledge of both Venusian and Jovian cuisine. My fillet of six-toed Nunbuck will find no equal in London.' Lord Brentford's ex-chef now became loquacious regarding his culinary skills, even recommending 'monkey's' adeptness in the art of the cocktail. 'Might I have a tad more champagne, please?' he asked at his conclusion.

'As much as you like, my dear fellow.' Mr Rutherford now approached with an unsteady sort of a gait. 'Just get fifty milligrams of this inside you and we'll see what's what.'

'What's that?'

'What's *what*?'

Mr Rutherford lunged forwards and rammed a hypodermic needle deep into the portly fellow's ample left shoulder.

'Ouch,' went the portly fellow. 'What in the world have you done?'

'It comes from the Amazon,' said Mr Rutherford, swaying slightly as he did so.

'What does?' asked the portly fellow, rubbing at his shoulder. 'What comes from the Amazon?'

'Water, mostly, I suppose. It discharges into the sea.'

'That isn't what I meant and you know it.' The portly fellow drained his glass and stumbled over to the newest champagne bottle which was located upon an occasional table, built from wood to serve at any occasion. 'You've spiked me,' he said.

The monkey screamed and bared his teeth.

'And spiked the monkey, too.'

'It might work,' said Mr Rutherford, nimbly evading the monkey's snapping teeth. 'After all, it *is* from the Amazon.'

'I feel somewhat queer,' said the man who now held the champagne bottle in an unsteady hand. 'You have poisoned me, sir, and I will have satisfaction. Fetch a brace of pistols, if you dare.'

Mr Rutherford was swaying more than slightly now. 'This really is *very* strong champagne,' he said in the tone known as 'tipsy'. 'Good stuff, though, don't you think?'

'I think that I am going to be sick.'

'Please do it in the wooden bowl,' said Mr Rutherford.

The portly bald and bearded ex-chef, and possibly the world's foremost consulting detective, staggered about clutching at his head. Something very odd was going on inside it.

'I think it is starting to work,' said Mr Rutherford. 'The endorsements for effectiveness on the bottle of ACME PATENT AMAZON-REMEDY UNIVERSAL MEMORY RESTORATIVE may well prove to be all they claim.'

'Oooh,' and, 'Aaah,' went the chef of mystery.

'Squeak,' and, 'Squawk,' went the monkey and he bobbed up and down.

Within the heads of man and monkey light pierced darkness, rushing forward, all-embracing, flooding over everything.

'Oh my dear dead mother,' cried Mr Cameron Bell. 'It's coming back. It's coming back. Oh yes, I remember it all.' And he stared as if from the present into the past. 'It all began last summer,' he said, 'in the long, hot summer of eighteen ninety-eight.'

6

*anana and Bell* read the nameplate on the door. A brightly polished plate of brass upon a painted door. Below the names were etched the words 'Consulting Partnership'.

The offices beyond the door were royally appointed. Which was to say that not only were the fixtures and fittings composed of regal stuffs, but the very establishment itself, the 'Consulting Partnership', had been accorded the official endorsement of Her Majesty Queen Victoria, Empress of both India and Mars.

The potential client, having tugged upon a brazen bell-pull that activated an electrical buzzer within, would find the door opened to them by a boy, smartly dressed in red livery, who would announce himself to be, 'Jack, and at your 'umble service.'

The first impressions of the potential client would be made favourable by a hallway opulent with gold-leafed papers patterned by William Morris. Jardinières that sprouted blooms which hailed from other worlds. Framed testimonials. A suave satyr of ebony that held a gong of bronze. An eclectic collection born of esoteric tastes, items for the eye to rest upon, yet briefly, for the potential client would have urgent reasons to be calling upon the offices of Banana and Bell. Reasons that would oft-times pertain to a crime.

For these were indeed the offices of the British Empire's foremost consulting detective Cameron Bell and his partner Humphrey Banana.

Having been led up a staircase carpeted in Royal Axminster, the potential client would be shown to a private curtained waiting booth from whence their *carte de visite* would be freighted upon a silver tray by Jack to the offices proper. The office of Mr Bell.

Mr Cameron Bell dwelt behind an exquisite desk that had once been the property of Louis XIV, the Sun King himself. The walls of this office were draped with pale swagged silks. Ornate and gilded furniture weighed heavily upon the eye and upon the lush pile carpetings. The effect was one of ostentation and grandiloquence. The titled clients adored it.

It was the summer of the year of eighteen ninety-eight and it was hot. Outside, London swam in the sunlight. Electrical hansom cabs purred through the heat-haze. Horses' hooves raised clouds of dust and gentlemen tugged at their collars. Those forecasters of weather tapped upon their leech prognosticators: the glass was rising, mercury bubbling, further heat was surely on the way.

Within the offices of Banana and Bell the temperature was moderated, cooled by conditioned air issuing from the patent ice grotto. The atmosphere was calm.

But for the shouting.

One voice boomed in a basso profundo.

The other one squealed in a shrill soprano.

Neither voice was pleasing to the ear.

There were no potential clients upon this summer's day.

Jack the boy servant, who freighted the *cartes de visite*, was in the downstairs pantry practising his ukulele, and the upstairs maid, a woman both spare and kempt, had gone to the market to purchase Lemon Pledge.*

The shouting that went on, went on between the partners. The shouting was quite loud, and sometimes bitter.

Humphrey Banana stood upon the desk of Cameron Bell. Humphrey was an ape of average height, whatever that might be for an ape, well clad in a hand-tailored pale linen suit of the Piccadilly persuasion that featured trousers with a tail-snood augmentation and a triple-breasted waistcoat in the very latest style. Humphrey was an ape of high fashion and an ape possessed of qualities that could be considered unique.

'I will not do it,' he squealed at this partner. 'No, not again, I will not.'

His partner, that famed detective Mr Cameron Bell, sat upon a golden chair behind his occupied desk.

'But it is such a simple solution and such an effective deception.'

'No!' shrieked Humphrey Banana. 'I will not do it! No indeed I will not.'

Cameron Bell sighed sadly. 'Our partnership has been most successful,' said he in a raised voice slightly less loud than a shout, but not much. 'I am sure you will agree.'

The detective's partner nodded his hairy head.

The ape's partner stroked at his beardless chin. The ape's partner wore a well-cut grey morning suit that flattered his portly form and a high wing-collared shirt with purple cravat. Spats and coal-black Oxford brogues adorned his

---

* *Not to be confused with the other Lemon Pledge.*

feet. A pair of golden pince-nez clasped the bridge of his snobby nose.

'You have prospered,' the ape's partner continued. 'I understand that you have recently purchased Syon House, the country seat of the late Lord Brentford, and have designed your own Bananary to place upon its rear.'

'I have.' The ape gibbered and bared his teeth. 'And you have prospered, too.'

'I am the detective.' The detective raised his voice somewhat. 'It is I who actually solve the cases.'

'Not without my help, you would not.'

'On that I beg to differ.'

'All right,' cried Humphrey, bouncing up and down. 'Who was it that stopped Big Bill McCrumby the Birmingham Basher dead in his tracks with a well-aimed piece of dung?'

'You,' said Mr Cameron Bell.

'And who caught Smiling Sam Dimwiddy the Pimlico Perambulator square in the earhole with a well-flung piece of dung?'

'You too,' said Mr Cameron Bell.

'And who, and I am sure you will remember this, brought down Senorita Rita the Hampstead Husband Beater by striking her slap-dap in the forehead with—'

'A well-tossed piece of dung,' said Cameron Bell. Most loudly. 'I remember it well.'

'There,' said Humphrey Banana. 'You see.'

'I *do* see.' Cameron Bell lowered his voice. 'But these people were not involved in any of the cases we were set to solving at the time. They were just casual bystanders to whom you took a dislike.'

'They were looking at me in a funny way,' cried Humphrey Banana.

'You were drunk,' shouted Cameron Bell. 'You had imbibed too freely of that banana liqueur of which you are so fond. You were singing a Music Hall song.'

' "Me One-Legged Nanna Is Home from the Sea and Wants the Loan of Me Foot",' shrieked the ape. 'It is a modern classic.'

'Could we not conduct this discussion in less heated tones?' asked Cameron Bell, clutching at his heart.

'It is *not* a discussion. It is an argument. And they *were* looking at me in a funny way.'

'You were *singing*.' Cameron Bell sighed. 'You are the world's one and only talking ape. It is supposed to be a well-kept secret. Certain elements of our partnership rely heavily upon this, as you know full well.'

'And one in particular.' Humphrey Banana raised his fists and bounced about some more.

'If I promise you that it is for the very last time,' said Cameron Bell, 'that you only have to do it until this case is concluded and then you never have to do it again?'

'I don't have to do it *this* time.' The ape took to the folding of his arms and the sticking out of his chin.

'You do if you do not want this partnership to be dissolved.'

'I might strike out on my own.'

Cameron Bell raised an eyebrow and sighed a little more. 'Is that *really* likely?' he asked. 'Humphrey Banana the monkey detective? Specialising only in cases that involve yellow tropical fruit, I suppose.' Mr Bell laughed loudly.

A wounded expression appeared on the face of the ape. His little mouth puckered and a tear formed in his eye.

'Oh, I am sorry,' said Cameron Bell. 'I did not mean it as a personal slight. Well, perhaps I did, but not to hurt you.' He reached out a hand to pat the ape's shoulder.

Humphrey Banana bit him.

Cameron Bell struck Humphrey Banana.

Humphrey Banana spat.

'Stop, stop, stop,' shouted Cameron Bell. 'There is nothing to be gained by this behaviour. I am on the verge of cracking an important case, one that will bring a considerable amount of money into the partnership. You can either assist me in this matter and benefit financially, or I offer you the choice of withdrawing from the case and forfeiting your share of the money.'

Humphrey Banana bared his teeth.

'And *that* does *not* impress me.'

The monkey made a sour face. 'Then just for this last time only,' he said, 'and never again.'

'Never ever again,' said Cameron Bell as he slyly disguised a smirk. 'We will don the appropriate apparel, blend in with the crowds and locate and follow our suspect to her lair. There we will place her under arrest and retrieve the stolen item.'

'The reliquary,' said Humphrey Banana. 'A very queer thing indeed, by all accounts.'

'A very queer thing,' agreed Mr Bell, 'and one of great value. We will be handsomely rewarded for its safe return. Now, are we agreed?'

Although still sour-faced, the monkey nodded his hairy little head. 'We are agreed,' said he.

'Then let us shake upon it, as gentlemen should.' Cameron Bell stretched out a hand and although he was not keen at all, Humphrey Banana shook it.

'Splendid,' said Cameron Bell, and he turned away to hide his spreading smile. 'Then I will fetch out the barrel organ while you slip off to get your fez and your little tin cup.'

★

Outside the noon-day sun shone down upon mad dogs and Englishmen. Within his office, Cameron Bell bit down hard upon his lower lip in an attempt to stifle the chuckles that sought to flee his mouth.

Humphrey Banana stalked from the office. A grumpy ape was he, for although Cameron Bell thought it something of a lark to have him wear a fez and dance about on a barrel organ waving an old tin cup in hope of funds, Humphrey did not find it funny at all. He hated that fez and tin cup, because they represented to him everything that was wrong with this world: the thraldom of one race to another – or in his case of one species to another. Man's inhumanity to Monkey.

Certainly, through the merits of his gift of speech, Humphrey had become an ape of means. But he was still an ape for all that, and he knew it. Still an ape and one who cared for his fellows.

'One day things will change,' he muttered as he stalked along. 'One day things will change, I know they will.'

And they would, they most certainly would. But not in any way that he could have imagined. For sometimes change comes in a shape that no one could possibly expect. And from a place most unexpected, too.

For change was coming now in the shape of a woman.

A shapely woman from the planet Mars.

7

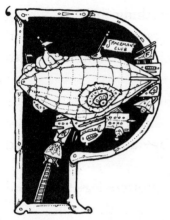'lanet Earth, all change,' called out the conductor. 'Please have your passports and travel documents ready for inspection and do remember to take all your luggage with you. Unattended bags and baggage may be destroyed upon the landing strip.'

The conductor called this loudly as he bustled down the central aisle of the second-class compartment. Thirty passengers occupied this cramped space, most of whom were employees of one big Martian mining conglomerate or another. These were the operators of steam-driven diggers and tunnelling equipment, the medics and mineralogists, surveyors and seismologists, navvies with a taste for travel, men with a thirst for gold.

Upon this homeward journey the latter category, those 'men with a thirst for gold', was represented by a single individual. A downcast fellow, this, whose thirst for gold had gone unquenched and who was now returning to his wife, although not expecting a particularly warm welcome.

'Excuse me, sir,' said this unhappy traveller. 'Why would unattended bags be destroyed upon the landing strip?'

The conductor turned and rolled his eyes. 'You've been down a Martian hole too long, mate,' he said. 'Haven't you heard about the anarchists?'

'I've *heard* about them, yes, but never actually seen any evidence of their activities.'

'They're everywhere,' said the conductor, and he tapped at his nose in that manner known as conspiratorial. 'They'd blow up the lot of us, given half a chance.'

The conductor turned to take his leave, but the passenger called him back. 'Have there been recent atrocities, then?' he asked.

The conductor sighed. 'Not as such,' he confessed. 'Not as such. But that is because we remain vigilant. Where do you hail from, sir?'

'Penge,' said the passenger.

'I have an uncle in Penge,' continued the conductor, who was now proving to be a man more enamoured with conversation than the tasks of his trade, 'and he's a vigilant fellow.'

The passenger nodded and wondered where exactly this was leading.

'He's a shaman,' said the conductor, to the passenger's considerable surprise. 'He supplies protective charms. I have one here about me.' And he fished this out from under his collar. It was a dull grey stone upon a silver chain. 'If an anarchist's bomb was to go off right here, this charm would turn red,' said the conductor.

The passenger's mouth opened, but no words came from it.

'The shaman sold my wife a charm that protects her from man-eating kiwi birds,' the conductor continued.

'There aren't any man-eating kiwi birds in Penge,' was the passenger's reply to this.

'Just shows how well it works, then, doesn't it.' And upon that excruciating note the conductor went off about his business.

The passenger settled back in his seat and glanced towards the porthole. It was really just a glance in the general direction of the porthole because it mostly alighted upon the shapely form of the female seated next to him. The passenger had sought to engage this elegant lady in conversation ever since the spaceship had left the port on Mars, but to no avail. Even his most well-rehearsed bons mots had received little more than a polite nod of acknowledgement.

The passenger had the opportunity to take one more furtive glance, so he took it. She was indeed a most striking woman, dressed utterly in black, her waist cinched by a silken corselet. Black gloves sheathed her delicate hands and a thick embroidered veil depended from a night-dark fascinator, girt about with the wings of tropical birds, wings in hues that were forever night. If black was to be the new black this season, the passenger considered, then this striking woman could claim to be at the very apex of fashion. She looked somewhat out of place in the second-class compartment.

'Well, it has been a pleasure,' said the passenger, but it had not. 'Might I offer my services as chaperone? We might take a hansom together.' As this offer received not even a polite nod of acknowledgement, the passenger folded his arms, closed his eyes and thought once more of how he might compose bons mots of sufficient suavity to temper his wife's ill humour when she learned of his penury.

The FASTEN SEAT BELTS PLEASE sign flashed on and off, the air brakes engaged and the spaceship named the *Marie Lloyd* dropped down towards the landing strip of the Royal London Spaceport. Where, with a crunch of Martian metals onto British cobblestones, it touched terra firma and came suddenly to rest.

The third-class passengers cheered from their cupboard and a parrot named Peter swore in the cargo hold.

Presently the outer ports were opened. The first-class passengers were assisted to a waiting covered landau that would carry them off in comfort to Customs and the arrivals lounge in Terminal One.

The second-class passengers stood upon the sun-blasted cobbles and awaited the arrival of the horse and cart. The third-class passengers remained in their cupboard, hoping that someone might remember they were there.

The lady in the veil sat primly postured next to the driver of the horse and cart, a black parasol shielding her from sunlight.

'Lovely day, ain't it?' said the driver. 'Is that all your baggage? You haven't got much.'

A Gladstone bag of atramentous aspect rested upon the driving seat between himself and the lady. The lady said nothing, so the driver stirred up his horse.

High above, on Sydenham Hill, the Crystal Palace sparkled in the sun. The heat-haze rising from the cobbles of the landing strip made it seem as some mirage, some vision of Fairyland viewed through crystal waters.

The driver of the horse and cart was about to remark upon the beauty of the building, but then considered this would probably be a waste of his breath. Here was a hoity-toity lass, thought he, and one with ideas far above her station.

The arrivals building at the Royal London Spaceport was certainly not without interest, being as it was the brainchild of Alfred Waterhouse, architect of the Natural History Museum, and based upon Charles Barry's neo-Gothic work of wonder, the Houses of Parliament. A tumble of tessellated towers crowned by complex cupolas, here was terracotta primped and teased into a plethora of foliate adornments that pleased the eye and touched the hearts of those who loved the Empire. To the Venusian or Jovian traveller new to the planet, the spaceport's buildings and the Crystal Palace rising on high to their rear conveyed an air of gravitas and grandiosity.

'This is England,' these architectural marvels seemed to say, 'and you must show her the respect she deserves.'

The horse and cart drew up before Terminal One and the sun-seared passengers stepped down from it. Two burly constables appeared from the terminal building and laid hands upon one of these sun-seared passengers.

'What of this?' cried the man who was now being held firmly in the grip of the two large constables. 'I have committed no crime. This is an outrage. Let me go.'

'We have you bang to rights, chummy boy,' said one of the constables, grasping the fellow by one hand whilst wiggling his truncheon with the other.* 'The conductor from the *Marie Lloyd* has told us all about you – asking him suspicious questions regarding anarchists and querying the efficacy of an English shaman's amulets. You would be one of those Bolsheviks, I am thinking.'

'I'm a gold prospector!' the passenger protested. 'Honestly, I am.'

'Then show us some of your gold.'

The remaining second-class passengers passed by without comment or concern. It was none of their business, after all, although it did bring a certain degree of comfort to know

---

* *More difficult than it might at first appear.*

that the British bobby could always be relied upon to protect them when the need arose.

As now it clearly had.

The interior of the Terminal One building was wondrous to behold. Tiled throughout in faux Islamic calligraphy, the walls were hung with mighty canvases depicting the victories of Albion. Marble statuary of military heroes stood hither and yon, along with busts of Queen Victoria in bronze and brass and gold. A kiosk offered tea to the weary traveller. A branch of W H Smith was manned by liveried servitors. The cash machine was sadly out of order.

Those first-class passengers who had arrived upon the *Marie Lloyd* had long since passed through the terminal building without needing to have their passports stamped. They were, even now, being whisked away in luxurious conveyances, bound in air-cooled comfort for their homes or hotels.

The second-class passengers formed a queue.

And this being England, the lady in black was ushered to the front of it.

A chap in a cap of officialdom sat in a glass-sided booth, a narrow desk before him, a rubber stamper upon this narrow desk. He appeared more interested in a penny dreadful magazine that was positioned upon his knees than he was in his duties and consequently did not look up as the lady in black placed her passport on his narrow desk.

'Nationality?' he asked, without so much as raising an eyebrow.

'British,' the lady in black replied, her voice sweet but muffled by her veil.

'Present planet of occupancy?' The chap in the cap could

not really have cared much less. He was far too preoccupied with the exciting adventures of Jack Union, monster-hunter.

'Mars, Sector Six,' said the lady.

'Visa then, please.' And the chap in the cap stuck out his hand to receive one.

'I was not told that I would need a visa. I hold a British passport.'

The chap in the cap let his penny dreadful slide from his knees to the floor. He took up the lady's passport and opened it before him.

'Violet Wond,' he read aloud. 'That is your name, is it? Violet Wond?'

'*Miss* Violet Wond,' said the lady in black.

'And your occupation? "Huntress", it says here. What does that mean?'

'It means that I hunt. Game. Big game.'

'You won't find much of that here,' said the chap in the cap. 'Penge was once the place for man-eating kiwi birds but the shaman shooed them all away.'

'I hunt bigger game than that,' replied the lady.

'Do you, now?' The chap in the cap looked up. 'Ah,' said he, a-sighting of the veil. 'You will have to lift that, if you please, so I might check your face against your photographic representation.' He flicked idly through the lady's passport whilst he awaited revealment. 'You do get about, do you not?' said he as he squinted at past rubber-stampings. 'Jupiter, Mars, even Venus. But you have not been here for some time, not since . . . eighteen eighty-nine! That is nine years ago. Here a-hunting then, were you?'

'Big game, yes,' said the lady as she slowly lifted her veil. 'The biggest game,' she whispered. 'The biggest game of all.'

'Africa, then, was it?' The chap in the cap smiled up at her.

'Whitechapel,' said the lady, her veil now fully raised.

'Oh my good God!' croaked the chap in the cap, his eyeballs bulging from his head. 'Why . . . you . . . are . . .' But he said no more, for with that he fainted, slipping from his chair and sinking upon his penny dreadful.

The lady in black lowered her veil. She reached forward, took up the rubber stamp from the narrow desk and applied it to her passport. Then she returned her passport to her atramentous Gladstone and, jauntily swinging her parasol, she tottered from Terminal One.

Within their cupboard aboard the *Marie Lloyd*, the third-class passengers' cries for release grew fainter as their air supply ran out.

8

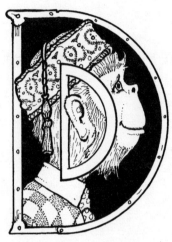ressed in a manner not unlike a
pirate, the organ-grinder stood in
Leicester Square. It was eight of
the evening clock and evening
clocks were busily striking eight
around and about.

The organ-grinder looked the
way an organ-grinder should,
with a battered tricorn and a long
frock coat. His dummy wooden
leg was nothing less than inspired
and he was a credit to his calling. Upon his barrel organ a
monkey sat, a monkey in a fez with an old tin cup.

The organ-grinder stood before a fashionable gentlemen's
club named Leno's and looked up at the modern flashing
neon. He placed his timber toe upon the first step leading to
this esteemed establishment but found his way barred by a
most imposing fellow.

He was a personage of considerable imposition, towering
over six feet in height and regally attired in robes and turban,
as would be some eastern potentate. A luxuriant beard, sewn
with pearls and semi-precious stones, depended nearly to his
waist where a gorgeous purple cummerbund encircled him.
Through this was stuck one of those short Sikh swords that

only Sikhs can remember the name of. He fixed the organ-grinder with an eye both dark and fierce and raised a mighty hand before him.

'You cannot come in here looking like *that*,' he said in a commanding tone. 'Away with you now before I summon a bobby.'

'But I have an invitation,' complained the organ-grinder. 'You *have* to let me in.'

The subcontinental commissionaire, for such he appeared to be, extended his mighty hand.

The organ-grinder dug into a bedraggled pocket and produced a gilt-edged card, which he handed up to the giant looming above.

The commissionaire read this aloud in a booming baritone.

The British Showmen's Fellowship

Annual Awards Dinner and Dance
8 until late

LENO'S   ADMIT ONE PLUS MONKEY

LEICESTER SQUARE   DRESS CODE: FORMAL

'Ah,' said the organ-grinder, a-grinding of his teeth. 'Dress code *formal*. I see.'

'You should have read the small print,' said the beturbanned enforcer of sartorial etiquette.

'But I am not to be blamed, for I have only the one eye,' pleaded the organ-grinder, and he pointed to an eyepatch which had received no previous mention.

'Don't come the old soldier with me, please, sir. And anyway, I can tell that you are not a *real* organ-grinder.'

'What?' The organ-grinder stepped back smartly and all but overbalanced on his dummy wooden leg. 'I have no idea what you mean,' he said.

The monkey looked up at his partner, and the monkey shook his head.

'You are William Stirling,' said the enlightened commissionaire. Which came as something of a surprise to man and monkey alike.

'Oh,' said Mr William Stirling, for it was indeed he and not some other organ-grinder impersonator. 'How did you know it was me?'

'Because I shared diggings with you for three years, while you were at the Royal Academy of Music studying to be a concert pianist and I was at RADA giving myself up to the muse.'

'Kevin Wilkinson?' said Mr William Stirling, and the two shook hands. 'Well, this is quite a surprise.'

'Certainly fate has not been so kind to us as it clearly has to others,' said Kevin. 'I might even now be treading the boards at Stratford, and you, dear boy, playing Tchaikovsky before a rapt audience at the Albert Hall. But instead I must play the part of commissionaire in turban and false beard, whilst you pose as an organ-grinder.'

'I prefer the term *chevalier musique de la rue*.'

'And well you might, dear boy. But regrettably I see a correctly attired gentleman approaching and so must bid you *adieu*. Please take your leave or I will be forced to strike you down with my kirpan.'*

William Stirling slouched away, pushing his barrel organ.

---

* *Ah,* that's *what those short curved swords are called.*

★

'Good evening, sir,' said the commissionaire who might once have played Hamlet. 'Might I see your invitation card?'

The gentleman in top hat and tails, white tie and white silk gloves proffered said card and smiled as it bore scrutiny.

His monkey was similarly attired and looked very dashing indeed. His trousers had a tail-snood made of silk.

'Go through please, sir,' said the commissionaire, returning the gentleman's card. The man and the monkey ascended the steps and passed into the club.

'You tricked me,' whispered the monkey to the man. 'You had me believe that I should wear the fez and shake the old tin cup this evening.'

'Only a good-natured jape, Darwin,' the gentleman whispered in return. 'And you look wonderful tonight.'

'And don't call me Darwin,' whispered the ape. 'I am now Humphrey Banana. Darwin was my slave name.'

'Darwin is a most dignified name,' said Mr Cameron Bell, for it was indeed he and none other. 'And you were never a slave, rather a respected servant of Lord Brentford. Who, if you will recall, left his lands and fortune to you in his will.'

Darwin made grumbling sounds.

'Which you then gambled away,' continued Mr Bell, 'but have lately been able to purchase once more with the wealth you have so far accrued from our partnership.'

'I miss Lord Brentford.' Darwin sighed a sigh.

Cameron Bell glanced down.

'I wish he wasn't dead,' said the ape. 'Perhaps he isn't. Perhaps he swam ashore somewhere after the *Empress of Mars* crashed into the sea and is now King of the savages upon a cannibal isle.'

Cameron Bell shrugged his shoulders at this. 'I suppose that is possible,' said he. Then: 'I wonder how exactly *this* works,' and he worried at the Automated Cloakroom System, a series of lockable boxes into which a gentleman might place his hat and gloves, thereafter to watch his chosen lockable box whirl away upon a jointed conveyor system into some far-away place in the gentlemen's club. 'I think I will carry my hat with me, in case we have to take our leave in haste.'

'Are you expecting some kind of trouble?' Darwin asked.

Cameron Bell shrugged his shoulders a second time. 'This is an awards dinner,' he said, 'and things can become a tad unruly at such events.'

Darwin was about to ask why, but Mr Bell shushed him to silence. A liveried servant was approaching to guide them to their table.

'If sir and his pet would kindly follow me.'

Darwin bared his teeth at this. Mr Bell did rollings of the eyes.

The dining room was suitably grand, with many marble pillars and alcoves where the bronze busts of eminent club members stood, to be respectfully admired. Once a year, the British Showmen's Fellowship hired this room for their special dinner to honour the achievements of the organ-grinding fraternity. It was a most exclusive event and although Mr Bell had managed to forge an invitation card, finding a seat at the numbered tables might prove problematic.

'Name?' asked the liveried servant.

'William Stirling,' said Cameron Bell, who had been close enough to catch the name of the piratically inclined ex-student of the Royal Academy of Music, who had, most conveniently, failed to gain entrance here.

'Follow me, sir,' said the liveried servant. 'And will your p—'

Cameron Bell put his finger to his lips. 'Best not to use the "p" word,' said he. 'My *assistant* does not take kindly to it.'

The liveried servant led Mr "Stirling" and his *assistant* to their seats, then departed, nose held high in the air.

'Thank you for that,' whispered Darwin, scrambling onto the vacant chair beside Mr Bell. 'My, what a lot of organ-grinders and what a lot of monkeys.'

There were twenty circular tables and each of these tables sat ten. That made for one hundred men and one hundred monkeys, by Darwin's calculation. And the thought alone of finding himself in a room with ninety-nine other monkeys was one sufficient to cause the simian no small degree of excitement. And Darwin was clearly not alone in this, for numerous others of his kind were already upon the tables squealing joyfully and getting up to what can only be described as monkey business.

The tables were spread with Irish linen cloths, adorned by floral centre-pieces and laid with a daunting array of cutlery. Clearly many courses were to come.

The eyes of Cameron Bell took in the room and the diners who sat therein. The great detective's remarkable natural intuition and honed observational skills enabled him to see much more than any average fellow might. He discerned subtleties in dress and disposition that informed him as to who was who and also what was what.

'Well,' said Mr Bell to his excited assistant, 'we have the very cream of London's underworld amongst us tonight. It would appear that I am not the only one who represents himself as an organ-grinder in order to move as if invisibly betwixt and between the London throng.'

'All men dressed in evening suits look the same to me,' whispered Darwin. 'Where is this suspect of yours?'

'She is seated over there,' said Cameron Bell. 'You cannot miss her.'

'A lady?' asked Darwin. 'A female organ-grinder?'

'She is dressed as a man when she grinds.'

Darwin viewed the woman in question. She was a slender woman, with hair piled high in an intricate coiffure. She was dressed in a tightly fitting gentleman's evening suit, which created a look that few men would find unappealing. She had the most extraordinary eyes the ape had ever seen. Mauve, they were, and glowing as if lit from within.

'She goes by the unlikely name of Lavinia Dharkstorrm,' said Mr Cameron Bell. 'She is a High Priestess of the Great White Lodge. A witch, she claims to be. She is also one of the most dangerous women in London.'

Darwin peered at this notable figure. Then he peered at the being sitting next to her. It was a monkey. A female monkey. A *beautiful* female monkey. She was chestnut-haired and hazel-eyed, with the prettiest of noses.

Darwin for once became speechless. He became entranced.

Cameron Bell had taken account of those who sat at his own table. He perceived them to be but minor criminals, who were showing him no interest at all and who did not present any significant threat. Those on Lavinia Dharkstorm's table were quite another matter. Two East End bare-knuckle fighters, an unconvicted poisoner and a Frenchman of sinister intent. Ugly customers all and their apes had menacing aspects.

'Now,' whispered Cameron Bell to Darwin, 'there is a certain important matter that I have to attend to. I shall return in five minutes. You *will* behave yourself while I am away, will you not?'

'Whatever,' said Darwin, who was not really listening, but possibly falling in love.

Cameron Bell followed the direction of Darwin's intense gazings, then smiled and nodded his head.

Mr Bell was gone far less than five minutes. But when he returned, he returned to no small chaos.

The liveried servant had Darwin by the scruff of the evening suit, and Darwin was protesting in monkey tongue to this. There was a great deal of cutlery all about the floor and many men in evening suits were holding back their monkeys, all of whom it seemed had very much to shriek about.

'Please keep your creature under control,' said the liveried servant, thrusting Darwin at Cameron Bell.

'He's very highly strung,' said the great detective. 'I am sure it was not he who started the trouble.'

The liveried servant made a sour face, turned upon his heel and marched away.

Darwin looked up at Cameron Bell and the man thought to detect a very guilty expression upon the monkey's face.

'For future reference,' said the detective, 'it is generally best not to anger the staff *before* they serve your meal, for they will often take a bitter revenge in your soup.'

'I don't want the soup,' said Darwin, and folded his arms in a huff.

Presently the soup arrived, but Darwin had fruit for his starter.

Cameron Bell leaned close to his partner and whispered into his little hairy ear. 'When the trouble starts,' he whispered, 'you stay close to me.'

'You are definitely expecting trouble, then?' said Darwin, with his mouth all full of fruit.

'*Expecting* it?' whispered Cameron Bell. 'I am *relying* upon it. For after all, I am the one who will be responsible for causing it.'

Cameron Bell did tappings at his snubby nose.

Darwin found sweet taste in a ripened kumquat.

9

‘Kentish Town Fried Chicken and chips,’ said Mr Cameron Bell, prodding same with a silver fork. ‘I am not altogether certain about this particular course.’

Darwin looked up from a-munching of mangos. ‘I don’t like chickens,’ he said. ‘In fact, I hate them.’

Cameron nodded as he prodded. ‘I don’t think anyone particularly likes chickens as such. Other than the eating of them.’

‘They have too many theories,’ said Darwin, pushing more mango than was strictly necessary into his mouth and chewing away with a will.

‘Too many theories?’ asked Cameron Bell. ‘What do you mean by that?’

As no one was paying either of them the slightest attention, the man and the monkey conversed freely. Other men in that elegant room did speak with other monkeys. Mostly, however, to offer threats of punishment for further unseemly behaviour.

‘I travelled briefly with the circus,’ said Darwin, when finally he had swallowed. ‘With Wombwell’s Menagerie. A showman named Figby exhibited a chicken act – Figby's Fantastical Fowl. They walked tightropes, danced the "fowl fandango", engaged in fencing competitions, all the usual sort of rigmarole.'

Cameron Bell speared a portion of Kentish Town Fried Chicken with his silver fork, brought it to his nose and sniffed at it.

'All the usual stuff,' said he. 'Carry on.'

'There was a cock,' said Darwin, preparing to tackle a pomegranate. 'A big black cock he was, named Junior, and he had quarters next to mine. He would go on and on and on about this thing and the other.'

Mr Bell peered down at Darwin. 'A talking cock?' said he.

'He didn't speak English,' said Darwin. 'He spoke "chicken", but it's not *that* hard to understand. But no one tries, because for the most part chickens are utterly boring. They just say "cluck" which means "food". It's not much of a conversation.'

Cameron Bell returned his chicken to his plate, lifted the glass of champagne he had been poured and took to the sniffing of that. Between such sniffings, he said, 'I do believe you are joking with me, young Darwin.'

'Not a bit of it.' The monkey considered the pomegranate then thrust the whole thing in at once. Mr Bell sipped at his champagne and waited patiently.

'That was a bit of a struggle,' said Darwin, rubbing at his throat. 'So where was I? Oh, yes. Well, as you probably know, chickens, like most birds, have their own religion.'

'They have *what*?' asked Cameron Bell, coughing into his glass.

'Religion,' said Darwin. 'They worship Lop Lop, God of the Birds. They believe that the universe was born from a giant egg.'

'And what laid this egg?' asked Mr Bell.

'The Great Mother Hen who's married to Lop Lop.'

'And where did this gigantic chicken come from?'

'Out of an egg,' said Darwin. 'There appears to be some debate amongst chickens as to which came first.'

'As there is amongst men. Please continue.'

'Lop Lop created the Earth, which is shaped like an egg.'

'A very *round* egg,' said Cameron Bell.

'A *very* round egg,' agreed Darwin. 'The Great Mother Hen gave birth to two chickens, a big black one and a little white one. Henny Penny and Chicken Licken, they were called.'

'You are making it all up,' said Cameron Bell. 'But continue with it if you wish. It is faintly amusing.'

'So,' continued Darwin, 'these two first-born of Earth lived in a beautiful chicken run. But they were tempted by a wily fox and fell out of favour with Lop Lop and his missus.'

'And a chicken told you this?'

'A big black cock named Junior, yes, he did.'

'Remarkable,' said Cameron Bell. 'The next time I bump into your namesake, Mr Darwin, I will pass this on to him.'

'I haven't told you about the theory yet.' Darwin looked hard at a pineapple.

'Dear God, *no!*' said Cameron Bell.

'The theory is this,' said Darwin, weighing up the pineapple between his hairy hands. 'Although chickens believe in Lop Lop, they also believe in Mr Darwin's theory of evolution. They believe that *some* of their forefathers evolved – into men. They believe that all men evolved from chickens.'

'That is absurd,' said Mr Bell, finishing his champagne and reaching towards the bottle, which stood in a silver Georgian cooler.

'I agree,' said Darwin. 'I believe that apes evolved from Man.'

'The other way around,' said Cameron Bell.

Darwin turned the pineapple the other way around.

'No, not the pineapple – the evolution. Man evolved from ape.'

'That is most magnanimous of you,' said Darwin.

'In what way?' asked Mr Bell.

'Well, according to your Old Testament, the first people of God were his most perfect creations – that is correct, is it not?'

Cameron nodded. 'Such is the belief,' said he.

'Then came Man's fall from grace, when he was forced to leave the Garden of Eden, and it has been downhill all the way ever since.'

'Spiritually, perhaps,' said Cameron Bell. 'But Mankind has attained many startling achievements. We live now in an age of wonders.'

'But the first man was the purest man and the first man knew God personally. He was therefore the most superior of all men.'

'If you put it like that,' said Cameron Bell.

'But you believe that Man is descended from monkeys, which therefore means that the first and most perfect being was an ape. Most magnanimous of you, thanks very much indeed.'

Cameron Bell did scratchings at his naked scalp. Somehow or other a monkey had just run theological and evolutionary rings around him.

'But,' continued this monkey, 'the chickens believe that Man is descended from the original fowls of the Great Mother Hen. Present-day Man eats present-day chicken, unaware that they are both of the same root race. The same stock. It is part of the punishment for Henny Penny and Chicken Licken committing Original Sin when tempted by the wily fox. And what is more, they also believe that this happened only a very short time ago.'

'Four thousand years before the birth of Christ,' said Cameron Bell, 'that is the date fixed by religious fundamentalists for the Creation. In fact, they have it down to a date and a day. James Ussher, the Anglican Archbishop of Armagh, famously stated that the Creation began at nightfall preceding Sunday October the twenty-third, four thousand and four BC.'

Darwin replaced the pineapple onto the table, much to the relief of Cameron Bell. 'The chickens consider it to be a lot more recent than that,' he said. 'They believe the world began on the twenty-fourth of May in the year eighteen nineteen.'

'That date sounds familiar,' said Cameron Bell.

'And so it should – it is the day on which Queen Victoria was born.'

Cameron Bell refilled his champagne glass. 'Priceless,' said he. 'And a fine tale, too, Darwin. Well done with that.'

'I am not making it up,' said Darwin. 'The chickens take it very seriously. They believe that there was *nothing* before the birth of Queen Victoria, that this age sprang into being with her royal birth and that *nothing* existed before it. And although I hate to say this, as a theory it is hard to argue against.'

'But it is clearly ludicrous,' said Cameron Bell. 'You yourself live in Syon House, designed by Robert Adam and built in the year seventeen sixty-two. There stands your house as proof against that theory.'

'On the contrary. You believe in the omnipotence of God, do you not? That God, by nature of being God, must be *all*-powerful, *all*-knowing, ever present and beyond all but the tiniest bit of human understanding?'

Cameron Bell looked hard at his partner and companion. 'It is very clear to me,' said he, 'that you have given these matters considerable thought.'

'I read the scriptures daily,' said Darwin.

'You do?'

'I would know what I can of the truth. I would seek to know whether I have a soul of my own.'

'Oh, Darwin,' said Mr Bell. 'I don't know quite what to say.'

'Then listen. I know that you believe in God. I know that you have experienced things that leave no doubt at all in your mind that God exists.'

'In truth, I have,' said Mr Bell. 'And although a rationalist, I have no personal doubts regarding the existence of God.' Mr Bell raised his glass and drank deeply of it. 'This is the sort of conversation I generally have at my club after umpteen ports and lavish helpings of brandy,' he said.

'The theory is this,' said the monkey, 'that everything prior to the birth of Queen Victoria, every ancient artefact, every piece of music, of art, of architecture, was brought into being simultaneously at the moment the God–Queen was born.'

'The *God-Queen*?' asked Cameron Bell.

'Queen Victoria is the manifestation of the Great Mother Hen on Earth. I might, as a slightly humorous aside, draw your attention to the fact that Prince Albert did look very much like a chicken.'

Cameron Bell gave thought to this. 'In fact he did,' he said.

'So,' said Darwin, 'an omnipotent God, who can do anything, creates a world and with it a history that stretches back and back.'

'But why?' asked Cameron Bell.

'To test the faith of his – or rather *her* subjects. If your grandfather could remember the Creation and told you all about it when you were young, there would be no need for faith, would there?'

Cameron Bell scratched once more at his head. 'I do believe,' he said, 'that I am getting out of my depth in this conversation. As a theory, I agree it is hard to logically refute. If God, or Goddess, *did* create the world a mere eighty years ago, complete with all previous artefacts, records, et cetera, et cetera, there would be no way of proving otherwise.'

'And that is why I hate chickens,' said Darwin. 'Their theory is as good as any other.'

'But it could not be true,' said Cameron Bell, and he scratched once more at his head.

'But it *could*,' said Darwin. 'That is the problem. It *could*. Which would mean, of course, that everything chronicled in the Bible, in both Old and New Testaments, never happened. That it is all allegorical, penned by God or Goddess, set down to test our faith. It makes you think, does it not?'

'It does,' said Mr Bell. 'And it is odd that we should have this conversation at a time like this.'

'Why so?' Darwin considered a pumpkin. Cameron Bell shook his head.

'Because the stolen item that I hope to lay my hands upon tonight is a reliquary said to contain some ancient piece of a saint. It is said to be one thousand years old. A priceless artefact. One wonders what value might be placed upon it if it was proved to be no more than eighty years old and the remnant of a holy man who never actually existed.'

'Best not to think too much about it,' said Darwin. 'The more I think about it, the more confused I become. Give me a piece of your chicken. Upon this occasion I will break from my strictly vegetarian diet. Damned chickens!'

Cameron Bell smiled and passed over the fork-load of fowl. 'I *will* present the theory in its entirety to Mr Darwin the next time I see him. He can at times be a rather smug fellow and it will be a pleasure to see him squirm.'

'The world has no shortage of smug fellows,' said Darwin, tasting chicken then spitting it out in disgust. 'It always tickles me to read the latest theories of how the universe began. They are so often penned by pompous persons who sincerely believe that they can fathom the mysteries of the infinite and gather together its eternal wonder in the form of equations set down on a piece of paper.'

'You are wise beyond your years, my friend.' And Cameron Bell filled his glass once more and toasted the monkey with it.

'Of course,' said Darwin, 'there would be one way to sort it all out and know the truth.'

'Would there?' asked Mr Bell.

'Go and find out for oneself.'

'And how might this miracle be achieved?'

'I have read lately,' said Darwin, 'a novelisation by Mr H. G. Wells. It is called *The Time Machine*. If one of these were to be built, perhaps I could travel back to the dawn of Creation and see what really happened.'

Mr Cameron Bell laughed gaily. 'What a wonderful thought,' said he. 'But I must veer towards the pragmatic now. Whether or not the chickens' theory is valid there is no way whatever of proving. But as to whether *you* will ever board a time machine and travel back to the dawn of Creation? Of this I am absolutely sure. You will *not*.'

'Absolutely sure?' asked the well-read monkey.

'*Absolutely* sure,' said Cameron Bell.

10

'ome to order if you will, please, gentlemen.' The liveried servant's voice rang out above the hubbub of men and monkeys alike. 'Be up-standing and make your appreciation felt for the chairman of the British Showmen's Fellowship, Mr Anthony Lemon-Partee.'

Amidst a great scuffling of chairs, men and monkeys rose to their feet and put their hands together as a gentleman of considerable girth, sporting a red velvet smoking jacket with matching cap and slippers, made several vain attempts to hoist himself onto the tiny stage that had been erected for the awards ceremony.

Several strapping grinders of the barrel organ rose from their stage-side seats and assisted the all-but-spherical chairman onto the hopelessly inadequate erection. Its floorboards groaned ominously, but Mr Lemon-Partee affected the bravest of faces.

It was a face that was not without interest, given its uncanny resemblance to a potato. And as cheering folk reseated themselves, certain thoughts now entered the mind of Mr Cameron Bell. Thoughts concerning his most recent conversation with Darwin. For if Prince Albert's resemblance to a chicken could be presented as evidence, no matter how improbable, that Mankind's genesis lay with feathered fowl, here was a man whose physiognomy surely put up a convincing argument that the origins of Man were to be found in the vegetable kingdom.

Mr Cameron Bell shook his own head, the one that bore an uncanny resemblance to that of Mr Pickwick, and sought further champagne. None, however, was forthcoming as Mr Bell had emptied the bottle.

'Gentlemen,' intoned Mr Anthony Lemon-Partee. 'My thanks for your kind applause. It is always a pleasure to receive a warm hand upon my opening.'

This remark received riotous mirth. Darwin the monkey looked baffled.

'If you are a member of a society and hoping for an award,' Mr Cameron Bell whispered to the ape, 'the chairman's jokes are always *very* funny.'

'I am still no wiser,' said Darwin.

The chairman continued, 'Another year has passed, another year when men of this world and of others have been brought to the very heights of pleasure by the sounds of that most tuneful of all instruments, the barrel organ.'

'It is not strictly an instrument, as such,' whispered Darwin.

Cameron Bell put his finger to his lips and shushed the ape to silence.

'Standards have once more risen.' Mr Lemon-Partee raised a hand, which in Darwin's opinion resembled a bunch of bananas. 'Upward, ever upward. Gentlemen, take pride in your achievements, for great achievements they are.'

And so the chairman's speech continued, extolling the

many virtues of the organ-grinding fraternity. Heaping praise upon those innovators who were perfecting new techniques in the art of hand-cranking. Offering up a panegyric to the courage of grinders who were even prepared to ply their trade in the rain, that the passers-by, though wet, should not be deprived of music. Eulogising—

Darwin rolled his eyes and ground his teeth. In his considered opinion, it was the organ-grinder's monkey who did all the *real* work. It was the monkey's dancing skills, the monkey's charisma that lured coinage into the old tin cup. But were the monkeys getting a mention? No, the monkeys were not.

The chairman was clearly exhibiting an outrageous bias towards the organ-grinder and Darwin felt a growing urge to protest on behalf of his species. Though not through shouted words, as he had no wish to publicly display his gift of human speech, but rather through a protest made non-verbally. One that would involve the hurling of faeces.

Darwin set to the dropping of his trousers.

Mr Cameron Bell restrained him. 'Please be patient,' he said.

'And so it gives me enormous pleasure – but then it always did—' The chairman screwed up his little spuddy eyes and grinned. The grinders laughed and Darwin made a most unpleasant face. 'For me to present this year's awards – the Eighteen Ninety-Eight Golden Grinders. Each an award of the highest merit. Each award an object of the dearest desire. Would you please bring forth the awards?'

The liveried servant appeared in the company of a four-wheeled dessert trolley. This he propelled with the exaggerated reverence of one pushing the monarch in a bath-chair. Aboard this trolley stood five awards, all identical, all gilded, all imaginatively crafted to resemble an organ-grinder standing proudly beside his 'instrument' with a monkey topping said organ, a fez upon its little head, an old tin cup (though gilded) in his hand.

Darwin viewed the awards as they passed by his table. At least there *were* monkeys, thought he.

The liveried servant steered the trolley to the over-crowded* stage and then took his place beside it, nose most high in the air.

'I hold in my hand an envelope,' the chairman continued, 'given to me this very evening. Its contents are unknown to myself, although the categories contained within are, of course, known to us all. Most Strident Rendition of a Popular Music Hall Tune. Best-Kept Organ. Liveliest Monkey.' Darwin's spirits rose somewhat at this. 'That award, of course, to be accepted by the pet's owner.' Darwin's teeth were grinding once again. 'Best-Dressed Grinder. And of course the most prestigious award – the much-coveted Organ-Grinder of the Year.'

The potato-head nodded, the diners cheered, then the chairman had more words to say. 'Winners are chosen through a democratic process governed by Fellows of the Showmen's Fellowship. Their decisions are final and not subject to alteration.' He waggled a big fat finger in a jovial fashion. 'So there. But you gentlemen are all aware of the rules, so now I will open the envelope.'

Mr Anthony Lemon-Partee now applied himself to the opening of the envelope. It was a yearly spectacle that the organ-grinders very much enjoyed. He went about it as one possessed, but given the largeness of his fingers and the smallness of the envelope, the performance could be likened to that of a pugilist in boxing gloves attempting to thread a

* *Overcrowded, that is, by Mr Lemon-Partee.*

needle. The chairman worried at that envelope. He fumbled and he fought with that envelope and eventually, to considerable applause, he rent it asunder and dragged from its ruination a crumpled piece of paper and waved it triumphantly aloft.

'The man is a buffoon,' whispered Darwin.

Cameron Bell agreed that indeed he was.

Now freely perspiring, Mr Lemon-Partee unfolded the crumpled sheet of paper and did that little professional cough and clearing of the throat which one does preparatory to delivering any speech of significant importance.

'Gentlemen, the Golden Grinders of Eighteen Ninety-Eight. First category – Most Strident Rendition of a Popular Music Hall Tune. The nominees are: Mr Bert Gussett for "We're Digging a Present for Granny".' Bert received some mild applause for this. 'Mr Eric Peercing for "Little Willy's Dead and Gone, But We Still Have His Stains to Remind Us".' There was slightly more applause here because, after all, that *was* a most popular song. 'Mr Danny Bucket for the evergreen "Don't Kiss a Corpse in a Coffin If You've Got Phossy Jaw".' The applause at this was polite, for Danny *had* won the award last year for the same song. 'And lastly—' And here Mr Lemon-Partee paused and peered hard at the paper, shook his head and peered again and then announced the final nominee. 'Miss Lavinia Dharkstorrm for "Sympathy for the Devil".'*

There came now some *tut-tut-tutting* and murmurs that all was not well.

'Gentlemen,' said the chairman, 'show decorum, please. The choices made are those of the Fellows. Allow me to announce the winner. And the winner *is*—' And once more

---

* *Not to be confused with the other 'Sympathy for the Devil'.*

he paused and he peered and he gasped somewhat, too. 'The winner is,' he said in a still, small voice, 'Miss Lavinia Dharkstorrm for "Sympathy for the Devil".'

Silence fell like a fire curtain and then there was warm applause. But it was a localised applause, coming as it did solely from the table of Miss Lavinia Dharkstorrm.

Cameron Bell cast a glance in her direction. The High Priestess of the Great White Lodge was grinning wickedly. She arose from her seat and, moving with an almost liquid grace, threaded her way between the tables to face the potato-headed man upon the stage. The liveried servant handed her the coveted award and she turned gracefully to face the diners.

'Gentlemen,' she said. 'I am so grateful. I would like to thank—'

'So, moving swiftly on,' said Mr Lemon-Partee.

'If you do not mind,' Miss Lavinia Dharkstorrm said, holding high her award, 'I really would like to say a few words.'

The chairman gazed down upon her, perspiration running freely over his lumpen forehead. The enormity of what had just occurred was causing him to tremble. A *woman* winning a Golden Grinder? It was unheard of. Unthinkable. It was an aberration. 'Madam, if you would please return to your seat,' he said, through gritted teeth, 'we have four more awards to get through. Move along, now – swiftly, if you would.'

Miss Dharkstorrm turned and looked up at the chairman, focusing her mauve eyes briefly upon him. Then she turned once more to face the diners, curtseyed politely and slipped away to her table.

'Next category,' said Mr Lemon-Partee, swaying slightly as he did so. 'Best-Kept Organ. Always a closely fought contest, this. Mr Danny Bucket has taken the award for three years in a row – will tonight be his fourth?'

The applause was . . . *measured*. 'Good old Danny,' said someone, without conviction.

'And the nominations are—' The chairman read once more from his sheet of paper. 'Mr Danny Bucket, Mr Mickey Muggins, Mr Arthur Sixpence and—' Syllables got stuck inside the chairman's throat. His face grew red as he slowly spat them out. 'Miss Lavinia Dharkstorrm,' he said, in a voice of utter despair.

The collective intake of breath sucked much of the oxygen out of the room. Darwin looked at Cameron Bell. Cameron Bell just shrugged. Ugly rumblings rumbled. Grumblings and mumblings of dissent. Made ever more so when the winner's name was announced.

'Gentlemen, gentlemen, please.' Mr Lemon-Partee sought order. His was not to reason why, he was just to read from the paper. The Fellows made the decisions and their decisions were final. Mr Lemon-Partee attempted to explain this to the mumbling grumblers. The mumbling grumblers made menacing faces. They were not at all pleased. As Miss Lavinia Dharkstorrm once more stepped forward to claim an award, someone blew a raspberry and another booed behind his hand.

Miss Lavinia smiled the sweetest smile. She fluttered her eyelashes, puckered her lips and blew the diners a kiss. And then in the company of her second award, she flounced away to her table.

Miss Lavinia Dharkstorrm did *not* win the next award. But then the next award was not given to a person. It was for a monkey. For the liveliest monkey. A monkey named Pandora won this award.

The monkey belonged to Miss Lavinia Dharkstorrm.

Cameron Bell leaned close to Darwin and spoke into his ear. 'I think we should be going now,' he said.

'Absolutely *not*,' said the ape. 'I would not miss this for the world.'

'There is going to be trouble,' said Mr Bell. 'Big trouble.'

'I am looking forward to it,' said Darwin as his little hairy hands steered themselves towards his braces.

'I have a cab waiting outside. We should be seated within it before Miss Dharkstorrm takes her leave and we will follow her.'

'Follow her?' said Darwin.

'Of course. Follow her to her lair, place her under arrest, retrieve the stolen reliquary—'

'And claim the large reward,' said Darwin.

'Precisely,' said Cameron Bell. 'We are professionals, after all.'

Darwin nodded thoughtfully. 'We *are* professionals,' he agreed. 'But if there is going to be trouble, at least allow me to hurl dung at that horrid Mr Potato.'

'Gentlemen, please, I must insist,' cried that horrid Mr Potato. 'The decisions of the Fellows, arrived at through a democratic procedure that admits to no bias or possibility of corruption, are final. To doubt the decisions of the Fellows would be to doubt the honour of this noble institution.'

The grumbling mumblers stilled to a sullen silence.

'Fourth award.' The chairman's hand was shaking fearfully. Perspiration dropped from his head and ran down the length of his waistcoat. 'Best-Dressed Grinder. And the nominations are—' He paused that he might draw breath. He was a big man, after all, and matters such as this were wont to put an unnecessary strain upon his heart. 'Best-Dressed Grinder,' he wheezed. 'And the nominations are –

Mr William Stirling for his "Pirate Bill".' Applause faintly rippled. Someone said, 'Good luck.'

'That's *you*, isn't it?' Darwin said to Cameron Bell. 'You're pretending to be Mr Stirling. I hope there aren't too many of his friends here if you win and have to go up and accept the award.'

Cameron Bell said nothing. The chairman wheezed some more. 'Mr Danny Bucket for his "Old Soldier Fallen Upon Tragic Times". Winner the year before last for that one, I recall.' Others recalled it, too, and no one offered applause. 'Mr Joe Leviticas for his "Coat of Many Colours".'

'Joe isn't here,' someone called out. 'He's fallen down a hole.'

The chairman nodded and gazed at his paper. Then he said, 'Oh my God!'

'If God's won one,' said Darwin, 'I hope a chicken comes forward to accept it on his behalf.'

Organ-grinders were now leaning forward in their seats. That sixth sense which animals and members of the lower working classes are believed to possess was suggesting to them that the fourth nominee would not be one to their particular liking. Mumblings and grumblings rumbled once again.

'Miss—' said Mr Lemon-Partee, all a-jelly-wobble on the stage. 'Miss Lavinia . . . Dharkstorrm.'

The mumblings and grumblings became howlings and growlings.

'And the winner is—' The chairman suddenly clutched at his heart and toppled from the stage onto the liveried servant. The combined sound as both bodies struck the floor was not one to inspire confidence in either man's chances of continued survival.

An organ-grinder near at hand leapt up from his seat and

sprang towards the fallen fellows, but not to offer help. Instead he tore the crumpled piece of paper from the chairman's lifeless hand and waved it at his organ-grinding comrades.

'Read it out!' cried someone. Others catcalled, and one person shouted, 'Bottom.'*

The organ-grinder perused the sheet of paper, then he climbed onto the back of the fallen chairman, that all might see him.

And cried aloud the name of Lavinia Dharkstorrm.

* *The reason for this has never been satisfactorily explained.*

11

ot since the year of eighteen hundred and five, when Lord Byron famously floored William Wordsworth during a literary luncheon, had a gentlemen's club in Leicester Square known such a brouhaha. His lordship had taken righteous exception to Wordsworth's poem 'The Solitary Reaper', which had pipped his own great work of verse, 'Opium for Breakfast, Laudanum for Lunch', to win some much-coveted medal or another that no one in the present age could even remember the name of. But they remembered the flooring of Wordsworth well enough. It was on a par with the Duke of Wellington's now-legendary thrashing of Isambard Kingdom Brunel at the Great Exhibition in eighteen fifty-one because, to quote the Iron Duke, 'That cove's hat was taller than mine and he looked at me kinda funny.'

There is always something memorable, if not admirable, about a really good fight. Especially if it takes place at a really impressive location. Take, for instance, Oscar Wilde's infamous bitch-slapping of Max Beerbohm in the restaurant at Fortnum & Mason. Or the occasion when Charles Dickens had the Pre-Raphaelite painter Dante Gabriel Rossetti held in a head-lock for almost ten minutes at the Royal Academy's Summer Show of eighteen forty-seven.*

Upon this warm summer's evening in the year of eighteen ninety-eight, the altercation at Leno's Gentlemen's Club in Leicester Square would prove to rank amongst the finest of the decade.

As Cameron Bell and Darwin looked on, organ-grinders great and small with monkeys at their elbows rose to their feet with loud cries of complaint. They were far from happy, these well-dressed fellows, these pleasers of passers-by, these musical bringers of joy, these *chevaliers musicale de la rue*. A terrible wrong had been done to them and they sought someone to punish.

Naturally their wrath did not turn in the direction of Miss Lavinia Dharkstorrm because, after all, she *was* a woman, and it was unseemly to hit a woman in public. The hitting of women being something one did exclusively in private, within the comfort of one's own home. And anyway, what was *she* actually guilty of? As a slender young woman, how could *she* possibly have influenced a judging panel comprised exclusively of men? It was unthinkable. No, if anything, this was most likely to be a conspiracy – the work of some jealous rival faction of the East End street-entertainment community. Probably one of those sinister organisations that lurked behind the mask of an amusing acronym, such as BUM, for example – the Bermondsey Union of Minstrels. Or WILLY, the Whitechapel Institution for Long-Legged Yodellers. It could be any one of a hundred such evil cabals. With the notable exception of the Meritorious Union For

* *For an in-depth analysis of this particular set-to, the reader is recommended to study John Rimmer's seminal work* When Authors Go Bad: Great Literary Punch-Ups of the Nineteenth Century.

Friendship, Decency, Individualism, Virtue and Educational Resources, who were above reproach.

The organ-grinders made and unmade fists; they needed someone to punch.

Exactly which one of the attendant monkeys hurled the first piece of dung, history does not record. History does record, however, that it struck home upon a certain Mr Danny Bucket, a gentleman most cruelly robbed of at least four awards in his own, most humble opinion.

Mr Bucket was not a man who, under any circumstances, would have taken kindly to a besplattering of monkey dung. And in his present fractious state of mind he struck out, as folk will sometimes do in such circumstances, randomly, but, him being a large man, with considerable force.

He brought down, by chance, a chappie named Chub, one of four brothers. All of whom were organ-grinders and all of whom were present in the room.

The brass knuckle-duster and the lead-weighted cosh were this season's concealed weapons of choice amongst the hoi polloi. And before one could say, 'Peace be unto thee, brother grinder,' a multiplicity of such martial artefacts were brought forth from their concealments and put to service in the art of war.

A war that grew and grew to almost biblical proportions.

For thusly then did grinder smite at grinder and loudly rang the cries of battle therewith. Great, too, were the weepings and wailings, and indeed the gnashings of teeth as Man's hirsute and humble cousin smote alike his own kind and the Sons of Adam,* too.

Mr Cameron Bell ducked smartly aside as a champagne

* *Chicken theory notwithstanding.* too.

cooler passed him by at close quarters. Darwin the monkey was up on the table, trousers down and eager for a tussle.

Mr Bell eyed the table occupied by Miss Lavinia Dharkstorrm and her associates: two East End bare-knuckle fighters, an unconvicted poisoner and a Frenchman of evil intent. Miss Dharkstorrm was loading her awards into an oversized reticule and appeared about to make an opportune departure. One of the bare-knuckle fighters knocked down a fellow named Chub. The fellow's brothers took to a bloody revenge.

Tables were now being overturned and chairs brought into play as weaponry. The Frenchman of evil intent was torturing a waiter. Then someone pulled out a pistol and fired it into the ceiling.

The purpose of this reckless act might not have been reckless at all; it might in fact have been one of good intention, an attempt to halt the altercation and to restore peace, order and good sense. It did not, however, achieve these noble ends. Rather it focused the attention of a passing bobby, who drew forth his truncheon and took to blowing his whistle.

The sound of a policeman's whistle was not one that signalled joy amongst the members of the club next door to Leno's. This was not a gentlemen's club per se, although it was a club frequented by gentlemen. The name of the club was Molly's and it catered to those who favoured wearing the apparel of the opposite sex and engaging in acts which, even in this most enlightened of times, were not strictly legal.

The police whistle, blowing as it did in the key of 'la', was disharmoniously accompanied by the sound of the large casement window of Leno's bursting asunder in the key of E-flat minor to admit the passage of several large organ-grinders locked in titanic conflict. As glass and timber and grinders too all toppled into Leicester Square, a new dimension of excitement was added to the turmoil within. A hurled champagne bottle struck a gas mantle, shattering same and causing a minor but significant explosion that set fire to the curtains with most dramatic effect.

A burly grinder tore down these curtains and took to stamping out the flames. He soon, however, found himself trampled beneath many feet as, fighting as they fled, the evening-suited combatants sought a hasty exit through the yawning maw that had once been a casement window.

The defenestrated grinders found themselves met all but head-on by the fleeing habitués of Molly's. Monkeys bounded onto the pavement, frightening the horses of a passing growler. The policeman, sufficiently distanced so as to avoid the danger of any personal injury, put new life into his whistle-blowing. Horses reared. The growler over-turned. Within the dining room of Leno's flames began to lick up the walls.

Mr Bell hauled Darwin from the table. The single table, so it appeared, that had not been overturned.

'Time to go,' he told the monkey. 'Miss Lavinia and her henchmen are taking their leave by the rear entrance. We should do likewise, I feel.'

As Darwin found flames fearful, he clung to Cameron Bell as the great detective threaded his way between broken furniture and battered bodies.

Miss Lavinia Dharkstorrm left the building.

Before Leno's, in the square named for Earl Leicester, mayhem abounded and misrule was the order of the evening. The lady-men of Molly's, believing the evening-suited grinders to be some company of plain-clothed policemen from the newly formed Vice Division, set about the grinders with a will. A party of Jovian sightseers found themselves drawn into the mêlée and, knowing from their guidebooks that London had a colourful history of riots and social unrest, joyfully took to the staving-in of a nearby hat shop and the looting of its contents.

Behind Leno's, in a back passage named for no particular historical personage and known only as Doggers' Alley, stood two horse-drawn conveyances. The first was an elegant four-wheeled landau, which seated six. Aboard this, in a fine scarlet uniform with matching high top hat, sat a straight-backed driver, facing to the front. The second was a hansom cab adorned by an ill-kempt sleeper who smelled most strongly of gin.

From the rear entrance of Leno's issued Miss Dharkstorrm, in the company of one bare-knuckle fighter, an unconvicted poisoner and the winner of the Liveliest Monkey Award, the chestnut-haired and hazel-eyed Pandora.

'Into our landau,' cried the High Priestess. 'We will away from this lunacy, as of now.'

Once all were aboard, she ordered the driver to put his whip to the horses.

'At your service, ma'am,' came the reply.

The landau set to a goodly speed, its wheels raising sparks on the cobbles of Doggers' Alley.

Now out from the rear entrance came Cameron Bell. Darwin was still clinging to the great detective, who threw himself aboard the hansom and ordered the driver to, 'Follow that cab as I have hired you to do.'

'Pardon?' said the driver, stirring somewhat from his drunken stupor.

'Follow the landau, man! Follow the landau!'

'Froggo the lighterman? Who in the Devil is he?'

'Oh my dear dead mother,' said Cameron Bell. 'Hold on tightly, Darwin, for I am going to drive this cab.'

It was but the work of a moment or two: the climbing down from the passenger compartment; the climbing up to the driver's perch; the forcible tossing of the drunken driver from his perch; the whipping-up of the single horse; and the setting off apace.

Doggers' Alley debouched into Leicester Square at a sufficient distance from Leno's that a passenger in a landau or a hansom, travelling from there to a further part of the square, might do so in comfort, enjoying the sight of what was now a full-blown riot without having their enjoyment in any way curtailed by actually becoming involved in it.

Not that rioters do not enjoy themselves. On the contrary, there is nothing quite like a good riot to set the pulse racing and the heart a-beating like a big bass drum.

Darwin took no small delight in viewing the antics of his fellow simians who, now perched high atop lamp posts, were raining faeces onto the crowds below. Two Black Marias entered Leicester Square. Flames were rising highly now from Leno's.

The landau was all but out of sight. But Mr Bell, aware of the general direction in which it was heading, stirred up the horse and pressed it on at a trot.

The little hatch above the passenger compartment popped open and Darwin stuck his head out.

'Well, I must say I enjoyed that,' said the ape.

'I thought you might,' said Cameron Bell. 'You are always going on about Man's inhumanity to Monkey. I felt it might be instructive for you to witness an example of Man's inhumanity to Woman.'

Darwin cocked his head on one side. 'You knew about the results,' said he.

'I knew about the results.'

'I suspect,' said Darwin, 'that if she really *is* a witch then the results were the result, as it were, of certain witcheries.'

Cameron Bell shook his head. 'Oh, bother,' he said. 'I left without my hat. But no, her witcheries, if such she possesses, played no part in the results.'

'Then she genuinely won the awards?'

'Not as such,' said Cameron Bell. 'I switched the envelopes, you see, when I left the table before the dinner began.'

'Oh, bravo,' said Darwin. 'Although—'

'Although *what*?' asked Cameron Bell, flicking the whip at the horse, which had slackened from a brisk trot to a stroll. 'Although *what*, exactly?'

'I counted at least two dead on the way out,' said Darwin. 'I expect the body count will have risen significantly by the morning.'

'Happily,' said Cameron Bell, 'if that word can be applied in such a context, the two fatalities were a bare-knuckle fighter and a Frenchman of evil intent – two of Miss Dharkstorm's henchmen. I had been hoping something like that might occur, to lessen the danger to us when we capture her.' Cameron Bell made a thoughtful face. 'However,' said he, 'I do not see how I could possibly be blamed for the altercation or the fatalities.'

Two fire engines, their bells ringing loudly, sped towards and past them.

'*You* substituted the results to allow a woman to win,' said Darwin. 'It is all your fault and no other's.'

'I recall clearly,' said Cameron Bell, 'that the fighting began when Mr Danny Bucket was struck by a hand-flung helping of dung.'

Darwin quietened somewhat. Then, 'Hold hard a minute,' he said.

'What now?' asked Cameron Bell.

'The original and genuine results,' said Darwin. '*I* might have won an award.'

'You didn't,' said Mr Bell. 'I checked. Although—'

'Although *what*?'

'*I* was nominated in the Best-Dressed category.'

'As "Most Badly Disguised Detective"?' asked the monkey.

'I must concentrate on my driving,' said Cameron Bell. 'Close the little hatch and sit yourself down.'

They had now reached the Victoria Embankment and were passing Cleopatra's Needle. The Moon shone from a cloudless sky and tinged the ancient obelisk with silver. Cameron Bell sighed and took a deep breath. Ahead now he could see the landau, slowed to an even pace and approaching Waterloo Bridge. On board was a witch, a High Priestess of the Great White Lodge. Possessed of magic? Possibly. Cameron Bell had encountered magic before, real magic, and its power had chilled him to the bone. He was a detective. A great detective. Greatest of the age, many claimed, and he was amongst this many. Show him an article of clothing and from it he could construct a description of the wearer that was little less than uncanny. Give him an item – a watch, a snuffbox, whatever – and he could divine from its perusal more inferences than any man alive. But match him against the powers of magic and he was oft-times lost.

He could have traced any normal criminal to their hideaway with comparative ease, but Miss Dharkstorrm, it so appeared, was no ordinary criminal. Again and again she had outfoxed him. He was certain she was responsible for at least three major crimes – the thefts of three valuable antique reliquaries, one of which he was presently engaged to retrieve. Exactly what a witch would want with a reliquary was beyond Mr Bell's powers to deduce. But he knew that she had them and he knew, *just knew*, that he would take them from her. For tonight he would employ the wonders of modern-day science to uncover the secret lair of the elusive Miss Dharkstorrm. Tonight he would succeed. Tonight he would triumph.

He would, he truly would.

A sudden coldness chilled the air and worried at his naked scalp. 'I wish I had not forgotten my hat,' said he.

Ahead the landau carried on along the Embankment past Waterloo Bridge, for although unknown to Cameron Bell, a true witch cannot pass over running water.

Miss Lavinia Dharkstorrm lolled upon perfumed pillows, Pandora snoring gently on her lap. She raised a star-shaped mirror in a delicate hand, gazed into it and found pleasure in the viewing.

'Tonight you will not lose me, Mr Bell,' said she, 'for tonight I have a score to settle with you.'

To the right the moonlight twinkled on the Thames. To the left a red glow showed above the rooftops as flames curled up into the sky from Leicester Square . . .

12

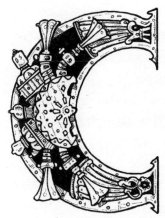

lip and *clop* went the horse's hooves, as a horse's hooves will do. The rhythmic beat on the cobbled street created an eerie mood. Cameron Bell found he was nodding off and shook himself into sensibility. He had imbibed too freely of the champagne this night and he knew it. And a most inferior champagne, too, hardly the Château Doveston he preferred. Ahead the landau moved at an even pace and there was little in the way of other traffic. An electric brewer's dray purred by, bound for taverns in Chelsea. Overhead an airship drifted, on course for the Royal London Spaceport at Sydenham Hill. Beyond the river, over on the South Bank, Cameron spied one of the new power stations and beyond that one of the tall Tesla towers that broadcasted electricity from a glittering sphere high above. The wireless transmission of electricity was the brainchild of Nikola Tesla, now *Lord* Tesla for his services to the British Empire. He and Lord Babbage had created so many marvels of the modern age. And so too had Mr Ernest Rutherford, a gentleman of Cameron Bell's acquaintance. A gentleman with a well-stocked cellar containing many bottles of Château Doveston.

'I must pay Mr Rutherford a visit,' said Mr Bell as the horse *clopped* on. 'In fact, I might visit him tomorrow to report the success or not of the little piece of science that may aid my cause tonight.'

With this said, Mr Bell dug into an inner pocket of his evening-suit jacket and brought into the moonlight a brass contrivance of intricate design and no immediately obvious purpose. From another pocket and amidst much juggling of the horse's reins, he extracted something resembling a small brass ear trumpet. With the reins now in his mouth, he proceeded to screw the two curious items together.

A tiny brass nameplate bolted to the queerly shaped contraption was engraved with the words

The Rutherford Patent Bloodhound

Which might have suggested a use to a few, but probably not to the many.

'So, let us see,' said Mr Bell, with the reins now in his right hand and the brassy apparatus in his left. 'If I have made the preparations correctly and this actually works, I will beard the lioness within her den. Now, the principle is this, if I remember correctly. Step one, create a unique fragrance by mixing a quantity of random scents which would not by chance be mixed together. Step two, apply a portion of it to the person or vehicle you wish to follow and place a similar portion within the Bloodhound. Earlier this evening I smeared such a portion on the rear of the landau. The Bloodhound has a range of three hundred feet and within this range can literally *sniff* out the portion you have pasted upon your target. Very clever indeed.

'Step three, switch on the Bloodhound and follow the direction indicators.' Mr Bell switched on the Bloodhound.

A dull hum rose from it and a needle upon a directional dial circled slowly, then stopped with its pointer aiming straight ahead.

'Splendid,' said Mr Bell. 'It appears to work in the open. The problem in the past has been tracing her through the narrow side-streets, so hopefully the Bloodhound will prove its worth amongst them.'

At which precise moment the landau ahead took a left turn into Temple Avenue and entered the notorious maze of streets that lay between the Temple and St Bride's.

'Now to prove your worth,' said Cameron Bell, feeling quietly confident as the directional pointer swung towards the left.

There were still many slums in London where poor folk lived in wretched squalor, prey to want and foulness and disease. Great social movements were in progress and there was always the promise that things would change for the poor, that their hopeless lives would be enhanced, their hovels torn down, new housing built, their children educated, a brave new world set before them.

But sadly it was mostly talk. Well-intentioned talk perhaps, but mostly only talk. The modern world with all its wonders favoured but a few. The rich got richer and the poor stayed poor.

Mr Bell lacked not for a social conscience, but what was *he* to do? He followed his calling. He was a detective. He brought justice. He did what he felt to be right. Honesty and integrity were his watchwords. He could do no more than he did.

As he steered the horse up Temple Avenue, his mood began to darken. A rank smell clothed the evening air and horrid sounds came to his ears. A woman's cry. A drunken oath. Mr Bell pressed on. The Bloodhound's needle swung to the right and Mr Bell tugged at the right-hand rein, but the horse wasn't keen at all.

'Come on, boy,' said Cameron Bell. 'There is far greater danger for me here than there is for you.'

Grudgingly the horse turned into a narrow side-street. There were many smells down here and all were nasty. As there was no street lighting, the great detective was forced to hold the Bloodhound aloft and follow its pointer by moonlight alone.

And so he followed its pointing down this narrow street and the next until he came to a little square illumined by the light of the Moon, at the centre of which was a single tall and narrow house. Before this stood the landau.

'Positively splendid,' whispered Cameron Bell, drawing the horse to a halt, dismantling his apparatus and returning the pieces to his pockets. From yet another pocket he drew out a sleek pistol of advanced design: a pocket ray gun known as the Gentleman's Friend. Mr Bell engaged the charge button and stepped quietly down from the hansom.

'Darwin,' he whispered, glancing into the cab. Darwin the monkey was fast asleep. Mr Bell smiled. 'Probably all for the best,' said he. 'I would not want you to come to harm. Your behaviour at times is outrageous, but I am very fond of you, my little friend.'

Darwin mumbled the word 'banana' in his sleep. Mr Bell pressed quietly on towards the narrow building.

It was an ancient affair, half-timbered with tiny windows of bottle glass, a sharply gabled roof and tottering chimney-pots.

Mr Bell crept to the landau and took a peep inside. It was empty. *All indoors, then,* thought the detective. Then another thought struck him, too, one that really should have struck him earlier. There could be numerous villains within, far more than those who had arrived in the landau. Entering the building might be extremely dangerous. So, what to do?

Mr Bell eyed the substance of the building. Predominantly timber. It would burn rather well. Mr Bell weighed up the pros and cons of this. It would be an irresponsible action, but it would probably have the desired effect, for when Lavinia Dharkstorrm fled the blazing building she would certainly do so in the company of the stolen reliquaries. And Mr Bell could pick off her associates with a few well-aimed blasts to their lower regions. Nothing fatal.

Mr Bell's left hand strayed towards his waistcoat pocket, wherein rested his silver match-case. It would be the work of a mere moment or two.

But then something struck him, and struck him *hard*. Mr Bell was pitched from his feet and tumbled to the ground. A hobnailed boot swung into contact with his belly, driving the breath from his lungs, and rough hands were laid upon his person.

'Up, you,' barked a cockney voice. 'Up onto your feet.'

Mr Bell floundered, gagging for air, as he was hauled from the ground.

'He's a heavy 'un, ain't 'ee?' the cockney voice said merrily. 'Like your nosebag, do you, Mr Pickwick?'

Cameron Bell clasped his stomach. He felt certain that he was going to throw up. He no longer held his ray gun and was now in serious trouble. He gaped red-faced at his attacker. The East End bare-knuckle fighter. But where had he sprung from? And who was with him?

The bare-knuckle fighter twisted Mr Bell's left arm up his back as the unconvicted poisoner approached.

'Well, well, well,' said this fellow. 'If it isn't Mr Cameron Bell, the world's most famous detective. Fancy meeting you here. Out for a bit of a stroll and got lost, did you? This is a dangerous place to be out on your own. How fortunate we've found you.'

The poisoner removed his black leather gloves, pushed them into a pocket and flexed long, sensitive fingers. 'My mistress tires of your attentions,' he said, wagging his fingers at Mr Bell. 'She says that we must punish you most brutally.'

Cameron Bell sought any escape, but he was firmly held and no escape was forthcoming.

'See,' said the poisoner, curling and uncurling his fingers before Cameron's face. 'See how each nail of my hand is sharpened to a tiny point, and each loaded with a different poison. One here—' and he thrust his forefinger towards the detective '—to kill you outright in seconds. Another—' and he displayed this '—to induce a lingering and painful death. Entertaining to watch, but most excruciating to experience. What shall it be, then? I have eight other options – I can run through them all, if you wish.'

'Just kill him quick and let's go for an ale,' said the bare-knuckle fighter. 'You waffle on too much before you do a killin'.'

'You lout,' said the poisoner. 'You have no style. No finesse. I studied under one of the last grand masters. I have learned techniques kept secret from the world for a thousand years.'

Mr Bell had regained his breath but was still helpless to escape.

'Spare my life,' said he, 'and I will reward you handsomely. Name your price and I will pay it.'

The poisoner slowly shook his head. 'Too late,' said he. 'I have removed my gloves and by the Poisoners' Code, they cannot be replaced upon my hands until a man lies dead or dying at my feet.'

'Then *do* get on wiv it,' said the bare-knuckle fighter, giving Mr Bell's arm a vicious twist as he did so.

Then, '*No!*' cried a new voice. The voice of Miss Lavinia Dharkstorrm. She stood in the open doorway of the tall narrow house dressed in robes of crimson velvet, a most dramatic figure in the moonlight.

'I do not want Mr Bell dead,' said she. 'Not yet. Disabled though, perhaps.'

The poisoner smiled, evilly, and raised the little finger of his left hand. 'A single jab,' said he, 'and our portly friend will lie like a jelly, torn with agony but unable to move a muscle or utter a word ever again.'

'Dear God, no!' cried Cameron Bell. 'I beg you, please have mercy.'

'And where is your God now?' asked Lavinia Dharkstorrm.

The poisoner looked towards her and waved his long, deadly fingers.

'I think,' said the High Priestess, 'that you should apply a combination of *coup de poudre* and mandrake to our uninvited guest.'

'Zombie Dust,' said the poisoner. 'Reduce him to a mindless slave. We will have sport with him then.'

Many thoughts now passed through the mind of Cameron Bell. Amongst these was one which informed him most accurately that although in the course of his duties as a consulting detective he had come up against many evil people, the woman and the poisoner before him were undoubtedly the two most abominable specimens of humankind it had ever been his misfortune to encounter.

'Poison him,' said Miss Lavinia Dharkstorrm, turning upon her heel and re-entering the tall narrow house.

The poisoner grinned and raised a hand, his venom-coated fingernails a-twinkle in the moonlight.

'Thus and so,' said he, his hand held high, 'our slave shall you be.'

Cameron Bell stood frozen with fear as the poisoner curled his fingers. And many many thoughts now entered his mind. Mostly to the effect that he really had not planned this evening quite as well as he might have.

And then things took a very terrible turn. A bright light flashed before Cameron Bell and warm liquid spattered his face. A scream of pain rang in his ears, but it did not come from the mouth of Cameron Bell.

The detective glanced towards the man who would horribly poison him. The man stood like a statue, gazing up.

Gazing up towards the spot where but a moment before his left hand had hovered.

For now that hand was no more to be seen.

And blood gushed freely from the severed wrist.

13

hilst engaged upon business in Paris the previous year, Cameron Bell had attended the opening night of *Le Théâtre du Grand-Guignol*. This curious palace of entertainment specialised in performances which were representations of naturalistic horror – torture, murder, disfigurement and gory revenge figured large. Mr Bell had left during the intermission and gone in search of a steadying absinthe or two.

And now, upon this summer's evening in London, the detective looked on with startled eyes as a scene that might well have stepped from the stage of *Le Grand-Guignol* played out right before him.

The poisoner, clutching at his bloody stump, sank to the ground, where he lay whimpering with pain. Then Mr Bell saw the woman who had destroyed the assassin's hand.

She was a most striking creature, spare and well formed, clad in high buttoned boots with tall, slender heels. An intricately decorated brass corset cinched her slim waist and curved up to cover her breasts. She wore a short skirt of segmented leather, which put Mr Bell in mind of those

martial garments worn by Roman legionnaires. Broad brace-
lets of brass encircled her wrists and a fearsome mask of
black India rubber covered her head and throat. Within the
blank and featureless visage were two circular glass eye-
shields and what appeared to be a mesh-covered breathing
hole.

The young woman, for such she clearly was, presented an
appearance that was both terrifying and tantalising by turn.

She held in her right hand a large ray gun of Martian
design which she now lifted slowly to her covered face in
order to blow the smoke from its barrel.

What happened next happened fast, but to Mr Bell, his
eyes now popping and his jaw hanging slack, it appeared to
occur in slow motion, as would one of those new bioscope
presentations produced by Nineteenth Century Fox which
presented moving pictures of varying speeds, depending
upon how fast one cranked the handle.

The masked woman holstered her ray gun, stepped forward, aimed a high-heeled boot at the fallen poisoner and
kicked him into unconsciousness, then literally fell upon the
bare-knuckle fighter who still held Mr Bell in his vicious grip.

The East Ender gave a good account of himself. He
bobbed about and swung his fists, did duckings and divings,
too, but he was simply no match for the wondrous woman.

She side-stepped every fist that was thrown and then in
what appeared to be a pure ballet of violence she leapt into
the air, swung high her legs and kicked him square in the
jaw. As he sank to his knees, she danced in close, turned up
his face between her delicate hands, then twisted his head
and snapped his neck with a hideous brutality.

Mr Bell saw the poisoner crawling towards her, his single
remaining hand held up to kill. The lady, however, was not

for turning and without even a glance behind her, she drew her ray gun from its holster and shot the poisoner dead.

Mr Bell gawped dumbstruck towards his female deliverer, who took a single step forward, raised a hand and lifted his chin to close his gaping mouth.

'My thanks, dear lady,' said Cameron Bell, when he could find his voice.

The angel of death who had saved his life had nothing whatever to say, but her hand snaked to the top pocket of Mr Bell's jacket and drew out his handkerchief, and this she held to his face.

'Oh, yes,' said Mr Bell, taking the white silk handkerchief and wiping it across his ample forehead. 'The blood's not mine, I hasten to add.'

The masked woman holstered her ray gun once more, took a step back, curtseyed prettily, turned upon her preposterous heels and swiftly marched away.

'Oh my dear dead mother,' said Cameron Bell.

Alone now in the moonlit square he stood, two bodies prone before him. He glanced towards the narrow house. Miss Lavinia Dharkstorrm lurked within. Had she seen any of this?

'Extraordinary business,' said Mr Bell, dusting himself down. 'And a most extraordinary woman. Whoever she was.' He stooped and retrieved his ray gun and on legs that were now most unsteady he ambled over to the front door. Where, having adjusted his gun to 'maximum', he shot this door from its hinges.

Mr Bell peered into the house, but found therein nothing but darkness.

'Miss Dharkstorrm,' called Mr Bell. 'Miss Dharkstorrm, your bully boys are dead. I have killed them all. I have no wish to injure you, but rest assured I will if the need arises.

Please step quietly from the house that we might discuss matters.' Mr Bell's words echoed within the ancient house but none were returned to him. In fact, there were no sounds at all.

The detective took a step into the darkness. 'Miss Dharkstorrm,' he called again. 'I really must insist that you give yourself up.'

No reply forthcoming, there was nothing else for it, so Mr Bell moved onwards into the darkness. As he felt his way forwards, his eyes slowly adjusted and vague impressions of his surroundings were to be had. The ground floor consisted of nothing but a single empty room with a narrow staircase set against its furthest wall. Mr Bell moved carefully to the foot of this staircase, then gingerly mounted it, slowly and with trepidation, one single creaking stair at a time.

On the first floor there was nothing. A single room, another flight of steps.

On the top floor, however, things were different. Mr Bell entered a pleasantly furnished garret lit by a solitary oil lamp upon a mahogany table. There were Gothic bookcases burdened by many leather-bound volumes, several small cupboards intricately inlaid with ivory and a fireside chair. A coal fire burned in a marble hearth, and upon its mantel shelf stood the three stolen reliquaries.

In the chair sat a small and slender child, a ragged girl who stared at the detective with round eyes filled with fear.

'Well,' said Mr Bell, 'and who are you?'

'My name is Emily,' said the child, 'and I belong to Miss Dharkstorrm.'

The corners of Cameron's mouth turned down. 'No longer,' said he. 'You are free.'

'Free?' asked the ragged child, wringing dirty hands. 'Free to leave this place?'

'Free,' replied Mr Bell.

'But where will I go?'

'I will find someone to care for you.' Cameron Bell now glanced with some concern about the room. 'Where is Miss Dharkstorrm?' he asked the child.

'My mistress has gone.'

'Gone? But gone *where*?'

'She left,' said the girl, but her eyes darted towards one of the cupboards and she raised a shaking finger and pointed with it, too. 'Mistress has gone away.'

'I understand.' Cameron Bell beckoned to the child. 'Go on,' said he, 'wait for me downstairs.'

'I am not allowed downstairs.'

'You are now. Go quickly and I will soon follow.'

The child crept away down the stairs and Cameron Bell approached the cupboard, ray gun at the ready.

'Kindly come out, Miss Dharkstorrm,' said he.

But there was no response.

'I am armed,' said Cameron Bell. 'You would do well to heed my words.'

The detective edged forward, his ray gun shaking some-what. This evil woman had him considerably rattled. 'For the last time,' said Mr Bell, 'come out!' And he reached with his free hand and flung open the cupboard door.

Miss Dharkstorrm was not in the cupboard.

Her little monkey was.

Darwin awakened in the hansom cab to the sounds of shouting, and the voice he knew to be that of Cameron Bell.

'Emily,' the detective was shouting. 'Emily, where are you? Please come back.'

Darwin sat up and stared. Mr Bell emerged from the narrow house and came shouting into the square. He was leading by the hand a chestnut-haired monkey that Darwin knew to be Pandora.

Darwin looked on as Mr Bell stepped over something – a corpse, was that? – and approached the hansom cab.

'Did you see anybody pass just now?' he asked. 'Did you see a small child go by?'

Darwin yawned and shook his head, then opened his mouth to speak. But did not. Instead he simply stared at the beautiful Pandora, and she in turn fluttered her eyelashes and demurely studied the ground.

Darwin was about to ask what he had missed and why he had been caused to miss it, but once again he did not speak. For it occurred to Darwin that should he give voice and speak the human tongue, such a thing would surely cause Pandora fear.

'I am a fool,' said Cameron Bell. 'Miss Dharkstorrm has escaped and a child she held captive has run away. I do, however, have the stolen reliquaries.' And he hoisted into view Miss Dharkstorrm's oversized reticule. 'Do you wish to take charge of this monkey? Or should we drop her off at London Zoo?'

Darwin nodded, then shook his head.

'I assume by the love-struck look on your face that you would like to take her home.'

Darwin's head bobbed up and down.

'Then I will drive you both to Syon House and from there drive myself to our offices. I have much to muse upon – strange things have occurred and I must have answers. Come, let us away.'

He lifted Pandora gently into the hansom. The female monkey made no fuss and sat down next to Darwin. Mr Bell climbed up to the driver's seat and stirred the snoozing horse.

And away he drove from the dismal square where two men lay in death.

14

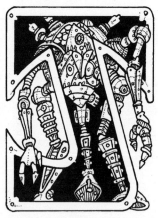 ones the troll swung open the door of Mr Ernest Rutherford.

'What do you want?' he shrieked. 'Waking this household up at eight in the morning.' He raised his little hairy fists and shook them all about. He was of that order of being whose likeness might be found in the gnomish illustrations of Arthur Rackham: big and bent of nose, squat and broad of belly, somewhat bowed about the legs and with large and pointed ears that thrust out from his swollen hairless head.

'You can't come in now, go away!' And Jones jumped up and down. Before him upon the doorstep stood a slim and elegant woman. She was dressed in the most funereal black, with a thick veil cloaking her face.

'I have an appointment to see Mr Rutherford,' she said politely. 'Please present him with my card.'

'He can't see anyone and anyway he's gone upon his holidays.'

The lady's blackly gloved hand extended towards the little bobbing figure.

'Please show him my card,' said she.

'He is not seeing anybody. Eeeeeeeek!'

The *eeeking* on the part of Jones was occasioned by him being suddenly lifted from his feet by a single ear and drawn up to the veiled face of the young woman who was standing upon the doorstep. This young woman now whispered certain words into the tightly gripped ear of the dangling troll called Jones, then let him fall to the steps.

Jones looked up with fear in his bloodshot eyes. 'I will fetch the master at once,' said he, meekly holding out his hand for the card. 'If you would care to wait in the hall?'

Miss Violet Wond entered the house of Mr Ernest Rutherford and stood in the hall, viewing the stuffed Maori with distaste whilst tracing runic figures upon the plush carpet with the tip of her black parasol. Jones the troll scuttled away up the staircase, down which presently came Mr Ernest Rutherford. The chemist had a broad smile on his face.

'Miss Wond, I presume,' said he, tucking the lady's card into the top pocket of his white work coat. 'I have no idea what you must have said to Jones, but he is most eager to make you a cup of tea.'

'I never take tea,' said Miss Wond. 'Except with the parson, of course.'

Mr Rutherford stopped dead upon the staircase, one foot hovering in the air. He had actually heard that, had he not?

Taking tea with the parson was a euphemism employed by the lower classes when discussing a sexual practice that even in these times of enlightenment could earn you at least six months' hard labour if you were caught at it in the back row of the music hall stalls.

'Excuse me?' said Mr Ernest Rutherford.

'Many of my relations are members of the clergy,' said

Miss Wond. 'One must observe the social graces when one is in ecclesiastical company, mustn't one?'

'One must,' said Mr Rutherford. And he lowered his hovering foot and continued down the stairs. 'I understand from your letter that you wish to discuss certain sensitive matters. We must do this in private, I feel.'

The chemist led the veiled lady to the door of many padlocks and then into the room that lay beyond. As he locked the door behind him, his guest seated herself on one of the oaken benches.

'This room certainly has wood,' said Miss Violet Wond.

'Would you care for a cordial?' asked Mr Rutherford. 'I generally offer my guests champagne, but it is somewhat early in the morning for that, I feel.'

'Champagne will be fine,' said Miss Wond. 'I have lately arrived from Mars and am still rocket-lagged, as I believe the expression goes.'

'Quite so,' said the chemist, repairing to his maple cabinet and drawing out a bottle and a pair of fluted glasses. 'I understand from your letter that your permanent residence is on Mars. Do you know Mr Septimus Grey?'

'The Governor of the Martian Territories is an intimate friend of mine.'

Mr Rutherford raised an eyebrow as he uncorked the champagne. There was no doubt in his mind that this woman's conversation was laced with suggestive remarks. But of course, as a gentleman, it was not for him to comment on this.

As he poured champagne, he said, 'Madam, by your veil and your attire, might one assume that you have recently suffered a loss?'

'One might *assume* so,' said the lady, accepting her champagne.

'But it is *not* the case?'

'*Not* the case.' The lady lifted her veil sufficiently to admit the champagne glass.

'Then you may raise your veil here.' Mr Rutherford set down the bottle and toasted with his glass.

'I wear the veil for protection,' said the lady.

'Ah, mosquitoes and suchlike. You will have no need of it here.'

'Not for *my* protection.' The lady lowered her champagne glass. Her champagne glass was empty.

'I see,' said Mr Rutherford. 'Or rather, I do not.'

'And it is better that way.' The lady in the veil held out her glass for a refill. Mr Rutherford took up the bottle and performed this pleasurable duty.

'Well, to business,' he said. 'According to your letter, you have a scientific project that you would like me to become involved with.'

'There is no man in the Empire more qualified than you to fulfil my desires.' The champagne glass disappeared once more beneath the heavy veil.

'Quite so. Perhaps you would be so kind as to outline your requirements – your letter was somewhat vague on details.' Mr Rutherford settled himself without comfort onto one of the uncomfortable chairs. His mysterious guest produced a large envelope from somewhere about her person and handed it to him. Mr Rutherford removed the contents and examined them with interest.

Time passed. Mr Rutherford became engrossed. The lady rose and refilled her glass. Further time passed and finally Mr Rutherford said, 'Well, I never did.'

The lady turned her veiled face towards him. 'Are you capable?' she asked.

'Capable? Well, yes. The theory appears sound, and I

cannot immediately fault the equations. But whether it is possible—'

'I know it to be possible,' the lady said.

'Well, anything is possible,' said Mr Rutherford. 'Except perhaps for Jones being crowned the Queen of the May.'

'Then you will do it?'

Mr Rutherford stroked at his chin. 'Let me understand this,' he said, 'so there can be no ambiguity of word or thought. This item you wish me to formulate – might it be described as a membrane?'

'That word is as good as any,' said the lady. 'It cloaks the wearer and confers certain properties upon them.'

'Indeed it would appear to.' The chemist topped up both glasses. 'It would confer upon its wearer abilities that could rightly be described as superhuman.'

'The power of flight,' said the lady, 'and a degree of invulnerability.'

'That might be a contradiction in terms,' said Mr Rutherford, 'like being *a bit* unique. Although this project is certainly *a bit* unique. The passage upon the absorption of light, for instance—'

'Invisibility,' said the lady. 'Light bent upon a molecular level.'

'I don't know what to say. It is a work of genius. This could revolutionise so very much – society could be changed for ever.'

'That is not my wish.' The lady shook her head. 'There are elements involved of which the general public must never learn.'

'Ah,' said Mr Rutherford. 'You are referring to the magical element.'

'Precisely.'

Mr Rutherford nodded thoughtfully. 'And there is the

"rub", as the bard once put it. For me to engage in this project would mean to flout interplanetary laws. The magic of Venus is deeply involved and it is illegal to practise Venusian magic upon Earth.'

'I won't tell if you won't,' said the lady, in a most coquettish tone.

'In all truth,' said the chemist, 'you tempt me. The physics involved is revolutionary. There is an atomic principle here that I would never have fathomed. But should I be discovered to be engaged in such a project I would be carted off to prison, probably thereafter to be dispatched to a court upon Venus at whose hands I would doubtless meet an ugly end.'

'I would reward you for your work in a manner you would not find disagreeable.'

Mr Rutherford raised an eyebrow once more. And sighed.

'Dear lady, I cannot,' he said. 'I am earning a reputation in my field of endeavour. I am presently engaged in something that in its own way might also change the course of history.'

'The Large Hadron Collider,' said the veiled lady, 'and the top-secret project attached to this.'

Mr Rutherford, who was sipping champagne, sneezed some into his nose. 'You know of *this*?' he said. 'How do you know of this?'

'I have friends in high places,' said the lady. 'Close friends who confide to me all manner of information.'

'Ah,' said the chemist. 'I must remain firm, I regret.'

'Peruse the equations once more,' the lady suggested, 'particularly the section regarding the negation of gravity – surely that has some resonance with your present endeavours.'

'Well . . .' said Mr Rutherford, and he scratched at his head.

'You would have my permission to apply them as you wish. And I will of course pay handsomely.'

'It is not the money,' said Rutherford. Although to a certain degree it is *always* the money. 'Although—'

'Do what I require and I will furnish you with something you require. Something physical.'

Mr Rutherford sighed anew.

'A spaceship,' said the lady. 'I am informed that in order to complete your present work you require a spaceship to convert into a vehicle that will travel through t—'

'No,' said Mr Rutherford. 'Do not speak the word, not even here. But yes, I do require a spaceship. And spaceships do not become available to purchase.'

'I own a spaceship,' said the lady. 'I arrived here in it yesterday. It is called the *Marie Lloyd* and it is yours to do with as you wish if you will create what I require.'

Mr Rutherford put down his glass and buried his face in his hands.

'Would you like some time to think the matter over?' The lady in black rose to her feet and placed her glass beside that of Mr Rutherford's.

'Well, yes. Well, no. Well, I don't know.'

'Then perhaps I can help you to make up your mind.'

The chemist sighed once more.

'Look at me,' said the lady in black, 'and listen to my words.'

Mr Rutherford looked up from his face-burying. 'What of this?' he asked.

'A terrible wrong was done to me,' said the lady, 'a terrible wrong that has made me the thing that I am. I will show you something that few have seen and fewer could possibly understand. It will shock you deeply to see this, but you, as a man of science, will understand what you see. Then you will know why I require what I do from you, and if you are possessed of a soul, you will do this thing for me. Prepare yourself.'

And with these words said, the lady slowly raised her veil.

Ernest Rutherford stared and stared in awe.

As the lady lifted high her veil, tears sprang into the chemist's eyes.

'Oh dear God,' said Ernest Rutherford. 'Oh, sweet lady, who has done this dreadful thing?'

'Will you do what I ask of you?' the lady said.

'All and more besides. Whatever I can.' Mr Rutherford's face was ghostly white and both his hands were shaking.

The lady in black lowered her veil and extended her hand to be shaken. 'I feel certain that we will enjoy a most satisfying relationship. You look as if you might have trouble getting up, so I will take care of myself. Farewell for now.'

And with that, Violet Wond took her leave, swinging her parasol.

15

rim were the thoughts of Cameron Bell and glum his disposition.

A night spent at his desk in the company of brandy had done nothing to lighten his mood. The cries from the street that awakened him to a new day brought no joy whatever.

'Leicester Square gorn up in smoke,' bawled newsboys. 'Read orl abaht it. Terrible conflagration. 'Undreds dead. Anarchists blamed.'

'Hundreds dead?' groaned Cameron Bell. 'Say it isn't so.'

'Oh, excuse me,' bawled the voice from the street. 'Only *two* dead, it's a misprint. Anarchists still blamed, however.'

The dejected detective stretched and did loud *clickings* of the neck. He scratched at stubble on his chin and arose with a grump and a grumble.

Beyond the office window London was stirring. There were all the makings of another hot day. Folk in pale linens were taking the air and a regiment of the Queen's Own Hussars rode by on magnificent greys.

Mr Bell steadied himself at the window, returned to his desk and drank down a remaining half-glass of brandy, then wandered off to change and wash and shave and make himself decent.

At a little after eight of the morning clock, looking well scrubbed and neat in pale linens of his own, Mr Bell was to be found marching in the direction of Scotland Yard.

Over the years, the great detective had cultivated many friendships within his sphere of professional influence. He had helped out more than a few, and more than a few knew he had done so. A certain chief inspector at Scotland Yard owed Mr Bell many favours.

The chief inspector's name was Chief Inspector Case, and recently he had been experiencing some difficulties. He had also recently been a commander, but he had fallen from grace.

Although on the outside dapper and well kept, with the military bearing of one who had served his Queen and country in the Electric Fusiliers, the chief inspector was a rather troubled man.

He had recently taken to the belief that the blood of the Aztecs flowed in his veins and as supposed proof of this demonstrated that he could crack walnuts beneath his armpits and sing 'songs of advancement' in a tongue of his own invention.

In times past, such behaviour and beliefs might well have had the man consigned to Bedlam. But as everyone nowadays did crack on about how enlightened were the times, the chief inspector was left to his own devices with words from his superiors being offered to the effect: 'We do not care if you think you're Monte-ruddy-zuma, just as long as you solve some crimes every once in a while.' Failure to do so, it was hinted, would incur further demotion.

Having gained entrance to Scotland Yard, Mr Bell sought

out the office of Chief Inspector Case and rapped a knuckle briskly on the door.

'Come unto me,' called a voice from within.

Cameron Bell sighed deeply and entered the office.

The chief inspector was sitting cross-legged upon his desk, and upon his head he wore a crown made from folded newspapers, which he had adorned with beer bottle tops. A gorgeous cloak of kiwi pelts was wrapped around and about him.

'Prostrate yourself,' said Chief Inspector Case.

Cameron Bell gave a foolish curtsey. 'That is all you are going to get,' said he.

'Bell,' said the chief inspector. 'It *is* you, is it not?'

'It is,' agreed Cameron Bell. 'Your powers of observation are, as ever, faultless.'

'They seek to destroy me,' said the cross-legged sitter.

'*They?*' asked Cameron Bell.

'Powers,' said the wearer of the paper crown. 'Dark powers. They are all about us, you know.'

'I know it all too well,' said Mr Bell, 'which is why I am here.'

'They say that I am mad,' said Chief Inspector Case. 'They say that I do not swim with both feet in the water.'

'You are as sane as I,' said Cameron Bell. Which worried him as he said it. 'And I come to you because you are all-knowing.'

The paper crown bobbed as the head beneath it nodded.

'I wish to consult your records – those in the "unsolved" file, I think.'

'That is a very large file,' said the sitter, snuggling into his cloak. 'I don't think you should look at it. It might upset you.'

'That is a very beautiful cloak,' said Cameron Bell. 'I have not seen its like since the last time I visited the British Museum. Were you not engaged upon an investigation there most recently yourself?'

'The filing cabinets over there will be the ones you want.' Chief Inspector Case hugged at his beautiful cloak. 'Help yourself.'

Cameron Bell surveyed the filing cabinets. They stood large and defiantly, as if saying, 'Open us if you dare.'

'Perhaps I might speed up the process,' said Mr Bell. 'I encountered a woman last night—'

'About time, too,' said Chief Inspector Case. 'Jolly well done to you.'

'Not in that way. This woman presented a most singular appearance.' A shiver ran through Mr Bell as he recalled the brutal slaying of Miss Lavinia Dharkstorrm's henchmen. 'A most violent woman.'

'No shortage of *them*,' said the chief inspector. 'Take my wife, for instance.'

'I would prefer not. This woman wore an armoured-brass corset affair and a black rubber hood with—'

'Round glass eyeholes,' said Chief Inspector Case. 'Oh no – not again. I hoped we had seen the last of her.'

'Then you know who she is?' Cameron Bell was most taken aback. This exotic creature was known to the police and yet unknown to him.

Chief Inspector Case climbed down from his desk and plodded to a filing cabinet, his magnificent kiwi cloak trailing wonderfully behind him. He slid open a drawer and tugged out a dog-eared file.

'There's not much in it,' he said. 'It was before my time and yours, too. She did what she did then went off-world, and she has committed a number of atrocities upon Mars since then. But they are, thankfully, out of my jurisdiction.'

He handed the file to Mr Bell, who seated himself on a visitor's chair and opened it up before him.

'It was in eighteen eighty-nine,' said the chief inspector, 'in Whitechapel. A gentleman was found, horribly mutilated. His name was Graham Tiberius Hill.'

Cameron Bell shook his head. 'That name means nothing to me,' he said.

'A relative of the then Prime Minister who was at that time under secret investigation for certain heinous crimes committed the year before.'

Mr Bell looked up at the chief inspector. 'Not . . . ?' said he.

The chief inspector nodded with his crown. 'The Metropolitan Police's prime suspect — we have every reason to believe that Graham Tiberius Hill was Jack the Ripper.'

'And this woman killed him?'

'Most horribly. You will see the rough sketch made by a Gatherer of the Pure who swore he had seen her emerge from the alley where Mr Hill was so cruelly done to death.'

Cameron Bell rifled through the papers until he came upon the drawing. It was crude but there was no mistake. He also came upon a photograph. 'What is this?' he asked.

'A wall,' said the chief inspector.

'But there is nothing on it.'

'Obviously not, because a constable washed the writing off.'

Cameron Bell sighed once again. 'So what *was* written upon this wall?'

'Words scrawled in chalk,' said Chief Inspector Case. 'Words that read —

LADY RAYGUN IS THE WOMAN THAT
WILL NOT BE BLAMED FOR NOTHING.

'Lady Raygun,' said Cameron Bell. 'Lady Raygun indeed.'

'Indeed, indeed, indeed, indeed, indeed, indeed, indeed.'

These 'indeeds' were spoken by the controversial cleric Cardinal Cox, for Cameron Bell's second port of call that morning was to the Bayswater residence of the colourful clergyman. A residence filled with wonders of the East in a gorgeous glittering clutter.

Indeed, it could be said that Cardinal Cox was a man that would not be blamed for nothing. Scandal attended to him as if a faithful servant, while outrage followed on as might a spaniel.

'Indeed,' said the cardinal once more as he viewed with interest those items that were placed before him.

'Reliquaries,' said Mr Cameron Bell. 'I felt that they might interest you.'

'You wish to sell them?' Cardinal Cox rubbed large red hands together. Everything about this man was large and red all over – his slippers, his raiments, his turban and his big red face.

'Where is my catamite?' he called, clapping those big hands in a loud smacking fashion. A youth of Arabian aspect appeared at the open door.

'Fetch us some hashish, if you will, young Ahmed.'

The boy departed, to return at length with a vast and beautiful hookah, which he placed upon the Afghan rug beside the Persian pouffe.

'A bit early in the day for me,' said Mr Bell, 'but don't let me stop you indulging yourself.'

'Indeed you will not,' said the cardinal. 'Indeed, indeed, indeed.'

'Tell me about the reliquaries,' said Mr Cameron Bell.

'How much do you want for them?' asked the cardinal.

'They are stolen property,' said Mr Cameron Bell.

'I am well aware of that. So how much do you want?'

'They are not for sale – they must be returned to their rightful owners.'

'You will have a long ride doing that, then.' The cardinal attended to the minutiae of lighting up the hookah.

'And why would I have a long ride?' asked the detective, looking on with interest.

'Well, that one is straightforward.' The cardinal pointed towards the smallest of the three, a jewel-encrusted thing of gold with a tiny glass enclosure at the top. 'That one has come from the British Museum.'

'Indeed it has,' the detective agreed. 'I was engaged by that worthy institution to recover it. I have also, by chance, this morning solved the case of the missing Maori kiwi cloak, but that is another matter.'

'Then let us not confuse each other with it here. The other two you have there are not from this planet – one is from Jupiter and the other from Venus. A collector's dream to see the three together. You do not know the whereabouts of the fourth one, I suppose?' The cardinal knelt down and lit up the hookah, sucked hard upon the mouth pipe then collapsed on the floor in a fit of coughing.

'A fourth one, you say?' said Cameron Bell, helping the cardinal onto his knees and patting away at his back. 'I was not aware that there *was* a fourth one.'

Cardinal Cox composed himself. 'Sit yourself down,' said he.

Cameron Bell settled onto a nest of cushions, kilims and subcontinental quilts.

'Tell me all about them, please,' said he.

The large red man relit his hookah and took the tiniest of

sucks. Breathing sweetly scented smoke, he told a curious tale.

'In the days of way-back-when,' said he, 'before science had triumphed over alchemy, it was believed that everything was composed of four elements in differing proportions – earth, air, fire and water. One can now consult the periodic table to test the inaccuracy of this medieval supposition. However, although many elements are now known and scientifically understood, the original concept of the four elements is not without its power, for a magical power it is.'

Cameron Bell groaned. 'Magic, you say?' he said.

'These are magical items,' said the cardinal. 'Or were, back in the days when folk believed in such nonsense. Each was said to contain the *Anima Mundi* – literally the World Soul – of its planet of origin, and each represents one of the four elements. Mars is fire. Venus is water. Jupiter is air.'

'And Earth is earth?' asked Cameron Bell. 'So where *is* the fourth reliquary kept?'

The cardinal shrugged as he puffed. 'Who can say? Perhaps it was broken up for the jewels that bestudded it – each of these is worth a fortune. And upon second thoughts I have no wish to purchase them. Venusians take most unkindly to their holy treasures being looted. You will do yourself a great deal of good when you return to them what is theirs.'

Cameron Bell took up the Martian reliquary and peered into the little glass enclosure atop it. Was that a flicker of flame he saw or just some trick of the light?'

'And the Earth one contains only earth?' he said.

'It is believed to contain the very substance of God. Have you ever heard of the Nazca Plains?'

'In South America? A high plateau carved with ancient patterns, if I recall correctly.'

125

'There are other beliefs. Some hold that the Nazca Lines are the fingerprint of God, left behind when he fashioned this world.'

'A fine tale,' said Mr Bell, now wafting at the air about him in an attempt to avoid any passive hashish-imbibement. 'So I suppose I must conclude that these items were stolen to order by some rich collector of outré paraphernalia.'

'Or a Master of High Magick,' said the cardinal.

Mr Bell groaned once more. 'And what would a High Master – or indeed a High Priestess – want with them?'

Cardinal Cox slapped his hands together. 'They would certainly be a witch's dream,' said he. 'If a High Priestess possessed all four, there is no telling what terrible witcheries she might perform. You return them to their rightful owners, old fellow-me-lad, and think no more about it.'

'Yes,' agreed Mr Bell. 'I will do that.'

Cardinal Cox gave Cameron Bell the very queerest of looks. '*Exactly* from where *did* you acquire these?' he asked.

'From a witch,' said Cameron Bell.

'And she let you take them from her? That I find unlikely.'

'She fled,' said Mr Bell.

'Fled leaving these?' Cardinal Cox did shakings of the head. 'Now that I find very hard to believe. Indeed, indeed.'

'It is a mystery, to be sure,' said Mr Bell. 'I followed her into a house that had but a single entrance. I searched it high and low but she was not there.'

'The house was utterly deserted?'

'There was a child,' said Mr Bell, 'but she ran away.'

'A child and she ran away?' And the cardinal laughed. 'That was no child, you foolish man – that was your witch employing her evil craft.'

'Oh, surely not,' said Cameron Bell.

'This child, did she inspire pity from you?'

Cameron Bell simply nodded.

'Then she had you fooled. She tricked you for reasons of her own.'

'I have the reliquaries,' said the detective, still fanning away with a will.

'And that puzzles me. What of the witch's familiar?'

'Her *what*?' asked Cameron Bell.

'Her familiar – every witch has one to serve her and obey her evil commands, the spirit of a demon trapped inside an animal by the witch.'

'An animal?' asked Cameron Bell, a terrible coldness entering into his voice.

'Certainly. A rat, a cat or some similar creature, normal without yet fearsome within. Beware the witch's familiar, my old friend.'

'A rat?' murmured Cameron Bell. 'A cat. Perhaps . . . a monkey?'

'Certainly a monkey. Indeed, indeed, indeed.'

'Oh my dear dead father, too,' cried Mr Cameron Bell. 'I have done a terrible thing. I must be going now. Farewell. Farewell.'

With fear upon his face, the great detective snatched up the reliquaries and made away from the smoke-shrouded room at the very greatest of speeds.

16

yon House slumbered in sunlight.

An uneasy slumber, this, however, for loud were the sounds of industry that issued from the rear of the ancient pile.

Mr Cameron Bell had engaged a hansom cab. Not the cab of the previous evening, which he had 'borrowed' from its gin-soaked driver and returned to its rank after dropping Darwin home. This was another cab with quite a different driver.

This driver, who smelled deliciously of bacon – having a wife who knew the value of a good breakfast – dropped Mr Bell off before the gates of Syon House, accepted his fare and went upon his way whistling that popular music hall tune 'A Carrot Is as Close as a Rabbit Gets to a Diamond'.*

Mr Bell did peepings through the big front gates. Beyond the newly planted groves of banana trees, a landau stood before the main entrance to the great house. The landau of Miss Lavinia Dharkstorrm.

---

* *Not to be confused with the Captain Beefheart classic of a century yet to come.*

Mr Bell did scratchings of the chin. Perhaps he was not too late. Perhaps he could rescue Darwin from the evil witch and her sinister familiar. Catching them unawares would be the order of the day.

Mr Bell ambled away to find a side-alley where he might scale one of the high surrounding walls of Syon House unseen.

As he ambled he cursed unto himself. 'This is all *my* fault,' he muttered. 'My carelessness, my thoughtlessness, my over-confidence, all have brought me to this pretty pass and put the life of my innocent companion in dreadful danger.' Mr Bell paused in his soliloquy whilst he ambled on. 'All right,' he continued, 'not wholly *innocent*, I suppose. Our partner-ship has been fraught with certain difficulties in that I do all the work and he does all the loafing about. And complains every time I need him for some special undercover assign-ment. Is it *really* too much to expect a monkey to im-personate a monkey?'

Mr Bell stopped and considered the wall. Much too high, it was.

'And how he has prospered,' the detective continued as he moved onwards. 'I do not possess a house as swank as this one, and *I* do all of the work.'

Mr Bell now stopped once more. 'I have a good mind just to leave him to it,' he said. 'The more I think about it, the more I become convinced that it is *not* my fault at all. If I climb a wall at the risk of my health and then confront that dreadful harpy, I might well end up dead. Better the loss of a mere monkey, I am thinking. Better I return these reli-quaries to their rightful owners—' he shook the oversized reticule '—accept all the reward money and, if I deem it necessary, at some time in the future team up with another partner. A man this time, and *not* a monkey.'

Mr Bell now ceased his ambling perambulations. 'My God!' said he. 'Did I really just say all *that*? Shame on me, for I am a terrible person. Of course I must rescue Darwin. Of course I must do what is right.'

And with that said he found that he had come to a place where the wall had partially fallen.

'All right, Darwin,' said Cameron Bell. 'Help is close at hand.'

With much scrambling, which precipitated no small degree of linen-suit besmerchment and an unfortunate seat-of-trouser tearing which brought a pleasant though unasked-for ventilation to Mr Bell's meaty loins, the great detective cleared the wall and dropped down into the garden.

The sounds of industry were now very loud in the ears of Mr Bell. Ears which, had they been located upon the head of an ordinary man, would have had between them a hangover of epic proportion. But it did have to be said that Cameron Bell was no *ordinary* man.

He straightened his apparel, dusted himself down as best as he could and mooched in the direction of the loud industrial clamour.

It was emanating from the all-but-completed Bananary.

Several sturdy artisans laboured upon this monstrosity. Cameron Bell had only been offered a brief glance at the plans. In real life and in the brightest of sunshine, it was far worse than he could ever have possibly imagined. It bulged in places where a glass-house should not and shunned all architectural conventions. Mr Bell, a man who harboured a strong appreciation for the classics in all their forms, in music, in art and in architecture, was rightly appalled.

The Bananary had him feeling faint.

'Good morning to you, guv'nor,' said a sturdy artisan as Mr Bell approached. 'Coming on a treat, is she not?'

Mr Bell did shakings of the head. 'It is not really to my personal taste,' said he.

'Everyone is entitled to their opinion,' said the artisan, studying the very plan that Mr Bell had once briefly glanced over.

'There is an old adage,' said Cameron Bell, 'that some things *are* better than other things and some people capable of making the distinction.'

'Whatever you say,' said the artisan, engrossing himself in the plan.

'Have you seen your master this morning?' asked Mr Cameron Bell.

'Never seen him at all,' said the artisan of sturdiness. 'Never even met him, as it happens. Seen his monkey often enough, but never met the master.'

Mr Bell nodded thoughtfully. So even those who worked for Darwin did not know that he owned Syon House. *A wise monkey indeed*, thought Cameron Bell.

'Where would the master and his monkey be found at this time of the day?' he enquired.

'In the drawing room beyond the kitchen. Some creepy woman came to visit. We were having our tea as working men rightfully should and she shooed us back to our labours.'

'Through that door there?' Mr Bell looked towards the indicated door.

The artisan nodded.

'Thank you,' said Cameron Bell. 'One last question – when do you expect to have the Bananary finished?'

'By lunchtime,' said the artisan. 'It took a bit longer than anticipated – things didn't fit as they should have.'

Mr Bell reached towards the plan, tugged it from the

artisan's fingers and turned it around. 'I will not mention it if you won't,' he said, 'but you have built it upside down.'

The great kitchen was very much as Mr Bell remembered it. Perhaps just a little untidier than it had once been and somewhat overcrowded by potted banana trees.

I do wish he would vary his diet, thought Cameron Bell as he drew out his ray gun and set its charge to 'maximum'. *If I were never to see or hear about another banana, it would in no way lessen the quality of my life.*

Mr Bell approached the door that led to the drawing room. He eased it open just a crack and peered into what lay beyond.

He viewed a room of couches and divans, of antique tables and tall jardinières. A Venusian carpet hugged a floor of polished oak and the walls were frescoed in the prettiest pastels. The curtains of this room were drawn, but modern electric torchères lit it with the brightness of the day.

Alone upon a couch sat Lavinia Dharkstorrm, reading a copy of *The Times*. She did not look up as Cameron Bell, with gun held high, came creeping into the room.

'I trust you have brought my reliquaries,' said the High Priestess. And then she neatly folded her newspaper and smiled up at Cameron Bell. 'Oh, do put away that silly pistol,' she said. 'Have you no manners? Pointing *that* at a woman!'

'Where is Darwin?' asked Cameron Bell. 'If you have harmed him, I will surely kill you.'

'Brave talk indeed.' Lavinia Dharkstorrm cocked her head upon one side. She was certainly a most attractive woman. And those mauve eyes were a most enchanting sight. 'You allude of course to your pet monkey, who calls himself Humphrey Banana,' said she. 'Such a clever little thing he is. And so very talkative. He had much to say for himself when we pushed him into the suitcase.'

'Release him immediately!' the detective demanded. 'I have never been forced to kill a woman but I will do it now with little force required.'

Miss Lavinia Dharkstorrm wagged a finger. 'I could not return him to you at this moment even if I chose to.' She pulled from her bodice a silver pocket watch. 'Ah, the ten o'clock flight,' she said. 'What times we live in – such punctuality. Your pet is even now on his way to Mars.'

'Then it is the end for you,' said Cameron Bell. 'Would you care for me to pause before your execution, that you might recommend yourself to your Maker and offer some apologies for the evil life you have led?'

'No, no, no,' said Lavinia Dharkstorrm. 'That is not the way it will be. I am booked aboard tomorrow's flight to Mars. If I do not arrive unscathed in the Martian terminal and in *your* company, a hideous fate awaits your little friend. A most prolonged period of torture during which pieces of his flesh will be removed and then posted to you. Eventually you should have enough to make yourself a nice pair of monkey-skin gloves.'

Mr Bell took two steps forwards. Never before had he known a time when he had wished so much to kill a human being.

'You will now return the three reliquaries to me and upon Mars you will seek and find the fourth. When I have all four in my possession, you will have your monkey. What say you to this?'

'I say, *why*?' said Cameron Bell. 'Why such a complicated rigmarole? Why did you not simply make good your escape last night in the company of the reliquaries? Why, if you have acquired three, can you not acquire the fourth? Why do you need to involve me in any of this?'

Miss Lavinia Dharkstorrm shook her beautiful head. 'And you call yourself a detective,' she said, smiling as she did so. 'I let you have the reliquaries last night so that you would do what I am sure you have done – take them to some expert for authentication and to provide you with some knowledge as to what they actually are. As for the subterfuge, I had intended all along to capture your partner to encourage you to find the fourth reliquary. I had you pegged all along, Mr Bell – that you substituted the real awards list at the British Showmen's Fellowship dinner and dance, that you might enjoy the ensuing chaos, all smug and filled with self-satisfaction at your cleverness. Well, I displayed a little cleverness of my own. Mine, it would appear, is superior to yours.'

And suddenly Miss Lavinia Dharkstorrm no longer sat before Mr Bell.

Instead there was a small and grubby girl, regarding him with large, reproachful eyes.

'Vile creature!' cried Cameron Bell. 'But if you are so clever . . . Why have you need of me?'

Miss Dharkstorrm reappeared and smiled a bit more. 'If I could have found the fourth reliquary myself, then so would I have done. But I have *not* been able to do so. The first three were relatively easy. I knew where they were – one in the British Museum, one upon Venus, one upon Jupiter. Stealing from the British Museum has never been particularly difficult – even chief inspectors of police get up to it. As for Jupiter, the Jovians, though affable, are a godless bunch, so I simply purchased theirs. Venus was more difficult. Theirs was kept in a temple, so I had a replacement crafted. They are still unaware of the exchange.'

'And where is the one upon Mars?' asked Cameron Bell. 'Is that kept in some holy place or in some private collection?'

'Ah, you are showing an interest. Good for you. The fourth reliquary containing the *Anima Mundi* of planet Earth has been stolen from its location on Mars.'

'Ha,' said Cameron Bell, and he almost laughed. 'By some rival coven, perchance?'

'Who can say?' Miss Dharkstorrm shrugged. 'Which is why the owner seeks to employ a detective.'

'And the *rightful* owner is who?'

'Princess Pamela,' said Miss Lavinia Dharkstorrm. 'Queen Victoria's sister.'

'The Queen has no sister named Pamela,' said Mr Bell.

'Oh yes she certainly does, and a wanton creature she is. Her existence has always remained unknown to the public in general. She was long ago installed in a palace on Mars where it was hoped she would not get into mischief. It is a very closely guarded secret.'

'But why?' asked Mr Bell.

'Because she is *the spare*. If anything was ever to happen to our all-good, all-reigning monarch — say, perhaps, the strike of an assassin's bullet — she would quietly be installed upon the throne in Victoria's place. You see, Mr Bell, she is Queen Victoria's very special sister. She is Victoria's identical twin.'

17

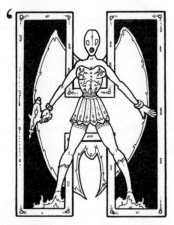

'ow are you to refuse me?' asked Miss Lavinia Dharkstorrm. 'An offer such as this one does not come your way too often.'

'I have served many royal households,' said Mr Cameron Bell, 'and be assured that when all this is done—' And then the detective paused.

'Oh yes.' The High Priestess smiled anew. 'I know just what you are thinking – an engagement from the Royal House of Saxe-Coburg-Gotha to seek a stolen reliquary and then to keep the secret of the owner's identity. A fine commission, that one, you are thinking, which will bring in many pennies and endear you to Her Majesty the Queen.'

'The Queen and I are already close friends,' said Mr Cameron Bell.

'I am, naturally, aware of this. Nevertheless, you are thinking, yes, I will take this job, I will seek and find this treasure. But when I do I will trick the wicked witch and effect my little friend's safe return, then deliver the treasure to its rightful owner and claim the large reward.'

It was Cameron Bell's turn to smile. 'Let us not forget the

reliquary stolen from Venus and the one belonging to the British Museum. This will be well-paid work indeed.'

'But of *course* that is what you would think. What you *should* think. But step carefully, Mr Bell, for I am more than your equal. Do me wrong and an awful death awaits your little monkey.'

'All right,' said Cameron Bell. 'I am aware that you are capable of many horrors. I will travel with you to Mars. I will take the commission from Princess Pamela. I will deliver the reliquary to you and you will return to me my friend.'

As Cameron Bell spoke the words *my friend*, it occurred to him that he had had few friends to call his own throughout his adult life. He had been a man driven by his occupation. He might well have unconsciously distanced himself from personal friendships, perhaps fearing just such an eventuality as this. And now the fate of his friend, his *only* friend, hung in the balance. Darwin's life depended upon him. But there was more to it than that and he hated himself for thinking it. He was an educated man and he believed himself to be an enlightened man. But he was clearly being beaten by a woman.

And, as with most gentlemen of his era, he greatly enjoyed having a woman physically beat him. The thought of one doing so mentally, however, was utterly appalling.

Miss Lavinia laughed. 'Men,' she said. 'Your thoughts speak so loudly to women. No matter how well or badly you dress, you are all the same inside.'

Miss Lavinia Dharkstorrm got up to leave.

Cameron Bell still held his pistol, but it was an impotent gesture. He tucked it back in his pocket.

'What time does our spaceship depart?' he asked. 'I have many affairs that must be put in order.'

'At ten tomorrow morning,' said the High Priestess. 'She

is called the *Phelamanga*, a rather pretty craft.' Lavinia Dhark-storrm stared at the detective. 'I know you will seek to play me false,' said she. 'How could it be otherwise? It will be sport for both of us. I wonder who will triumph.'

'I will triumph,' said Cameron Bell. 'I will bring you to justice.'

'We shall agree to differ on that. Now kindly hand me my bag.'

Cameron Bell looked down at the oversized reticule which contained the three reliquaries.

'Hand it over,' said Lavinia Dharkstorrm. 'It really doesn't suit you at all, you know.'

Cameron Bell handed it over.

Miss Lavinia Dharkstorrm held it up and gave it a sniff. 'Ah, we are off to a fine start,' she said. 'You have tainted it with an ointment that your Rutherford Patent Bloodhound can follow. Happily I have another with me.' She transferred the reliquaries from one bag to the other. 'You will have to do far better than *that*, Mr Bell. Until tomorrow, then, farewell.'

And she left the detective all alone to stand and grind his teeth.

Darwin the monkey was all alone. All alone in a locked suitcase in the cargo hold of a spaceship travelling to Mars. Darwin was a most unhappy monkey, so he stuck his thumb into his mouth and had a little cry.

Jones the horrid troll was all alone. He had a nest beneath the stairs, although he bethought that he deserved a four-poster bed. That woman in the veil had treated him roughly this morning and she had whispered such words into the ear that she held as to make the troll very afraid.

Jones the troll curled up in a ball and had a little cry.

Ernest Rutherford was all alone. Alone in his laboratory. Upon a work bench before him were the papers the veiled lady had left. Ernest studied them thoughtfully. It was all here – literally a new branch of science, which incorporated something described as the transperambulation of pseudo-cosmic anti-matter, which caused a positronic cross-polarisation within something described as a flux capacitor.* It was the missing piece in the jigsaw puzzle of time, and it was right there before him. All he had to do in exchange for this priceless knowledge was to formulate the curious membrane that fused science to magic. That could enable a woman to fly and to be in a state of near invulnerability. Why should any woman want such a thing? The chemist's question was swiftly answered as he recalled in terrible detail what he had seen when she had lifted her veil.

Mr Ernest Rutherford poured champagne and had a little cry.

Chief Inspector Case sat upon his desk, huddled in his kiwi cloak. He rocked gently back and forth and sang a 'song of advancement' in a language all of his own. She was back in London, that terrible woman. Back after nearly ten years and back to plague *him*. What had *he* done to deserve *her*? He was the King of the Aztecs. People should not mess about with such a chap as he. They should show him some respect.

Upon his desk, next to the file he had shown to Cameron Bell, was a nice fresh police report, freshly written up by a nice fresh policeman. It was a report of two bodies found in a square near St Bride's church, outside a tall and narrow house. A late-night Gatherer of the Pure had discovered the

* *Obviously not* that *one. As that would be a breach of copyright.*

bodies and he had given a description of the woman, wearing an armoured corset and a black rubber headpiece. He had seen her leaping over the rooftops, laughing as she leapt.

Chief Inspector Case wasn't laughing. That brass-bound lady was a one-woman crime wave and now she was in *his* manor. The chief inspector rocked some more and had a little cry.

Miss Violet Wond walked all alone towards Trafalgar Square. The sun raged down upon her parasol. From beneath her veil she viewed the comings and goings of those who trod the streets of the Empire's capital. She saw the nannies in their lace, pushing at their prams. The nurses wheeling dames in old bath-chairs. Young lovers with their arms entwined, Jovians with large behinds, Venusian ecclesiastics whispering their prayers. Here walked poor and ragged children. There was a barrel organ played by a man dressed up as if a pirate. Soldiers rode proudly by upon their beautiful mounts. Hansoms clattered, new electric-wheelers purred upon their rubber wheels. An airship passed in glory overhead and now the young lovers tossed coins into a fountain as jets of water flung their rainbows to the sky.

All was commonplace and though this was the city of her birth, still now all was alien to Miss Wond. She was a stranger in her own land. A woman who could love no one, nor be loved by anyone. There were things that she had to do, scores that had to be settled before she could ever hope for absolution. Or find love of her own.

Miss Violet Wond strode swiftly on. But beneath her veil she had a little cry.

Cardinal Cox sat all alone in his Bayswater residence. His catamite was out at Boots, purchasing hashish. The cardinal quaffed thickened Turkish coffee. Thickened with hashish, that coffee was. Seeing those three reliquaries together had quite upset the man in the robes of red. There was much regarding them that he had not disclosed to Mr Bell. Much regarding the prophecy.

He had studied many religions, had the cardinal. Many faiths and many practices and many magics, too. Upon his knee rested an annotated copy of the Talmud, annotated by the prophet Abu Ben Addam. There were notes here regarding the Creation and what occurred upon the evening of the very first Sabbath. It was said that five things were given then to Man. Four bejewelled caskets, each containing an *Anima Mundi*, one for each of the inhabited planets that the Lord God had made. Four caskets and the rod of Moses. The staff that would one day part the Red Sea as the old patriarch led the Chosen People from the fleshpots of Egypt. Abu Ben Addam wrote of the four caskets. Each was a gift from God, each containing the soul of a world and each to be kept on another world entirely.

'And never should the four be brought together,' warned Abu Ben Addam, 'for then shall the End Times come to each and every world.'

Exactly how and exactly why, Abu Ben Addam did not say. But it *was* clear that he believed the End of the World would occur.

'O woe unto the Sons of Adam,' wailed Cardinal Cox. 'And woe unto my catamite, for surely shall he receive a box about the ears for taking so long.'

Cardinal Cox laid down the Talmud and had a little cry.

Cameron Bell stood all alone upon the first-floor landing of Banana and Bell. He had said his farewells to the lad known as Jack and the maid who was spare and kempt. He had given each of them two months' wages in advance to continue maintenance of the offices, then sent them home for the rest of the day. So all alone was he now in the building. He slouched to his office and opened the door. The office smelled of last night's alcohol. Cameron Bell let forth a mighty sigh, crossed to the desk and lifted from its tooled-leather top a photograph in an ornate silver frame. It was a sepia print of a man and a monkey, stiffly posed beside a potted plant. The man and the monkey made stern and noble faces, but there was laughter in their eyes.

Cameron Bell peered hard at the sepia print. 'I am putting on weight,' he said, 'but you, my little friend, look just the same.'

He slid the photograph from its frame, took out his wallet and placed it therein. Then he set to do what had to be done.

Mr Bell placed a Gladstone bag onto his desktop, opened up the concealed wall safe and emptied it of its contents, which he then heaped all into the Gladstone bag. He sought out his passport and papers that authorised him to carry a handgun.

He entered the tiny room where he mostly slept and filled a pigskin valise with clothes, then changed his suit for one without holed trousers.

Now clad in travelling tweeds, a sword-stick tucked beneath his arm and a Tyrolean hat upon his head, he took up the Gladstone and valise and strode towards the stairs.

But upon the landing he paused and stood once more. From beyond came the sound of the city. Within there was nothing to be heard.

A thought struck Mr Cameron Bell that he might be leaving these offices for the very last time, for although he would certainly seek to foil the plans of Lavinia Dharkstorm, rescue Darwin, return the reliquaries to their rightful owners and claim gold for his reward, he knew full well that the witch intended to see him dead. Once he had performed the duties she had set him, she would have no compunction in having him done to death.

In all truth, he might not survive this particular challenge.

'I am so sorry,' said Cameron Bell, 'so sorry that this came about, my little monkey friend. But I *will* save you. Yes, I *will*. No matter what the cost.'

A tear welled up in Cameron's eye, but he blinked it away. 'I have no time for *that*,' said Cameron Bell.

18

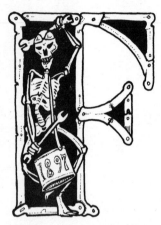iercely the heat-haze shimmered above the landing strip. That expanse of cobbled stone at the Royal London Spaceport.

Mr Bell travelled there upon the New Electric Railway. The sleek silver train with its elegant carriages swept silently through the countryside at a speed that Mr Bell found most alarming. It was fast and it was clean and it was efficient, too, but the great detective much preferred the puff-puffs of his youth. There was just something special about a steam engine. Something almost magical.

And thoughts of things that were magical were very much on the mind of Cameron Bell.

He had not wasted the previous day. He had engaged in research. He had visited the British Library to try to make sense of this reliquary business. It all sounded so complicated, so confusing. Mr Bell had a contact there who allowed him access to the Restricted Section, wherein lurked all those books forbidden from public scrutiny – works that might upset a library-goer, works of smut and sauciness, but works of magic, too.

The Restricted Section was a closely guarded secret, although most folk suspected its existence, just as most folk suspected that it held a copy of the loathsome *Necronomicon*. Which, naturally, it did. Mr Bell, however, had not come to the Restricted Section to view *that*. He wished to consult works regarding the confusing reliquaries.

The detective's contact, a bespectacled librarian, scoured the shelves of the dark little room. There really didn't appear to be too many books within. 'I know we had a copy of the Talmud here,' he said, 'one annotated by Abu Ben Addam, but it appears to have been mislaid.'

Mr Bell showed no surprise at this.

'What *do* you have?' he enquired.

'All manner of things. I have a copy of the *Chicken Kabbala* which contains most extraordinary theories regarding the Creation.'

'Perhaps another time,' said Cameron Bell. 'I need to learn whatever I can about the four reliquaries of the elements.'

'Then this is the book you're looking for.' And the librarian hefted down a mighty tome and held it on his palm. 'This one never ceases to amaze me,' he said. 'Look at the size of this book, but it is as light as a feather. How would you explain that?'

'I would not think to try.' The great detective accepted the book, all leather-bound with clasps of gold. It certainly did not weigh any more than an ounce.

'I will slip off for a cup of tea now,' said the librarian. 'Promise you won't steal anything.'

'Of course I promise,' said Cameron Bell.

The librarian smiled. 'That is one thing I really love about being in charge of this section,' said he. 'Everyone is so honest. Everyone makes me that promise. I just wish I knew where all the books keep vanishing to.'

Mr Bell sat himself down and studied the book. It appeared to be handwritten in a language of which he had no knowledge. But the more he stared at the pages before him, the more they appeared to be in English and very simple to read. Mr Bell closed the great tome and read aloud its title.

The Book of Sayito

He returned to its text and in the simplest terms he gleaned this.

In the beginning, God created the Heavens and the Earth. He brought forth the flowers and the trees, the fish and the fowl and animals of every description. And life he gave to Adam and Eve to tend the Garden of Eden.

But in his wisdom God did not only create an Adam and Eve upon this Earth. So, too, he created such a pair of first folk upon Mars, Venus and Jupiter.

Just to be on the safe side.

To each of these worlds God sent a tempter in the shape of a serpent to test his Adam and Eve. On Earth, Eve failed the test.

Upon Mars, the Martians, who were simply born evil, apparently, worshipped the serpent. God turned their world the colour of blood.

Upon Jupiter, the Jovians, a naturally jolly bunch and hearty eaters all, cooked up the serpent for dinner and ate him. But God ejected them from the Garden because of the mess they made.

Upon Venus, it was said, their Adam and Eve resisted the serpent's evil temptations and God rewarded them by expanding the Garden of Eden to cover all of their planet.

'But what about those reliquaries?' asked Mr Cameron Bell.

And he was somewhat surprised when the next page turned by itself.

It had been God's original intention that the inhabitants of each of his four worlds would never know of each other's existence, that the folk of each planet would believe they were the chosen people of God and that no other beings existed in all of the universe.

But God gave free will to his people and as time passed they grew in knowledge and eventually conquered space.

'But what about the reliquaries?' asked Mr Bell once more.

The pages of the book flicked backwards and forwards, but eventually settled down.

' "For in those days",' read Cameron Bell, ' "there were but four elements from which God created all things. And God consigned to each world an element of their own upon which they should base their meditations and their thoughts for good.

' "For Mars he chose the element of Fire.

' "For Jupiter, the element of Air.

' "For Venus, the element of Water.

' "And for Earth, the element of Earth.

' "And God placed a little piece of each of these elements, which were little pieces of himself, into a Holy Casket, that it might be kept in the chief temple of each world and venerated as a sign that God was all-seeing, all-knowing and never too far away to notice when you got up to something naughty.

' "God flung the Holy Caskets out into the void of space, that they might fall upon whichever planet they would.

' "That of Earth fell upon Mars.

' "That of Jupiter, upon Venus.

' "That of Mars, upon Earth.

' "That of Venus, upon Jupiter.

' "And God in his wisdom made this decision, that he would no longer have any involvement with his creations. That they should be allowed to go about their business and do things in their own way.

' "*But* that he would not allow this to go on for ever.

' "It was his decision that as long as his peoples paid reverence to the Holy Caskets, he would remain aloof from their ways. But should the four Holy Caskets ever leave their temples and be brought together in an unhallowed place, he would know that his creations had fallen for ever from grace and God would turn his back upon them all." '

'And what might happen then?' asked Cameron Bell.

A page turned and Cameron read from it.

' "Should these very relics of God himself be brought together in an unhallowed place, then the Gates of Hell will be opened. And upon the turn of the next millennium, the Evil One will be given dominion over all the worlds." '

'Oh my dear dead mother,' said Cameron Bell. 'But the *next millennium* – that would be when this century turns into the next. When eighteen ninety-nine becomes nineteen hundred. At least *that* is eighteen months away.'

The pages flicked once more.

Cameron read once more.

' "In those End Times before the turn of the millennium, great evil will fall upon the planets all. Great plagues will occur, great Empires will fall. The good will be at evil's mercy. And things of that nature, generally." '

The book slammed shut by itself.

'Well indeed,' said Cameron Bell. 'Well now, yes indeed.'

★

The sleek silver train of the New Electric Railway drew into Crystal Palace Station. Cameron Bell gathered his luggage together and alighted from his carriage.

It was all too much to think about. Too difficult to encompass. But wasn't that always the way with theology? What man could ever hope to fathom the mind of God? What He did, He did for reasons of His own. For after all, He *could* do as He wished, because He *was* God.

But no matter the whys and wherefores of it, one thing was clear as a crystal ball: the four reliquaries must *not* be brought together into an *unhallowed* place for fear of hideous consequence and the possible extinction of each and every one.

'So,' said Cameron Bell, wearily, 'this *would* be the Big One, then. The biggest case that ever there was that any detective could ever be set to solve.'

This thought, for some reason, gave him certain comfort. But it was comfort laced with terrible fear.

Mr Bell drew up short before the ticket barrier.

'And so,' said he, 'I will not just be saving a monkey but all of the human race besides and all of the universe, too.'

'Well, of course you will, sir,' said the ticket-collector. 'And well done to you. Now please move on through the barrier. There are sane people here who need to get on with their business.'

The sun beat fiercely down upon Cameron Bell as he strode from the station to the Royal London Spaceport. Above him rose the Crystal Palace in all its noble glory. It had been a while since Mr Bell had visited the Crystal Palace. The last time, in fact, had been while he was pursuing another case. And upon that occasion he had been *partly* responsible for reducing the mighty edifice to ashes.

But accidents *will* happen.

Beads of perspiration ran into the eyes of Mr Bell. He blinked them away and continued onwards.

The departures building of the Royal London Spaceport was not unduly crowded. Travelling to other planets was an expensive business and very few could afford it. Employees of the great mining conglomerates travelled at their companies' expense. But when it came to tourism, however, that was another matter.

Of Venus, Mars and Jupiter, Mars was the most popular destination for the wealthy tourist. Venus, through interplanetary treaty, remained closed to all but a few. Jupiter welcomed all-comers, but the heavy gravity made for an exhausting stay. Mars, however, was quite the place to be, with its romantic crimson sunsets and its network of canals that spanned its globe. Upon these placid waters, great pleasure boats moved, water-borne casinos that had much to offer their well-tailored clientele. Then there were the big-game hunts, for although the race of Martians was now happily extinct, the wildlife of the planet remained to provide exotic trophies for a gentleman's study walls. Yes, there were fine times to be had upon Mars for those who could afford to travel there.

The *Phelamanga* stood upon the cobbled landing strip, a beautiful spaceship of the new Excelsior Class.

Mr Bell espied it through the window next to the ticket booth. He nodded approvingly.

'Bell,' said he to the menial who manned the booth. 'Cameron Bell, booked aboard the *Phelamanga*, I believe.'

The menial did sortings through his papers.

'Yes indeed,' said he eventually. 'Booked aboard by Miss Lavinia Dharkstorrm. What a charming lady – such beautiful eyes. And travelling first class. How wonderful that must be.'

'I'll let you know,' said Mr Cameron Bell.

'I have no idea how you will,' said the menial, pushing Mr Bell's ticket towards him, 'for you have been booked into steerage with all those smelly miners.'

The menial raised a finger and thumb to his nose. Mr Bell did grindings of the teeth.

19

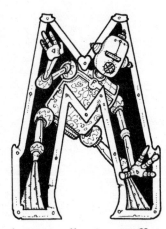

r Bell did *not* travel steerage to Mars, but neither did he travel in the First-Class Saloon. He was prepared to pay the considerable difference, but the First-Class Saloon was all sold out.

'It's the season, ain't it?' said the fellow in the second–class seat next to his. He had introduced himself to Mr Bell as, 'Luther 'Iggins, as may be, traveller in snuff, tobaccos and "things what a gentleman might require for private circumstances".' And as Mr Bell settled himself into the lumpen seat next to Mr 'Iggins, as may be, Mr 'Iggins felt the need to regale his fellow peregrinator with tales of the travelling life.

'Mars is a regular stop for me,' said Mr Luther 'Iggins. 'I suppose you might say it is one of the last frontiers, as were perhaps the Americas when the wagon trains moved west. A man might still make 'is fortune on Mars, if 'e 'as 'is wits about 'im.'

'If you must speak to me at all,' said Mr Bell, affecting a tone of indomitable condescension, 'please confine your discourse to explicit knowledge of the High Echelons of Martian Society.'

'The toffs, like?' said Mr Luther 'Iggins.

'The toffs, like,' Mr Bell agreed.

'Well, as I was saying, it's the season, ain't it?' Mr Luther 'Iggins wore a pair of those long and trailing side-whiskers which are known as Piccadilly Weepers and a suit of beige twill in the tartan of Lord Burberry. The pomade upon his hair had a bluebottle-stunning range of approximately five feet. 'The season,' said Mr 'Iggins, 'when the toffs take to the water, like.'

'Go on,' said Mr Bell, patting himself in search of cigars. In search of *anything*, in fact, that might stifle Mr 'Iggins' pomade.

'They 'as palaces, sir,' said the noxious Mr 'Iggins, 'big as ocean liners and they sails the canals in right regal splendour, with balls and masquerades and promenade concerts and soirées. All the toffs of London do be goin' to Mars at this time of year. I 'as my carpet bag chock full of gentlemen's requirements.'

Cameron Bell found his cigars and thrust one into his mouth. A blessed relief was on its way, thank God.

'Ah, look,' said Mr 'Iggins as a sign began to flash. 'No smoking in the cabin, please, the ship is about to depart.'

The *Phelamanga* boasted many of the latest innovations. A Wiff-Waff court with an electrical scoreboard. A Turkish bath. Tri-planetary cuisine and female serving staff who wore bright red tightly fitting bodices with matching culottes and fascinator hats and sported tiny aeronaut's goggles, and who were already affectionately referred to as the 'Scarlet Harlots'.

As the NO SMOKING sign took to flashing, one of these lovelies appeared.

'Ladies and gentlemen,' she said, in the voice of one not unacquainted with a finishing-school. 'please fasten your safety belts, extinguish all cigarettes, pipes and cigars and join me in a prayer for our salvation.'

Cameron Bell was not alone in raising an eyebrow to this.

'Take no notice,' said Mr 'Iggins. 'Spaceships 'ardly ever explode nowadays. I 'aven't been in a serious crash for almost three weeks.' And he nudged Mr Bell in the approximate area of his ribs. 'Always tickles me that the toffs sit up front. I always sit well back, me, because I've never 'eard of a spaceship *backing* into a mountain, 'as you?'

'Madam,' called Mr Bell to the Scarlet Harlot. 'Would it be possible for you to check first class, just in case a seat has unexpectedly become available?'

But the Scarlet Harlot was praying softly as the spaceship rose into the sky. There was none of that sickening shaking-all-about that you got with old hulks like the *Marie Lloyd*. The *Phelamanga* swept smoothly aloft, borne as it were upon the wings of angels.

'And please remain seated until the NO SMOKING sign ceases its illumination,' said the Scarlet Harlot, having made her peace once more with the Almighty, 'at which time the spaceship will have taken to revolving, creating a state of artificial gravity without which you will float about and get yourself all in a mess. Anyone caught using the water closets prior to this time will be prosecuted by the management.'

With that, the Scarlet Harlot took herself off to a seat with a safety belt.

Mr 'Iggins opened his mouth to speak once more. Mr Bell, however, informed him that this was his particular hour for silent meditation, so quiet as the eternal grave must Mr 'Iggins be.

It was a three day-voyage to Mars and there was no sleeping accommodation provided for the second-class passengers. In first class there were elegant little private booths, with fitted wardrobes and hammocks where the wealthy might spread out and relax when they had exhausted themselves from too much Wiff-Waff.

Few of the second-class passengers had thought to withdraw clothes from their luggage before this luggage was stashed away in the hold. And so, by the second day, the atmosphere within the second-class accommodation was not one conducive to good health.

The food, though basic, served as it should and Mr Bell ran up a considerable bill for brandy and cigars.

As the *Phelamanga* moved imperceptibly through the aether of space, those who had never travelled between the planets before gazed in wonder through the portholes whilst those more seasoned to off-world perambulation affected blasé dispositions, read journals, drank themselves to insensibility or congregated in the gentlemen's water closet for illicit games of Snap.

With so many things upon his mind, Mr Cameron Bell found the journey tedious at best and when Mars was finally sighted, he joined in what cheering there was.

The Red Planet slowly swelled to fill the endless void and the *Phelamanga* fell into orbit about it. The Scarlet Harlot made several speeches concerning the officious nature of those who manned the customs hall and read from a long list of prohibited items, which ranged from tooth powder to tennis balls.

The illegal importation of apes, Mr Bell duly noted, carried with it a long prison sentence.

Mr Bell gazed towards the porthole. How much did he *really* know about Mars? *Very little*, was the answer to this. He knew, as did all men of the age, that it was girded about by vast canals; that the now happily extinct Martian race had been an amphibious species, part sentient cephalopod, part reptile; that the lands were predominantly jungles, where all the trees were red and where walked, crawled and scampered many mysterious beasties which provided sport for big-game hunters.

Of the Earth-folk who lived there, he knew a little. He was acquainted with Mr Septimus Grey, Governor of the Martian Territories – and a gentleman with a colourful past. And he was aware that members of the British aristocracy favoured Mars as a summer resort and dwelt there upon spectacular floating palaces. The social divide was extreme upon Mars between the toffs and the working class, which consisted of servants and those who toiled in the mines for the great conglomerates or chanced their luck in the uncharted jungles, seeking the mother-lode. And there were always rumours that a revolution was about to break out, that there were anarchists hiding behind every red bush, waiting to blow something up.

Oh yes – and then there was Princess Pamela, identical twin sister of Queen Victoria. A secret so well kept that even *he* had not heard of her until now.

Not even a rumour, thought Cameron Bell. *Somewhat surprising, that.*

Regarding law and order upon the Red Planet, the wealthy maintained small private armies and considered themselves above the law. For the rest, a thuggish militia in the pay of Her Majesty's Government dispensed a summary justice, which was open to negotiation. Mars certainly had the 'frontier' feel, and that caused Mr Bell a certain degree of alarm.

The NO SMOKING sign began to flash and Mr Bell fastened his safety belt.

The Scarlet Harlot appeared once more and called upon

the second-class passengers to join her in prayer, then made good her escape from the evil-smelling cabin.

The *Phelamanga* entered the atmosphere of Mars with little more than a few angelic flutterings, then wafted down and settled upon the landing strip of the planet's capital city.

The imaginatively named VICTORIA.

Mr Bell craned his neck to view what lay beyond the porthole. He had only been off-world once before, when he found himself amongst an illegal hunting party upon the planet Venus. Mars would be a very big adventure.

Would he succeed? Rescue Darwin, foil the witch and bring her justice, then return the stolen loot to its rightful owners? All depended first upon him finding and acquiring the last reliquary. Stolen by whom? And located where? It was a very big planet out there.

The first-class passengers disembarked and were carried off towards the arrivals hall aboard a six-wheeled charabanc drawn by several creatures which Mr Bell assumed to be the Martian equivalent of the horse. Three-legged beasties were these, which perambulated in a spiralling balletic fashion. Their heads were small, their bodies sleek and speckled.

Mr Bell now became aware that everything upon Mars appeared to be hued in shades of red. The dust that arose from the charabanc's wheels was a rich and rusty ochre, while the beasties' pelts were in tones of pink that matched the cloudless sky.

Presently the outer door of the second-class cabin opened, releasing the fetor within and admitting a dry and pleasant air laden with curious essences, all new to Cameron Bell.

An open cart pulled by an alarming spider the size of a brewer's dray horse arrived at the *Phelamanga* to collect the second-class passengers and their luggage. The driver of this cart and a swarthy assistant went about the loading of the baggage in a calm, unhurried fashion possibly indicative of a philosophical frame of mind that embodied syncretisation and spiritual placidity.

The driver's shirt cuffs, however, informed Mr Bell that it was nothing more than wilful malingering and the great detective offered Mars his very first sigh of the day.

The journey to the arrivals hall passed without incident. But as Mr Bell stepped down from the cart, he became aware that he was now coated with a thin layer of Martian dust. Two 'dust boys' appeared from the building and with the aid of long-handled brushes, and in exchange for a small remuneration, flicked the passengers into a semblance of normalcy.

The arrivals building was a piece of original Martian architecture. Constructed in an unforgiving and unaesthetic manner, it was all bold buttresses and stanchions with high blank ceilings and small circular windows. A large crude 'A' had been painted upon the facing wall. Menials were scratching away to remove it and grumbling the word 'anarchists' as they did so.

Now began a process which appeared expressly designed to upset the incoming passenger, involving as it did out-rageous public body searches accompanied by much shout-ing and barking from brutal officialdom. Mr Bell managed a long and lingering anticipatory sigh but was mercifully spared from it all, for upon displaying his passport to a ferocious flat-headed individual, he was informed that he had a 'priority clearance' and that his friends were waiting for him in the First-Class Saloon.

Mr Bell humped his luggage to this First-Class Saloon, there to be greeted by Miss Lavinia Dharkstorrm and two henchmen new to Cameron Bell.

Miss Dharkstorrm was seated at a table topped by red local

marble and supped at a cocktail held in a long pale glass. She raised her eyes to Mr Bell, then dabbed her fingers to her nose.

'Why, sir,' said she, 'you smell most rank indeed.'

Mr Bell smiled through teeth most tightly gritted. 'Your fragrance remains unchanged,' he observed.

'Compliment or insult?' Miss Dharkstorrm shrugged without interest. 'I have booked you into the New Dorchester,' she said. 'There you may bathe and make yourself respectable. I have also arranged an audience with Princess Pamela at ten o'clock local time tomorrow morning. Princess Pamela is aware of your reputation – after all, it was *I* who recommended you to her as the ideal fellow, both discreet and thorough, to retrieve her stolen property. I know you will seek to recover the reliquary as quickly as possible to save your little monkey friend from undue suffering. Once you have done so, you will place it in a safety-deposit box here at the spaceport. Give Mr Bell the key, please, McDuff.'

The henchman named McDuff stepped forward and tossed the key at the feet of Mr Bell. The detective stooped to pick it up.

'I would ask—' he began.

But Miss Dharkstorrm shook her head. 'All that needed to be said has now been said.' She smiled. 'You will do as I have instructed. The matter is neither open to negotiation nor subject to equivocation. Depart now, if you please, for your rankness offends me.'

The New Dorchester was but a short stroll from the arrivals building.

The New Dorchester had opened the previous year and was a faithful reproduction of the Grand Hotel in

Eastbourne. The whiteness of its walls might be tinged Martian pink, but it stood all proud and British upon this alien soil.

Before the hotel was a steam charabanc that the hotel's residents might hire for days out. Also there loafed a group of boys, grubby boys, these, and somewhat wild of eye. As Mr Bell approached they fell upon him with offers to carry his bags, or indeed his person, and to do certain things that were quite illegal on Earth. Mr Bell fended them off with his sword-stick and entered the hotel. The plushly costumed doorman was similarly offended by Mr Bell's rankness but tipped his hat to the detective, for it was more than his job was worth to turn away paying clients.

A suite of rooms had been booked for Mr Bell, a splendid bedroom with a study area and a bathroom with a hydrostatic health spa, which was as fearsome an arrangement of piping-showerhead-water-jet paraphernalia and brass stopcocks as had ever daunted Mr Cameron Bell. The instruction manual ran to thirty-six pages and the detective suffered chills and scaldings by turn, but eventually emerged from the bathroom a cleaner and a wiser man.

Having attended to all the minutiae of male hygiene, he dressed in his pale linen suit and put his travelling clothes outside the door, with a note to the effect that they should receive immediate attention.

By local time it was now early evening and Mr Bell's stomach grumbled for dinner. He stood in the bedroom and examined his reflection in a tall ornately framed looking-glass.

He was determined that he would succeed in his endeavours. He was, after all, Mr Cameron Bell, widely recognised to be the greatest detective of his day. A man who through mere observation of a gentleman's attire could deduce with unerring accuracy a host of intimate details and reveal the truth, thereby determining guilt or innocence.

He peered at this reflection. What could he deduce from *that*? It was slightly out of focus, for from a misplaced vanity he rarely wore his pince-nez. But he could read much about himself from his reflection.

Here stood a man of average height, a portly fellow with a large bald head. A fellow who looked as Mr Pickwick did. A fellow, furthermore, whose turn-ups spoke of his self-doubt, and his lapels of his failings on this, that and the next thing, too.

Mr Bell was distracted from his reverie by a knock at his door.

He answered this to find a messenger boy in a pillbox hat and brightly buttoned waistcoat holding a silver tray that bore a long white envelope upon which Mr Bell's name was scrawled.

Mr Bell accepted the envelope and tipped the messenger.

Alone in his room, he examined the envelope.

It had travelled through many hands and the Gothic script had been penned by a woman. An evil woman. Miss Lavinia Dharkstorrm.

Cameron Bell tore open the envelope, drew out a sheet of scented paper and read aloud what was written upon it.

DO EXACTLY AS I HAVE
INSTRUCTED YOU TO DO
OR ELSE.
Love L.

There was something more inside the envelope and this Mr Bell tipped into his hand.

A tuft of brown hair. A tuft that had not been cut but rather *torn* from the skin of its owner.

There was blood upon this hair.

The blood of Darwin the monkey.

20

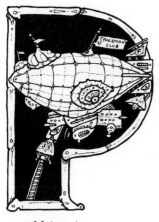

rincess Pamela's floating palace was painted peachy pink and had tiers and tiers of tessellated turrets. Amongst its architectural anomalies were also to be found a conglomeration of crimped cupolas, a multiplicity of marble minarets and a superabundance of staggering steeples. All sufficient, in fact, to beg for abominable alliteration as a hungry hound might beg for a bonemeal biscuit.

Or indeed a simpering slave for the mercy of a monstrous master.

Mr Cameron Bell, whose tastes in architecture were of the classical persuasion, considered the palace to be of such overwhelming ostentation and ghastly grandiloquence that he was lost for all alliteration.

As he approached aboard the royal steam tug, the great detective stood at the prow, as if some stoic figurehead, viewing the outrageous construction as it slowly filled the skyline.

This portly figurehead with his pale linen suit, straw boater aslant upon his baldy head, a Gladstone bag in one hand and a sword-stick in the other, was not the Mr Bell of the previous day. Which is to say that a substantial change had come over him since he had viewed the horror delivered to his hotel room in a long white envelope. This Mr Bell was the Mr Bell of old. A man supremely confident of his powers. A man determined in his attitude. A man who would not be shaken from his purpose.

A man who was a force to be reckoned with.

The steam tug's engine *chug-chug-chugged* as the bulbous boat, its registration plate naming it as the *Maggie* of *Cubit's Yacht Basin, London*, moved over the placid waters. The Grand Canal was five miles wide at this point and had more of the look of a lake or an inland sea about it.

Mr Bell called back to the man at the helm. 'How many folk inhabit his extraordinary creation?' he called.

'Thousands,' the helmsman replied. 'The princess maintains a vast retinue of servants. There's flunkeys and footmen, castellans and courtesans, equerries, courtiers and chatelaines, too. Then there's the shield-bearers, train-bearers, cup-bearers, wine-bearers, bare-bearers—'

'*Bare*-bearers?' asked Mr Bell.

'Did I say *bare*-bearers?' said the helmsman. 'Naturally I meant *bear*-bearers – the chaps who carry little bears around. Then there's the laundry maids and parlour maids and chambermaids and—'

'I think I get the picture,' said Cameron Bell.

'Jamadars and bheesties,' said the helmsman. 'Not to mention the major-domos, lordly lamplighters and twisted firestarters.'

'Twisted firestarters?' enquired the detective.

'I told you not to mention them.'*

---

* *This line can apparently be dated back to the Battle of Trafalgar, when Nelson told Hardy not to mention the tongues.*

Mr Bell leaned back towards the helmsman and smote him smartly upon the head with the business end of his sword-stick.

'Enough of your impertinence, my fine fellow,' he said.

'Well, pardon me, guv'nor,' said the helmsman in a tone that vaguely echoed contrition, 'but sometimes I cannot contain myself, what with the joyousness of life on this here canal.'

Mr Bell raised an eyebrow but spared the helmsman a further smiting. He glanced the fellow up and down and drew deductions from here and there and also the next place, too.

'You have served the princess for a very long time,' said he to the man at the helm, 'yet you have never been allowed to enter the floating palace.'

'Man and boy I have served the royal lady,' said the helmsman, adjusting a stopcock which put Mr Bell in mind of those within his bathroom at the hotel. He had received a particularly violent scalding this morning but felt confident that he was getting to grips with the theory of it all.

'Perhaps your eldest son will find a place in the Royal Household,' said Mr Bell. 'He appears to be a bright enough lad.'

'Ah,' said the helmsman. 'I see.'

'You do?' asked Cameron Bell.

'You are a thaumaturge, one of them as can read the minds of men. Come for some congress at the palace, I suppose it would be.'

Mr Bell's face expressed no emotion. 'And what do *you* know of such congresses?' he asked.

'No more than I should, sir. No more than I should. But it is common knowledge that the princess enjoys the company of magicians. The princess fears the anarchists, just as everyone else does, and she has been known to employ magicians to protect her. I boat them out to the palace all the time. Backwards and forwards I go, backwards and forwards, year after year after year, but never allowed inside that big pink palace.'

'You follow a noble calling,' said Mr Bell. 'When I speak with the princess, I shall recommend that she raise your salary. And also that she employ your son, when he is of a suitable age.'

'Why, thank you, sir. Why, thank you very much.' The helmsman tipped his cap to Cameron Bell.

'So tell me,' said the detective, 'has the princess received many visitors and guests of late? Anyone of singular interest you have ferried across?'

'None but the usual lords and ladies as comes for the season. But for that one woman, and I did not take to her.'

'Please go on,' said Cameron Bell.

'Skinny creature with mauve-coloured eyes. You could smell the magic upon her. I takes her over and she's all smiles, but on the way back she's cursing fit to fracture a rib and threatens to turn my face inside out if I don't put more speed to her passage.'

Mr Bell smiled somewhat. Lavinia Dharkstorrm, he presumed with correctness. Travelling happily to the palace with the intention of stealing the reliquary. Then returning in fury when she discovered that someone else already had.

'The palace was originally the property of Martian nobility, I assume,' said Mr Bell.

'You assume correctly, sir. Once the Martians were all dead, the London toffs took over the floating palaces. The princess had hers painted pink. Everything's pink with the princess, so I've heard.'

Mr Bell chose not to comment upon that remark. 'When will the palace be setting sail, as it were?' he asked.

'In two days' time,' said the helmsman. 'And I'll travel with it, moored to the jetty, but not permitted to set a toe upon her.'

The floating palace now loomed all-consumingly above and the helmsman drew the little craft close to the jetty upon which he could never set a toe.

'Do you wish for me to await your return, Master Mage?' asked the helmsman, saluting as he did so.

Mr Bell climbed with care from the royal tug to the royal jetty and turned to face the helmsman. 'What if other folk come to the shore, awaiting you to ferry them across?' he asked.

'Then they'll just have to wait, sir, won't they?'

'Splendid,' said Mr Bell. 'Then settle yourself down for a nap and I will awaken you gently upon my return.'

The helmsman offered another salute and Mr Bell went on his way.

He trudged up a gravel drive that led to an unprepossessing door. Knowing well the societal niceties of court, Mr Bell was aware that only those of royal blood could expect to use the grand main entrance. As his shoes crunched on the gravel, he wondered at the wonder of it all. This palace was constructed of marble and stone and had to weigh literally millions of tons and yet it floated as would an ocean liner. There was much to understand upon this rose-red world and there would be little room for error if he was to succeed in his enterprise.

Mr Bell faced up to the unprepossessing door and rapped upon it with the pommel of his sword-stick. The door swung instantly open and the detective gazed at the being who stood within. Gazed *down* at this being. This rather wonderful being.

For she was a woman of oriental appearance, her hair teased into the style of the geisha, her sylph-like body embraced by a gorgeous kimono. A perfectly proportioned woman, this, but one standing less than three feet in height.

'Mr Bell,' said this delicate creature, in an accent that was unknown to the great detective. 'Princess Pamela is expecting you. Do please follow me.'

Mr Bell entered the palace and as he followed this enchanting little person up a spiral staircase, which she climbed with practised ease, he recalled an article he had read in *The Times* newspaper several years before. An article which concerned certain alarming discoveries that had been made upon this planet once it had been freed from its warlike inhabitants. Human beings were found upon Mars. Human beings who had been altered in various ways and pressed into the service of their loathsome masters. The evidence suggested that for a considerable period of time prior to their abortive invasion of Earth, the Martians had been surreptitiously visiting our world with the purpose of kidnapping human children. Evil things had been done to these innocents, ungodly experiments carried out upon them. Mr Bell had shuddered considerably when he read this account. It was truly the stuff of nightmare.

The tiny woman moving briskly before him was, however, anything *but* the stuff of nightmare. She was as one of the elfin folk, wafted from the realms of Fairyland.

At length they gained a high hallway, the little lady button-bright but Cameron Bell a-puffing like a steam tug. As he regathered his breath, the elfish being indicated a door, bowed politely and departed from his sight.

'So be it,' said Mr Bell, removing his straw boater,

dragging from his pocket an oversized red gingham hand-kerchief and drawing it over his brow. He straightened his tie and, with shoulders back, knocked gently upon the door.

Which was immediately drawn open by yet another tiny figure, this one even tinier than the first. He looked to be a gentleman of considerable age, with a bright bald head and a noble beard that reached from his chin to the floor. He wore a loose red long-sleeved garment secured at the waist by a silken cord, and he looked every bit the way a storybook wizard should look.

Only smaller.

Mr Bell gained knowledge from his fingernails and foot-wear. The little fellow glared at him with ill-concealed contempt.

'Bell, is it?' he said, in a voice all shrill and reedy. 'Follow me and hurry, too – the princess won't be kept waiting.'

The bald and bearded fairy-man set off at the scamper and Mr Bell marched behind, swinging his sword-stick and taking in his surroundings.

These were certainly pleasant enough, although colour-wise they did lean rather heavily towards the pink. There was a medieval feel to it all, with hanging tabards and crested shields smothering walls of unplastered stone. Unplastered perhaps, but painted pink. Mr Bell marched onwards.

Ahead, from on high, hung curtains of pink. 'Go through between them,' said the bearded manikin.

Cameron Bell pressed through the curtains and entered a wonderful room. A wonderfully *pink* room it was, all filled with wonderful things that were wonderfully pink.

The furnishings were eccentrically eclectic, drawn from many ages and all expressing an overwhelming opulence. Renaissance thrones rubbed gilded shoulders with high-backed settees that must once have graced the drawing room of the Sun King. There were paintings, too, by Constable and Turner, by Gainsborough and Landseer and also Richard Dadd. Their frames were pink but the oils remained untouched. Pinkly patterned kilims pelted the polished floor and a chandelier so overwrought with crystals as to be some ice-capped mountain flung light from a thousand modern bulbs in ten thousand directions.

Somewhere in the distance arose a baroque table upon which was spread a banquet of heroic proportions. Glazed hogs' heads, roasted turkeys and local game that defied easy description lay heaped in their steaming masses. And somewhere to the rear of it all a lady lounged a-feasting on a jellied tentacle.

'*Bell*,' called out this lounging lady. 'Bell, do hasten here!'

Cameron Bell, with head humbly bowed, hurried as best he could. As he reached the table he peered between a haunch of something or other and a loin of something else.

'Mr Bell at your service, Your Royal Highness,' said Mr Cameron Bell.

The lounging lady leaned forward. She was a vision in pink from crown to gown, from lacy cuff to bulging blowsy bodice. Her fingers flashed with rare rose diamonds and a pearl the size of a copper penny, though pink as a pony's pizzle, shimmered at her throat. The only note of sobriety in all this perfusion of pink was the little black domino mask that hid the upper part of her face.

This, however, did little to offer disguise, for the feasting female was in every way but dress the very double of Her Royal Majesty Queen Victoria, Empress of both India and Mars.

'Hast thou eaten, chuck?' asked the princess in that accent known to most Londoners as 'Northern', but to a few, Mr

Bell included, as the accent of Jupiter, where Princess Pamela had clearly spent most of her formative years. 'If thou art hungry, then roll up thy sleeves and get thyself stuck in.'

21

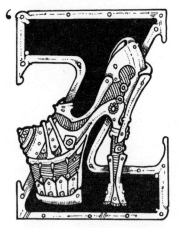oos?' asked Cameron Bell, in response to a question posed to him by Princess Pamela. 'Do I like them? Well, yes, I suppose I do.'

'So dost I,' said the regal lady, laying about a haunch of grilled galliguffin* with the carving knife. 'I think they're champion. I'm having one installed on the forward promenade deck.'

'A fascinating novelty,' said Mr Cameron Bell.

'Close to kitchen,' said the princess.

'Ah,' said Cameron Bell.

'Art thou enjoying thyself?' Princess Pamela topped up Mr Bell's glass from the bottle of vintage Château Doveston that lazed in a bucket of pinkly tinted ice.

'Very much so.' Mr Bell had his sleeves well rolled, no stranger he to an old-fashioned trenchering-down.

'Champion. Champion. Champion,' said the pinky princess. 'I've read all about thee, Mr Bell. And dear Lavinia says that nowt will stand in thy way when it comes to retrieving my reliquary.'

---

* *A three-trunked Martian mammoth.*

'Nowt,' said Mr Bell, sipping champagne between great gulpings of grub. 'You can rely on me completely.'

'Aye, that I can, or it will be the worse for thee.'

'Excuse me?' said Mr Bell, a leg of something hovering now before his open mouth.

'Mars,' replied the princess, loading her plate with grilled galliguffin and sweet potatoes, too. 'Mars, lad, Mars!'

'I fail to understand, fair lady,' said the gallant Mr Bell.

'Not like Earth, lad. Thou canst do what thou wilt 'pon Mars. Well, not thee, but me. I can chop off thy head and eat thy meat and toss thy bones into Grand Canal and none will care nowt. How's that to be goin' on with?'

'I am confident that you will have no cause to employ such extreme measures,' said the dining detective.

'Extreme?' The princess fell about in mirth. 'That's not extreme. I'll tell you what's extreme.'

'Perhaps not while I'm eating,' said Cameron Bell.

'Dost thou choose to argue with a princess?'

'Perish the thought,' said Mr Bell. 'It is simply that I am eager to begin my quest and solve for you the case of the purloined reliquary.'

'Dear Lavinia tells me that the Sherlock Holmes stories are actually based upon thy exploits.'

Mr Bell nodded as he once more ate.

'And that Dickens based the looks of Mr Pickwick upon thine?'

Mr Bell nodded dismally this time. 'It did sound like a good idea at the time,' said he.

'I like my men plump,' said Princess Pamela, a-patting at her belly. 'Holmes is slim as a whippet. Thou wouldst not get a sandwich out of he.'

Mr Bell took up a napkin and gave his chops a good wiping over with it. 'Well, I must be up and about my business,' he said. 'Could someone show me to the scene of the crime, as it were?'

'Thou'll not be staying for pudding?' The princess made a kittenish expression. 'Topped off with a Martian coffee.'

'A Martian coffee?' said Mr Cameron Bell.

'It is like an Irish coffee, only red.'

Mr Bell laughed politely.

'Why dost thou laugh?' asked the princess. 'Dost thou mock the royal person?'

'Oh, on the contrary,' said Mr Bell. 'I laugh at myself for being so ill-informed as to know nothing of a Martian coffee.'

'Two days,' said Princess Pamela.

'Two days?' queried Mr Bell. 'What two days might these be?'

'The two days it will take thee to solve the case of the purloined reliquary and return it to me, before my floating palace sets sail.' The princess smiled a greasy smile and drew a lacy cuff across her mouth. 'In the meanwhile, in fact from early this morning, t'spaceport is closed to thee. And a bounty be upon thy baldy bonce, if thou comest not back with my treasure.'

'You will have no need for that,' said Cameron Bell. 'If the perpetrator is on this planet, I will find him, have no fear, sweet lady.'

'Fear?' the princess chuckled. Then, 'Belmont!' she cried out in a bellowing tone. 'I am firm but fair,' she told Mr Bell, whilst she waited impatiently. 'Thou playest fair with me and I'll play fair with thee. Return my treasure and thee'll get a big reward. Fail and it'll be the worse for thee.'

Away beyond the confusion of furniture, the tiny bearded man poked his tiny bearded face between the curtains.

174

'At your service, ma'am,' he called in his tinkly little voice.

'Take Bell to t'chapel and let him search for clues. Then send him on his way and 'appen back 'ere to serve my pudding.'

'Yes, ma'am, yes.' The manikin beckoned Mr Bell, who backed from the room, a-bowing as he did so.

Belmont scuttled forward and Cameron Bell fell in behind. 'How far away is the chapel?' he asked the scuttling figure ahead.

'We're not going to the chapel,' said Belmont, casting his beard scarf-like over his left shoulder. 'We're going to the machine room.'

'And why might we be going there?' asked Mr Cameron Bell.

'You want to solve the case, don't you?'

The scuttler did not turn, but Mr Bell still nodded.

'And so do we all. She's a regular horror since the burglary. She had my brother poached last week and munched him up for supper.'

'Oh my dear dead mother,' said Cameron Bell.

'So we'll all be happier when she gets her blessed reliquary back.'

'And the solution lies in the machine room?' said Mr Bell.

'Absolutely,' said Belmont. 'I could have sorted all this out for the princess, but oh no, she has to listen to that harpy Dharkstorrm. "Bring in the famous detective, Cameron Bell, let him take on the case."'

'Is *this* the chapel?' asked the detective. 'This looks very much to be a chapel door.'

'It is,' said Belmont, turning and hunching up his shoulders. 'But it is the machine room you want – believe me on this, you surely must.'

'I have no cause to doubt you,' said Mr Bell. 'But as we *are* at the chapel, what harm would there be in letting me take a swift look around before we visit the machine room and all is revealed?' Mr Bell did grinnings down towards the tiny man.

'Oh, as you wish – it's your rump she'll have served on a silver platter.'

'Key?' asked Mr Bell.

'Isn't locked any more,' said Belmont. 'No point now the reliquary is gone.'

Mr Bell made a thoughtful face. 'Who held the key at the time of the robbery?' he asked.

'My brother,' said Belmont. 'The Keeper of the Keys. Those keys never left his hands. He swore to that throughout the long, slow poaching.'

'How many other entrances to the chapel?' asked Mr Bell.

'None, and no windows.'

'Then please wait here while I examine the interior of the chapel alone.'

'As you wish.' Belmont folded his arms in a huff and made a grumpy face. 'But before you do, let me warn you – it isn't nice in there.'

'Would you care to elaborate?' asked Mr Bell.

'The murals on the wall are horrid,' said Belmont. 'The princess should have them painted over.'

'Horrid in what way?' asked Mr Bell.

'Violent. Nasty,' said Belmont. 'You see, many now believe that the war the Martians waged upon Earth was a holy war. A crusade. The Martians believed themselves to be God's Chosen People and the folk of Earth idolaters and fallen beings, little more than animals, fit for nothing better than enslavement or death.'

Mr Bell nodded at this. The Martian invasion had been notable for its brutality if nothing more.

'After the Martians were all put to death,' Belmont continued, 'scholars from Earth gained access to the libraries of Mars. They deciphered the Martian sacred scripts and were surprised to find that the Martian Creation stories closely mirror our own. And they discovered that the prophets of old were not born upon Earth but had descended from the sky. They had come from Mars. Moses, it transpired, was a Martian and even—' Belmont whispered '—Jesus, too.'

'That is surely blasphemous,' said Cameron Bell.

'For now, perhaps,' said Belmont, 'but not perhaps to future generations. Who can say what they might choose to believe? They might even incline towards a theory that God did *not* create the universe, but rather that the universe created itself out of nothing, in a great big bang or suchlike.'

'I doubt that,' said Cameron Bell, 'for such a theory would be laughable. But it is all food for thought. So please wait here while I look into the chapel.'

And with that said he left Mr Belmont, entered the chapel and closed its door behind him.

The smell of the chapel surprised Mr Bell, for it was the smell of any chapel on Earth, and the interior decoration was most familiar, too: Gothic arches, pews of pine, though broad these pews to accommodate the Martians' beastly bottoms. The depictions of the saints, however, came as a body blow, as did the sight of the tentacled horror that adorned the cross above the altar.

And as for the frescoes, they were frightful throughout. Hideous depictions of Earth people toasting in Hell whilst Martians swanned about on the Heavenly plains.

'Ghastly,' was Mr Bell's opinion, 'but hardly out of place in this appalling palace.' And without saying more he turned his attention to the job in hand and did what no man of the Earth did better.

Mr Bell removed from his Gladstone bag several items of scientific interest, one of which at least had been the invention of Ernest Rutherford. Mr Bell approached the altar and conducted certain experiments upon the area where the reliquary, its absence accurately denoted by a bright and dustless ring, had rested for many long years.

'Removed twelve days ago,' said Mr Bell, consulting dials and employing a slide-rule. 'So what of this thief, whom locked doors trouble not?'

Mr Bell peeped here and there, stroked at his chin and scratched upon his head. He dropped to his knees and examined the floor. Climbed upon pews and scrutinised the ceiling.

And then he began to pace about in ever-decreasing circles. 'No,' he said as on he paced. 'No, this cannot be.'

He turned and paced the other way, a-no-ing as he did so.

And when finally his ever-decreasing circles had reduced to only himself, slowly rotating and shaking his head, he drew to a halt and sighed a mighty sigh.

He then repacked his Gladstone, placed his straw boater onto his head, tucked his sword-stick under his arm, took up his Gladstone, cast one final all-encompassing look around and promptly left the chapel.

'Done, are you, then?' asked Belmont. 'Seen all you needed to see?'

'I have indeed,' said Cameron Bell.

'And identified the thief?'

Cameron Bell made noddings of the head.

'You *have*?' piped Belmont. 'You have *not*!'

'I have,' said Cameron Bell. 'But I must confess to puzzlement.'

Belmont twisted fingers into his beard.

'You see,' said Cameron Bell, 'there is no doubt in my

mind as to who stole the reliquary. The evidence is all there, most strikingly apparent, almost as if the criminal was aware that I would take the case and so left, for reasons all of his own, the clues necessary for me to identify him.'

Belmont's beard was all in a-tangle. 'So who did the crime?' he asked. 'And do you know the villain's name?'

'I do,' said the great detective. 'The villain's name is well known to me. As such it might be, for it is *my own*.

'The name of the villain is Cameron Bell. It would appear that *I* stole the reliquary.'

22

‘*ou* did it?’ Belmont laughed. ‘That is priceless,’ he said.

‘It is ludicrous,’ said Cameron Bell, ‘but it would appear to be true. I have recently published a monograph regarding the unique configuration of fingerprints.’

‘What did you call it?’ Belmont was doubled up with mirth.

‘I called it *A Monograph Regarding the Unique Configuration of Fingerprints.*’

‘Excellent title.’ Belmont was now upon the flagstoned floor, giggling like a mad thing and thrashing his legs in the air.

‘No two men have identical fingerprints,’ Mr Bell continued, unabashed. ‘And I have studied this intently. I know my own as well as . . . well . . . I know the back of my own hand.’

‘Please stop.’ Belmont raised a feeble hand. ‘You’ll be the death of me.’

‘This is *no* laughing matter!’ Mr Bell did stampings of the feet.

‘Oh, it is . . . it really is.’ Belmont rolled about upon the floor.

A single swing of the foot is all it would take, thought Cameron Bell, *to send this laughing gnome upon his way.*

'Have you ever seen me before?' he asked the rolling laughster.

'Seen you before, what of this?' Belmont wiped tears from his ancient eyes.

'I have never been here before, have I? You have never seen me in this palace before now?'

'Absolutely never.' Belmont rocked gently, clutching his stomach.

'I am at a loss to explain this.' Cameron Bell shook his head.

'Oh . . .' went Belmont. 'Oh . . .'

'What?' asked Cameron Bell.

'Well, have *you* ever seen *me* before?'

Cameron Bell took to shaking his head once more.

'Then how do you know it's *me*?' Belmont creased in further convulsions of mirth.

Mr Bell swung his foot and kicked him down the corridor.

At length, order was restored and both made free with their apologies. Mr Bell's sounded the more convincing of the two, but even *he* did not really mean it.

'So,' he said with a heartfelt sigh, 'it appears I must investigate myself.'

Belmont chewed upon his lip and twisted his fingers into his long white beard. 'The machine room should settle it,' he said.

Mr Bell tapped his sword-stick upon the flagstones. 'What is this machine room all about?' was the question that he asked.

'I am the Keeper of the Royal Engines,' said Belmont,

pulling back his shoulders and thrusting out his pigeon chest. 'It is my duty to—'

'Clean and maintain them,' said Cameron Bell. 'And you have asked repeatedly for an assistant to aid you in your duties but so far one has been denied you.'

'Uncanny,' said Belmont. 'How did you know all that?'

Cameron Bell shrugged. 'Observation,' he said.

'Yes, well, all true. The engines are old – they belonged to the Martians. I am the only one who knows how they work.'

'And you believe that through the use of one of these machines we might divine the truth of all this?'

'Precisely.' The little man made a weary expression. 'I said as much to the princess, but as I told you, she wouldn't listen.'

'*I* am listening,' said Cameron Bell. 'Lead me to this machine room of yours and we shall see what we shall see.'

'We shall,' said the bearded Belmont.

The machine room was long and low and offered up that smell of oil and brass polish that would forever bring joy to generations of young and old men alike.

Mr Bell sniffed approvingly and viewed the machine room. It was indeed a room of many engines, all highly polished and highly complicated, a veritable panorama of brazen tubing, cogs and gubbins and buffed-up brass stop-cockery.

'A most impressive collection.' Mr Bell made a smiling face and sniffed once more at the air.

'You wouldn't want the job of polishing it all,' said Belmont bitterly.

'But what do they do?' asked Cameron Bell, whose knowledge of engineering was scanty at best.

'All manner of things.' Belmont beckoned to be followed and pointed as he walked. 'This one transmutes gold into base metal,' he said. 'That one creates unnecessary friction. That one there can bring chaos out of order. And *that one*—' he pointed to one quite near at hand '—that one makes apples out of cider.'

'They all do the reverse of what they were intended to do,' said the enlightened Mr Bell.

'On the contrary – they all do *precisely* what they were intended to do. It is more difficult to untie a knot than it is to tie one, would you not agree?'

'I would,' said Cameron Bell, reaching out to touch a particularly pleasing contrivance.

'And don't touch anything!' cried Belmont, spinning around. 'That one unpicks people as a grandma might unpick knitting.'

Cameron Bell withdrew his hand. 'Regarding knots,' said he.

'Like I said, it's harder to undo a knot than to tie one, so imagine how skilful would be the inventor who constructed a de-printing press?'

'*De*-printing?' queried Mr Bell.

'It removes the printed words from paper then reduces the paper to its component parts. Years of work went into that one, I am sure.'

'But to what end?' asked Mr Bell.

'To make all well with the world,' said Belmont in a most exasperated tone. 'Have you never heard anyone say "things were so much better in the good old days"?'

'I say it myself every once in a while,' admitted Mr Cameron Bell.

'So these engines were designed to make things the way they were before they got all messed about with and spoiled.'

'I understand the logic,' said Cameron Bell.

'Good,' said Belmont. 'These engines, if set running twenty-four hours of every day, would eventually return the worlds to the state of paradise that existed at the dawn of Creation. Now do you see their cleverness and purpose?'

'Yes, indeed,' said Mr Bell. 'Yes, indeed I do.' And his head went bob–bob–bob and then he asked, 'Who invented these marvels of retrograde machinery?'

'Ah,' went Belmont and took to tapping his nose. 'A Martian invented these engines and you know his name well enough.'

'It was not *me*, I suppose?' said Cameron Bell.

'What a foolish thing to say,' said Mr Belmont. 'Let us pretend that you never said it and go on with our conversation.'

'So who did invent these machines?'

'A Martian by the name of Leonardo da Vinci.'

Cameron Bell gave thought to this. 'That should have been followed by a drum roll and a symbol clash,' was his observation.

'Were you dropped at birth?' asked Mr Belmont.

'Which is the machine that would have solved the case without the need for my involvement?' enquired Mr Bell.

'This fellow here,' cried Belmont, making expansive gestures before an exceedingly large and very wonderful engine. A symphony in brass, it was, with cogs a-twinkle all about and pistons tall and pistons short and lettered key plates poking out.

'Behold,' said Belmont. 'The Patent Post-Cogitative Prognosticator.'

The detective beheld this. '*Post*-Cogitative?' said he. 'Am I to assume that this contraption predicts the *past*?'

'With unerring accuracy. Behold the lettered key plates.'

184

Mr Bell had already beheld the lettered key plates, but he was prepared to behold them anew if necessary.

'There are key plates with letters and others with spaces,' said Belmont. 'Although I cannot see them from down here, I've been up there polishing them often enough.'

'All right,' said Mr Bell. 'What is it that I must do?'

'Ask it a question,' said Belmont. 'Tap the letters on the keys and spell out your question. Ask it who stole the reliquary.'

'But I know who stole it,' said Cameron Bell. 'Somehow it was me.'

'Listen,' said Belmont, 'I am sorry that I laughed so much in the corridor.'

'And I'm sorry that I kicked you along it,' said Cameron Bell.

'Quite so. But the reason I did is this. You may be a detective, and a good one, too.'

'Some say the best,' said Cameron Bell.

'And you, no doubt, would be one of those. But you are on Mars now and things are different here. Look at *me* – did you ever see anything like me on planet Earth?'

'I once saw General Tom Thumb,' said Cameron Bell. 'I had dinner at Windsor Castle, with the Queen and Mr Phineas Barnum.'

'You're not paying attention. Did you steal the reliquary, or did you not?'

'The evidence—' said Mr Bell.

'Forget the evidence. Did *you* steal it?'

'Not to my certain knowledge,' said Cameron Bell.

'Then whatever your evidence tells you, it must be wrong. The Patent Post-Cogitative Prognosticator, however, is *never* wrong. It was built to be right. It is *always* right.'

'So if I ask it who stole the reliquary, it will furnish me with the *correct* answer?'

'That is what I have been trying to tell you all along.' Belmont cast his hands aloft. 'People just don't listen to you when you are little. They boss you about and don't take any notice of you. They do not care about your feelings.'

'I am sorry,' said Cameron Bell. 'But – and please bear with me on this – what if I enquire who stole the reliquary and it *does* spell out my name?'

'Then I will eat my beard,' said Belmont. 'Peppered and salted. Perhaps upon toast.'

Mr Bell considered that although he could not really spare the time, he would be prepared to set an hour or two aside to watch *that*.

'Right,' said the detective. 'I will tap in the question.'

'Not so fast,' said Belmont. 'You should pay a forfeit if you are wrong.'

'But I am *not* wrong,' said Cameron Bell. 'I have yet to explain matters, but essentially I am *not* wrong.'

'Then you won't mind paying a forfeit if you *are* wrong.'

'Not at all,' said Cameron Bell. 'What do you have in mind?'

'Well,' said Belmont, stroking the beard that he soon might be having for lunch. 'Ah yes, quite so. If I am to dine upon my beard, then you, if you are wrong, must eat your hat.'

Mr Bell laughed somewhat at this.

'Promise that you will,' said Belmont. 'I assume you to be a man of your word.'

'All right,' said Mr Bell. 'I promise.'

'Then tap the keys and spell out your question.'

Mr Bell gave thought to this and then tapped out his question.

WHAT IS THE TRUE NAME OF THE MASTERMIND BEHIND THE ROBBERY OF THE RELIQUARY?

'Are you sure you wish to phrase it like that?' asked Belmont.

'Absolutely certain,' said Cameron Bell.

Belmont tutted loudly. '*Mastermind*,' said he. 'Giving yourself all airs and graces.'

'Just trying to keep it accurate,' said Cameron Bell.

'Oh, it will be *that* all right.' Belmont climbed a small staircase, took hold of a key that was almost the size of himself and wound up the clockwork motor that powered the Patent Post-Cogitative Prognosticator.

The engine came to life with wonderful *whirrings* and *clickings*, with a spinning of ball governors and the enigmatic moving of parts that few men knew the names of.

Mr Bell watched it as it went about its mysterious business.

'Just one question for you,' he said to Belmont. 'How far back into the past can this contraption delve in search of answers?'

'Until the year eighteen nineteen,' said Belmont, who had found an oily rag to wipe his hands upon in the manner that engineers find so pleasurable. 'Back until that year only. It expresses no knowledge of anything prior to that time.'

'And how would you account for that?'

Belmont now wiped his beard on the oily rag. 'Either the engine was built during that year or *nothing at all* occurred before that year. I am in two minds myself.'

Click-click-whirr-and-whizz went the wonderful engine and then it ground to a standstill. There was a sound that resembled a thunderous burp and a strip of brass popped out of a little slot.

Belmont caught it, blew upon it – for it was hot – then without so much as a glance passed it up to Mr Bell.

'You read it out,' said he.

Cameron Bell glanced at the strip of brass. Letters were embossed upon it, so Cameron Bell read out what they spelled. But read it to himself.

'Out loud,' said Belmont. 'What does it say?'

Mr Bell took a very deep breath. 'It says,' said he, and he took another breath. 'It says: "THE TRUE NAME OF THE MASTERMIND BEHIND THE ROBBERY OF THE RELIQUARY IS—"'

'Go on,' said Belmont. 'Let's hear it.'

'"DARWIN THE MONKEY,"' read Cameron Bell.

'Do you want mustard on your hat?' asked the grinning Mr Belmont.

23

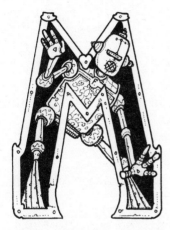ustard, Mr Bell spread on his hat, and then consumed it.

'You are a man of your word,' said Belmont. 'I certainly would *not* have eaten my beard.'

'Perhaps not *willingly*,' said Mr Bell, his face both pale and grey.

'You missed a bit of the hatband,' said Belmont. 'And might I enquire – who is this criminal mastermind who calls himself Darwin the Monkey? Carlos the Jackal,* I've heard of – he's one of those anarchists that the princess is a-feared of – and Hopp the Frog-Boy. And I once met a parrot called Peter, but that, as they say, is quite another story.'

Mr Bell swallowed the last of the hatband. It was a matter of principle, really. Darwin the monkey indeed. But somehow he could find no cause to doubt it. The Patent Post-Cogitative Prognosticator could, had it been simply randomly generating names, come up with anything, even Hopp the Frog-Boy at a push. But it had come up with Darwin, so Darwin it somehow must be.

* *Not* that *Carlos the Jackal.*

But how? And Mr Bell wiped boater from his chin.

'Ah,' said he, of a sudden. 'I have it.' And he flung aside his knife and fork and pushed his plate away.

He and Belmont were sharing a table in the servants' quarters. There was much busyness here, much straightening of uniforms and ironing of clothes.

'What do you have?' asked Belmont. 'Please tell me it is the whereabouts of the stolen item.'

'That is what I am thinking,' said Cameron Bell. 'Let us ask your wonderful machine where the reliquary is at this moment.'

'Brilliant,' said the tiny man. 'I wish I had thought of that.'

Cameron Bell made a certain face.

Belmont made it also.

And then Belmont shook his head and said, 'Sadly, it cannot be done.'

Cameron Bell asked why this was and Belmont told him why.

'The engine has to recalibrate itself,' he said, 'and that takes time. And before you ask, a very great deal of time – twenty-five years, I'd say, give or take a month.'

'Then I shall have to apply logic to this situation.' Cameron Bell drained the pint pot of porter that Belmont had recommended as the perfect complement to his boater. 'The I, that is me here, did not commit the crime, and as I cannot be in two places at the same time, it therefore follows that there must be another I, which is identical but not the same as the one here. Are you following this?'

'I am probably way ahead of you,' said Belmont. 'Your reasoning goes—'

'Please let me say it,' said Mr Bell, 'for *I* am the detective.'

'The *I* that is *you*, or the other *I*?'

Mr Bell's temper was growing short, but he kept his anger in check.

'My reasoning goes,' said he, 'that if this other *me* is so very *me* that his fingerprints are identical to mine – that he *is me*, in fact – then *I* have every reason to believe that *he* would act as *I* would act and that *he* would carry the reliquary off to a place and leave it for *me* to collect.'

'The two yous are working together, then, is it?' asked Belmont.

'I know *exactly* where *I* would take it,' said Cameron Bell. 'And if I am wrong I will gladly eat my jacket.'

Belmont now bounced up and down. Which put Mr Bell in mind of Darwin and set him to wondering many things about his little friend.

'Oh, do tell,' said Belmont. 'I have never before seen a man eat a jacket. A flowerpot, once, I recall, and upon another occasion—'

'I have to go,' said Cameron Bell, rising from his seat. 'I have a theory regarding this. A fanciful theory, certainly, but a theory nonetheless. If I am correct, all will shortly be explained to me.'

'Well, lucky old you,' said Belmont. 'I for one do not think I could survive much more of your company. Mystery and chaos surround you like false friends who have learned of your lottery win. You will eat your jacket if you're wrong, though, won't you?'

'I promise I will,' said Mr Bell.

But Mr Bell did not always tell the truth. When he returned to the royal steam tug and gently awakened the helmsman, this fellow enquired of Mr Bell whether he had, as promised, spoken with Princess Pamela and broached the subject of a pay rise and a job for his eldest son.

'I certainly did,' said Cameron Bell. 'She said she would think about it. She said also that you were to hurry me back to the shore as speedily as possible.'

'As speedily as can be,' said the helmsman. 'I notice that you have your bag and sword-stick, but fear that you have forgotten your fine straw boater.'

'As speedily as can be,' said Mr Bell.

The helmsman stoked up the boiler, diddled with stop-cocks and set the tug in motion.

Once more upon dry land, Mr Bell tipped the helmsman and went upon his way. It was a long walk back to the hotel, for the driver who had conveyed him to the steam tug's mooring had long since departed with his cart. Mr Bell was forced to trudge the road. A long and winding road was this, which led through deep-red forest. Odd things swung about in the trees, calling their curious calls. Other things that might well have been predatory scampered through the undergrowth and the detective put a certain spring into his step.

As he marched along, he pondered on the strangeness of it all. He could only draw one single conclusion and this was one he did not like at all, for it was one that could surely be the cause of all kinds of chaos.

Something shrieked in the forest and Mr Bell hurried on.

The New Dorchester gleamed in the Martian sunshine. Lackeys on ladders flicked red dust from the stately walls of white whilst others laboured to remove a large red 'A' that someone had painted upon a wall. The work of the dreaded anarchists, Mr Bell supposed. The hotel's steam charabanc had been similarly disfigured.

The loafing boys once more approached Mr Bell to offer him their personal services. Mr Bell pushed past them and entered the hotel.

The detective was somewhat damp about the brow and other regions, too, when finally he reached the reception desk. A gaunt and dark-faced fellow stood behind it, who looked up from his doings and glanced at Mr Bell. Then stiffened and stared and cried, 'Oh my!'

'Apologies for my appearance,' said the dusty and bedraggled detective. 'A rather long walk back.'

The gaunt and dark-faced fellow gawped at Mr Bell, then glanced towards the lift, then back once more to Mr Cameron Bell. 'But . . .' said he. 'How did you . . . ? I do not understand.'

'Would I be correct in thinking that *I* have already gone up to my room?' said Mr Bell.

The dark-faced fellow nodded gormlessly.

'My twin brother, Sam,' said Mr Bell, the lie springing easily to his lips. 'He is always getting up to such tricks. He took my room key from your peg, I suppose.'

'Yes indeed,' said the dark-faced fellow. 'Your twin brother Sam? Ah, yes, I understand.'

'Is there a spare key?' asked Mr Bell. '*I* would like to surprise *him*.'

The dark-faced fellow nodded then went to seek it out. Upon his return, Mr Bell snatched the key from his hand and made off with haste towards the lift.

When shortly thereafter he stood before the door to his hotel room, the detective was breathing heavily. He pressed his ear to the door's panelling and hearing nothing pushed the key into the lock.

Turned it and flung the door open.

All was as it had been, though a maid had tidied the room. But there had certainly not been that great big brown-paper-covered parcel on the bed before. The one with the note tucked into its twiney bindings.

Mr Bell glanced beneath the bed, into the wardrobes, here and there. There was no one hiding. He sat down on the bed and tapped the parcel. He had absolutely no doubt as to what it contained. The stolen reliquary. He was very interested, however, to read what the note that accompanied it had to say.

He took it up and examined what was on the sheet of paper. The small and neatly written script was, as he had expected it to be, his own handwriting. Mr Bell took his pince-nez from their case, as this writing was small, and read aloud the missive that he held now in a rather shaky hand.

' "Note to self," ' it began. ' "As you are now aware, it was you who stole the reliquary. You did this in order to foil the evil schemes of Miss Lavinia Dharkstorrm, an adversary who is proving to be most problematic. You were able to do this because the you sitting there reading this note and the you who wrote it are one and the same person, but you inhabit different time frames. The you who wrote this note travelled back into the past in a time-ship created by Mr Ernest Rutherford and piloted by Darwin, who masterminded this particular attempt to foil the evil witch. I told him that it would not work. But he told me (that is the *you* in the future) that it was his turn to have a go and as he was pilot his decision was final.

' "There have been difficulties –" ' Mr Bell laughed just a little at reading this ' "– and if this particular attempt to alter the past fails, Darwin and I have agreed that it will be the last. I cannot tell you what you must do with the reliquary now that it is in your possession. I am hoping you will do something inspired, because if you do not then things will go very badly for the you that is me now. Please try very hard not to get me killed this time!" '

'*This time?*' Mr Bell turned over the paper. There was nothing more to be read.

'You cannot leave it like *that*!' he cried. '*I* would not leave it like *that*! I would explain a plan. One that was guaranteed to work. I would have written it all down here. Unless—'

And here a terrible thought struck Mr Bell.

'Unless the actions I am about to take will cause the death of the me from the future. Oh, calamity.'

A refrigerated cupboard in the study area was well stocked with champagne. Mr Bell drew out a bottle and dragged forth its cork. He could not as yet toast success, but he sorely needed a drink.

As the contents of the bottle found its way into Mr Bell's stomach, he gave great thought to the matter in hand.

'It is certainly *not* the way I would have gone about it,' he said, as he tossed back champagne. 'I would have stolen the reliquary from the British Museum before Miss Dharkstorrm acquired it and hurled it into the deepest ocean.' Mr Bell thought of the Martian canals. 'Well, at least I can dispose of this one,' he said.

But here great problems loomed.

If the reliquary was not returned to Princess Pamela, the spaceport would be closed to him and a price put on his head. And if it was not passed to Lavinia Dharkstorrm she would butcher Darwin most dreadfully. But if it *was* given to Miss Dharkstorrm, she would reunite it with the other three reliquaries in an 'unhallowed place' and bring about the End of Days when the clock struck twelve on the thirty-first of December, eighteen ninety-nine.

It was all something of a dilemma.

Cameron Bell poured further champagne down his throat. 'But I am Bell,' said he, his voice somewhat slurred now by drink. 'Cameron Bell, the world's foremost consulting detective. If anyone can solve this thing, then I am the one who can.'

The champagne bottle was empty, so Mr Bell sought out another.

And he was half the way through that when the great thought hit him.

'Oh yes,' said Mr Bell. 'Oh yes indeed.'

There *was* a solution to this. A dangerous one, certainly, and one that might involve the destruction of a great deal of property. But sacrifices sometimes had to be made, and in a cause such as this, in which so very much was at stake, there was always likely to be − now what was that term *The Times*' Bioscope Reviewer had so recently coined? − ah, yes, 'collateral damage', that was it.

Mr Bell held up his champagne glass. It was afternoon now and sunlight slanting through the casement windows tinged the sweet champagne a bloody red.

The rather drunken detective took himself off in the company of both bottle and glass to the desk in the study area and there put pen to paper. He scribbled away as one possessed, and when he was done reading through what he had scribbled, he made jottings here and there then pushed aside the paper.

'Now *that* is what *I* call a *plan*!' said Cameron Bell. 'And now I shall take a shower, change my clothes, go down to the lobby and hire the hotel's steam charabanc for the day tomorrow, put certain propositions to the loafing boys outside, then take supper and have an early night. Tomorrow will, I feel, bring a very big adventure.'

The sun wallowed low in the Martian sky and strange beasts howled in the distance.

24

ery early the next morning, Mr Bell awoke hangover-free, as was the way with him. He eschewed today the bathroom spa, taking instead a cold-water wipe-down, then dressed and descended to the dining room for the earliest of breakfasts.

Then he returned to his room, where for the next hour he inter-viewed a number of the loafing boys, paying some for services already rendered and receiving from them certain illicit goods; thanking others for jobs well done and dispensing coin of the realm in a carefree, generous fashion.

When all was done and he was once more left alone, he attended to certain pressing duties, then took up the brown-paper-covered parcel and his Gladstone bag and marched from his room in a most determined manner.

Although it was still relatively early and the Martian sun was only just upon the rise, there was a very great deal of activity before the New Dorchester. A very great deal of rubbing and fussing and cursing from hotel staff.

During the night, vast works of vandalism had been performed upon the building's façade. Huge red painted 'A's were in evidence and the ominous line had been wrought many times in letters large and red.

A driver, all swaddled in blankets, sporting a big black beard and a high top hat, stood to the rear of the hotel's steam charabanc, adjusting stopcocks and scalding his hands. Of the loafing boys who usually loafed, none was to be seen.

Mr Bell climbed aboard the gleaming automobile, which offered its fragrances of polish and oil to the great detective's nostrils. He seated himself upon the luxuriously appointed forward leather couch, tucked the Gladstone between his feet and placed the parcel carefully upon his lap.

'The spaceport,' said he. 'if you will be so kind.'

The driver yanked levers, tugged upon enamel thingama-jigs that resembled vast organ stops and drove the steam charabanc the short distance to the spaceport.

Where further vandalism of the anarchic persuasion was plainly to be seen.

TODAY IS THE DAY

was heavily painted all around and about.

The driver of the charabanc had no comment to make about any of this. Nor did Cameron Bell, although he nodded once or twice in a manner that might almost have been described as 'approvingly'. But for that, he strictly kept his own counsel.

Before the arrivals building stood a row of carts and carriages harnessed to curious creatures, the drivers standing idly by, smoking cigarettes and making ill-informed com-ments about the apparently forthcoming revolution.

'We'll 'ave all the toffs up against the wall, come the

revolution,' Mr Bell heard one remark as he stepped down from the charabanc.

'We'll string that Septimus Grey up from a lamp post,' announced a cabbie with a proud moustache. 'We all know what *he* has been up to.'

Mr Bell did *not* know, but neither did he care. Leaving his Gladstone bag aboard the steam charabanc, he hefted his brown-paper-covered parcel, said loudly, 'Please wait for me here, driver,' then strode into the arrivals building, whistling merrily.

High upon a wall a great clock, its dial advertising the virtues of a popular laxative, ticked loudly in the all but empty hall, its minute hand approaching twelve, its hour hand at the eight.

Mr Bell halted his perambulations, drew his pocket watch from his waistcoat, flipped open its case and perused its face. Then, nodding with thought, he returned it to his waistcoat. Ahead were the left-luggage lockers – large brass cages capable of accommodating considerable bags and trunkage. Mr Bell took out the key that Lavinia Dharkstorrm had given him.

And then, from the corner of his eye he spied a henchman draped upon a bench, but all alert. A strange henchman this time and one quite new to Mr Bell. A moment's perusal, however, of the Campbell tartan kilt, the scuffings on the gumboots and a tidemark about this fellow's neck told Mr Bell all he needed to be told. This was the witch's associate who was presently on duty at the spaceport awaiting Mr Bell's return in the company of the reliquary.

Mr Bell half-turned towards this henchman and waggled the parcel about.

Then took a step towards the left-luggage lockers.

At which point—

A mighty explosion, coming from the direction of the landing strip, rocked the building. Several tiny windows shattered and smoke began to billow over the concourse.

Mr Bell clutched the parcel to his chest as the henchman in the Campbell plaid leapt from his seat and rushed towards him.

Another explosion echoed and the detective did duckings of the head.

'Give me that parcel!' shouted the henchman. 'Give me that parcel now.'

'That is not what was agreed,' said Mr Bell, his arms wrapped tightly about the parcel. 'I demand in exchange the return of my partner, Darwin.'

The henchman now drew out a ray gun, and quite a substantial ray gun it was, too. 'Give me that parcel or die,' he said in a tone which expressed that no further words needed saying.

Another explosion nearer at hand had Mr Bell staggering sideways. The henchman snatched the parcel from him and fled at speed from the building. Mr Bell sat down on the floor and covered his face with a handkerchief.

The henchman ran out to the carriage rank just in time to see the driverless carriages racing away at speed.

'Explosions have scared the damn animals!' he was told by a driver.

The henchman clubbed him down.

Sighting the New Dorchester's steam charabanc, the henchman leapt aboard it.

'Drive,' was his command.

The driver mumbled into his beard. 'This vehicle is hired,' said he. 'If you wish to engage it at some future date, please make arrangements with the management at—'

The henchman displayed his ray gun. 'Drive or die,' was all he had to say.

The driver adjusted stopcocks, and then he drove.

Folk were now fleeing in many directions, most of these being *away* from the spaceport, jamming themselves up in the doorways as folk will do in such situations and generally behaving in the manner of 'every man for himself'. When Mr Bell finally issued into the early-morning sunlight, his handkerchief over his face, he was just in time to see the steam charabanc merrily puffing away with the henchman aboard.

Mr Bell's face wore a placid expression as he dusted at himself then walked away.

Fire-alarm bells were now ringing and flames licked up from the flammable parts of the arrivals building.

'Faster,' demanded the henchman. 'Get a move on, do.'

The driver once more mumbled into his beard. Words to the effect that with a maximum speed of five miles per hour, it would probably be to the henchman's advantage to step down and walk if he was in such a hurry.

The henchman hunched and shouted out directions. The charabanc rumbled on.

Presently it rumbled down a paved track into the forest and at the henchman's orderings drew up before a tall, narrow house of ancient aspect.

The henchman stepped down. 'Now sling yer hook,' he said.

'I'll need to stoke up the boiler,' said the driver.

The henchman turned and slouched away.

The driver stepped down from his perch.

★

On the topmost storey of the tall, narrow house was a very nice room indeed. Nicely furnished with a nice fire in the grate, a nice chair beside that and a very nice table, upon the top of which was an exceedingly nice brass parrot's cage which contained a sleeping monkey named Darwin. This monkey's dreams were not very nice. Nor indeed was the woman who sat beside the nice fire in the nice chair toasting a nice-looking muffin on a rather nice toasting fork.

The henchman pushed open the door to this room without knocking.

Miss Lavinia Dharkstorrm made the fiercest of faces.

'Sorry, mistress,' said the tartaned henchman. 'There's trouble at the spaceport. The revolution has begun.'

'And you have abandoned your duties and brought me a present to celebrate this?'

'I have brought you the stolen reliquary,' said the henchman, puffing out his chest and doing a sort of arrogant head-wobbly thing.

Miss Lavinia Dharkstorrm grinned the wickedest of grins. 'So quickly,' said she, tossing her muffin and toasting fork into the fire and rubbing her slender hands together. 'Place it upon the table, if you will, next to our slumbering friend.'

The henchman placed the brown-paper-covered parcel onto the table, stepped back, made a proud face—

Then shouted, 'Ouch!' and fell down onto the floor.

Lavinia Dharkstorrm stared in surprise at the chap in beard and blankets who smelled somewhat of brass polish and oil. This fellow held in his hand the heavy spanner which he had just brought down upon the head of Miss Lavinia's henchman.

'What of *this*?' cried the mauve-eyed witch. 'What do you think you are doing?'

'He didn't pay me, ma'am,' said the driver.

'*What?*' shrieked Miss Lavinia Dharkstorrm.

'In truth,' said the driver, now removing his blankets and pulling from his face his big black beard, 'I am not normally a driver by trade.'

'Mr Bell,' said Lavinia Dharkstorrm. 'This is quite a surprise.' The witch's hand moved towards her corset.

Mr Bell dropped the heavy spanner and drew his ray gun swiftly from his pocket. 'No tricks, please,' said he. 'I merely wish that we transact our business and then I will take my leave – in the company of my companion, of course.'

Miss Lavinia Dharkstorrm nodded her head but had nothing to say.

Mr Bell viewed the sleeping monkey. 'You have drugged him,' he said.

'I tired of his conversation.'

'And where is your familiar today?'

Miss Lavinia winked. 'That would be telling.'

'Well, no matter,' said Cameron Bell. 'But just one thing before I depart. I have, as you are aware, done my research regarding the four reliquaries and I know what the sacred texts foretell will occur if they are all brought together into an unhallowed place. Do you truly wish to bring destruction upon humanity? Is there nothing that I can do to persuade you from this abominable course of action?'

Miss Lavinia's eyes seemed to glow as she fixed them on Cameron Bell. 'Do you love your country and your Queen, Mr Bell?' she asked.

'With certain reservations,' said the detective.

'Many consider that if left unchecked, the Empire will inevitably wage war upon the other planets. History surely informs you that this is a strong possibility.'

'Yes, it does,' said Cameron Bell, in sadness. 'But this does not give you the right to bring death to millions of innocent people.'

'Innocent?' Lavinia Dharkstorrm laughed. 'I would kill a billion if my mistress ordered it.'

'Your mistress?' asked Cameron Bell.

'We have spoken enough. See, my henchman is starting to stir and his colleague awakens in the cupboard over there. They might wish to punish you. Best you depart at once. Our business is done – take your monkey and go.'

Mr Bell bowed his head politely. 'So nothing I can say will sway you from your evil ways?'

'Depart *now*,' said Lavinia Dharkstorrm.

Mr Bell lifted the parrot's cage from the table and with his ray gun still aimed at Miss Dharkstorrm backed swiftly from the room.

Down the stairs at speed went Cameron Bell, then out through the front door and over to the steam charabanc. He placed the parrot's cage containing his slumbering friend beside it and drew from beneath the passenger couch his Gladstone bag.

Within the tall, narrow house, Miss Lavinia Dharkstorrm kicked the stirring henchman. 'Get up, you buffoon,' she shouted at him.

Cameron Bell rooted in his Gladstone. Darwin snored now in his cage.

Miss Lavinia Dharkstorrm tore the brown paper wrappings from the parcel and opened the lid of the box that lay revealed. The reliquary casket golden glittered, and Miss Lavinia smiled.

Cameron Bell removed from his Gladstone bag a small brass box and extended from this a slim and telescopic rod of steel.

Miss Lavinia Dharkstorrm took up the holy casket and gently eased open its lid to reveal—
  The dynamite.
  And the brass mechanism.

Mr Cameron Bell ducked down behind the charabanc and planted his finger upon a button marked FIRE. The tall and narrow house exploded with a deafening roar that raised queer birds from roosts around and about. Mr Bell curled up in a ball as debris tumbled hither and thither.

At the spaceport, the other Mr Bell (the one who had stolen the reliquary from Princess Pamela and delivered the bomb into the hands of the tartan-clad henchman – the Mr Bell from the future*) strolled across the landing strip and boarded a battered Martian hulk named the *Marie Lloyd*.
  At the controls and awaiting his return sat an elderly monkey. This monkey's name was Darwin.
  'Did it work?' the future monkey asked the future Mr Bell. 'Did your former self rescue me and blow up the wicked witch and not get either of us killed?'
  'Apparently so,' said the future Mr Bell, 'for we are both still alive.'
  'Splendid,' said Darwin. 'Then, as agreed, we will tamper no more with the past.' The monkey pilot plucked up a banana from a case that rested beside his seat. 'When shall we

---

* *It is all so regrettably complicated. But isn't that always the way when time travel is involved?*

go to next?' he asked. 'Any particular time that takes your fancy?'

Mr Bell had been giving this matter some thought. 'I would like to travel back to the year eighteen-eighteen,' he said. 'I would really like to know whether the chicken's theory about the Creation is actually correct.'

'Good idea,' said Darwin, between great munchings of banana. 'I had quite forgotten about the chickens. Let's go travelling back and take a look.'

25

uietly waited the present-day Mr Bell until the flames died down. Then, ray gun in hand, he kicked amongst the wreckage. If anything had lived through the explosion, the detective had every intention of seeing that it lived no longer.

The thought that he had actually been responsible for the death of a woman was not one that Mr Bell savoured. But he *had* offered her the chance to change her evil ways and she *had* refused him.

But what of the *mistress* she claimed to serve?

Cameron Bell did further kickings amongst the wreckage and presently uncovered the bejewelled reliquary. It sparkled unsullied, completely unmarked.

'I rather suspected it would be indestructible,' said Mr Bell, lifting it from the ashes. He delved into a pocket, took out the holy relic itself and dropped it back into its casket. Then, satisfied that all was now safe, removed the still-snoring Darwin from his imprisonment, placed him on the passenger couch and, having stoked up the boiler with only minor scaldings, drove the steam charabanc back to the New Dorchester Hotel.

Here Mr Bell tucked Darwin into bed and paid off the lounging boys who had formed an orderly queue at his door.

He paid each in turn according to services rendered. Two for painting anarchist graffiti upon the walls of the hotel and the arrivals hall. One for acquiring dynamite for Mr Bell and another three for setting off charges at the spaceport upon the stroke of eight. When all was done to Mr Bell's satisfaction, he shook the hands of the lounging boys, advised them to maintain the stoniest of silences regarding their endeavours and bade them all a fond farewell.

Darwin slept on and after lunch Mr Bell set out aboard the steam charabanc to the berth of the royal tug.

The helmsman looked quite happy to see Mr Bell once more. 'I have heard nothing regarding my wage rise,' he said. 'Perhaps you might broach the subject again when you next see the princess.'

'I would be pleased to do so,' said Mr Bell. 'Make haste now, if you will.'

Princess Pamela was also happy to see Mr Bell once more. She was enjoying a prolonged lunch all by herself and beckoned him to join her.

'I have just eaten, thank you, ma'am,' said the detective, tapping at his belly as he did so, 'but only to restore my energies after the protracted but successful struggle to re-acquire your precious reliquary.' And he displayed the treasure in all its glittering twinkliness.

'Ey-oop, lad,' cried the princess, laying down her eating irons and clapping pink palms together. 'Thou art a credit to thy calling. Didst thou bring the culprit with thee? We'll spit him oop for a roast.'

'It was a struggle to the death,' said Cameron Bell in a

tone that implied that it *really really* was. 'Only I survived to tell the tale.'

'Well done, lad.' The princess clapped her hands some more. 'I won't get up, so pat thyself on the back.'

Mr Bell attempted this but found it quite impossible.

'Regarding two matters,' said he. 'Firstly, I desire that the spaceport be reopened to me, as I am anxious to return to Earth. And—'

'And secondly thou'd like thy pay?' asked the princess, tucking into further lunch.

'Correct,' said the detective, eyeing tasty morsels as he did so. And noting that Château Doveston was the lunchtime choice of champagne.

'In truth, lad,' crowed the princess, 'I never 'ad the space-port closed to thee.'

'Ah,' said Mr Bell.

'But then neither did I 'ave any intention of eating thee.'

'Ah, indeed,' said Mr Bell.

'But then neither did I 'ave any intention of paying thee a reward.'

'Ah, indeed, indeed,' said Mr Bell.

'So all's well that ends well, eh?'

Mr Bell cocked his head on one side. He was not quite sure about *that*.

'Might I take a glass of champagne,' he asked, 'to celebrate the return of your precious item?'

Princess Pamela smiled and poured the detective a glass. 'If truth be told,' she said as she passed it over, 'I couldn't give a pigeon's doodah for that reliquary.'

'Oh?' said Cameron Bell.

'It was the principle of the thing. Folk canst not steal from me. That's not on t'cards, my lad. No, and again I tell thee, no.'

'I understand,' said Cameron Bell, a-tasting of champagne.

'Tell thee what,' said Princess Pamela. 'How's about this, then? How'dst thou care to join me on my cruise? Six months here in t'palace, all the way round Mars on t'Grand Canal?'

Mr Bell tasted further champagne. 'That is a very tempting offer,' said he.

'We might get t'know each other more closely.' The princess winked lewdly at the drinking detective.

The drinking detective coughed champagne up his nose. 'That,' said he, 'is an offer no man could refuse.' And his eyes strayed towards the exits. 'I shall return to the hotel and collect my baggage.'

'Aye, thou doest that.' The princess raised her glass and blew Mr Bell a kiss.

'Shall I return this to the chapel?' asked the now rather freely sweating Mr Bell, and he pointed to the casket that lay upon the table next to the sprouts.

'Wouldst thou be a love?' The princess smiled. 'Belmont is no longer available to show thee the way, but I'm sure thou canst remember.'

'No longer available?' Mr Bell whispered these words and glanced along the table. Several dishes were loaded high with steaming roasted meat. Was that one at the far end possibly garnished with beard?

'Your wish is my command, fair lady.' Cameron Bell took the reliquary and backed from the dining room.

Darwin the monkey stirred and yawned and then said, 'Where am I?'

Mr Bell gazed down upon the ape. 'Ah,' said he. 'You have finally awoken. Would you care perhaps for a banana?'

'Very much indeed,' said Darwin, rubbing at his eyes in that very dear way that a kitten does. 'But *where* are *we*?'

'Aboard a spaceship,' said Cameron Bell. 'Travelling first class. Only first-class passengers are being allowed to leave the planet Mars at present.'

There had been some unpleasantness at what was left of the Martian spaceport. It had all become rather complicated and Mr Bell *was* in quite a hurry to return to Earth.

'First class,' said Darwin, and then, 'I am free!' he cried in sudden realisation. 'You saved my life, my friend – my thanks to you.'

Mr Bell smiled and put his finger to his lips. 'It is probably best if the other first-class travellers do not become aware of your particular gift,' he whispered.

'Why?' asked Darwin, glancing all around.

'There was a bit of trouble on Mars,' said Cameron Bell, 'something to do with an anarchist uprising. The military are now in control of the planet. We wouldn't want some nervous passenger overhearing you and taking you for a French spy or something, would we?'

Darwin gave Mr Bell the queerest of expressions. 'Did *you* have anything to do with this?' he enquired. 'Did it involve anywhere being blown up or engulfed in flames?'

Mr Bell made so-so gestures with his free hand. His other hand held a glass of champagne, Darwin noted.

'Is that Château Doveston?' he asked.

Mr Bell nodded. 'And I will give you a glass if you are *very* quiet.'

'And a very big bunch of bananas?' said Darwin.

'A *very* big bunch of bananas,' said Cameron Bell.

It was hotter than ever in London and the Crystal Palace was quite steamed up inside. But as first-class passengers travelled in air-cooled luxury across the cobbled landing strip from spaceship to Terminal One, Mr Bell whistled between sippings of champagne and cared not one jot for the climate.

Darwin gazed out of a window; it was good to be back.

'Mr Bell,' he whispered to the detective. 'You have not told me anything about what happened upon Mars – why not?'

Mr Bell whispered in return. 'All you must know,' he whispered, 'is that the wicked witch is dead and that unless something most unexpected occurs, you and I will enjoy many years of happy acquaintanceship together.'

'That is a very odd thing to say,' whispered Darwin.

'It would all be very complicated to explain. Shall we dine at the Ritz tonight?'

'Oh yes,' said Darwin. 'I'd like that very much.'

First-class passengers enjoying those privileges accorded to them were soon aboard further luxurious carriages and away towards the metropolis.

'Do you want to be dropped at Syon House?' asked Mr Bell as the new electric runabout propelled them at speed along the highway.

'No,' said Darwin. 'I don't want to return there on my own for now. Let's go to our offices. Perhaps someone has sent us a letter inviting us to take on an exciting case.'

'You still wish to carry on in our partnership, considering all that has happened?'

'You *do* still want me?' asked Darwin, gazing up at his partner.

'Of course I do,' said Cameron Bell, and he knew in his heart that he did.

'Our offices, then,' said Darwin.

Mr Bell took up the speaking tube and gave the driver the address of Banana and Bell.

'No one here,' said Cameron Bell. 'No maid who is spare and kempt. No boy named Jack. I gave them each two months' salary in advance before I left for Mars and this is how they reward me for my kindness.'

'It smells a bit in here, too,' said Darwin, wrinkling his nose.

'I have champagne in my office,' said Cameron Bell.

'How could it be otherwise?' said Darwin. 'Let us crack a bottle and raise glasses to the future.'

'Yes, indeed,' said Mr Cameron Bell.

Together they entered Mr Bell's office, then drew as one to a halt.

Seated behind Mr Bell's desk, with feet upon its top and flanked by a pair of monstrous henchmen, was Miss Lavinia Dharkstorrm.

'Welcome back to London, boys,' she said.

26

'ery pleasant indeed to see you,' said Miss Lavinia Dharkstorrm. 'I assume by the jolliness of your tones that things went well upon Mars.'

The eyes of Cameron Bell were wide and his mouth hung hugely open.

'That is a most unflattering expression,' said Miss Dharkstorrm. 'I would almost go so far as to call it "gormless".'

'But *how*?' went Mr Bell, when he could find his voice. 'How are you here, when you were on—'

'*Mars?*' asked Miss Dharkstorrm. 'But I was *never* on Mars, Mr Bell. Did you see me on the spaceship when you travelled there?'

Cameron Bell shook his head.

'But only when you arrived there and met me in the First-Class Saloon.'

Cameron Bell now nodded his head.

'That was *not* me,' said Miss Dharkstorrm. 'That was my familiar, Pandora — like myself, a most accomplished shape-shifter. Why would I wish to travel to Mars when I could simply wait here for you to return, bringing with you what I seek?'

Darwin looked up at Cameron Bell. Darwin was an ape most baffled. 'What of this?' he asked.

'You do not confide in your little friend, Mr Bell?' Lavinia Dharkstorrm shook her head and smiled in Darwin's direction. 'He carries the holy relic with him,' she said to the monkey.

'What what *what*?' went Darwin. 'What of this, I ask?'

Cameron Bell sighed deeply and took to shaking *his* head.

'You see, Mr Bell,' said Lavinia Dharkstorrm, 'I have always been one step ahead of you and always will be because I have second sight. I can view the future as others remember the past. I knew precisely what you would do upon Mars – although I must confess that there are certain dark areas, as if you were assisted in some way by yourself. I do not fully understand this, but I viewed your actions as if in a scrying glass. And *you* destroyed my familiar, Mr Bell, and *I* do not take kindly at all to *that*.'

Mr Bell's right hand was snaking towards his trouser pocket, wherein rested his ray gun.

'Oh, do,' said Miss Dharkstorrm. 'Do pull it out. Let us all have a look at it, please.'

Mr Bell delved into his pocket, felt something slimy, then pulled out a very large toad and gaped at it.

'Out of your league, Mr Bell.' Lavinia Dharkstorrm laughed. 'Now hand the holy relic to me, if you will.'

'*You* have the relic?' asked Darwin. 'You have brought it back from Mars?'

Cameron nodded gloomily. 'It was my intention to discharge it into space during the journey home. But there was no way that could be done, so I intended to toss it into the Thames this very evening.'

'He stole it from Princess Pamela,' said Miss Dharkstorrm. 'He was a trifle miffed when she refused to give him a reward. And greatly afeared when she offered her amorous attentions.'

'Who is Princess Pamela?' asked Darwin.

'No one you need worry your furry little head about.' Miss Dharkstorrm turned her alarming eyes once more upon Cameron Bell. 'Hand me the holy relic,' said she, 'or I will have my men take it from your lifeless body.'

Mr Bell dug into his waistcoat pocket and brought forth something resembling a glass marble, within which strange lights flickered and twisted.

'I cannot let you have it,' said Mr Bell. 'Darwin,' he shouted, 'take it and run!' And he flung the sphere to the monkey.

But it did not reach the monkey's hands.

The sphere drew up short in the air, then flashed across the office and into the hands of Miss Dharkstorrm. 'Thank you very much indeed,' said she.

Cameron Bell shook his head in dismay. 'How could I be such a fool as this?' he asked.

'How indeed,' said Miss Dharkstorrm. 'But I will let you make amends. I will not kill you, Mr Bell, for that would be a waste, but I cannot have you pursuing me and getting in my way – I have far too many important things to do. So I will tell you what. I have already dealt with your maid and your servant-boy in a certain way and I will deal in this way too with you and your monkey. I have a drug, Mr Bell, a combination of *coup de poudre* and mandrake known as Zombie Dust, which will erase your memories and put you into a deathlike trance. I will have you, your monkey and servants boxed up to be sold as slaves to the gentry. You will never again know who you truly are. But you will serve your new master without question.'

Darwin bared his teeth at this and prepared to put up a struggle.

Cameron Bell raised high his fists and prepared for a struggle of his own.

1899

Once more in the present day,
in the house of Ernest Rutherford.
Following on from Chapter 5,
when Mr Bell's memories of the previous
year were returned to him . . .

27

'et me refresh your champagne glasses,' said Mr Ernest Rutherford. 'That certainly was a very big adventure.'

Cameron Bell rose to his feet and stared into a mirror. 'I am bearded,' he said. 'I have never grown a beard in my life. Although it *does* rather suit me.'

'No, it does *not*,' said Darwin, accepting a top-up to his glass. 'But does this *really* mean that we have been lying unconscious in boxes for almost a year?'

'I am afraid it does,' said the chemist, administering champagne. 'And you probably would still be doing so now had Lord Brentford not returned from the dead, as it were, and ordered one chef, one monkey butler, one maid both spare and kempt and a boy named Jack to polish boots and suchlike.'

'Oh yes,' said Darwin. 'Lord Brentford.'

'I recall you saying how you missed his lordship.' Cameron Bell toasted further champagne. 'You should be pleased that he is back in Syon House.'

'*Pleased?*' said Darwin. 'You jest,' said Darwin. 'Syon House was *my* house until *he* returned,' said Darwin.

'Ah, yes,' said the detective. 'I see how that might be a problem.' And then he had a bit of a think and said, 'Oh my dear dead mother, I am homeless, too.'

'*You* did not live at Syon House,' said Darwin.

'*I* lived at our offices,' said Cameron Bell. 'The salubrious and expensive-to-maintain offices of Banana and Bell. The offices for which rent has not been paid for a year.'

'Oh your dear dead mother indeed,' said Darwin. And then he too had a bit of a think. 'Could I just get something straight,' he asked, 'so that everything is made clear?'

Cameron Bell did shruggings of the shoulders while he sipped champagne.

'Well,' said Darwin, 'all the foregoing that Mr Bell has just recalled, all the foregoing that brings us up to this present day . . .'

Cameron Bell and Ernest Rutherford nodded.

'Well, it pretty much covered everything,' said Darwin, 'including things that happened to other people when Mr Bell and I were elsewhere.'

Cameron Bell and Mr Rutherford glanced somewhat at each other.

'Well,' said Darwin, 'should I be aware of all those things, too? Even the things that occurred when I was unconscious, drugged by Lavinia Dharkstorrm, on Mars when Mr Bell blew up the spaceport and so on?'

Cameron Bell and Mr Rutherford took to shaking their heads. 'Let us assume you should *not*,' they agreed.

'Good,' said Darwin. 'Because otherwise I think I would become very confused indeed, what with Mr Bell being helped out by another Mr Bell from the future – I might start to wonder how they both got together to release me. You see, I can think of a number of reasons why that would not work—'

'More champagne?' asked Cameron Bell. 'Mr Rutherford, please give my partner another glass of champagne.'

'I'm still drinking this one,' said Darwin. 'And furthermore—'

'Let us assume,' said Mr Bell, 'that you know absolutely nothing whatever about *anything* that happened when you were not there to see it happen.'

'That is a great weight off my mind,' said Darwin.

'But not mine,' said Mr Bell, who could find numerous things with which to find fault regarding his dealings on Mars with his future self.

'Well, all is almost well that ends well.' Mr Rutherford upended a champagne bottle. 'And that, I regret, is the last of my stock,' said he, 'so that ends well as well.'

Mr Cameron Bell said, 'Then I think we must be going.'

'Going where?' asked Darwin. 'We are homeless and office-less. Do you have any money?'

Mr Bell now patted at himself. 'My pockets are all but bare,' said he. 'I have but a guinea or two at most.'

'What do you have in the bank?' asked Darwin.

'Nothing,' said the downcast detective. 'And you?'

'Not a penny to call my own,' said the monkey. 'Bananaries are most expensive to build.' And then he thought about the destruction that had been wrought upon his Bananary and this thought made him tearful. 'And Lord Brentford shot me dead,' said Darwin.

'Come now, my little friend.' Mr Bell did kindly pattings

on the monkey's shoulder. 'There must be some way that the two of us can turn some coin and get ourselves back on our feet.'

'I have it,' said Mr Rutherford. 'I am working very hard at present to complete my time-ship. The one that I know will work because the two of you have (or will have) travelled upon it.'

'Ah,' said Mr Bell. 'You would like us to work on the project with you.'

'In a manner of speaking,' said Mr Rutherford. 'You see, the work can sometimes be very tedious and it would be wonderful to lighten it in some fashion.'

'Go on,' said Mr Bell.

'Well,' said Ernest Rutherford, 'the solution is obvious. The two of you could acquire a barrel organ and play outside my window.'

'Now *that* was uncalled for,' said Mr Bell as he and Darwin strolled along the Strand. 'Attacking poor Mr Rutherford like that. Pulling his ears in such a frightful fashion.'

'It was *not* uncalled for,' said Darwin, sniffing away at the London air and finding the sniffing pleasant. 'And it made you laugh, so do not pretend otherwise.'

Cameron Bell did sighings and scratched at his beard. 'I suppose I should shave this off,' said he. 'I look more like a sailor than my usual handsome self.'

Darwin raised a quizzical eyebrow. 'I expect that was the point,' he said. 'That Lavinia Dharkstorrm thinks of everything. Without the beard, friends of Lord Brentford for whom you had solved cases in the past would have recognised you, even dressed like a chef as you are.'

It was a fine hot summer's day but thoughts of the evil witch made Cameron shiver. 'I have sufficient money for us to dine in a chop-house,' he said. 'Dressed as I am, the Ritz is out, I regret.'

'You could apply for a job as a chef,' said Darwin.

Cameron Bell hunched his shoulders as he and the ape strolled on.

They dined in a chop-house down on the Charing Cross Road. They sat by a window and gazed at London beyond. Costermongers hauled carts that were burdened with bread and beef and biscuits while newsboys recommended the midday editions in loud and piping voices. Electric cars purred unheard amidst the clatter of horses' hooves as hansoms, drays, pantechnicons and landaus moved this way and that in steady streams. Overhead, one of the new electric flyers drifted steadily, a sleek platform with wealthy patrons leaning over the guard-rails sipping cocktails and smoking blue cigarettes.

Mr Bell drained the last of a pint of porter. 'This is the end, my only friend,' said he of a sudden.

Darwin, dining on roasted potatoes, looked up at Cameron Bell.

'I regret,' said the detective, 'that it is time for us to dissolve our partnership.'

'You don't want me any more?' said Darwin.

'It is not that I do not want you. It is simply that I do not wish you to come to any more harm. You might well have died upon Mars and it would have been all my fault.'

'But you rescued me. I am well.' Darwin made the jolliest of faces and waved his little hands about with vigour.

'It is the end,' said Cameron, shaking his head. 'There is no more Banana and Bell. In fact, there is no more Cameron Bell, the world's greatest consulting detective. I failed, Darwin. Lavinia Dharkstorrm won.'

'Technically, perhaps,' said Darwin, 'but you cannot give up your calling. You *are* the world's greatest detective and the Case of the Stolen Reliquary has yet to be brought to a successful conclusion.'

'I am tired,' said Cameron Bell, 'and I will not put you in any more danger.'

'I thrive upon danger,' said Darwin. 'I am an ape of courageous disposition.'

'My mind is made up,' said Mr Bell.

'But what about *me*?'

'Remember,' said Cameron Bell, 'you are unique – the world's one and only speaking monkey. Find a manager and exhibit yourself at the Egyptian Hall and you will soon be wealthy once more.'

'Would you manage me?' asked Darwin.

'No,' said Cameron Bell, 'because for one thing I rather like the Egyptian Hall, and I am sure that somehow or other if I managed you there, it would inevitably get blown up or burned down.'

'I am very upset about this,' said Darwin. 'I really liked being a detective.'

'No you did *not*,' said Cameron Bell. 'You liked the money but you hated the job. I recall the fuss you made.'

'Yes yes yes,' said Darwin. 'But I can change. I will work hard. I have worked hard before and I will work hard again.'

'I will tell you what,' said Cameron Bell. 'I *will* return to my true calling as detective if *you* agree to return to yours.'

'And what is *my* true calling?' asked Darwin.

'You know perfectly well what it is. The job you loved the best.'

'Ah,' said Darwin, and, taking up his half-pint of porter between his little hands, he drained it to the dregs. 'Return to Lord Brentford,' he said and he smiled, 'and serve as his monkey butler.'

Outside the chop-house, Mr Bell and Darwin said farewell. Both of them had a tear in the eye and neither tried to hide it. It started with a polite handshake but ended with a cuddle.

'When you have an office once more,' said Darwin, 'you write to me at Syon House and I will come to visit.'

'And we will take tea at Fortnum and Mason,' said Mr Cameron Bell. 'And when Lord Brentford has another social soirée, perhaps you could see to it that my name appears upon the guest list.'

'Nothing would bring me more pleasure,' said Darwin.

And after shaking once more his ex-partner's hand, he turned and scampered away.

Mr Bell watched as the ape vanished into the crowd.

'Fare thee well, my one and only friend,' said Cameron Bell.

28

‘he Lord of the Isles will see you now,’ said the broadly grinning policeman, pressing open the storeroom door and pushing Mr Bell into the dismal room that lay beyond.

A raddled soul looked up from a miniature desk. He wore a tam-o'-shanter of Boleskine plaid topped by an eagle's feather, a ginger beard that was not his own and yards and yards of tartan. In his left sock, unseen behind his tiny desk, there lurked a dinky dirk, and upon this desk there lay a mighty claymore.

‘Oh dear me,’ said Cameron Bell. ‘Dear oh dear oh me.’

‘A chef!’ cried the ersatz highlander. ‘Who let a chef in here?’

‘I am not a chef,’ said Cameron Bell, ‘and you are not a Scotsman.’

‘I am Donald Ferguson, the Laird of Lasmacrae, and I'll fight any Sassenach who dares to say I'm not.’

Cameron Bell released a sigh that came from his very soul.

The Lord of the Isles stared hard at the bearded chef.

‘I know that sigh,’ said the Lord of the Isles. ‘I'd know it anywhere.’

'I am Cameron Bell,' said Cameron Bell, 'and you are the pride of Scotland Yard – the famous feted Chief Inspector Case.'

'*Bell?*' cried the famous feted one. 'Is that really you?'

'It is,' said the sleuth in chef's clothing.

'But I have been on your case for nearly a year.' Chief Inspector Case tore off his beard. 'Missing, presumed dead. No trace of you. We thought you had perished in the fire.'

'What fire?' asked Cameron Bell.

'At the offices of Banana and Bell,' said the chief inspector. 'They burned to the ground on the day you went missing.'

Cameron Bell chewed on his lower lip. Miss Lavinia Dharkstorrm, he presumed.

'So where *have* you been?' asked the chief inspector. 'And why the beard and chef's get-up? Have you gone stark raving mad?'

The irony of this remark was not lost on the detective. 'A secret undercover mission,' he said, recalling now what a pleasure it always was to lie to the chief inspector. 'For Queen and Empire. I wish I could tell you more.'

Chief Inspector Case nodded enthusiastically. 'I suspected that was the case,' he said.

Cameron Bell rolled his eyes.

'I'd shave off that beard, though,' said the chief inspector. 'Between you and me, what with your baldness and every-thing, it looks as if you are wearing your head upside down.' And the chief inspector laughed, a shrill and most alarming laugh that set Mr Bell's teeth all upon edge and caused his ears to ring.

'I must ask you for the twenty-five guineas in advance,' said Cameron Bell.

Chief Inspector Case expressed surprise.

'I feel,' said Mr Bell, 'that as an old and greatly valued

friend, you should take the credit for solving the mystery of my disappearance.'

'Ah,' said Chief Inspector Case. 'And in return for me taking all the credit, I will be expected to secretly sign over to you twenty-five guineas from the petty-cash box.'

'A trifling sum,' said Cameron Bell. 'But if you feel that more is in order—'

'I do *not*,' said the chief inspector, coldly sober now and removing his tam-o'-shanter. 'But in truth, it *is* good to see you once more. London is a duller place without you around, setting it on fire.'

Mr Bell smiled. 'I said twenty-five guineas *in advance*,' said he, 'because for the present the fact of my reappearance must remain a secret. I have a most important and uncompleted case that needs my attention and it will be far easier for me to go about my business if the villain in question does not know that I am going about it.'

'She's a bad 'un, for sure,' said Chief Inspector Case.

'*She?*' said Cameron Bell. 'You know of whom I speak?'

'If you are speaking of this vigilante strumpet Lady Raygun, then yes, I do,' said Chief Inspector Case.

'Ah,' said Mr Bell. 'There have been more of her comings and goings while I have been away?'

'Do you recall the Kray Triplets?' asked Chief Inspector Case.

'Ronald, Reginald and Dorothy,' said Cameron Bell. 'Dorothy is the most dangerous of the three, I surely recall.'

'Done to death most horribly,' said Chief Inspector Case, 'with the words LADY RAYGUN WAS HERE scrawled in their blood across the paving stones.'

'Nasty,' said Cameron Bell. 'But no great loss to the world, if truth be told.'

'Do you remember Professor Moriarty?' the chief inspector asked.

'The Napoleon of Crime,' said Cameron Bell. '*I* gave him that title, you know.'

'I *did* know,' said the chief inspector. 'You *have* mentioned it before, *many* times.'

'He retired, did he not?' said Cameron Bell. 'I heard he makes a living now by signing photographs of himself for enthusiasts of the Sherlock Holmes stories.'

'Dead,' said Chief Inspector Case. 'She stuck his head on the railings of Buckingham Palace.'

'She appears to be a rather angry woman,' said Cameron Bell.

'The file on her grows daily.' The chief inspector mimed a growing file. 'Crime rates *are* dropping, however.'

'Ah,' said Cameron Bell. 'Well, it is the matter of crime rates that has brought me here today.'

And indeed it was, because Mr Bell needed to know whether there had been a growing number of evil deeds committed during the time he had been all boxed up in suspended animation. Evil deeds precipitated as a result of the four reliquaries being brought together in an 'unhallowed place', as sacred texts predicted. Mr Bell just *had* to know.

'It is only really *her*,' said the chief inspector. 'She has had a sobering effect on the criminal population – they rarely venture out after dark nowadays. I cannot recall the last time anyone was brutally slain in a Whitechapel alley. Sometimes I miss the good old days, don't you?'

Cameron Bell agreed that sometimes he did. 'I am very glad to hear this,' he said. 'Very glad indeed.'

'Then I am very glad indeed that you are glad to hear it.'

'I am glad of *that*,' said Cameron Bell.

'Then I am sure you will be utterly delighted to know that I would be pleased to engage your services, in order that you may track down this rogue female and bring her to justice.'

'That might prove to be something of a challenge,' said Mr Cameron Bell.

'Would a fifty-guinea retainer and an open expense account nudge your elbow in the direction of such a challenge?' asked the chief inspector.

Cameron Bell tugged at his beard. His most pressing unfinished business lay with Miss Lavinia Dharkstorrm. But fifty guineas *was* fifty guineas and although the mysterious Lady Raygun was clearly a most violent creature, at least she was not possessed of supernatural powers. Such an adversary, although clearly most dangerous, he could surely deal with.

'I will accept the challenge,' said Cameron Bell.

Chief Inspector Case stuck out his hand and Mr Bell shook it. A deal was a deal, as both men understood.

'Did I mention,' asked the chief inspector, a rather sly look creeping onto his face, 'that not only is this murderous woman now able to fly, but she is, so it would appear, also invulnerable to bullets?'

Lord Brentford looked particularly vulnerable as he lay in his hospital bed. He had much of the Egyptian mummy about him, swathed as he was from head to toe in bandages of white. Many much-prized parts of his lordship were broken, but the noble man maintained his stiff upper lip. He was presently engaged in a private conference with a Venusian ecclesiastic and although his mouth was moving, the rest of him stayed still.

'The Wonders of the Worlds,' said his lordship. 'The Tri-Planetary Exposition. It would open upon the stroke of midnight on the thirty-first of December, to welcome in the new century in a manner most fitting – do you not agree?'

The Venusian ecclesiastic stood before his lordship's bed of pain, an enchanting creature, tall and slender, high of cheekbone, broad of mouth and large of golden eyes. She, for surely such was her gender, wore a gown that seemed as wisps of smoke and walked upon shoes with dizzying heels whose soles were specifically sanctified to permit her to step upon a planet that Venusians deemed unholy.

'Your lordship,' she said, in a voice surely that of some echoing choir, 'although your motives are pure, there is danger in this enterprise.'

'Danger?' puffed his lordship. 'A lot of organisation, perhaps, but no danger that I can see.'

'It is not a propitious moment for such a venture.' The Venusian ecclesiastic swayed backwards and forwards, her long and shapely fingers drawing queer and ghostly patterns in the air. 'If you wish, I could cast a horoscope and tell you the precise day and hour of that day which would serve you and your Empire best.'

'I have no time for all that hocus-pocus. We did not have witch doctors rattling their bones about when the Crystal Palace opened. A fanfare and horsemen and Her Majesty the Queen was all it took.' Lord Brentford tried to ease himself about. He hurt in places he had quite forgotten that he owned. 'I am not asking much,' he said, 'only that your people play some part in it. Exhibit some of your woven carpets, your handicrafts, your famous orchids. You know the drill. Put on a bit of a show for the public. Do yourselves a bit of good. A lot of tension exists between the worlds at present, what with all that revolution business on Mars last year and the military junta taking over and all. Peace between the worlds and all that carry-on – do you catch my drift?'

The ecclesiastic's fingers described a pentacle above the head of Lord Brentford. 'I will see what can be done,' said she, 'but know that there are signs and portents in the Heavens. Omens of the Coming of Ragnarök.'

'Just tell me that you will do your best,' said his lordship, 'that you and your people will cooperate. I ask no more than that.'

'I will do what I can,' said the Venusian ecclesiastic. 'But now I must go – it is time for my devotions. My blessings upon you, Lord Brentford. I hope that you will soon be well once more.'

The enchanting creature turned to leave.

'Before you go,' said his lordship.

The enchanting creature turned once more towards him.

'What is your name?' asked his lordship. 'I do not know your name.'

'My name is Leah,' said the Venusian. 'But you may only use this name when the two of us are alone and no others are present to hear you speak it to me.'

'Leah,' said Lord Brentford. 'A very beautiful name.'

The Venusian ecclesiastic swept away from the hospital room, leaving nothing behind but her name upon Lord Brentford's lips and a haunting fragrance hanging in the air.

His lordship made a pained expression beneath his bandages, then gently turned his head towards the window.

'Come in here,' he called as best he could.

The curtains twitched and a foolish face peeped in at the bed-bound lord.

'Darwin,' said Lord Brentford. 'It *is* you, Darwin boy.'

Darwin grinned and waved at his lordship.

'Come on in,' called the noble lord. 'I have no idea how

you found me but I'm damned glad that you did. Come on in and share this bowl of bananas.'

Darwin's smile widened and he danced into the hospital room.

'And then you can help me with my bedpan,' said Lord Brentford.

29

'h, please leave it be,' cried Mr Ernest Rutherford, flapping his fingers at the troll named Jones. 'We have a very busy day ahead of us and you are not helping by fiddling with *that*!'

Jones made the face of shame then put away the thing with which he fiddled. 'What is it I can do for you, O master?' he asked in a greasy tone. 'Your wish is my command, as well you know.'

'Jones,' said Mr Rutherford, 'you arouse mixed feelings in me – abhorrence and disgust in equal measure.'

'Master flatters me,' said Jones, finding something else to fiddle with.

'I feel certain,' said Ernest Rutherford, 'that I could reverse the process which brought you from your world to this. What say you – shall we give it a try?'

'I would prefer not,' said Jones. 'Great things here will shortly be mine, of this I am most certain.'

Ernest Rutherford peered into the wall mirror. His ears still smarted from the tweakings that Darwin had given them. The chemist rubbed at the left one and tugged at the right.

The doorbell rang and Mr Rutherford waved to Jones to answer it. The troll, however, stood his ground, picking at his nose.

'Door,' said Mr Rutherford. 'It will not answer itself.'

'It will be *her*,' said Jones the troll. 'The beast in human form.'

'That is no way to talk about the delightful Miss Violet Wond.' Mr Rutherford straightened his tie, took off his work coat and slipped on a velvet smoking jacket. Topping this off with a matching fez, he said, 'She's a charming woman.'

Jones ground yellowed teeth together. 'I can't stand the sight of her,' he muttered.

'Without her help I do not believe I could ever have come so far with the present experiment. She has been invaluable.'

'She's horrible,' said Jones, examining the yield from his nose and popping it into his mouth. 'Promise you will get rid of her as soon as the time-ship is finished.'

The doorbell rang once more and Mr Rutherford glared at the troll called Jones.

'All right,' said the ugly creature. 'I shall let her in.'

Mr Rutherford watched as Jones left the work-room, slamming the door behind him. In truth the chemist had grown quite fond of the strange Miss Violet Wond. As the months had passed he had grown more and more attached to her. She had allowed him to take her to dinner on several occasions and the conversation had been polite, at times extremely interesting, but never as yet of the intimate persuasion.

Miss Wond was a woman of mystery. Mr Rutherford had so far failed to draw her out regarding the matter of what lay beneath the veil she always wore. Nor had he learned anything of her past other than that she had spent much of it upon Mars. Miss Violet Wond was a mystery wrapped up in an enigma and cinched at the waist by a very fetching corset.

The door banged open and Miss Violet Wond stood in the opening, black parasol in hand.

'Fair lady,' said Mr Rutherford. 'My apologies for keeping you waiting. I will chasten that Jones, have no fear.'

'I took the liberty of doing so myself,' said Miss Wond, lifting her parasol and waggling it about. 'He has retired to his nest beneath the stairs. Although he will not be sitting down for quite a while.'

Mr Rutherford coughed politely. 'So he will not be joining us upon our journey today,' said he, and he smiled as he said it. 'Just you and I.'

'Just you and I,' said Violet Wond. 'I think we can manage by ourselves.'

'We certainly can.' Mr Rutherford now hastily removed his velvet jacket and matching fez and replaced these with a sober morning coat and high silk top hat.

'If you will walk this way,' he said to Miss Wond.

'If I could walk *that* way . . .' she replied, but did not finish the sentence.

Mr Ernest Rutherford felt tiny hairs stand up in certain places. 'To Crystal Palace,' said he.

'A regular palace,' said Chief Inspector Case. 'I am sure you will agree.'

Mr Septimus Grey gazed up at the grand façade of Syon House. 'It is a most imposing building,' said he. 'But you have yet to explain to me why I have literally been dragged here from the Martian Embassy to join you in looking at a country house. I *am* the Governor of the Martian Territories, you know.'

'I do, I do,' said Chief Inspector Case, dipping into his

tweed shooting jacket and drawing out his pipe. Sensibly clad now, was the chief inspector, although he had toyed with the costume of a Jovian potentate, to put Mr Grey at his ease, as it were.

'Something occurred here last night,' said Scotland Yard's finest. 'A spaceship crashed down out of the sky into the rear of this house.'

Septimus Grey fixed the chief inspector with a beady eye. 'A spaceship?' said he. 'A spaceship crashed? What has this to do with me?'

'The reports are,' said Chief Inspector Case, 'that it was a *Martian* spaceship. And as Mars is under your control—'

'*Never* under *my* control!' Septimus Grey spoke sharply. 'I was the administrative head until the July Revolution of last year. A military junta now *controls* the planet. *I* inhabit the Martian Embassy in London.'

'I'll wager you would like to return on Mars.'

Septimus Grey gave Chief Inspector Case the full force of both beady eyes. 'When the generals now in control are sent on their way,' he shouted, 'then *yes*, of course I would like to return! Mars is a beautiful planet. There are many op—' He paused in mid-flow.

'Opportunities?' asked the pride of Scotland Yard. 'Financial opportunities?'

'I was going to say many op— Many op— Oh, what word is it that begins with "op"?'

'Opportunities,' said the chief inspector, lighting up his pipe, 'and I applaud this. Heaven knows, existing upon the meagre pay of the Met, I would be grateful for a few "opportunities" myself.'

'Ah,' said Septimus Grey. 'I think then that we understand each other.'

'I think, sir, that we do.'

'But I still do not understand exactly why you have brought me here.'

'Let us visit the rear of the building where we might discuss matters in privacy and you might view the wreckage and the extent of the damage done.' Chief Inspector Case drew deeply on his pipe and blew out tiny puffs of purple smoke.

'Martian hashish,' said Septimus Grey.

The chief inspector nodded.

As Lord Brentford could not nod at all, he just said, 'Yes,' when asked.

'Would you care to return to your home?' asked the nurse, in that overloud and over-precise manner that those of the medical professions choose to employ upon the elderly and infirm.

Darwin nodded his head for the noble lord.

'Aw,' went the nurse. 'Your little pet, bless him.'

Darwin bit the nurse, scaled the curtain, seated himself upon the pelmet and hurled down invective in fluent monkey.

The nurse howled loudly and under his bandages Lord Brentford managed a grin.

'I'll summon a doctor,' said the nurse, 'and have you discharged at once.'

There were papers that had to be signed, medicines that had to be dispensed, much fussing that had to be done over the moving of Lord Brentford, much unnecessary bother, much fawning by staff who wished to curry favour with nobility. Much of much and so much more, but finally all done.

By four of the afternoon clock, his lordship had been carefully lowered onto many pillows in the rear of a new electric-wheeler. Darwin had been settled down beside him, with a box of pharmaceuticals to guard and the now-hated bedpan to watch over. Orders were given that the driver should proceed with care to Syon House.

The electric motor whirred and purred and off went Darwin with his bandaged master.

'Master time,' said Violet Wond, 'and a man might be master of all.'

She and Ernest Rutherford were also being propelled by electrical energy aboard the New Electric Railway that ran from Victoria Station to Crystal Palace. The two sat in a first-class carriage, air-cooled and pleasing, watching the world through the plate-glass windows, speaking of this and that.

'A Master of Time,' said Ernest Rutherford, thoughtfully. 'It does sound rather like something from a novel by Mr Wells.'

'Would you not enjoy being *masterful*?' Miss Wond's voice took on a *certain* tone. It was a tone that Mr Rutherford found confusing. This woman's talk was full of innuendo, yet there was something about her which said *do not touch* – and so forcibly, too, at times that it put a certain fear into Mr Ernest Rutherford. But there was something about her that fascinated Mr Rutherford, intrigued him, tantalised him. Mr Rutherford had, over the past year, been falling utterly in love with Violet Wond.

'What might a man do,' asked the smitten chemist, 'if he was a Master of Time?'

'He could right wrongs!' said Miss Wond. 'He could travel back into the past and put right things that had been made wrong.'

'Dear lady.' Mr Rutherford gazed at the woman in black,

gazed towards the heavy veil that smothered her face and hid what lay beneath from a world that would know only fear if it was revealed. 'If I could, sweet lady, I would,' said Ernest Rutherford.

'We shall see what we shall see,' said Violet Wond.

'You see what I mean,' said Chief Inspector Case. 'A jolly fine mess it has made.'

'A *jolly* fine mess,' agreed Septimus Grey. 'Whatever was this building that it tore down with such force?'

'Something called a Bananary. Built by a lunatic recluse, apparently, who was in charge of Syon House until Lord Brentford returned as if from the dead to claim what is rightfully his.'

'And I will wager he was not best pleased by the Bananary.'

'Not best pleased at all.' Chief Inspector Case puffed somewhat at his pipe. Red smoke fled its bowl and turned in spirals in the air of afternoon.

'The wreckage of the spaceship,' said the chief inspector. 'It is the wreckage of a Martian spaceship, is it not?'

'Very hard to tell,' said Septimus Grey.

'On the contrary,' said Chief Inspector Case. 'Even in this pitiable state the contours are clearly visible. I was called here last night and arrived an hour after the crash, when the firefighters were still at work and the ambulance men were carting away Lord Brentford.'

'It fell upon him, then?' asked Septimus Grey.

'Not as such. It crashed. He was furious as he was having a soirée in the hope of raising money for some Wonders of the Worlds project he has in mind. He fetched his shotgun, entered the wreck and let free both barrels at the pilot.'

'Goodness me,' said Septimus Grey.

'His gunshots caused a bit of a ruckus in the mechanical gubbins of the spaceship and his lordship hadn't got far before it exploded. Nearly had his bum blown off, apparently.'

Septimus Grey made a pained expression. 'You have not, as yet, explained to me precisely what *my* involvement in this unfortunate incident might be.'

'It is simplicity itself,' said Chief Inspector Case. 'A spaceship has crashed into the home of one of the Empire's most notable members of the aristocracy. One whose mission, with his Wonders of the Worlds project, would appear to be a peacekeeping affair designed to bring accord amongst the planets.'

'This much I know,' said Septimus Grey.

'Indeed you do,' said Chief Inspector Case, 'because I acquired a copy of the guest list when I arrived here last night. Your name is upon it. You were present last night when this occurred.'

'I never said I was not,' said Septimus Grey.

'But you left swiftly enough after the crash – you had gone before I arrived.'

'And so too had many others. I left as I feared for the safety of my daughter.'

Chief Inspector Case perused the guest list. 'Your daughter is not listed here,' he said.

'She chooses to use her mother's surname.'

'Ah, I see.' The chief inspector sucked some more at his pipe. 'I am a modest fellow, Mr Grey,' he said. 'I am not one for airs and graces. I doggedly follow clues. I work upon logic.'

'And when all those fail you call upon the services of Mr Cameron Bell.'

'Oh, harsh words,' said Chief Inspector Case. 'But I note well that you are clearly a gentleman who is "in the know", so let us bandy no further words. Why was this deed done, Mr Grey? Why would you do such a thing?'

'*Me?*' said Mr Septimus Grey. 'You are accusing *me?*'

'As I told you, Mr Grey, I work in a dogged fashion. A spaceship crashes into a country house. Not an everyday occurrence, you will agree. But the thing about spaceships is that there are only a limited number of them, and each is registered. This craft here . . .' Chief Inspector Case stepped carefully over banana skins and wreckage, took up something that he had discovered the previous night and carried it over to Septimus Grey, who stood looking very grumpy.

'And what is *that?*' asked the Governor of the Martian Territories.

'This,' said Chief Inspector Case, 'is the nameplate of the crashed spaceship, dented but quite readable. Its name, as you see—' he displayed this nameplate '—is the *Marie Lloyd*, a spaceship, Mr Septimus Grey, that is registered to *you*.'

30

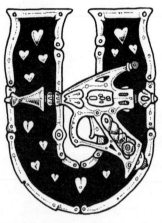pon the cobbled landing strip of the Royal London Spaceport stood a single spaceship. It was a battered old Martian hulk and its name was the *Marie Lloyd*. It was, of course, the same *Marie Lloyd* that had crashed into the Bananary at Syon House on the previous evening. Although *that Marie Lloyd* had been converted into a time-ship and launched back into the past from a point five months in the future.

Proving how simple things can be when they are explained with precision.

The spaceport shuttle cart moved over the cobbled strip towards this spaceship. Aboard were Mr Ernest Rutherford and Miss Violet Wond.

'And you actually *own* this spaceship?' asked the lovesick chemist. 'You are the mistress of it, as it were?'

'It was given to me as a present,' said Miss Wond, 'by an acquaintance, in return for services rendered.'

'Oh,' said Mr Rutherford.

'An acquaintance had wronged the gentleman who owned the spaceship. I set matters right.'

'Ah,' said Mr Rutherford. But he did not understand. Miss Wond did have rather definite ideas regarding *right* and *wrong*. The chemist, who dreamed of her at night, felt that he truly had no wish *ever* to get upon her *wrong* side.

'Might I ask,' said Mr Rutherford, almost touching a silk-gloved hand, 'regarding the special membrane and body-coverings that I formulated for you at your instruction – all is satisfactory there, I trust?'

'The membrane functions perfectly,' replied Miss Wond. 'It negates gravity and allows the wearer to travel through the sky.'

Mr Rutherford clapped his hands together. 'How very exciting that must be,' he said.

'I imagine so,' said Miss Wond.

'And the body-covering that makes one impervious to bullets?'

'Perfect,' said the lady all in black.

'Splendid. Splendid. Splendid.' The chemist patted the arm of Miss Wond. 'Oh, do please pardon me,' he said. 'I got rather carried away there.'

'It is of no consequence.'

The shuttle cart drew up before the *Marie Lloyd* and Mr Rutherford stepped from it, extending a hand towards Miss Wond in the hope of helping her down.

The lady in black, however, leapt nimbly from the shuttle and dropped onto the cobbles several yards beyond.

'Most athletic,' said the chemist approvingly and, after dispensing coin to the shuttle's driver, he followed the lady in black.

Things were suddenly looking black for Mr Septimus Grey. 'What are you suggesting?' he asked, for he was not without fight.

'Questions *will* be asked,' said Chief Inspector Case. 'Awkward questions. Most likely in the House of Commons and also the House of Lords. "How," these questions might be put, "did a spaceship owned by Mr Septimus Grey, a man who was forced from his exalted position on Mars, come to crash into the house of a member of the aristocracy? Is this some act of revolutionary anarchism, perhaps?"'

'Stop right there!' said Septimus Grey. 'This does not make any sense at all.'

'Oh, it will once I have tidied up all the loose ends,' said Chief Inspector Case. 'You would be surprised how good we hard-working and sadly underpaid detectives at Scotland Yard are at tying up loose ends into nice tidy bundles. Where even the most unlikely pieces of jigsaw can be made to fit.'

'Rather too many metaphors there for my liking,' said Septimus Grey, 'but things are indeed becoming crystal clear. How much do you want for that nameplate there, Chief Inspector?'

'*This* nameplate?' asked the pride of Scotland Yard.

'The very same. One hundred, two hundred pounds?'

'Did you say two hundred *guineas*?' asked the chief inspector.

'Guineas, then,' said Mr Septimus Grey.

'A little louder please,' said Chief Inspector Case. 'I punctured an eardrum swimming in the Thames as a boy.'

'I will pay you two hundred guineas for that nameplate,' shouted Septimus Grey.

'Wonderful stuff,' cried the chief inspector. And, 'You are nicked, chummy,' he also said. And, 'Slap the handcuffs on him, lads,' as well.

Septimus Grey gaped in horror as several young

constables, with truncheons held aloft, leapt from hiding and placed him very firmly under arrest.

'Try and bribe an officer of the law, would you?' crowed Chief Inspector Case. 'We'll add that charge to the one of attempted murder by spaceship.'

'Well done, sir,' said a constable, striking down the Governor of the Martian Territories with his truncheon. 'You certainly solved this one pretty smartish. If you will accept the compliments of myself and my fellow officers, you are a regular Cameron Bell.'

Cameron Bell was taking tea at the Ritz. No longer clad as a chef was Cameron Bell. In a suit of pale linen now sat the detective – a suit off-the-peg, it was true, but one that fitted well.

The beard had been shaved away by his favourite barber, giving him that baby-faced look that just-shaved men with hairless heads so easily carry off.

A young and inexperienced waiter who had welcomed him as Mr Pickwick and enquired after the health of Sam Weller* had been summarily cautioned. Tea was being served by a turbaned Sikh.

Mr Bell had before him the file from Scotland Yard. The big and bulging file with the name LADY RAYGUN printed large upon its cardboard cover. Mr Bell leafed through this file, whistling now and then as he did his leafing.

This woman had been most busy during the year that Mr Bell had spent boxed up in a cellar. The number of underworld figures that she had brought to justice was quite extraordinary. Although "brought to justice" was not a

---

* *Mr Pickwick's famous valet in* The Pickwick Papers.

particularly accurate way of putting it — "brutally slaugh-tered" was more appropriate. She had methodically, coldly and dreadfully carved her way through London's most dangerous criminals. Mr Bell was very much impressed.

He flicked back to the very first page of the file: the murder of Graham Tiberius Hill, Jack the Ripper as possibly was.

Then there had been a gap of ten years before she began once more her one-woman campaign of summary justice. And after she had dealt with the East End bare-knuckle fighter and the unconvicted poisoner who had threatened the life of Cameron Bell on the night of the British Show-men's Fellowship awards dinner and dance, she had made a regular weekly sortie into the more dangerous areas of London to seek and destroy the villains lurking there.

And she had gone about it—

'Oh my dear dead mother,' said Cameron Bell. 'In alphabetical order.' He delved backwards and forwards through the assembled papers. She was methodically work-ing her way through Scotland Yard's filing system.

'Someone on the inside, then,' said Mr Cameron Bell.

Inside the *Marie Lloyd*, Mr Ernest Rutherford seated himself on a comfortable cockpit couch. 'Who will pilot this ship for us?' he asked Miss Violet Wond.

Miss Wond was adjusting flyer's goggles beneath her black veil. 'I will fly the spaceship,' she said. 'Just tell me where to land.'

'Oh,' said Mr Rutherford. '*You* will pilot the ship?'

'Do you have any objections to that?' Miss Wond took hold of the joystick.

'None whatsoever, I suppose.'

'Then tell me where you wish me to fly this ship.'

'It has to be dropped down into a siding on the Circle Line but it must be done at night, when no one will see it happen.' Mr Rutherford mimed a tricky landing.

'Then we have several hours that must be killed.'

'I am sure there will be a Wiff-Waff table somewhere aboard, if you would care for a game.'

'I would care for a game indeed,' said Violet Wond. 'But not one of Wiff-Waff, I am thinking.'

'I am thinking,' Lord Brentford said to Darwin as the electric conveyance, moving in a gentle rhythm on its rubbered wheels, pressed on towards Syon House, 'that I will soon be needing the bedpan again.'

Darwin the once-more-monkey-butler viewed his aristocratic employer. The sharing of lordly bananas he favoured, but *not* the business with the bedpans. He opened his mouth to remonstrate with Lord Brentford, but then thought better of it. He would keep the secret of his special gifts until some time that was suitable. The shock Lord Brentford might experience upon hearing his monkey butler reply to him in the Queen's English could at this particular moment be too much for the broken, bandaged fellow spread out so helplessly upon his pile of pillows.

Darwin viewed the bedpan and then the injured lord. If duty called, then he would heed its calling.

Cameron Bell called presently for his bill. He graciously paid it, took up the file and left the restaurant.

But he did not leave the Ritz. He entered the foyer and enquired at the reception as to whether any rooms were presently available. Upon learning that one was and that the price for the night was not above his purse, Mr Bell signed the register and was led to a splendid room.

'I will seek more humble accommodation upon the morrow,' said he as he blew into a speaking tube to order champagne from below. 'But tonight a little indulgence, perhaps. A trip to the music hall. Some light entertainment. Things of a frivolous nature. Lady Raygun will not easily be brought to book. So tonight, as once more I am all myself, I shall enjoy the city I love, dear old London Town.'

At the Royal London Spaceport a single craft stood on the landing strip. Within this craft a couple embraced most passionately.

A gentleman's fingers sought a corset's fastenings. A lady's felt for buttons to release.

Mr Ernest Rutherford had never made love in a spaceship before. He felt utterly confident, however, that he would thoroughly enjoy the experience.

Septimus Grey was not enjoying the experience of being forcibly detained in a Scotland Yard cell. He was bitterly bewailing his lot to a Gatherer of the Pure who had been incarcerated for seeking the pure of the Queen's dogs at Windsor without the appropriate licence.

'I will have my revenge!' cried Septimus Grey. 'And don't think that I won't.'

'Damn and blast all coppers!' said the Gatherer of the Pure, a big and burly fellow with a horrid broken nose. 'Come the revolution we'll have all their heads on the block.'

Septimus Grey kicked out at the door then hobbled about in pain.

'You are a fine young gentleman,' said the burly and broken-nosed one. 'A very handsome fellow, it would appear.'

Septimus Grey sank down on the only bed and rubbed at his damaged foot.

'I could give that a little rub for you,' said the unlicensed Gatherer. 'What about a little kiss and a cuddle?'

Constables heard the shriekings of Septimus Grey. But they were very busy constables and so did not have time to go and see just what he was shrieking about.

In an unhallowed corner of Highgate Cemetery, something evil shrieked. It shrieked the barbarous names of those who never aloud should be called. And naked ladies danced by candlelight. Lavinia Dharkstorrm danced amongst them, mauve eyes glowing brightly in the gathering of night.

There appeared to be much of an erotic nature occurring upon this hot July evening in the year of eighteen ninety-nine.

Some of it joyful, some not, and some just plainly hideous.

31

ardinal Cox's catamite had gone for a healthy swim in the Thames at Kew. The cardinal was knitting socks for soldiers of the Queen. He was making slow progress, though, as his most recent delivery of hashish had been of a particularly potent blend. Some of the socks had two foot-holes and others none at all. When a knock came at the door of his Bayswater dwelling, he gladly set his needles aside and called, 'Please enter indeed, indeed.'

The door swung open, as doors will do, and in came Cameron Bell.

'By the Lord, indeed indeed indeed,' cried Cardinal Cox. 'Cameron Bell, as I live and breathe and do much more besides.'

'It has been a while,' said Mr Bell.

'A while, good Bell? It's been a year – we thought a sorry end had come to you.'

Cameron seated himself upon a Persian pouffe and viewed the cardinal's handiwork. 'I have been away upon business. Secret business. I have, however, been back for a month and thought I would look you up.'

Cardinal Cox gazed up towards a calendar a-hanging on the wall. ' 'Tis August, I see,' he said. 'Saint Artemus, patron saint of pantomime dames, is the saint of the month.'

'Would not December be a more appropriate month for such a seasonal saint?' asked Cameron Bell.

'You would think so,' said the cardinal. 'But who am I to fathom the vagaries of the calendar-maker's craft?'

'Who indeed,' said Cameron Bell. 'Is this a sock or a hat for a three-eared donkey?'

'That one *is* a hat,' said Cardinal Cox. 'But tell me, please, why are you here? Much as I do enjoy your visits, I tend to find our conversations a trifle one-sided, with you asking all the questions and me providing all the answers.'

'There will be no change today,' said Cameron Bell.

'No, I thought as much.' The cardinal sighed. 'There is, however, a great change coming, Mr Bell. There are signs and portents in the Heavens. The Astrological Columnist in *The Times* newspaper speaks of the End of Days. There is some alarm upon Venus, I understand – something to do with a planetary alignment that will occur at midnight upon the final day of this century. All the planets arranged in a single line pointing directly to the Sun. A once-in-a-million-years event, or so I am assured.'

Mr Bell picked up a sock of such gross deformity as to make him sick at heart. 'When last we met,' he said, 'I was in possession of certain reliquaries.'

'Three of the four,' said Cardinal Cox. 'I well remember that.'

'And knowing well your sacred texts, you will therefore also be aware of what is prophesied to occur should all four reliquaries be brought together in an unhallowed place.'

Cardinal Cox made the sign of the cross, lifted his rosary to his lips and gave it a passionate kissing.

'Should this blasphemy occur,' said Cameron Bell, 'what might we expect to experience?'

'That evil would be set free upon the fields of Men.' The man of God looked hard at the detective. 'Am I to understand,' he said, 'that *you* have allowed this to occur? That the three reliquaries in your possession, under your care and protection, have been reunited with the fourth of their kind and conveyed to a place of unholiness?' The cardinal's voice had been rising in pitch and volume as his red face grew even redder and his eyes became most round.

'Regrettably,' said Cameron Bell.

'*Regrettably*, man? You will be the death of us all.'

'Assuming,' said Mr Bell, guardedly, 'that these reliquaries *are* what they are purported to be and not merely some manufactured medieval fakes.'

Cardinal Cox was puffing and panting and looked upon the point of passing from consciousness. 'They are real enough,' he cried. 'My God, man, what have you done?'

'Please don't rub it in,' said Cameron Bell. 'Things have been difficult, to say the very least.'

'Spaceships,' said the cardinal, making the face of one who had been granted enlightenment. 'As old Father Noah led two of every kind into the ark, so must we gather up likewise and load all into spaceships. Then, when the Time of Terrible Darkness comes, we can flee to the stars, seek out a new world and start all over again.'

'I am sure that will not be necessary,' said Mr Cameron Bell.

'Are you?' asked the cardinal. 'Well, that has set my mind at rest.'

'I'm glad,' said Cameron Bell.

'I am *joking*!' shouted Cardinal Cox. 'Probably the last joke I will ever manage.'

'It was not a very good one,' said Mr Bell. 'But, under the circumstances—'

'We are all doomed!' declared the cleric. 'Bell has murdered Mankind!'

'That's quite enough of *that*,' said Cameron Bell. 'Might I light for you a pipe of kiff? Its effects can be most calming.'

Cardinal Cox had no objection to that and looked on as the detective set about the business with a surprisingly practised hand.

'Your Grace,' said Cameron Bell.

'A long time since anyone's called me *that*.' The cardinal folded his arms and made a huffy face.

'Your Grace,' said Cameron Bell once more, 'I come to you because I believe you are the one man in London who can help me in this matter. Your erudition in such occult knowledge is well known to me.'

'You smarmy toad,' said Cardinal Cox. 'Hurry please with the pipe.'

Cameron Bell completed his narcotic labourings, lit the pipe, sucked upon its stem then passed it to Cardinal Cox.

'I would know,' said Mr Bell, 'precisely what we might expect to happen if the worst was to occur.'

The cardinal in crimson drew deeply on the pipe and plumes of smoke escaped his ears and nostrils. 'The Seven Plagues, of course,' said he. 'The Seven Plagues of Egypt.'

'Seven minutes in the pan, not six, not eight, but seven.'

Darwin the monkey butler licked his lips as Lord Brentford's chef cooked up a banana fritter.

With the unexplained departure of the bald and bearded chef from the kitchen at Syon House, his lordship had been forced to hire another. Geraldo was a veritable wizard.

Although he hailed from the Isle of Wight, where he had been raised by kiwi birds,* he was master of most of the world's cuisines and a chef of growing reputation who had already invented three new gateaux, two pork pies and a parsnip in a pantry.

And he harboured a deep love of monkeys, which suited Darwin well.

The banana fritter danced in the sizzling butter, and the smell alone had Darwin in a daze.

'A dusting of cinnamon,' sang Geraldo, 'and a sprinkling of crisp cane sugar. Then hey jigger-jig.' And he tossed the fitter onto a plate and presented it to Darwin.

Darwin's eyes were wide and his mouth was smiling. He took up a knife and fork and—

'*Darwin!*' came a cry. 'Come, Darwin, hurry.'

'Aw.' Geraldo snatched away the plate. 'Lord Brentford calls. Perhaps another time.'

Darwin's mouth was now wide open and he waved his knife and fork.

'Come back tomorrow, perhaps,' said the chef, lifting the fritter carefully, blowing upon it and popping it into his mouth. Then, 'Mmph mm mm mph mmph,' which, loosely translated meant, 'And I will cook you another then.'

Darwin watched in horror as the fritter vanished away.

His lordship cried his name once more and the monkey left the kitchen.

'Ah, there you are, my boy.' Lord Brentford was not quite so bandaged as he had been. His legs were still in plaster, though, and one arm in a sling, and there was a curious collar

---

* *It was a genuine heartstring-tugger of a tale. A child abandoned at birth, taken into the nest by birds that had escaped from a circus sideshow. A jealous monk. A fairy princess, three wishes wasted, but a pig who would know better in the future.*

affair with much brass gubbinry holding the nobleman's head in a fixed position.

He had attained a state of some mobility, however, inhabiting as he did a steam-powered bath-chair. Darwin's duties in this regard extended to boiler-stoking, maintenance and very careful steering. Darwin greatly feared the steam-powered bath-chair.

There had been the occasional upset. The occasional piece of unpleasantness. There had even once been a hurling of faeces. Darwin and the bath-chair did not get along.

'Time for a morning snifter, Darwin,' said Lord Brentford. 'Be so good as to fix me a gin and tonic.'

As Darwin sloped off to the drinks cabinet, the bath-chair backfired noisily and Darwin jumped in the air.

Chief Inspector Case was taking the air in the company of Mr Septimus Grey. The erstwhile Governor of the Martian Territories had lately been released from Wormwood Scrubs through the intercession of Chief Inspector Case.

'There will be Hell to pay for all this,' said Mr Septimus Grey. He was a man most put upon, it appeared. A man who had lost a certain something. A man who had experienced things that he dearly wished to forget.

'I have gone to a great deal of trouble on your behalf,' said Chief Inspector Case. 'I hope you appreciate this.'

'But it was *you* who had me convicted on trumped-up charges.'

'Hardly trumped-up,' the chief inspector replied. 'You *are* the owner of the *Marie Lloyd* and you *did* try to bribe an officer of the law.'

'I am *not* the owner of the *Marie Lloyd*.' Septimus Grey made fists and waved them about. 'I gave this evidence under oath in court. I gave the *Marie Lloyd* to a certain Miss

Violet Wond. What she chose to do with it I neither know nor care.'

'And herein lies great interest,' said Chief Inspector Case. 'The jury found against you because no trace could be uncovered of anyone by the unlikely name of Violet Wond.'

'Unlikely?' asked Septimus Grey.

'Never mind. You were sentenced to six months for careless driving and being drunk in charge of a spaceship.'

'Ludicrous,' said Septimus Grey. 'All ludicrous.'

'All ludicrous indeed,' agreed the chief inspector, 'because by diligent police work I uncovered something most curious. The *Marie Lloyd* docked at the Royal London Spaceport upon the day of Lord Brentford's party. The supposition would be that it was then flown to Syon House and there crash-landed.'

'And?' asked Mr Septimus Grey.

'Well, clearly this was *not* the case for according to the flight logs at the Royal London Spaceport, the *Marie Lloyd* was still standing on the landing strip in plain sight at the time it was doing its crashing.'

'I do not understand,' said Septimus Grey.

'Nor me. But apparently the *Marie Lloyd* took off from the spaceport the following evening. A woman in a black veil boarded her in the company of a well-dressed gentleman.'

'A black veil?' said Septimus Grey. 'That thoroughly hid her face?'

'Such was the description given. In order to gain access to the spaceship, she of course had to display documents of authority.'

'It was *her*, was it *not*?' cried Septimus Grey.

'Miss Violet Wond,' said Chief Inspector Case. 'How can the *Marie Lloyd* crash into an English country house one evening and then take off from the spaceport quite unscathed upon the next?'

'I am most confused,' said Septimus Grey.

'Confusion! Ruination! And damnation!' cried Cardinal Cox.

'Would those be three of the Seven Plagues?' asked Mr Cameron Bell.

'Not as such,' said Cardinal Cox, drawing very deeply on his pipe. 'But all will be included when the Terrible Darkness falls.'

Cameron Bell sniffed at the smoke. 'Might I have a little puff of that?' he asked.

'Certainly not!' said Cardinal Cox. 'You are an iconoclast.'

'Speak to me of these plagues,' said Cameron Bell.

'The scriptures differ regarding this. Some say ten plagues, others merely seven. Seven is the accepted figure, particularly when relating to the End of Days. They run as follows –

'A plague of Blood.

'A plague of Frogs.

'A plague of Lice.

'A plague of Flies, or Wild Animals.

'A great Pestilence.

'The Time of Terrible Darkness.

'The Death of the First-Born.'

'All very grim,' said Cameron Bell. 'Let us hope very much that none of these come to be.'

'Oh, they'll come to be!' shouted Cardinal Cox. 'They *will* come to be.'

'Which is why I am here,' said Cameron Bell, 'to ask for your help and advice.'

'Spaceships would be my advice.' The cardinal hunched his shoulders. 'Spaceships, you blackguard, spaceships.'

'And that is all you can offer?'

'What more can there be? If the Seven Plagues come upon us, no one on Earth will be spared.'

'Then let us hope for all of our sakes that they do not.'

Cameron Bell rose from the Persian pouffe. 'I am sorry if I have been the bearer of bad tidings,' he said, 'but I remain confident that all will be well in the end.'

Mr Bell might well have had further platitudes to offer had not his flow been interrupted by a sudden commotion.

Cardinal Cox's catamite burst through the doorway and flung himself into the room. He was all in a terrible state, be-gored from his head to his toes.

'Sweet baby Jesus on the cross or otherwise.' Cardinal Cox caught the catamite, who fell in a horrible heap upon his lap.

'My boy!' cried the cardinal. 'My dear boy. Who has done this terrible thing to you?'

'No man,' the catamite blubbered. 'But we were having a swim in the Thames at Kew for the good of our health, we were.'

'And were you struck by a steam launch or some such?' asked Mr Cameron Bell.

'No, sir,' moaned the catamite. 'One moment all was well and good, the next the River Thames had turned to blood.'

32

ed ran the Thames beyond the gates of Syon. Within the great house, Darwin poured a gin and tonic for his bandaged master.

'Well done there, my boy.' Lord Brentford accepted the glass in his serviceable hand and toasted Darwin with it. 'Now steer me out the back and into the grounds.'

Darwin mounted to the rear of the steam-driven bath-chair and gingerly tweaked a lever or two. The thing took off as a bath-chair possessed. Darwin ground his teeth.

'Slow down, boy!' called Lord Brentford. Darwin struggled and finally took control.

In a manner most sedate they moved along the high-windowed gallery that led to where the Bananary had been.

'Must say you look very smart today.' Lord Brentford took a glance into the wing-mirror. 'Those weird clothes in the wardrobes upstairs appear to fit you very well.'

Darwin turned his eyes towards the ceiling. Exactly why it was that Lord Brentford had failed to recall that he had willed Syon House to Darwin in the first place was anyone's guess. And how, upon returning, as from the dead, to discover the Bananary, the banana groves and the wardrobes filled with clothes that could only be worn by a monkey, he still had not reasoned it out was anyone's guess also. And the fact that he had totally failed to recognise Darwin until the ape had visited him in his hospital room was ludicrous at best. None of this made the vaguest sense to the monkey butler. Although, so his reasoning went, Lord Brentford *was* a member of the aristocracy and as such did not think quite the same way that other men were wont to think.

Darwin today wore a grey silk morning suit with matching top hat and gloves. He really was a very dapper Darwin.

'Steer me outside, if you will.'

As the double doors were open, Darwin steered Lord Brentford out from the house and onto the flat foundation area where the Bananary had until so recently been standing.

Naught was there now to be seen of the architectural anomaly, naught either of the twisted wreckage of the *Marie Lloyd*.

'At least they've done a decent job clearing up,' Lord Brentford observed. 'If I ever catch the scoundrel who built that atrocity . . .'

Darwin wore a downcast face. He had really truly loved that Bananary and considered it to have been a thing of rare beauty.

Certainly he *had* been aware that the artisans he had employed to erect it had built it upside down, but that, if anything, had enhanced its beauty rather than detracted from it.

Well, in Darwin's opinion, anyway.

'Do you know who's coming to visit today?' asked Lord Brentford of his ape.

Darwin shook his hatted head.

'The Queen of England,' said Lord Brentford. 'What do you say to that?'

Darwin could have had plenty to say, but instead he made *oo-oo-ooh*-ing sounds indicative of delight.

'Quite so. And she's bringing a cabinet minister and that young Mr Churchill. It will be quite a lunch. And you will have the honour of serving at table.'

Darwin had mixed feelings regarding this, for he was still torn by the matter of Man's inhumanity to Monkey. But the thing was he *did so* enjoy his role in Lord Brentford's household. And to serve Victoria, Empress of both India and Mars, *was* an honour, of that there could be no doubt.

Darwin did further *oo-oo-ooh*-ings to signify that he was pleased with this.

'Much to discuss over lunch,' said his lordship. 'And as it is such a fine sunny day, I think we'll take it al fresco.'

Birds sang merrily in the trees and beyond the garden's high stone walls the River Thames ran red.

It created a most startling appearance and had halted all traffic on London's many bridges.

Opinions were various and many.

'It is caused by the rich red ochre of the soil in the Indus Valley,' announced a gentleman of advanced years who knew little of geography.

'Martian dust wafted in on solar winds,' said his companion.

'It will be the anarchists,' opined a lady in a straw hat, 'poisoning our English waters with their Bolshevistic ways.'

'The crimson clay of Kentish Town,' remarked a costermonger.

'The dirty dogs of Dagenham,' said a Gatherer of the Pure.

All agreed, however, that it was definitely something 'upstream', but as few Londoners knew the source of the Thames, their guesses were blurry at best.

''Tis the first of the Seven End Times Plagues!' cried a cleric, wild of eye and white of hair.

But as these were sensible modern times, nobody listened to him.

'Now listen,' said Lord Brentford to his staff – an upstairs maid both spare and kempt, a boy of all trades known as Jack, Geraldo from the Isle of Wight and monkey butler Darwin. 'Several of the gentry are coming here today – lords and ladies *and* Her Majesty the Queen.'

He paused that his staff might go, 'Oooooh.'

'We know what happened the last time I held a little soirée here. Damned Martian spaceship crashed down upon us. Mad anarchist plot, or so the story goes.'

Darwin made a sorry little face. He was not likely to forget that Lord Brentford had shot the monkey butler's future self quite dead with his twelve-bore shot gun. Not that he held it against Lord Brentford.

But—

'Pay attention, Darwin,' said his lordship. 'I do not want anything to go wrong this time. So very much depends upon it. So very much indeed.'

And so it clearly did. Darwin had attended to his lordship throughout his many meetings over the last month. He had peered furtively at top-secret plans for a titanic glass-house to contain the Tri-Planetary Exposition, a glass-house of such magnitude as to dwarf the Crystal Palace on Sydenham Hill. Work was already in progress in foundries up and down the country, casting the sections that would link together to form the giant whole. But the question that remained to be

262

answered was, where was it going to be erected? No doubt this question would figure large throughout the coming lunch.

'Geraldo,' said Lord Brentford. 'As you know, there will be a pair of Venusians present today. They must find no red meat upon their plates. Chicken only, and green vegetables, do you understand?'

'The favourite dishes of Venus are most well known to me.' Geraldo lifted his high chef's hat and gave a sweeping bow.

'Darwin, your duties will be those of wine waiter.'

Darwin preened at his lapels, for that was a rather posh job.

'Boy named Jack,' his lordship continued, 'you will be on cloakroom duty, and will also serve the guests their lunch – with no upsettings of soup into laps or any of that kind of caper.'

The boy named Jack raised high his thumbs and said, 'Aye aye, your lordship.'

'Upstairs maid, both spare and kempt, you will drift around in an enigmatic fashion, catching the eye of the young lords present but remaining aloof to their advances.'

The upstairs maid curtseyed in a manner spare and kempt.

'And all will go perfectly, will it not,' said his lordship. And as this was a statement rather than a question, none of his staff replied.

The very first carriage arrived around twelve and the boy named Jack opened the door.

Upon the step stood Mr Winston Churchill, briskly scrubbed and baby-faced and sporting the bright blue uniform of the Queen's Own Electric Fusiliers. Splendid with his golden braideries and medals that sparkled on his breast, a sword in an ornamented scabbard made him look even more dashing. Although only in his early twenties, Mr Churchill presently held a position of great responsibility. He had been appointed Her Majesty's Defender Throughout the Period of the Anarchist Threat. A post he had accepted humbly, asking only that he be permitted full control over all of Her Majesty's armed services, including the newly founded Air Force.

Mr Winston Churchill bustled past the boy named Jack, drew his sword and went in search of anarchists.

The next to arrive were the Ambassador of Jupiter and his wife Doris. The ambassador *had* been present at the previous soirée and had no intention of missing this one in case something else fell out of the sky and he wasn't there to see it. The ambassador, a rotund chap with skin toned Earthly pink, slapped his wife on her comely backside and entered Syon House.

Sir Peter Harrow, Member for Brentford North and Minister for Home Affairs, appeared upon a penny-farthing bicycle of his own design and construction. It was not one likely to tickle the public's imagination, however, having as it did the little wheel at the front.

Leah the Venusian ecclesiastic stepped daintily from an electric-wheeler and, moving with care and grace upon her towering heels, she entered Syon House in the company of an unnamed individual – a Venusian too with high-teased hair who swung a smoking censer.

Queen Victoria's arrival was attended by all the necessary brouhaha that befitted the appearance of a great Head of State.

A platoon of the Household Cavalry accompanied her carriage along the drive and she was aided down from it by two huge Sikhs done up in golden apparel. Mr Churchill noted ruefully that their mighty swords put his own to shame.

Her Majesty had today brought two members of the Royal Household with her: her monkey maid named Emily and her augmented kiwi bird Caruthers.

Caruthers was a notable kiwi bird who was very much the darling of high society. A generous gift from a Maori chief, he had sadly suffered the loss of a leg during an altercation with Prince Edward's gun dog Wilkinson at Sandringham.

Lord Babbage had been commissioned to create the clockwork-powered wheeled prosthesis that afforded Caruthers considerable mobility.

Caruthers wheeled into Syon House and hand in hand with Emily, Queen Victoria followed.

A table had been placed in the midst of the banana groves, set with linen and doilies and silver cruets and crystal glass and antique knives and forks. Geraldo had arranged floral decorations along the table's length, and the redolence of roses, blended with the heady musks of late flowering bananas and the incense of the Venusian's censer, created perfumes of intoxicating enchantment.

Lord Brentford, in his bath-chair, sat at the table's foot, facing Queen Victoria at its head. Between them were arranged, upon Lord Brentford's left, Leah the Venusian, her companion and Mr Winston Churchill; and to his right, Sir Peter Harrow, the wife of the Jovian ambassador and the Jovian ambassador himself.

It was as correct as it was possible to be, within the strict and formal protocols required by such an occasion as this.

Darwin dispensed champagne, stepping carefully over the table in soft silk slippers. The monkey butler was greatly taken with Emily, an ape of considerable charm, who sat upon the lap of her royal mistress making coy expressions at Darwin.

Geraldo aided Jack in the serving of soup. The sun shone down with gentleness upon the elegant assembly and although beyond the walls the Thames ran red, no more pleasant a luncheon could be imagined. The company was charming, the foods and wines superb. The Empress Queen reigned all supreme and God most surely loved the British Empire.

33

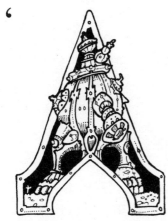

'mused are we,' said the royal personage, reducing the table hubbub to a deep respectful silence as she dunked her biscuit into a cup of tea. 'Undoubtedly the finest Treacle Sponge Bastard that one has tasted since one's dear Prince Albert passed away. One's compliments to the chef.'

Geraldo had been enjoying a conversation with Caruthers in their common tongue of kiwi bird, but at the regal compliment he stiffened to attention.

The hubbub returned with a vengeance and Lord Brentford attempted to make himself heard above it. 'Would you care for a little post-prandial, ma'am?' he shouted. 'One of those round chocolate sweets, or a pipe of opium, perhaps?'

Queen Victoria raised the royal hand.

'I would gladly try the opium,' said Sir Peter Harrow.

Lord Brentford affected a languid Byronic gesture towards his monkey butler. Darwin set off in search of opium.

'One reads with interest your plans for this Grand Exposition,' said Her Majesty, drawing attention all around. 'Will you speak to us of this venture now, Lord Brentford?'

'With the greatest pleasure, ma'am.' Lord Brentford shooed away a bee that had settled upon him. 'It is my wish to bring Your Majesty joy,' said he, 'by bringing together the arts and crafts and industries of the three inhabited planets into a wonderful exhibition within an equally wonderful building.'

'One hears,' said Her Majesty, 'that you plan to have constructed a glass-house three times the size of the Crystal Palace.'

'Such is my intention, ma'am.'

'And where will it stand, this Wonder of the Worlds?'

'I had hoped in Hyde Park, ma'am, on the original site of the Great Exhibition.'

Sir Peter Harrow raised his hands. 'If I might say a word,' said he.

'Please do,' said the monarch, smiling.

'Too big,' said Sir Peter. 'Won't fit,' said Sir Peter. 'The site is already booked by the Chiswick Townswomen's Guild for a firework display to celebrate the dawn of the twentieth century,' said Sir Peter, too.

'Would have been handy for the Albert Hall,' said the Queen, 'but one has many dear friends amongst the Chiswick Townswomen's Guild. Put it somewhere else, Lord Brentford, do.'

'Ah,' said Lord Brentford, swatting at the bee. 'Then I have Your Majesty's formal approval for the scheme.'

'What will it cost the Crown?' asked Queen Victoria.

'Precisely nothing, ma'am, not a single penny.'

'Then one gives one's blessings.'

'Thank you very much, ma'am,' said his lordship.

Mr Winston Churchill spoke. 'A question or two, if I might.'

Queen Victoria nodded and Lord Brentford, too.

'Security,' said Winston Churchill. 'We live in troubled times. Such a mighty edifice would present the ideal target for anarchists.'

'One cares not for anarchists,' said Her Majesty the Queen.

'And,' continued Mr Churchill, 'there is the matter of importation. What goods will be arriving from the other worlds? What threats to the nation might these pose?'

The Queen gazed down her nose towards Lord Brentford.

His lordship worried a little more at the bee, which had somehow crawled its way into his sling.

'The Grand Exposition,' he said, 'is a mission for peace between the worlds. I would ask the noble representatives from Venus and Jupiter who sit amongst us to speak of what they would care to display.'

Leah's golden eyes gazed at Lord Brentford. 'What has the Ambassador of Jupiter to say on these matters?' she asked.

'I?' said the ambassador. 'Thou askest me, lass? Well, I'll tell thee.'

And with that the ambassador started to sing:

> We have cakes and pies and sausages and pastries and
>   preserves.
> Pots of honey, marmalade and jam.
> Bread and buns and big baguettes.
> Toffee shaped like cigarettes.
> Cuts of pork and beef and leg of lamb.
>
> Our pies are the size of the Sun in the skies.
> Our pork is the talk of the town.
> Our butter, I'll utter, will make thy heart flutter
> And our cheese will please as thou swallow it down.

We have brisket, we have biscuit, we have chocolate gateau,
And thou'll not want for sweeties, I can say.
We have bubble gum to please thy tum
And we can offer everyone
The finest foods this universe could put upon display.

Queen Victoria clapped her hands; she always had a soft spot for the Jovians.

'I know a rather saucy song about a lady lighthouse keeper,' said Sir Peter Harrow.

'Not now, Sir Peter,' said the Queen.

Darwin arrived with the opium pipe and the chastened Sir Peter accepted it gratefully.

'So,' said Lord Brentford to the Jovian ambassador, 'I envisage the area assigned to the arts, crafts, produce and commerce of Jupiter to be one resembling a greatly magnified version of Harrods' food hall.'

'Only tastier,' said the ambassador.

Darwin offered a tray of marshmallows to Queen Victoria's monkey.

'And might we hear now from the Venusian representatives?' asked his lordship.

'We will be contributing nothing,' said Leah.

'*Nothing?*' said Queen Victoria. 'What is one to understand by this?'

'The ecclesiastical elders have discussed this matter at length,' said Leah, her voice as some Arcadian ghost murmuring amongst the towering plants. 'It has been agreed that we will put upon display one of our greatest treasures: a sphere containing nothingness – which is to say, the purest thing in the entire universe.'

'One wishes for enlightenment,' said the Empress of India and Mars.

The golden gaze of Leah touched the monarch. 'Between our world and yours,' she whispered, 'exists the realm of space. But space is not an empty place, for it is popularly understood that space is filled with the aether, an electric though impalpable *something* which conducts the heat of the Sun and the light from the stars. If space was an empty vacuum, devoid of all molecules, molecules even of space itself, then light and heat could not be conducted through it.'

Sir Peter might have taken issue with this, but he had the opium pipe upon the go and his eye had fallen upon the upstairs maid, both spare and kempt, who was drifting about in an enigmatic fashion.

'And your sphere,' said Lord Brentford to Leah, 'contains absolutely nothing – pure unadulterated nothingness?'

Leah's gaze rested upon him and her wide mouth formed a smile.

'What does it look like, this nothingness?' asked Her Majesty the Queen.

'Quite unlike anything you could imagine,' said Leah. 'To gaze upon it is to gaze into celestial purity. Those who gaze upon it will be touched for ever.'

'Then they can come t' our bit later for lunch,' said the Jovian ambassador.

'Ooooh,' went Lord Brentford of a sudden.

'Ooooh?' queried Her Majesty. 'What is the meaning of "ooooh"?'

'A bumblebee's gone up my sleeve,' said his lordship.

'Winston,' said Her Majesty, 'go and swat the bee that's bothering Brentford.'

Winston Churchill rose and drew his sword.

'No need for swordplay,' said Lord Brentford.

'Say I'm the only bee in your bonnet,' sang Sir Peter Harrow.

Queen Victoria looked on with interest as Winston Churchill began to buffet Lord Brentford with the pommel of his sword.

'I've never been to the Isle of Wight,' said Caruthers to Geraldo in the kiwi tongue, 'but I've heard it's a very nice place.'

Darwin popped a marshmallow into Emily's mouth. Emily munched and fluttered her lashes at Darwin.

Sir Peter blew kisses to the upstairs maid, but she remained aloof from his advances.

Presently Queen Victoria said, 'One tires of all this hitting, Winston. Surely the bee must be done for by now.'

Winston Churchill cracked Lord Brentford over the head. 'One can never be too sure, ma'am,' was his answer to that.

'Stop it now, Winston,' said the Queen. 'There are matters of state to discuss.'

'I hate to pour cold water on this,' said Mr Churchill, clouting Lord Brentford one more time before sheathing his sword and returning to his seat, 'but frankly, ma'am, this entire enterprise is simply ludicrous.'

'How so?' asked Her Majesty the Queen.

'Ma'am, the Jovians seek only to open a restaurant and the Venusians have *absolutely nothing whatsoever* to contribute. Added to which no location can be found to accommodate this monstrous anarchist's delight of a construction.'

Queen Victoria stroked her monkey's head. 'These are good points,' she said to Lord Brentford. 'How do you answer them?'

Lord Brentford, however, was still preoccupied with the bee, which had outmanoeuvred Mr Churchill's assault and taken refuge in his lordship's trousers.

'Well?' went the monarch. 'Well?'

'Ma'am,' said Lord Brentford, feeling at himself beneath

the table, 'Mr Churchill seeks to obfuscate the issue. Jupiter offers us the finest viands in the solar system, everything that can delight the palate. Venus offers us spiritual sustenance, affording us a view into the infinite. Should these two not be sufficient for all to marvel at, the British Empire will contribute the cream of its arts and industries. There will be a great concert hall and within it, to celebrate the dawn of the new century, the London Symphony Orchestra, with full chorus, will perform Beethoven's Ninth Symphony – surely one of Mankind's highest attainments. All these wonders of the worlds gathered together in the heart of the Empire could not offer a nobler tribute to England's most beloved monarch. Namely yourself.'

Winston Churchill made a sullen face.

Queen Victoria said, 'We are convinced.'

'Ha,' said Winston Churchill. 'There is still no place in London to accommodate this errant aberration.'

'We will raise it next to the Mall,' said Queen Victoria. 'The parklands there belong to the Royal Household. Lord Brentford has one's permission to construct his hall for the Great Exposition there.'

'No,' cried Winston Churchill, rising once more to his feet. 'Such a thing is dangerous folly, ma'am.'

'Do you argue with your monarch, Mr Churchill?' Queen Victoria made the face of sternness.

'No, ma'am, please, but—'

'*Waark!*' went Lord Brentford as the bumblebee stung him hard in a personal place.

'Allow *me*,' said Mr Churchill, once more drawing his sword.

Darwin, whose eyes were only for Emily, heard Lord Brentford's, '*Waark!*' but felt that it was probably none of his business.

273

His lordship's cries of, 'Stop hitting me, you blackguard!' drew the ape's attention.

As Winston Churchill raised his sword to clock Lord Brentford one in the eye, Darwin flung the tray of marsh-mallows aside and leapt along the table's length to aid his helpless master.

Sir Peter Harrow's hand snaked out towards the upstairs maid both spare and kempt. This unasked-for intimacy was rewarded with a blow to the head that sent Sir Peter sprawling.

He sprawled across the bountiful lap of the Jovian ambassador's wife, a woman who had been asked to contribute precisely nothing to the foregoing conversation and as such was happy to strike out at anything that came her way, in the spirit of pure frustration.

She raised Sir Peter from her lap, hauled him upright, then flung him onto the table.

Queen Victoria stared aghast as Darwin set about Mr Winston Churchill, who in turn set about Lord Brentford, who in turn was setting about himself and punching repeatedly at his groin. Sir Peter rolled over the table and fell onto the Venusian ecclesiastic who accompanied Leah.

As *to be touched by those of an impure race* was considered by Venusians an act of such gross personal violation as might only be redressed by the extinction of the perpetrator, the Venusian ecclesiastic uttered the words of a magical spell to draw down fire from Heaven.

Flames rolled out from the empty sky and set ablaze the table decorations.

Geraldo, seeking someone to punish for this, chose the Jovian ambassador.

As 'Great Fights in Inappropriate Places' went, it did not rival the now-legendary 'Battle of the British Showman's

Fellowship' of the previous year. But as Queen Victoria later wrote in her diary:

> Luncheon today at Lord Brentford's.
> Treacle Sponge Bastard for pudding.
> Splendid punch-up afterwards.
> Tea at Claridge's later.

34

ameron Bell gazed down at the River Thames. The bloody hues of the previous day were gone and the majestic watercourse flowed pure and crystal clear once more. Salmon sported and ducks went dabble-dabble.

The detective stood upon London Bridge, an early-morning newssheet spread before him on the parapet. Cameron Bell glanced at the headline, printed big and bold.

LORD BRENTFORD RETURNED TO HOSPITAL
UNHAPPY LORD ADMITTED WITH
BROKEN NOSE AND BEE-STING

Cameron Bell turned pages in search of some reference to the blooding of the River Thames. On page four he located a small piece penned by the paper's Thames Correspondent, who through diligence and determination had tracked down the cause of the horror:

A chance combination of soil from the Indus Valley, dust from Mars brought in on solar winds,

the crimson clay of Kentish Town and
the dirty dogs of Dagenham.

So that was that and the capital of the Empire had nothing whatever to fear.

Cameron Bell flipped pages back and forth. He had been hoping to see some crime reported, some major crime that would baffle Scotland Yard. Not that he wished to solve it himself, oh no. Rather it was his hope that such a crime would lure the Nation's Most Wanted, Lady Raygun, out to destroy the criminal.

And in doing so, allow herself to fall into some cunning trap laid for her by Mr Cameron Bell.

For during the month that had passed since Mr Bell's return to sensibility, there had been no further outrages from the woman the gutter press referred to as the Mistress of Mystery and the Angel of Death. In fact she had attained to a certain celebration, with penny dreadfuls dedicated to her exploits and Lady Raygun dolls for sale on the market stalls of Brick Lane.

At present, Mr Bell had nothing to go on and a growing sense of unease that as the nation appeared to have taken this murderous female to its heart, the detective who brought her career to an end would not be a popular man.

'Best let Chief Inspector Case take *all* the credit for that one, then,' said Cameron Bell to himself.

But there it was, and now there was simply no crime in London Town. The pages of the news-sheet painted the prettiest picture of the metropolis, a crime-free utopia and one, it appeared, that within several months would be treated to something altogether superb.

THE GRAND TRI-PLANETARY
EXPOSITION
Wherein will be displayed
THE WONDERS OF THE WORLDS

The announcement had been made this very morning. The news-sheet displayed a detailed engraving of the planned structure within which this fabulous exhibition would be displayed. It spoke of the concert hall at which Beethoven's Glorious Ninth would be performed and hinted at many marvellous things to be seen. And the mighty edifice was to be raised literally within Her Majesty's front garden, in the park stretching the length of the Mall.

'Now that *will* be something to see,' said Cameron Bell, and he raised his eyes from the news-sheet and looked up at the city he loved, a thriving city and one blessed with miraculous technologies. Around and about the power station at Battersea arose the tall, slim Tesla towers, transmitting, without the need for wires or cables, electricity to power the capital and those marvels of the modern age that rose from within it. For above and swimming in the sky of blue were great silver airships and the sleek pleasure-craft of the wealthy. And all about in the architecture there was evidence of the new. Of the coming century. Of hope. And all about, too, Londoners pressing on about their business as ever they had and hopefully would ever do. As Mr Bell watched them passing him by over the famous bridge, he found his thoughts turning unexpectedly to Beethoven's Ninth and its libretto drawn from Friedrich Schiller's *Ode to Joy*:

Endure courageously, millions!
Endure for the better world!
O'er the tent of stars unfurled
A great God will reward you.

A gentle breeze lifted Mr Bell's news-sheet and flung it down to the crystal waters below. The great detective marshalled his thoughts. She was out there somewhere, that Lady Raygun. Out there somewhere and *he* would surely find her.

The knock upon the door of Ernest Rutherford's house was swiftly answered. A well-dressed troll with polished teeth greeted the lady all in black who stood upon the step.

'A joy to see you once again, sweet madam,' crooned the troll, noting well the swing of the lady's dark lace parasol. 'Mr Rutherford awaits – I will lead you to him directly.'

The troll named Jones led Violet Wond to the door of Mr Rutherford's study, knocked upon it, stepped back, announced, 'I will fetch you tea and biscuits at once,' and made a smart departure.

Mr Ernest Rutherford opened the door. 'Dearest Violet,' said he. 'This is an unexpected surprise and a most delightful one, too.'

'Ernest,' said the lady in black, inclining her head towards the chemist that he might kiss his loved one on the veil. 'I have come to see what progress has been made on your grand enterprise.'

Mr Rutherford smiled. 'Then would you care to come and see?'

'I would be delighted.'

'Then I will fetch my coat.'

As the two approached the front door, Jones the troll

descended the staircase, tray of tea and biscuits in his horny little hands.

'A splendid job there, Jones,' said the chemist, 'but we are going out.'

Mr Rutherford turned away to open the front door and as Jones stepped from the staircase to the hall, an accident occurred.

Miss Wond's parasol swung between the legs of Jones, causing him to trip, upend his tray and fall in a heap to be painfully scalded by tea.

Mr Rutherford turned to view this calamity.

'You really are a clumsy fellow, Jones,' said he. 'Please fetch a cloth and clear up all that mess.'

Jones glared daggers at the lady all in black.

As, swinging her parasol once more, she swept into the street.

'We are making considerable progress,' said Mr Rutherford as he helped Miss Wond to enter a hansom cab. 'I have engaged the help of two of the Empire's most notable scientific minds.' Mr Rutherford climbed into the cab and settled himself next to Miss Wond. 'Victoria Palace Theatre,' he called out to the driver.

'You are taking me to the music hall?' asked the lady of his heart's desire.

'You will see – it is my surprise.'

Clip and *clop* went the horse's hooves and the cab travelled over the cobbled streets of London.

'Did you read the papers today?' Mr Rutherford asked.

'I did,' said Miss Violet, taking his hand and giving it a squeeze. 'Absolutely no crime to speak of in the capital at present.'

Mr Rutherford raised an eyebrow. 'You say that almost as if it is a bad thing,' he observed.

'Of course not, dear. But what was it that interested you in the morning's press?'

'The Grand Exposition,' said Ernest, 'wherein will be displayed the Wonders of the Worlds.'

'And what is this to you?' asked Violet Wond.

'The greatest opportunity that ever there was,' the chemist replied. 'Would it not be just the thing to unveil the time-ship at the Grand Exposition?'

'I thought the project was to be conducted in the utmost secrecy?'

'It is, my dear, it is – at least until it has reached a successful completion. I have given this very much thought and I do believe that the time-ship will be the single most important invention in the history of Mankind, and one that will ensure peace between the worlds in our time and for ever.'

Miss Violet Wond set free her loved one's hand. 'Perhaps you should give it a little more thought,' said she.

At length they reached the Victoria Palace Theatre and Mr Ernest Rutherford paid the cabbie.

A large sign above the doors to the theatre read: CLOSED FOR RENOVATION.

'I do not believe,' said Violet Wond, 'that Little Tich will be entertaining us today.'

'Come, please,' said Ernest Rutherford, pushing open a door and ushering his sweetheart into the darkened theatre.

They passed through the foyer and entered the auditorium and here Miss Violet Wond beheld a great wonder which caused her to cry aloud.

'The *Marie Lloyd*,' cried she.

And indeed, there stood the battered Martian hulk, filling the interior of the music hall. The stage, the seating, the balconies were gone and nothing was contained within but a great big spaceship.

Miss Wond gazed up to the frescoed ceiling, a wild rococo romp of pink-bottomed cherubs and a five-tier chandelier, a perfect match for that which lit the music room of the Royal Pavilion in Brighton.

'But how,' she asked, 'did you get it in? The ceiling is untouched.'

'Through the floor,' said Ernest Rutherford, with pride in his voice. 'You steered it down into a siding of the Circle Line. I had it eased through the tunnel then raised upon hydraulic ramps into this disused theatre. No more fitting place for Miss Marie Lloyd, surely?'

'Very impressive,' said Miss Violet Wond. 'And who are these bright fellows, might I ask?'

For two bright fellows had indeed issued from the open port of the *Marie Lloyd*, a robust avuncular figure and a tall and pinch-faced man with a fine dark shock of hair.

'Please allow me to make introductions,' said Mr Rutherford. 'Lord Charles Babbage and Lord Nikola Tesla, pleased be to meet Miss Violet Wond.'

The avuncular fellow bowed and said, 'Babbage.'

The other bowed and said, 'A pleasure to meet you.'

'Well, now,' said Miss Wond. 'Two most distinguished *members* of the scientific community.'

Lord Babbage glanced at Lord Tesla. There was something about the way that this young woman had just articulated the word 'members' . . .

'How goes it, gentlemen?' asked Mr Rutherford, taking a businesslike approach.

'For the most part, well,' said Lord Babbage. 'We have linked the inter-rositor to induce a cross-polarisation of beta particles which should result in a transperambulation of pseudo-cosmic anti-matter.'

'That's easy for you to say,' said Miss Wond.

'Quite so, madam.' Lord Babbage shook his head. 'But things keep coming through, as it were, which tend to cause confusion.'

'Things?' asked Mr Rutherford. 'Coming through?' he said also, for the memory of a certain troll named Jones, who had 'come through' during a previous experiment, was ever fresh in his mind.

'Each time we switch on the inter-rositor, one of them comes through,' said Lord Tesla. 'We did not mind the first time – Babbage had it for dinner.'

'And very tasty it was,' said the famous inventor of the famous Difference Engine, 'but the novelty has worn off. I am a scientist, not a farmer. Something must be done.'

'I would appreciate it,' said Mr Rutherford, 'if you would explain to me clearly and precisely exactly what you mean.'

'Step this way,' said Lord Tesla, 'and we will show you.'

The two eminent scientists led the chemist and the veiled lady in black into the *Marie Lloyd*. Here was to be found all that electronic trickery-dickery and brass-tubed hubbing-gubbing that had filled the *Marie Lloyd* when the aged Darwin from the future had crashed it into the Bananary at Syon House, one month before this day.

'It is all so very shiny,' said Miss Wond, affecting the manner of the scatterbrained female that big roughty-toughty men find so endearing. Scientists in particular. 'What does that big wiggly thing do?' asked Miss Wond, pointing to the flux capacitor for which she had drawn up the plans.

Lord Babbage said, 'Please allow me to demonstrate.'

'What are you intending to do?' asked Mr Rutherford.

'Create a minor temporal anomaly within strict boundaries and lure, if you will, a tiny piece of the past into the present.'

'How very exciting,' said Miss Violet Wond. 'But isn't that rather dangerous? From what location are you ensnaring this tiny piece of the past?'

'From our present location,' Lord Babbage explained. 'I assume Mr Rutherford has explained to you the nature of this project – in a manner that a lady can understand?'

'He has,' replied Miss Wond. 'That power here is drawn from the Large Hadron Collider beneath our feet, which is built into the Circle Line, a particle accelerator designed to create a situation where the speed of light is slowed to below walking pace, in order that this vessel can overtake it and travel through time.'

'Yes,' said Lord Babbage. 'That is indeed the case. The experiment that we have been conducting creates this effect on a limited scale, bringing a bit of yesterday into today.'

'But,' said Lord Tesla, 'we cannot take a piece of yesterday as such. This theatre was built in eighteen twenty and folk have sat in this auditorium since then. We do not want to snatch one of them from the past into today – that would be most impolite.'

'So you have set your controls to fish for something back beyond the year of eighteen twenty?'

'Indeed, madam,' said Lord Tesla. 'We have set it to seventeen twenty, sixteen twenty, fifteen twenty, so on and so on and so on—'

'And?' said Miss Violet Wond.

'Oh yes,' said Lord Babbage, 'let us see. What do we have it set at presently, Lord Tesla?'

'Twenty-seven thousand and twenty BC,' said his scientific lordship.

'And I will wager it comes up the same.'

'Gentlemen, please get on with it,' said Mr Ernest Rutherford.

'As you will.' Lord Babbage threw a lever.

There was a flash and a big cloud of smoke.

Which cleared.

To reveal a big fat chicken.

'There,' said Lord Tesla. 'Another one! It just doesn't make any sense.'

35

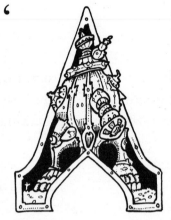

'chicken!' said Ernest Rutherford. 'And it is *always* a chicken?'

'Always a chicken,' said Lord Babbage. 'No matter how far back in time we go, we always turn up a chicken.'

'Perhaps there have been chicken farms upon this spot since the very dawn of civilisation,' was Mr Rutherford's suggestion.

'Perhaps,' said Lord Babbage, 'perhaps.'

'I cannot think of any other likely explanation.'

'I hate flaming chickens, I do,' said Lord Nikola Tesla.

'Flaming chicken,' said Lord Brentford. 'Flaming chicken for lunch.'

Darwin looked up at his lord and master. What was *this* all about?

They sat side by side in a hansom cab parked at the kerb of the Mall.

'I will take you for lunch,' Lord Brentford explained, 'to the very latest and most fashionable eatery in town. It is called Patrick's Flaming Chickens. You have no objection to eating chicken, I suppose?'

Darwin shook his hairy little head.

'Mean to say, not as if they're your ancestors or any-thing.' Lord Brentford chuckled merrily, then clutched at his wounded nose. 'Anyhow,' he continued, 'this is where the Grand Exposition will be held. The great house of glass stretching all the way from there—' he gestured towards the archway that led to Trafalgar Square '—to there.' And they viewed the palace of the Queen. 'Construction will start next week. We'll pop down every day or so to keep an eye on things.'

Darwin thought this a pleasant enough prospect and smiled as he nodded his head.

'We will be making history, my boy,' said Lord Brentford, patting his monkey butler upon his nodding head and nearly knocking his hat off. 'Making history, what do you think about *that*?'

Darwin raised a thumb approvingly.

'Splendid stuff. Then let us go for lunch.' Lord Brentford shouted up to the driver, 'Patrick's Flaming Chickens, man.'

It was a rather swank affair, was Patrick's Flaming Chickens. It served a most nutritious delicacy: farm-fresh chicken pieces cocooned in a batter of secret herbs and spices, then plunged into a boiling vat of health-giving lard and cooked to a tasty turn.

Willing waiters lifted Lord Brentford from the hansom cab and conveyed him to the seat he had reserved.

'I am sure you have no objection to standing while you eat,' said his lordship to Darwin. 'Pretty swank affair, this – seats are hard to come by.'

And indeed it *was* a pretty swank affair. The literati and glitterati and indeed the obiterati were all well represented here this lunchtime. On behalf of the literati, Lord Brentford drew Darwin's attention to Mr Oscar Wilde, who sat sharing a milkshake with Sir Arthur Conan Doyle.

The glitterati glittered as they should. There was Dame Nellie Melba and there too Little Tich and several other stars of the music hall. And all were setting about their tucker in a most poetic manner:

> Sammy 'Sherbert' Schwartscof sucked a stripy sweet.
> Freddie 'Fat Boy' Firkin favoured fowls.
> When it came to pudding, Birdie Pinkerton could claim
> That he ate it while impersonating owls.

Of the obiterati only one was present today: the late great Duke of Wellington. Looking pale, but interesting.

'Tuck in me napkin, do,' said Lord Brentford to his monkey butler.

Darwin climbed onto the table and attended to the lord.

'Would sir care to see the wine list?' asked a liveried waiter.

'Just bring me a bottle of Château Doveston,' said his lordship, 'and *squawk!*'

'I don't think we have *squawk* on the wine list, your lordship.'

'It's not a damn drink,' said Lord Brentford. 'It was a damn *squawk* – damn monkey butler's tucked me napkin in too tight.'

Darwin scuttled smartly from the table.

'Dining with a lady today,' said Lord Brentford, 'so bring two glasses.'

Darwin made a hopeful face and tugged at his master's leg.

'And a bowl of water for the ape.'

Cutlery clattered and toothsome viands were munched

upon with relish. The setting was of the modernistic persuasion, with the very latest thing in red flocked wallpaper, neon strip-lighting and Bakelite chairs that grated musically upon the pink linoleum floor. It was chic beyond chic and they even served Treacle Sponge Bastard.

Leah the Venusian entered the eatery. Ravishing in high-heeled shoes, with high cheekbones and high-plumed hair, she had the heads of high-born fellows turning.

Lord Brentford greeted her with much enthusiasm. 'So happy to see you, most beautiful lady,' he gushed. 'So sorry about all the misunderstandings yesterday at my luncheon. No hard feelings upon the part of your companion, I trust.'

Three waiters aided Leah into her seat, then began to fuss at her with napkins.

'Sling your hooks, waiters!' bawled Lord Brentford. 'Trying to have a bally conversation here, don'cha know.'

Darwin grinned. He actually quite liked to watch Lord Brentford throwing his weight around and bullying the menials. Why? Darwin shrugged. He did not know, but still it made him smile.

The waiters departed. Then returned in the company of the waiter who was bringing the champagne. Lord Brentford shooed the lot of them away and called upon Darwin to open and pour out the bubbly.

Darwin willingly obliged and sneaked a glass for himself.

Lord Brentford took his in his good hand and toasted the delightful Leah.

'My dear lady,' said he in a confidential tone, 'I really am so glad that you chose to dine with me this lunchtime. Terribly embarrassed about yesterday and everything. Especially in front of Her Majesty. I consider it all Sir Peter Harrow's fault. Man's a scoundrel, should have seen it from the first.'

'It is of no consequence,' said Leah, tasting champagne. 'And regarding my companion, he underwent rigorous purgations to repurify himself. He has had his skin scoured and powerful laxatives—'

'Well,' went Lord Brentford, humming and hah-ing, 'let us not dwell upon such a personal matter. Do you find the champagne palatable?'

Leah nodded, her golden eyes fixed upon his lordship.

Lesser men might well have wilted, but Lord Brentford was the son of sterling noble stock. 'It is a delicate matter,' he said, 'that I wish to broach. You see, yesterday at the luncheon table, your companion caused certain events to occur.'

Leah's gaze remained unfaltering.

'The fire,' said Lord Brentford, 'that fell from the Heavens. Narrowly missing Sir Peter Harrow but playing merry havoc with my table decorations.'

'It was a regrettable occurrence,' said Leah.

'It wasn't a bad shot,' said Lord Brentford. 'It only *just* missed him.'

'Regrettable,' said Leah, 'as it is against interplanetary agreement for Venusians to practise magic on Earth.'

'I know, I know,' said Lord Brentford. 'Darwin,' he called to his ape, 'top up the lady's glass, if you will.'

Darwin hastened to oblige and also topped up his own.

'It is forbidden,' said Leah. 'My companion will be punished for his undisciplined behaviour – fifty strokes of the Poomdanger's Pizzle, followed by—'

'I do not wish to know,' said his lordship, who knew nothing of Poomdangers, but having served in the Queen's Own Electric Fusiliers was no stranger to a flogging with a pizzle. 'Never seen such stuff myself before,' said his lordship, placing his empty glass before him. 'Fire falling out of an empty sky. Most impressive.'

The golden eyes were focused on Lord Brentford.

'Question is,' said he, 'what would it take to persuade you to teach me a trick or two like that?'

'Trick?' said Leah.

'And a damn fine one, too. Would certainly put the wind up the chaps at the Explorers' Club if I knew how to do it.'

Leah stared hard at Lord Brentford. 'I think you fail to understand,' she said. 'These are neither parlour tricks nor stage illusions as might be displayed before an audience at the Electric Alhambra. This is magic of the purest kind. This is genuine magic.'

'Genuine magic, you say?' Lord Brentford rattled his glass on the table and Darwin swiftly refilled it. '*Genuine* magic?'

'How can you doubt it?' asked Leah. 'Interplanetary treaties have been drawn up regarding it. Laws passed.'

'Hmph,' went his lordship. 'Well, I *have* been away for a couple of years. Airship crash. Stuck on cannibal island. Long story, won't bore you with it here.'

'It is genuine magic,' said Leah.

'Is it, by Jingo?' his lordship said.

Presently meals were ordered, and further champagne. Mr Patrick, the suave and debonair proprietor of the establishment, even happened by to offer a rose to Leah and present her with a voucher which enabled her to eat for half the price on Monday evenings.

By the serving of the Treacle Sponge Bastard, Lord Brentford was somewhat into his cups. As was Darwin, who now could see two Lord Brentford's and an infinite number of Leahs.

Which set him to wondering whether an infinite number of Shakespeares might be able to write a really good monkey.

'So, would you teach me?' asked Lord Brentford, swaying in his chair. 'A little piece of genuine magic. I promise that I'd only use it for good.'

'Absolutely not,' said Leah. 'It is quite forbidden.'

'But if it *is* genuine,' said Lord Brentford, within whose head many ideas were now percolating, 'then it is right and proper that you share it.'

'No,' said Leah. 'It cannot be done.'

'For the sake of peace,' said Lord Brentford. 'I am a man of peace, you know this.'

'I do,' said Leah. 'We Venusians are gifted with an ability to discern character. Yours, although severely flawed in many areas, is intrinsically good.'

'I'll take that as a compliment. And if I might be permitted to offer you one, might I say that you are the most fascinating creature that it has ever been my honour to dine with.'

'I am flattered,' said Leah, and a flash of pink came to her ivory cheeks.

'Pity, though,' said his lordship, 'about the magic. The Empire and the Crown have enemies, you know, upon this planet and possibly upon others. If there was a magical spell which, say, could protect our dear Victoria from harm, as a loyal subject I would do all in my power to gain the knowledge of it. I know I probably appear a bluff kind of body, but I care. I really do care. Know it's not perhaps a manly thing to say, but I do care, yes, I do indeed.'

Leah looked thoughtfully upon Lord Brentford. 'I do believe you to be sincere,' she said, 'but it *is* forbidden.'

'And I would not wish to get *you* into any trouble. Nor wish to see the pizzle inflicted upon you, or any of that frightful stuff.'

'I know,' said Leah. And she stared long and hard at her host. 'Perhaps,' she said slowly, 'something might be arranged. Something of a secret nature.'

'Really?' said Lord Brentford. 'Well—'

'No one must ever know. I might teach you certain things, certain minor cantrips and invocations.'

'Really?' said Lord Brentford once more.

'Absolute secrecy.' Leah took up her champagne glass, her golden eyes reflected in the golden sparkled liquid. 'It would mean death for me if I were discovered.'

'Then it is out of the question,' said Lord Brentford. 'Please forget that I ever broached the subject.'

'And *that* is the only answer I could have hoped for.' Leah smiled at his lordship. 'I am considered by my parents to be somewhat irresponsible and skittish, for I hold to opinions that are not strictly to their liking. One of these opinions is that magic is a universal force that can benefit all if used correctly. I will school you in the thaumaturgical arts, Lord Brentford, for I know that you will use them wisely.'

'Well,' said his lordship. 'Wasn't expecting *that*. Don't know quite what to say.'

'What is your Christian name, Lord Brentford?'

'Albert,' said his lordship. 'But folk who are close call me Berty.'

'Well, Berty,' said Leah, reaching forward to touch her glass to his, 'you can say thank you to me, if you will.'

'Thank you, Leah,' said the lord called Berty. 'Thank you, beautiful lady, very much indeed.'

Although history would never record it, this intimate agreement between two beings born upon separate worlds would set in motion a series of events that would culminate in an event of such cosmic significance as to be considered by most historians, had they known of it, the very turning point of humanity.

Berty and Leah gazed at each other and shared a moment of magic.

Not so Darwin, however, who lay in a drunken stupor on the floor.

36

avinia Dharkstorrm was never far from the thoughts of Cameron Bell. All lines of investigation had brought the great detective to one dead end or another. The evil witch was nowhere to be found. It was possible, of course, that she had gone off-world, to Mars perhaps, or even Jupiter. Mr Bell had no wish at all to return to Mars and he knew little or nothing about Jupiter.

'Why cannot things just be the way they were?' asked Cameron Bell of himself. 'I recall a time when a criminal was a criminal and not some sorceress casting spells and making life so difficult. This magic business has me most perplexed.'

Ernest Rutherford was perplexed as he gaped aghast at chickens.

'So many chickens,' he said to Lord Babbage, 'and all of them making a frightful mess of the five-star dressing room.'

'We didn't know where else to put them,' said Lord Nikola Tesla. 'This is the only dressing room with a lock on the door.'

Ernest Rutherford drew the door closed as chickens, sensing a chance for escape, came about him in a clucking horde.

'There is one thing that strikes me,' said the chemist, 'and I assume that it has struck you, too.'

'The similarity between them?' asked Lord Babbage.

Mr Rutherford nodded. 'They appear to be identical,' he said. 'See the spot on the left wing there – they all have it, do they not?'

The pair of scientific lordships nodded harmoniously. 'Which leads me to a conclusion,' said the tall one with the shock of hair.

'And what is that, Lord Tesla?' asked the chemist.

'Either that they are all *very* closely related. Or—' And here Lord Tesla paused. 'That they are all, in fact, the *same* chicken.'

'What of this?' asked Mr Ernest Rutherford.

'Some temporal anomaly,' said Lord Tesla, 'some singularity created by the transperambulation of pseudo-cosmic anti-matter that reproduces with exactitude the selfsame chicken again and again and again no matter what time we set upon our controls.'

Ernest Rutherford scratched at his head. Lord Babbage shrugged at his shoulders.

Miss Violet Wond said, 'There might be another answer.'

Ernest Rutherford glanced towards the lady in the veil.

'That before eighteen twenty,' said Miss Violet Wond, 'nothing existed but chicken. *That* chicken there.' And she pointed. 'And all these other chickens, too. They are all *one* and nothing existed before them.'

Darwin the monkey butler was perplexed. Although, had he been present at the Victoria Palace Theatre, he might well have heeded the words of Miss Violet Wond. Because, after all, he *had* been told about the Chicken Theory years before by that big black cockerel Junior. But it *was* only a theory and one articulated by *a chicken*! And Darwin greatly preferred the one put forward by his namesake, that Mankind was descended from monkeys. That sounded to him a *much* better theory.

The perplexity that Darwin was presently experiencing was not in any way connected with chickens.

It was connected with magic.

'Come on in, boy, don't be shy,' Lord Brentford said. Out of his bath-chair and on crutches now, but still in need of Darwin's help when it came to the terrible bedpan. 'Need your assistance, hurry, do.'

Darwin entered the study of Lord Brentford, which had undergone some recent and drastic redecoration. All the furniture, paintings and precious carpets had been removed. The walls, floor and ceiling had been painted the deepest of blues and curious white sigils had been inscribed upon the floor, including a great pentacle, and a candle burned on what appeared to be some kind of altar. The smell of incense cloaked the air. There was a certain atmosphere and Darwin did not like it.

Darwin looked up at Lord Brentford. He wore a long white robe that put the monkey butler in mind of a nightshirt.

'You recall this enchanting lady from the other week at the chicken restaurant, do you not?'

Lord Brentford directed Darwin's gaze to Leah the Venusian.

The lady of another world turned golden eyes upon him.

The look of those eyes made Darwin giddy, so he looked hurriedly away.

'Going to conduct a little experiment,' said Lord Brentford to his monkey butler. 'All very hush-hush. Don't wish to get any of the other staff involved. Know you won't go blabbering about it to anyone, eh?'

Darwin said nothing and wondered, in fact, when was the last time he had spoken. More than six weeks ago, when he had said his farewells to Mr Cameron Bell.

Darwin looked up once more at Lord Brentford.

'Going to engage in a bit of magic,' said his lordship. 'That will be exciting for you, won't it, Darwin?'

Darwin shook his head with vigour and made grumbling sounds.

'Wonderful, isn't he?' said Lord Brentford to Leah. 'It's as if he understands every word I say.'

Leah nodded, smiling as she did so.

'Going to speak a few words that I've been taught by the lovely lady here,' said Lord Brentford. 'Well, chant them, really. So you just be a good boy and stand there and we'll see what we shall see.'

Darwin shuffled uneasily. He wore today a rather dashing military ensemble – bright red jacket, khaki jodhpurs, high black riding boots. When a monkey of substance, he had never skimped at his tailor's.

'Right, then,' said Lord Brentford, drawing breath. And then he called aloud a vocal evocation in a tongue that was queer to Darwin.

'Once more, Berty,' said Leah. 'And try not to contract the vowels. Go on.'

Lord Brentford shouted out the words with vigour.

Darwin blinked and then felt suddenly strange.

There was something most definitely going on with his lower regions. A certain numbness, a lightness of limb.

Then—

'Oooooooooooooooooh!' wailed Darwin as he was swept from his feet, borne upward on invisible wings and flattened against the ceiling.

Cameron Bell lay on his bed and stared up at the ceiling. A ceiling far too close, in his opinion. The sloping ceiling of the tiny garret room he now inhabited. Once he had owned a beautiful house, and later a beautiful office, but now he had been reduced to *this*? A cockroach crossed the linoleum floor, its legs most loudly clicking. It vanished into a mouse hole from which issued the sounds of a fight.

Cameron Bell rolled a cigarette. Once he had smoked the finest cigars. *And* drunk the finest champagne. This was a very sorry end to a fine career. Mr Bell lit his cigarette and blew smoke towards the ceiling. He had an appointment shortly with Chief Inspector Case and he knew full well why *that* was.

He had been scraping this meagre existence at the expense of the Metropolitan Police Force with funds from the petty-cash box of the chief inspector. But as Mr Bell had nothing to show, even this pittance would soon be withdrawn.

'There has to be an answer to this,' said Cameron Bell. 'If I could bring Lady Raygun to justice, that would impress the chief inspector. If I could recover the stolen reliquaries, I could claim the rewards outstanding upon them and engage in a far better style of life. *And* avert the End Times, which is frankly no small matter and one that I find most troubling. But it has all become so desperately difficult that—'

And here Mr Cameron Bell ended his heartfelt soliloquy, for a thought had suddenly struck him, a thought that expanded all but instantaneously into a supposition and thence into a proposition encompassing a plan of campaign which found much charm with Mr Cameron Bell.

He had been going about this all the wrong way. Fire should be fought with fire.

'Oh yes, indeed,' cried the garret-dweller, frightening both mouse and cockroach and the bed-bugs, too.

'Sorry to frighten you, Darwin boy. We'll have you down in a jiffy.'

Lord Brentford looked towards the beautiful Leah. 'How *do* we get him down?' he asked. 'I haven't learned that bit.'

'Reverse the invocation.'

'Ah, indeed.' His lordship called out words towards the ape upon the ceiling. The ape dropped a foot or two, then swung about in a lofty arc, travelled with speed the length of the room and buffeted into a wall.

Lord Brentford chewed upon his bottom lip. 'Sorry, pardon, Darwin,' he said. 'Let me have another go.'

Leah laid a hand upon his lordship's arm. 'Let me,' said she. 'You would not want to cause your servant harm.'

'Quite so,' puffed his lordship.

Leah whispered words of magic and Darwin drifted gently down to rest upon the floor.

In his office, Chief Inspector Case paced the floor, dressed today as a Chinese Mandarin. Mr Bell knew well enough that things generally boded ill when the chief inspector was in costume. That the chief inspector was a troubled man.

'Sit down, please.' Chief Inspector Case affected that mock-Chinese accent so popular with second-rate music hall mimics. 'You likee cuppa tea?'

'Me likee glass of Scotch,' said Cameron Bell.

Chief Inspector Case looked sternly upon the detective. Mr Bell observed that he had employed a wax crayon to render a travesty of a Chinese moustache beneath his nose.

The look was *not* appealing. Mr Bell gazed sidelong glances at the chief inspector's thumbnails and at a smudge upon his left ear.

'It is lucky indeed that I was able to come here at such short notice,' said Mr Bell, in a manner both chipper and confident. 'A regrettable circumstance regarding your wife. But things will probably work out for the best.'

'My wife!' cried Chief Inspector Case. 'She's not *here*, is she?'

'Happily not,' said Cameron Bell. 'I perceive that she left the marital home some seven days ago.'

Chief Inspector Case took to flustering at the papers piled upon his desk. 'Damnable woman,' he said. 'I am glad to see the back of her.'

'She was not worthy of you,' said Mr Bell. 'You, the pride of Scotland Yard and everything.'

'Don't try to get around me, Bell.' The foolish Chinese accent was no more. 'I blame *you*. I don't know why, but I do.'

'I have never met your wife,' said Mr Cameron Bell.

'I don't mean my wife and you know it.'

'If you mean the case, then I am happy to inform you that a breakthrough is imminent.'

'A familiar phrase,' said Chief Inspector Case, now leafing through the pages of his diary. 'Oh yes, I knew that I recognised it. You have offered it to me at least once a week for the past four—'

'Ah,' said Mr Bell. 'But this time I actually mean it.'

'And that phrase, too. I am sorry, Bell, but it just won't do.'

'How would you like to solve the Crime of the Century?' asked Cameron Bell.

'I am certain I already have. At least twice.'

Cameron Bell recalled these occasions. 'I remember that *I* provided invaluable assistance upon both occasions,' said he, 'and let *you* take the credit.'

'And all but bankrupted Scotland Yard into the bargain.'

'I incurred heavy expenses.'

Chief Inspector Case made grumblings.

'It is now September,' said Cameron Bell. 'Only four months remain of this century. Now would be the time to solve the greatest case of all and place yourself into the annals of history.'

'How much will it cost?' asked the chief inspector. 'And more to the point, *what case*? What is this Crime of the Century that has been committed and of which I know nothing?'

'It is a crime that has yet to be committed.'

'Well, this is new,' said Chief Inspector Case. 'Have you taken to travelling through time, then?' And he laughed.

Cameron Bell did *not*. 'As a matter of interest,' he said, of a sudden, 'I understand that you have been investigating the matter of the Martian spaceship that crashed into Lord Brentford's Bananary. Any breakthroughs in that case?'

'We know the name of the spaceship's owner,' said the chief inspector, with pride.

'*We?*' asked Cameron Bell.

'That ne'er-do-well Septimus Grey is assisting me. Although I haven't seen him for weeks, the ungrateful blighter.'

'The name of the spaceship's owner?' asked Cameron Bell.

'Miss Violet Wond,' said Chief Inspector Case.

The name rang no bells at all with the great detective.

'And you have apprehended this anarchist?' he asked.

'An arrest is pending,' said the chief inspector. 'We'll have her any day now.'

'Well, good luck with that. But in the meanwhile you must turn your attention to the Crime of the Century.'

'The one that has yet to be committed?'

'It will be committed next week,' said Mr Bell. 'And next week you will solve it. I can see the papers now.'

And he could.

CELEBRATED CHIEF INSPECTOR SOLVES CRIME OF THE CENTURY

'I just reasoned it out,' says
the era's most-noted detective.

'And,' continued Cameron Bell, 'I would expect also to read words to the effect:

CHIEF INSPECTOR CASE TO RECEIVE KNIGHTHOOD IN THE NEW YEAR'S HONOURS LIST
A NATION APPLAUDS

'Tell me more,' said Chief Inspector Case. 'I am liking what I've heard so far.'

'The Crown Jewels will be stolen,' said Cameron Bell.

'*The Crown Jewels?*' cried the chief inspector. 'And this you know for a fact?'

'I do,' said Cameron Bell. 'I have given the matter considerable thought and I am absolutely certain it will occur.'

'Incredible,' said the chief inspector. 'And *I* will solve the case?'

'It will certainly look that way,' said Cameron Bell.

Chief Inspector Case smiled broadly and pictured himself

being knighted by Her Majesty the Queen. 'And there was me about to cut your wages,' he said.

'I was hoping for a rise, as it happens.'

'And you shall have one. As long as I take *all* the credit for solving the case and bringing the criminal to justice.'

'I promise you that,' said Cameron Bell. 'Shall we shake upon it?'

He extended his hand and the chief inspector shook it.

The deal was done and could not be undone.

'I have things to do now,' said Cameron Bell. 'I will call by in a couple of days and tell you what is on the go.'

Chief Inspector Case rubbed his hands together.

Cameron Bell turned to take his leave.

'Oh, just one thing,' the chief inspector called. 'As you know that this Crime of the Century will definitely occur – do you also know the name of the criminal mastermind who will be responsible for it?'

'He is known as the Masked Shadow,' said Mr Cameron Bell.

'Sounds like quite a character,' said Chief Inspector Case.

'Yes,' agreed Cameron Bell. '*Character* would most certainly be the word.'

37

he Masked Shadow's Manifesto came as something of a body blow to the God-fearing citizens of the Empire's capital. They were growing used to a London without crime and talk was only of the Grand Exposition and the Wonders of the Worlds that would be seen therein.

That this monstrous criminal should spring out from nowhere with no history but claiming many sinister qualifications was indeed an outrage. Something must be done. This creature must be stopped.

Copies of the Manifesto had been posted up all over London – posted even onto the walls of St Paul's Cathedral and Scotland Yard itself. Shameful, it was. Quite shameful!

Cameron Bell perused the one that had been posted onto a postbox at the corner of his street.

'Quite a character,' said Cameron Bell. 'And a most unpleasant character at that.'

The Yellow Press were having a field day. An anonymous source, who signed himself only as *SWORD OF TRUTH*, had dispatched to their offices a number of stories regarding

HA! PEOPLE OF LONDON

KNOW OF ME AND BE AFRAID

I AM

THE MASKED SHADOW

AND THIS IS MY MANIFESTO

* * * * *

I WILL BRING CHAOS TO YOUR STREETS

I WILL BRING DOWN YOUR MONARCHY

I WILL TAKE FROM YOU YOUR MOST PRECIOUS THINGS

I WILL WREAK ANARCHY

AS I DID UPON MARS

I WILL EAT YOUR CHILDREN

AND RAVISH YOUR WIVES

* * * * *

I AM

THE MASKED SHADOW

KNOW OF ME AND BE AFRAID

HA!

the Masked Shadow. Shocking stories, these, of his evil exploits upon Mars, and suggesting that he was responsible for many unsolved crimes, including – and this was hinted most strongly – that he was Jack the Ripper.

'Appalling fellow,' said Chief Inspector Case, wearing tweeds today and with ne'er a hint of Red Indian warpaint or the tribal markings of a Watusi chief. 'Glad we're ahead of the game on this one, Bell.'

'Well ahead,' said Cameron Bell, seated in the chief inspector's chair and tasting the chief inspector's five-year-old malt whisky.

'And you are convinced that he will strike soon?' The chief inspector paced a bit, pounding his right fist into the palm of his left hand.

'Upon Friday the thirteenth,' said Cameron Bell, 'he will strike for the Crown Jewels. I would wager my reputation upon this.'

'Hm,' said Chief Inspector Case. 'Well, we will be waiting for him. I will have the Tower of London surrounded by an impenetrable ring of bobbies. I'll have an airship stationed overhead with one of those new death-ray jobbies mounted upon it. A squadron of the Queen's Own—'

'Have to stop you there,' said Cameron Bell. 'With such martial forces in evidence, no criminal would come within five miles of the Tower of London.'

'Then we will have foiled the blighter,' said Chief Inspector Case.

'If you will remember,' said Cameron Bell, refilling his glass, 'our intention was to capture the Masked Shadow in order that you gain your knighthood.'

'Ah, yes, indeed.' The chief inspector took to stroking his chin.

'It will be,' said Cameron Bell, 'what Mr Churchill, I believe, refers to as "an undercover operation" – just you, me and a single constable.'

'*Are you sure?*' cried the chief inspector. 'I have no fear for myself, naturally, for I am a fearless fellow. But you are not a young man, Mr Bell.'

'I *am* a young man,' said Cameron Bell.

'Quite so,' said the chief inspector. 'But this fellow appears to be some fiend in human form.'

'He certainly appears so,' Cameron Bell agreed.

'So, just the two of us and one constable?'

'And make him a small one,' said Cameron Bell. 'And young. And no one but me is to carry a firearm.'

'*What?*' cried Chief Inspector Case.

'I don't want there to be any accidents. Now you put the word around Scotland Yard that the crime will occur on the thirteenth of September and that we need a volunteer. I will meet you on that night at eight o'clock. And do bring the keys to the Jewel Room.'

'And what are *you* going to be doing in the meanwhile, Mr Bell?'

'I am going to be investing some of the fifty guineas that you are now about to pay me.'

'Investing?' said Chief Inspector Case.

'Investing,' said Cameron Bell. 'Just trust me, do.'

'Trust me,' said Lord Brentford. 'You will not come to harm.'

Darwin the monkey butler stood in Lord Brentford's converted study and shook in his bright white spats. He was coming to dread these little sessions.

'Nothing to knock you about this time,' said his lordship. 'In fact, this one should appeal to your sense of fun.'

If I am turned into a clown, thought Darwin, *I shall kill Lord Brentford and run away with the circus.*

'Just stand there,' his lordship said, 'while I call out the business.'

Lord Brentford stepped away from his ape and took his place beside Leah. Darwin saw the Venusian lady put out her hand towards that of his lordship and grip it tenderly. That at least made Darwin happy, for he was a monkey who thought a lot about love.

He had led a solitary existence, had Darwin. He had no recollection of his mother or family. He had awoken, as it were, in a cage at Tilbury Docks, and was taken from there to an auction house and sold to a sideshow proprietor. He travelled for a while with the famous Wombwell's Menagerie before deciding to strike out on his own. He escaped one night from his cage and made his way to London, there to be captured by Lambeth Borough's Monkey Catcher in Residence and sold at yet another auction. But this time to Lord Brentford.

But throughout all this toing and froing he had never known love of his own. He had never met a lady ape with whom he could raise a family. He had been tricked by the evil Pandora, Lavinia Dharkstorrm's familiar, and politely rejected by Queen Victoria's monkey maid, Emily. Although he did have thoughts to pursue that comely creature . . .

But Darwin was a simian who still searched for love.

'Wake up, boy,' said Lord Brentford. 'Falling asleep on your feet, by the looks of you.'

Darwin arose from his reverie to face the world with dread.

Lord Brentford chanted words of Venusian and waved his free hand about in a fanatical fashion.

Darwin considered the study door and wondered if he should make a break for it now.

'And . . . *so!*' cried Lord Brentford, raising his hand in the air.

Darwin the monkey felt very queer indeed. He felt giddy and strangely not–all–there. He lifted a hand to clutch at his head, then gaped in horror at his hand.

And through it!

His hand was vanishing right in front of his eyes.

'It is working,' called Lord Brentford. 'He is fading away.'

And Darwin was. He was fading. And then gone.

Just gone.

'Are you there, boy? Can you hear me?'

Darwin was there somewhere. Was he *here*? The now-unseeable monkey butler stamped his feet on the floor. He *was* still here, still in the converted study, but he was utterly transparent.

He was the Invisible Ape.

'Invisible, or so they says,' the newsboy said to Mr Cameron Bell. 'They says the Masked Shadow can turn himself invisible. He is in league with the Devil, so they says.'

The great detective paid for a paper and bore it away to a coffee house to peruse it at his ease.

The Masked Shadow was quite the talk of the town, it so appeared. Mr Bell overheard heated conversation regarding this mysterious fellow all around the coffee house.

'They say he's the very last living Martian out for revenge on the human race,' said someone.

'I heard he was the victim of a dreadful medical experiment and that he has an elbow instead of a face.'

Cameron Bell raised his eyebrow to that one and ordered a coffee.

'They say that he's a werewolf,' said an ancient lady of Eastern European extraction. 'The thirteenth is the night of the full moon, you know – he'll strike upon the thirteenth, mark my words.'

Cameron Bell just nodded his head to that one. The Masked Shadow was certainly making his presence felt in London. Given that none but a few had known about his existence prior to this day, news of him and his depredations were spreading in the manner of a plague.

The thought of a plague distracted Cameron Bell. It had now been weeks since the Thames had turned blood-red and most folk had now forgotten it. But *if* that really *was* one of the Seven End Times Plagues, the next one would shortly be on the way.

Although the day was mild and the coffee shop electrically heated, a cold and icy shiver crept the length of Cameron's spine.

It was quite cold, being invisible. A draught from the door crack seemed to blow right through the unviewable ape.

Lord Brentford clapped his hands in glee. 'That really is most wonderful,' he said.

'I know you have promised before,' said Leah, 'but I would ask that you promise again that you will never demonstrate the magic I am teaching you unless your life, or the life of someone that you love, depends upon it.'

'You have my most solemn vow,' said Lord Brentford. 'I got a bit over-joyous there, but believe you me, I take all this stuff most seriously. Know what would happen to you if it came out you'd been teaching me. Wouldn't want anything bad to happen to you. Care very much about you, as it happens.'

And then Lord Brentford screamed.

It was a piercing scream. Almost feminine, it sounded.

The scream of a man who had, perhaps, been headbutted hard in his private parts by a quite unseen attacker.

'You scoundrel!' cried his lordship, knees bent, eyes

crossed and face grown rather red. 'You'll get a thrashing for that, you saucy fellow.'

SAUCY FELLOW WILL TAKE
A DARE FROM GENTLEMEN

Cameron Bell was reading the small advertisements upon the rear of his newspaper.

MISS CAINE'S ACADEMY
FOR THE TRAINING OF
PONY-GIRLS

Cameron Bell ran a finger down the page.

ILLUSIONS UNLIMITED
SUPPLIERS OF FIRST-RATE
MAGICAL ACCOUTREMENTS
FOR THE MUSIC HALL

'*That* is the one I am looking for,' said Mr Cameron Bell.

38

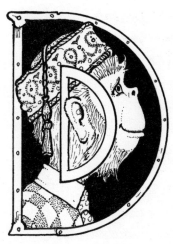arwin was not severely chastened
by Lord Brentford. The noble-
man's humour had not deserted
him, and although it is always easy
to affect a detached attitude to the
problems of others, it takes a man
of character to accept a blow to
the testes and still keep a smile on
his face.

'Come out, you scoundrel, or
I'll fetch my gun,' Lord Brentford
shouted, in a manner that was possibly ironic.

Leah laid a calming hand upon Lord Brentford's head.
It was more, it appeared, than simply a calming hand, for
the pain of his pummelled private parts fled the noble
lord.

'Why, thank you, m'dear,' said Lord Brentford. 'Wish I'd
known that particular piece of magic when I was playing
rugger back at Winchester. Used to get biffed in the three-
piece-suite most every game.'

Leah said, 'I feel we should restore your ape to sight.'

His lordship made grumbling mumbling sounds, but these
were sounds of assent.

'It is known as the Glamour,' said Leah, 'whereby that

which is seen can go unseen. But never for too long, for fear that they be lost to us for ever.'

'Humpty-tumpty,' said Lord Brentford. 'Don't want that for Darwin. Very fond of the little fellow.'

Which probably spared Lord Brentford a biting to the bottom.

Darwin, who had been quite enjoying himself pulling unseen faces at his master and pondering upon whether his dung might be invisible, should he produce some and then hurl it, came to sudden order when Lord Brentford said, 'Stand before me, Darwin, if you want to reappear.'

Leah aided his lordship with the words to reverse the spell and Darwin wavily appeared from nowhere.

'Fetch us up cocktails, you little blighter,' said Lord Brentford, 'and we'll say no more about it. Go on, now.'

Darwin made off to the kitchen, *ooh-ooh-ooh*-ing in ape.

Cameron Bell made off to ILLUSIONS UNLIMITED, a workshop housed beneath an archway near London Bridge Station. A small and weaselly man replied to his knockings and ushered him into the very weirdest of rooms. Within the span of bricked archway were to be found things of a magical nature.

But not Venusian magic, this, rather stage illusions born from the cunning of man.

Things that might best be described as if sung as a music hall song.

> There were dragons that were made of papier-mâché
> That could breathe and move their little eyes about.
> A contraption that would make you laugh
> In which to saw your wife in half.
> A box that was much bigger on the inside than the out.

There were hats from which to pull a bunny rabbit
And a rabbit that could turn into a cow.
A clockwork Turk that would impress
By beating you each time at chess
But nobody could really tell you how.

There were oriental wonders in the corner,
A rope trick that had come from Indi-ah.
There were cups and balls and cards and rings
And many many magic things
Everything to please your heart's desire.
(As long as you paid in guineas. And in cash.)

The small and weaselly fellow announced himself to be
Caracticus Crawford, creator of wonders and owner of a
whippet.

Cameron Bell had once owned a wiener dog, but it had
taken to chasing hansom cabs and an irate driver had shot it.

Mr Crawford smiled upon Cameron Bell. 'Something for
the ladies?' he asked.

'Excuse me?' said Cameron Bell.

'Some little card trick, perhaps, to impress the ladies of
your social circle? Or perhaps a comedic boil fashioned from
gutta-percha that can be affixed to your nose to alarm the
ladies at supper? Or perhaps an India-rubber cushion which
mimics flatulence when sat upon by a lady? Or—'

Cameron Bell raised his hands. 'I want you to create for
me an illusion,' he said.

'Ah, you wish perhaps to compress a lady into a Gladstone
bag. Or perhaps something involving a very fat lady who
becomes two slim ladies when literally torn in half by a
special machine which—'

Cameron Bell stared hard at the weaselly man and observed his shirt cuffs and trouser-buttons.

'Yours was *not* a happy marriage, then,' he said.

The weaselly man's eyes grew wide. 'You are a mentalist,' said he. 'Your act is one of mind-reading.'

'No,' said Cameron Bell. 'I need you to create for me a certain illusion. It is most important that it works perfectly. You might say it is a matter of life and death.'

'I have a guillotine effect that appears to remove a lady's head from her body—'

'I will show you the plan that I have drawn up,' said Mr Cameron Bell.

Over cocktails, in the Garden Room – a room which presently lacked for certain essentials, in Darwin's opinion, now that all the potted banana trees had been removed from it – Lord Brentford sat in a wicker chair.

Next to him sat Leah, upright, elegant, mysterious and thoroughly enticing, and the two were studying a plan that was spread before them upon an occasional table.

'The hall of the Grand Exposition,' said Lord Brentford, with no small pride in his voice. 'Three times the size of the Crystal Palace. A single large hall, as you see, that extends the length of the Mall, with a hall at either end, extending at right angles from the main hall. The concert hall in the centre of the main building, and to either side of that, displays of the Arts and Commerce of the British Empire. I recently received a letter from the eminent chemist Ernest Rutherford – he has apparently created an invention of staggering implications and has asked my permission to display it.'

Leah raised a golden eyebrow.

'It will be a surprise, my dear,' said his lordship. 'And

here—' and he pointed '—in the very centre of this hall, you can place your magical sphere of absolute nothingness. I cannot position it any further away from the Jovian food hall, but believe me, that is as far away as it is possible to get from it.'

Darwin viewed the plans. He had overheard the name of Mr Ernest Rutherford being mentioned, and also that he wished to exhibit something with staggering implications. To Darwin it could mean nothing other than the time-ship that his elder self had flown from the future and into the Bananary.

Eventually, said Darwin to himself, *I feel certain that everything will become clear.*

'I feel,' said Lord Brentford, 'that if everything goes according to plan, if the building is constructed on time and all correctly assembled within, this should be the greatest exhibition that any of the worlds has ever known. Thousands come daily just to view the construction. When it is opened, I am confident that millions will attend.'

Leah nodded her beautiful head, her long, slim fingers toying with her cocktail glass. 'Might I ask a question?' she enquired.

'Ask anything, my dear, ask anything.'

'As you are of course aware, I was present at your al fresco luncheon when Queen Victoria gave the venture her approval. I now know that even before this time you had foundries working upon the cast-iron frameworks of the building—'

'Had to get ahead,' said Lord Brentford, 'otherwise it would not be ready on time.'

'I recall well,' said Leah, 'that you told Her Majesty that the Crown would not be expected to pay a penny towards this enterprise.'

'Ah,' said Lord Brentford.

'Then might I ask,' said Leah, 'just where the money is coming from to finance this enormous venture?'

'Ah,' said Lord Brentford once more.

'Ah,' said Mr Caracticus Crawford. 'An illusion such as that will not come cheap.'

'A labourer is worthy of his hire,' said Cameron Bell. 'I believe the colonials have a phrase – "If peanuts are the remuneration, then one can only expect to gain the employment of simians," or something similar.'

'Quite so,' said Mr Crawford. 'An illusion of this magnitude will cost you fifty guineas.'

'Forty,' said Mr Bell.

'Forty-five,' said Mr Crawford.

'Pounds then, not guineas.'

Palms were spat upon and then smacked hard together. 'It must be ready and crated by next Thursday evening,' said Cameron Bell.

'Next Thursday evening? Only a week away? That is an outrageous demand!'

'Shall we say guineas, then, instead of pounds?'

Palms once more received spit and were slapped together.

Mr Bell smiled and went upon his way.

Days went on their way and time passed by. Days passed into a week and then were gone. Chief Inspector Case was quite excited.

'You see *this*, Bell,' he said with glee and opened up his shirt.

Cameron Bell had been standing at the window of the chief inspector's office, viewing London going about its business. Several airships slowly crossed the sky, huge sections of cast iron slung beneath them, bound for the Mall and the halls of the Grand Exposition.

'That building is coming on a storm,' said Mr Bell, and, turning, added, 'Oh my dear dead mother.'

Chief Inspector Case was stripped to the waist but appeared to be sporting the breast-plate of a Roman legionnaire.

'Dare I guess that you have recently discovered yourself to be the reincarnation of Nero?' said Mr Bell.

'Not one bit of it.' Chief Inspector Case did tappings at his breast-plate. 'The very latest thing in Metropolitan Police issue, this is. It is called a bullet-proof vest.'

'Ha,' said Cameron Bell, drawing out his ray gun. 'Shall we put it to the test?'

'For the love of God, no!' cried Chief Inspector Case. 'It is only for emergencies.'

'And what if it fails in emergencies for lack of adequate testing?'

'Shall we test it on a constable?'

Cameron Bell shrugged shoulders. 'If you do the shooting. Answering to the charge of murder is something I would only wish to do in the event of having shot an officer of a higher rank.'

'Let us call in Williams,' said Chief Inspector Case. 'It is he who will be accompanying us to the Tower of London tomorrow night.'

'Williams being the knock-kneed constable with the rounded shoulders and the advanced acne?'

'He's *very* willing,' said Chief Inspector Case.

'Then why not call him in.'

Williams was duly summonsed and matters explained to him.

'Certainly not!' said Williams. 'Do I appear such a fool?'

'I will fire from right across the room,' said Chief Inspector Case.

'And probably shoot me in the head,' said Constable Williams. 'Why not prop the bullet-proof vest upon your chair and we'll all take potshots at it?'

'Do you have a gun, then, Williams?' asked Cameron Bell.

'The chief inspector said—' The lad paused as the chief inspector shook his head. 'Yes, I *do* have a gun,' said Williams in a guilty tone.

Cameron Bell sighed sadly. The term 'friendly fire' had recently passed into common usage. It sent large shivers up the spine of Mr Bell.

Chief Inspector Case de-bullet-proof-vested himself and placed the protective garment upright on his chair. He stepped back and winked at Cameron Bell. 'Let us draw out our pistols like those cow chaps of America,' he said. 'Go for your gun.'

Cameron Bell drew out his ray gun.

Williams unsheathed something that resembled a miniature cannon.

Chief Inspector Case brought forth his old service revolver.

And the three men drew down fire on the bullet-proof vest.

The ambulance arrived quite soon with the bell on its roof ringing loudly. The bloodstained Williams was stretchered away in the very nick of time.

'Worked better than might have been reasonably expected,' said Chief Inspector Case, tapping at the scarcely dented bullet-proof vest on his chair. 'Shame about the ricochet, though. Poor Williams.'

'All in a good cause,' said Cameron Bell, trying very hard not to smirk.

39

n Thursday the twelfth of September at eight o'clock in the evening, Mr Cameron Bell parted with
forty-five guineas.

He was very sad to see those
guineas go, but understood that it
was all in a good cause. For if one
sought to match wits with the
Masked Shadow, a veritable demon
in human form for whom no godless
atrocity went unindulged in, it was better to do it with a
trick or two up one's sleeve.

Mr Bell was loaned the use of a horse and cart by Mr
Crawford, which he returned first thing the next morning.
The horse looked chipper, for it had had a sleep. Mr Bell
looked much the worse for wear, however, for he had been
hard at work all night.

'You constructed it all by yourself!' said Mr Crawford as
he shook the hand of Mr Bell.

'Of necessity,' said that man. 'I trust one day our paths will
cross again.'

'I am presently engaged in creating a cannon that can hurl
a lady at least halfway across Lake Windermere,' said Mr
Crawford.

'The best of luck with *that*,' said Cameron Bell.

Mr Bell returned to his garret and got his head down for a nap. At six he rose, packed certain items into his Gladstone bag, armed himself with his ray gun and sword-stick and, dressed in his finest hunting tweeds, set out for Scotland Yard.

Chief Inspector Case was having a very bad day. His estranged wife had paid him a visit at his office and berated him in a voice so loud as to be heard by his superiors. Be they even three floors up above.

She had cursed the chief inspector for his thoughtlessness and failure to show her affection. Criticised his manhood and extolled that of Señor David Voice, the London-tram-conductor-turned-architect, with whom she was presently enjoying 'love unsullied'. She concluded her diatribe with the hope that her soon-to-be-ex-husband would encounter the Masked Shadow at the earliest eventuality and that said Masked Shadow would thrust a weapon of considerable magnitude into an area of the chief inspector's lower regions where 'shineth not the sun'. She had then flung things of his all around his office.

And with that said and done, she had left with a slam of the door.

Mr Bell passed the indignant woman on the stairs and came immediately to the conclusion that, should her present liaison with the dashing Señor Voice come to a bitter end, he would *not* be offering the turbulent woman his shoulder to cry upon.

'It will serve her right,' said Chief Inspector Case to Cameron Bell, upon his arrival at the most dishevelled office.

'I shall make sure we are divorced before I accept my knighthood. Let's see how she likes *that*!'

'Bravo,' said Mr Cameron Bell. 'Are you all prepared for tonight?'

The chief inspector tapped at his chest, evoking a dull metallic clang. 'And I have my trusty service revolver, a pair of handcuffs, some sandwiches and a Thermos flask of tea.'

'Most thorough,' said Cameron Bell, who had not quite given up hope that he would be the only one armed. 'And the keys to the Jewel Room, so we might get in?'

'Well, bother me,' said the chief inspector. 'I knew I'd forgotten something.' And then he patted his trouser pocket. 'Only joking,' he said. 'I have a full set of keys.'

'You are the very acme of wit,' said Cameron Bell. 'And you have another constable, to replace the one you shot the other day?'

'I have it down in the accident book that he shot himself,' said the chief inspector. 'I took the liberty of forging your signature as a witness.'

'Very thorough,' said Cameron Bell. 'Then let us gather your latest constable and head for the Tower of London.'

The Tower of London squatted four-square with its feet dug into the capital. No more solid and beastly a building ever stood by the side of the River Thames. The wing-clipped ravens muttered 'nevermore' as ravens will always do when given half a chance. The ghost of Anne Boleyn walked the Bloody Tower with her head tucked underneath her arm. Beef-eating guardians sat in their wardrooms smoking cigarettes and discussing the legs of music hall girls. The full moon rose high in a starry sky and cast deep shadows about the ancient structure.

A hansom dropped the three bold enforcers of the nation's law before the big imposing doors to the sinister building.

'I don't like it here,' said Constable Reekie. 'Perhaps it would be better if we came back in the morning.'

Cameron Bell shook a head behatted by a tweed deerstalker. 'Tonight must be the night,' said he. 'Please be alert and let's not shoot each other.'

After a degree of key confusion, the chief inspector unlocked a big imposing door and the three men slipped into darkness.

'Best lock it again,' said Cameron Bell.

The chief inspector eventually found the key once more.

They crept across the courtyards and down stone lanes, at last to arrive at the Jewel House.

'You will stand outside the door to the Jewel House,' Cameron Bell told the trembling Constable Reekie. 'Chief Inspector Case and I will lock ourselves inside and lie in hiding.'

'*What?*' gasped Constable Reekie. 'The Masked Shadow will most certainly carry me off to his cave of horror and perform hideous deeds upon my young and tender person.'

'Whose idea was it for you to join the police force?' asked Chief Inspector Case of the babbling boy.

'My mother's,' said Constable Reekie. 'She told me that nice girls like a man in uniform.'

'Happily not only *nice* girls,' said the chief inspector, recalling happier times when he was still young and still in a smart uniform. 'Go and find somewhere to hide, lad – we'll call you if we need you.'

'Would that be after you have the handcuffs on him?'

'Just go and hide,' said Chief Inspector Case.

The constable scuttled away with speed while Chief Inspector Case located the key to the Jewel Room door.

Moonlight fell in silvered shafts through windows high above, touching upon most wonderful jewels and ornaments of gold.

Chief Inspector Case lit up his bull's-eye lantern and flashed it about at jewel-bedecked crowns, orbs and other precious things.

'Do you know what?' said he, a-making a thoughtful face. 'Perhaps the two of us should just steal all the jewels and abscond to the Americees to live the life of Riley.'

'Let us start filling our pockets,' said Cameron Bell.

'Are you serious, *man*?'

'Of course not,' said the great detective. 'But then neither were you.'

The chief inspector shook his head. 'Shall we hide over there?' he said. 'And I'll put out the lantern.'

It is always the waiting that does for you. When whatever is going to happen, no matter how horrid it might be, *does* happen, it's almost a relief, really. The actual waiting is the worst part of all.

'Do you hear *that*?' whispered Cameron Bell.

Chief Inspector Case did not reply, but a curious lip-smacking sound was to be heard.

Cameron Bell struck out in the darkness. 'Wake up, there!' he muttered.

'I was only resting my eyes. What time do you think it might be?'

A nearby clock struck midnight. An owl asked, 'Who?' A bat flew upside down.

'There,' whispered Cameron Bell. 'Look up.'

The chief inspector peered towards the windows high above as a shadow fell upon them, stood still for a moment, then moved on.

'Somebody up there,' whispered the chief inspector. 'I trust you have your ray gun, Mr Bell.'

'Raised and ready,' said Cameron Bell. 'And a few more things besides.'

It happened so fast that none could say exactly what happened for certain. One moment the chief inspector was huddling next to Mr Bell and the next minute he lay unconscious on the floor. There were brisk movements, a struggle in the darkness and then the Jewel Room door was flung open and a figure in a high top hat, a death's-head mask and a long and trailing cloak sprang from the Jewel Room bearing a bag marked SWAG.

He took off along the stone lane that led to the outside world at extraordinary speed, moving with queer and bouncing strides. Constable Reekie raised his gun. The man in black with the death's-head mask clubbed the constable down.

Out across the courtyards, into shadows and out again.

Down from the Tower of London and on towards Tower Bridge.

Above, something glittered in moonlight. A tiny airship secured to the uppermost ironwork of the tower – a getaway craft for the modern-day criminal mastermind.

Into the north tower went the figure and up the many flights of steps that led to the topmost structure of the bridge.

Alarm bells now sounded from the Tower of London. Lights were flashing on in tiny windows. Beef-eating guardians were awakening from unauthorised slumbers. Constable Reekie was out in a courtyard blowing hard on his whistle.

The cloaked and frightful figure of the Masked Shadow issued from a tiny doorway in a lofty peak of the bridge's northern tower and sprang onto one of the iron maintenance gantries that spanned the bridge from one side to the other. Fifty yards ahead of him, the tiny airship hung, moored to the gantry, awaiting him to make his sleek departure.

The Masked Shadow merged with darkness.

Beneath another shadow now and one cast from above.

Something rather wonderful was moving through the sky.

It appeared to flutter, as might a falling leaf, but then to ripple and twist, as a flock of starlings. It looked as some aerial jellyfish, transparent then opaque, and at its centre a single figure.

That of a striking woman.

Short of skirt and high of boot, with a corset of brass and a black rubber headpiece, Lady Raygun drifted down from above.

The Masked Shadow was gone into darkness, then re-appeared beneath his tethered airship.

He turned and beheld the vision that dropped to the gantry.

The curious jellyfish-something appeared to dissolve into nothingness and the Mistress of Mystery, the Angel of Death, stepped lightly forwards on towering heels, a ray gun in her hand.

'So,' said she, 'the Masked Shadow. Prepare yourself for death.'

40

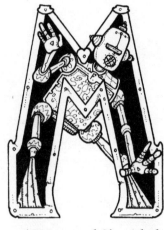oonlight tinted Tower Bridge with silver.

High upon an iron gantry figures stood defiant, one a shapely woman in most exotic garb, the other clad in cloak of black, with high top hat and death's-head mask. A chill breeze blew and an airship hung above.

'Any last words?' asked Lady Raygun.

'*Last* words?' said the man in black. 'Now why would I say those?'

'Because you are about to die.' The lady's ray gun pointed at the death's-head mask.

'You cannot kill *me*!' cried the figure in black. 'I am the Masked Shadow.'

'Evil men die as easily as do the good.' Lady Raygun squeezed upon her trigger and electrical fire darted forward. Struck the figure all in black. Passed completely through him and crackled against ironwork beyond.

The lady's shoulders stiffened. She fired her ray gun once again, then fired it many times more.

The Masked Shadow laughed and waved his arms.

The lady clicked her trigger, but the ray gun's power was spent.

She cast aside the dissipated weapon, strode forward and kicked the Masked Shadow straight in the death's-head mask.

To find herself kicking at nothing whatever at all.

'It is a fine illusion, is it not?'

The Mistress of Mystery turned at these words to find the Masked Shadow behind her.

She paced forward and he aimed a ray gun towards her.

'Fire it, do,' said Lady Raygun. 'Then prepare yourself for death, as you can harm me not.'

'Then take not a single step forward or I will press this button.'

The Masked Shadow held in his other hand a small polished-brass contrivance.

'Look down,' said the Shadow. 'To your feet, my dear.'

The Angel of Death glanced down. Beneath her feet and secured to the gantry were sticks of dynamite.

'I am aware that you are immune to bullets,' said the man in black. 'I suspect, however, that dynamite will be the match for you.'

'You will die, too,' said the lady.

'That is a risk I am prepared to take.'

The two stood staring, one at the other. Figures frozen against the backdrop of London and the star-strung sky.

A long minute passed and then the Shadow spoke.

'I only wish to offer you a proposition,' he said, 'and I hope you will take it, Miss Violet Wond.'

The lady drew back and cried, 'How do you know this name?'

'I know that it is a name you choose to go by. I doubt that it is the name that you were christened with.'

'I was never christened,' said the lady on the bridge.

'And you have so very much anger. Give me your word that you will listen to what I say and I will put this aside.' The Masked Shadow waggled his brass contraption.

Lady Raygun slowly nodded her head.

'Then firstly, know this,' said the Shadow, removing his mask. 'My name is Cameron Bell.'

'Mr Bell, are you there?' Chief Inspector Case did flounderings in darkness. And then the light of a bull's-eye lantern fell upon his face.

'Are you all right, sir?' asked Constable Reekie.

'I've a bump on my head,' said the chief inspector. 'Where is Mr Bell?'

'Perhaps chasing after the Masked Shadow, sir. There's an awful lot of confusion.'

'Come on, then,' said the chief inspector. 'Let's get up and at it.'

Up upon high, Cameron Bell removed his high top hat. The moonlight glinted on his baldy head. 'I have gone to a very great deal of time and expense to arrange this meeting,' said he, 'for it is most important.'

Lady Raygun clapped her hands together. 'And why not?' said she. 'How perfect, this, a famous detective, and I know well of you, Mr Bell, for I once saved your life from an East End bare-knuckle fighter and an unconvicted poisoner.'

'And I am grateful, fair lady,' said the gallant Mr Bell.

'But how perfect that *you* should be the Masked Shadow.'

'There *is* no Masked Shadow,' said Cameron Bell. 'He is pure invention.'

'And yet you have robbed the Jewel House at the Tower of London and are preparing to make your getaway aboard this airship.'

'Firstly,' said Mr Bell, 'my SWAG bag contains nothing more than Chief Inspector Case's sandwiches and Thermos flask. And secondly, I do not believe that the tiny airship hanging there could actually carry my weight, do you?'

'Then you have gone to all this effort simply to arrange a meeting with me?'

'I could think of no better way of drawing you out. I had the Masked Shadow's Manifesto printed and posted up around London by a close acquaintance who owed me a favour. I leaked stories about the Masked Shadow to the press under the name of SWORD OF TRUTH. I put the word around Scotland Yard that the Shadow would strike tonight because, having studied your file, I drew the conclusion that you have a contact inside Scotland Yard who supplies you with information.'

'You are very clever,' said Lady Raygun.

'Thank you,' said Cameron Bell. 'But I am not quite done yet. I moored the little airship here on one of the highest points in London where a female avenger who has the gift of flight could clearly see it. I acquired a pair of Rutherford Patent Spring-Heels, designed for the military to enable infantrymen to double their marching speed. Believe me, I could not have climbed all those stairs without them. And of course I paid out a great deal of money for the illusion. An improvement upon the popular Pepper's Ghost of the theatre. It creates a most lifelike image, does it not? I stood below. It is all done with mirrors. I reasoned that you would be employing your ray gun. I decided it better that you use it upon an image rather than myself.'

'Have you quite finished blowing your own trumpet?' asked Lady Raygun.

'I just felt things might need an explanation,' said Cameron Bell. 'Oh, and I might also mention that another reason for the creation of the Masked Shadow character was so my associate Chief Inspector Case could apprehend this criminal mastermind, take all the credit and earn a knighthood in the New Year's Honours List.'

'And continue to pay you a handsome salary,' said Lady Raygun.

'Well, now,' said Cameron Bell, 'your informant at the Yard is *most* informative.'

'And as *you* are in such an informative mood,' said Lady Raygun, 'then tell me this. How could you possibly know that I use the name of Violet Wond?'

'Ah,' went Cameron Bell. 'Well, I have the chief inspector to thank for that. He had discovered that a Miss Violet Wond was the owner of the Martian spaceship that crashed into Lord Brentford's Bananary.'

Lady Raygun stiffened slightly. She knew nothing of *this*.

'I knew,' continued Mr Bell, 'that Ernest Rutherford was the brains behind this particular spaceship's interior workings. I wondered what he might tell me about this Violet Wond, so I paid him a visit two days ago. But I did not speak with him because I saw him leaving his house in the company of a heavily veiled lady. I took the liberty of following this veiled lady – *you*, madam – to your lodgings. And I took the further liberty of searching your lodgings during the next time you were away. I discovered a portmanteau beneath your bed containing the Lady Raygun costume.'

Lady Raygun took a step forward. 'Then know this, too, my clever fellow. My informant at Scotland Yard has told me that Chief Inspector Case is presently employing your services to solve a certain case for him that he is unable to solve. To wit, that you bring Lady Raygun to justice.'

'Of course,' said Cameron Bell. 'But I do not wish *that*!'

'*What?*' cried Lady Raygun. 'All this subterfuge, all this deception, the employment of a stage illusion atop Tower Bridge and you do *not* wish to capture me?'

'Absolutely *not*,' said Cameron Bell. 'Quite the contrary, in fact. I wish you to continue your crusade. The streets of London are far safer when villains fear to step from their doors as the Mistress of Mystery might take them.'

Lady Raygun shook her head. The tightly fitting rubber hood with its circular eyeglasses and queer mouth grille created a most fearsome sight by moonlight, or indeed any other.

'You went to all this trouble simply to speak to me,' said she. 'Would it not have been easier just to have had a note delivered to the lodgings of Miss Violet Wond?'

'Considerably so,' said Cameron Bell. 'But not nearly so much fun.'

'*Fun?*' cried Lady Raygun.

'Come, come,' said Mr Bell. 'What greater fun can there ever be but danger?'

Lady Raygun shook her head once more.

'And,' said Cameron Bell, 'on a serious note, I wished to make it plain to you that should I set out in earnest to track you down, I could accomplish this task.'

Lady Raygun shook her head yet again. 'No,' said she. 'That will not happen and I will tell you why. I avenge the good by destroying the evil and I will not be held from my crusade. You know my identity and so, regrettably – because I do not kill the good as a rule – regrettably, you must die.'

'I think *not*,' said Cameron Bell and *he* now shook *his* head. 'You see, my gift, as it were, is one of perception. Give me an article of clothing and I will disclose to you all manner of personal details regarding its owner, details that the average person would find truly amazing. Miss Wond, I spent a considerable time in your private lodgings. I studied your articles of clothing with considerable care.'

'You foul creature!' cried the lady. 'I will do for you.'

'Please.' And Cameron Bell displayed once more the brass contrivance. 'Such is the reaction I expected from you. You are a most secretive creature and for good reason, considering all you have experienced in your life. But I would have you as a friend and not an enemy. I have penned a letter regarding yourself that will be opened should I come to an untimely end.'

'Do your worst!' cried Lady Raygun, taking a single step forwards. 'I have no fear of death. I hate all.'

'And that is not strictly true,' said Mr Bell, 'because in fact you are in love with Ernest Rutherford, and it is your hope that he can reverse the wrong that was done to you.'

'You are a remarkable man, Mr Bell,' said Lady Raygun.

'My thanks,' said the great detective. 'And when you have heard what I have to tell you, it is my hope that we might form a partnership and work together.'

'I work alone,' said the lady.

'Please delay your final decision until you have heard my proposal.'

'Go on, then,' said Lady Raygun. 'But do make it brief, for you are surely the most loquacious fellow I have ever met.'

Cameron Bell now suddenly took a step back. 'They are coming,' he whispered. 'Up the stairs. Policemen. Fly, Lady Raygun, please. Meet me tomorrow for luncheon at one, at the Savoy Grill. Now – please go.'

Lady Raygun swayed upon her towering heels, then sprang up onto the gantry railings and flung herself into the sky. The curious membrane swam about her and she was borne off into the London night.

'Bell,' puffed Chief Inspector Case, issuing through the tiny doorway of the northern tower. 'Are you all right, man? Where is the Masked Shadow?'

'Dead,' said Mr Cameron Bell. 'We had a bitter struggle. He was a most terrible opponent, fought as a thing possessed—'

'Extraordinary,' said Chief Inspector Case.

'He said,' continued Cameron Bell, 'that the only man he truly feared was *you*.'

'*Me?*' said Chief Inspector Case.

'He knew I was working for you. He knew you were the man who would bring him down.'

'But *you* brought him down.'

In the moonlight, Cameron Bell raised an eyebrow.

'Ah, yes,' said the chief inspector. '*I* brought him down.'

'After a bitter struggle,' said Cameron Bell. 'Which I witnessed. While you were saving my life.'

'Quite so, Bell. Quite so.'

'So bravo to you and good luck with that knighthood.'

Chief Inspector Case did preenings of his lapels. 'A good night's work,' said he. 'Although—'

'Although?' asked Mr Cameron Bell.

'Well, just two things,' said the chief inspector. 'Firstly, there appears to be no immediate evidence that this Masked Shadow fellow actually stole anything out of the Jewel Room.'

'And secondly?' asked Cameron Bell.

'Well, secondly, why is it *you* who is wearing that cloak?'

41

atisfactory explanations were offered up by Cameron Bell and gladly accepted by Chief Inspector Case. The two men descended from Tower Bridge and stood once more upon terra firma.

'You have done a man's job, Bell,' said the chief inspector and gave Mr Bell a very manly hug.

It was a hug of such manliness, in fact, as to press down hard upon the pockets of Mr Bell. One of which contained a brass contrivance.

The explosion that then occurred high above upon Tower Bridge had that famous London monument and artery of traffic closed for a week for repairs.

'A damnable anarchist, that Masked Shadow,' the chief inspector said, whilst ducking his head. 'London Town is a safer place without him.'

The morning papers were greatly in accordance with this sentiment and much praise was heaped upon Chief Inspector Case for ridding the Empire's capital of this Devil-made-flesh, and demands were put about that a knighthood should be forthcoming.

'That man is a credit to England,' a waiter at the Savoy Grill told Cameron Bell as he sat nervously awaiting the arrival of Miss Violet Wond. Nervously because he feared that she might well have packed her goods and chattels and gone off-world, never again to be seen upon this planet. And while this might have its benefits, possibly financial in the case of Mr Bell if he could concoct some convincing tale for the chief inspector of how he had personally managed to defeat her, it would be of far more benefit to Mr Bell to have her remain in London and team up with him.

The Savoy Grill was bustling with life. Its wall mirrors, richly etched and ornately framed, reflected the very cream of London society. There sat Lady Elsie Grover, the glamorous personal dresser to Her Majesty. It was this lady's job to design and fit the monarch's fetching attire, and this season it appeared that black was once more to be the new black. There, too, sat a romantic brooding character of the Byronic persuasion, and surely this was the enigmatic Herr Döktor, a figure who moved within high society doing only good, for he was the creator of a clockwork apparatus designed to act as a panacea for ladies' hysteria. Holding court was Sir Peter Harrow, lately released from a stay in hospital brought on by major burnings and his 'nerves'. Sir Peter was, as it happened, extolling the virtues of Herr Döktor's clockwork apparatus.

At a distant table sat the Laird of Dunoon in his distinctive newspaper bonnet, sharing a joke with Count Otto Black, a gentleman of leisure presently in London to promote vampirism.

Lords and ladies came and went, sat and dined and chatted.

Cameron Bell sat all on his own and sipped a little champagne.

And as the clock struck the half-hour past one, a lady veiled and all in black entered the glamorous restaurant swinging a parasol. She whispered words to the maître d', who guided her to the table of Cameron Bell. The great detective rose from his chair as the maître d' assisted the lady into hers.

Cameron Bell reseated himself. 'I am very glad that you chose to honour me with your presence,' he said. 'Might I enliven your empty glass with champagne?'

The lady nodded that this would be acceptable and Mr Bell poured out a generous glass.

'I have many important appointments,' said Miss Violet Wond. 'Let us make this meeting brief, if you will be so kind.'

A waiter brought menus. Mr Bell and Violet Wond perused them.

'I am informed that the chateaubriand is particularly delicious,' said Mr Bell, toasting the lady in black with his glass of champagne.

'Then that will serve,' said Violet Wond. 'Now tell me what you wish of me.'

Cameron Bell drew the attention of the waiter. 'Two of the chateaubriands,' he said. 'I shall have mine medium-rare. What of you, Miss Wond?'

'I will have mine raw,' said Violet Wond.

'With a side order of those French-fried potatoes that are all the current rage,' said Cameron Bell.

The waiter departed, worrying over raw meat, and Cameron Bell looked long and hard at Miss Wond.

'Seeking to discern my inner feelings from the study of my outer garments?' asked the lady in black. 'You have surely learned all you need to know from my personal underthings.'

Cameron Bell's cheeks pinkened at this. 'My sincere

apologies for encroaching upon your privacy,' said he, 'but so it must be, for such is my line of work.'

'I have not yet decided whether *my* line of work will include your execution,' said Miss Violet Wond, toasting Mr Bell then sipping champagne beneath her veil.

'It is in neither of our interests to make an enemy of the other.'

'I can never be your friend,' said Violet Wond.

'Indeed. And is there not a popular axiom: "Keep your friends close and your enemies closer"?'

'Please just tell me what you want,' said Violet Wond.

'Peace between us and that we can work together.'

'I work alone. I told you that.'

'What do you know,' asked Cameron Bell, 'of Miss Lavinia Dharkstorrm?'

The stem of Miss Wond's champagne glass shattered in her hand.

Champagne splashed upon her black silk glove.

Mr Bell offered assistance, but this was declined.

'I am unharmed,' said Violet Wond. 'But you speak a name that is not unknown to me.'

'And I would gather that you hold no affection for this particular female.'

'What is she to you?' asked Violet Wond.

'My greatest enemy,' said the great detective, in all candour. 'A fearsome adversary who is presently engaged upon a course of action that may well destroy this world and all the others.'

'Really?' said Miss Wond. 'And I thought that *I* was the Angel of Death.'

'Miss Dharkstorrm is the most evil creature I have ever met.'

'I feel perhaps on that we are agreed.'

A waiter had hastened forward to offer Miss Wond a replacement glass and fill it. Another was worrying at broken glass with a tiny brush.

'Please leave us,' said Violet Wond, in a tone that left no room for misinterpretation. The waiters scuttled away at speed. Miss Wond sipped further champagne.

'You know much, Mr Bell,' said she, at length, 'but you know far from all. Speak to me of Lavinia Dharkstorrm and what she means to you.'

The chateaubriands arrived upon a gilded trolley drawn by a monkey servant dressed as for the hunt. A human counterpart served at Cameron's table, then snapped his fingers and waved the monkey on.

'Are you sure you can eat that raw?' asked Cameron Bell.

'I have *very* strong teeth,' said Violet Wond.

And so these two ate chateaubriand and during this eating Cameron Bell told Violet Wond all that he knew of Lavinia Dharkstorrm. He spoke of how she had acquired the four sacred reliquaries that when 'brought together into an unhallowed place' would precipitate the arrival of the End Times with the Seven Plagues, terminating in the Time of Terrible Darkness, the Death of the First-Born and the Coming of the Apocalypse, which wasn't a very nice thing.

And he went on to say that Lavinia Dharkstorrm had informed him that she performed her unspeakable actions in the service of another – *her mistress*. Mr Bell confessed that he did not know who this personage was, but suspected her to be someone of all-surpassing evil.

Violet Wond dined upon raw chateaubriand, which she consumed with loud munching sounds, but spoke no words whilst Cameron told his story.

Once the story was all done and the plates all cleared away, she spoke.

'I know well Lavinia Dharkstorrm,' she said, 'for she and I were girls together at Roedean. And I know well the hag she serves – her name is Madam Glory. She was the head-mistress, who was dismissed for unspeakable cruelties.'

Cameron Bell, who had been educated at a minor public school, raised his eyebrows to this. Unspeakable cruelty was the order of the day in every public school. It was considered character-building. It was a tradition and an old charter and simply the way things were done.

'I have no doubt,' said Violet Wond, 'that Lavinia Dhark-storrm is a woman most evil and that her mistress Madam Glory would be capable of any abomination. My question would be the obvious one. What would they have to gain by destroying this world?'

Cameron Bell shrugged his shoulders, drew the cham-pagne bottle from its silver cooler and poured out glasses for Violet Wond and himself. 'There is much about this business I find puzzling, so I must ask you this. Having listened to what I had to say, and having as you do a prior knowledge of Miss Dharkstorrm, will you aid me in bringing her to justice and halting her evil schemes?'

'That you might profit by claiming the rewards for the stolen reliquaries?'

'This is no longer about money,' said Cameron Bell, 'if indeed it ever was. But I will split the rewards with you, if you wish.'

'That will not be necessary. I am a person of independent means.'

'Will you consent to help me in tracking down this evil woman?'

Violet Wond toyed with her champagne glass. 'She has stolen certain precious items,' she said, 'which makes her a criminal. And I have no love for criminals.'

342

'Splendid,' said Cameron Bell.

'I have not finished,' said Violet Wond. 'You have had your say, so let me have mine. As you are aware to some degree, a great wrong was done to me. This wrong may never be put to rights, although I remain hopeful that with the help of Mr Rutherford, it may. But I have set myself a task, Mr Bell – to right the wrongs that are done to those less able than myself. I take an eye for an eye. I kill those who have killed.'

'Lavinia Dharkstorrm is certainly capable of murder,' said Cameron Bell.

'I am speaking!' said Miss Wond. 'And Miss Dharkstorrm is more than just capable, I assure you. I will enter into this partnership, Mr Bell, if you will agree to three things.'

Cameron Bell said, 'Go on.'

'Firstly,' said Violet Wond, 'when this matter is resolved, we go our separate ways. I will leave London and you will agree not to pursue me.'

'Gladly,' said Cameron Bell.

'Secondly, as I have no need for money, you may take *all* of the rewards.'

'I am certainly in agreement with that,' said Cameron Bell.

'I had not entirely finished. Because thirdly, you may only take all the money if I am allowed to deal with Miss Dharkstorrm directly.'

'Directly?' said Cameron Bell.

'I mean, in as few words as need be spoken, that I intend to kill her.'

There was a certain silence then and Cameron Bell did scratchings at his chin.

'Let me say this,' said Violet Wond. 'I do not believe in any of this End Times hocus-pocus. The Thames turned blood-red for a day but that means nothing at all. I have reasons of my own for dealing with Miss Dharkstorrm.'

'Then we are agreed upon all points,' said Cameron Bell.

'Most fortunate for you,' said Violet Wond.

Cameron Bell looked puzzled.

'I hold upon my lap a ray gun,' said Miss Violet Wond, 'and had this meeting not gone to my liking, I would have had no compunction about shooting you dead with it, here and now.'

'Oh my dear dead mother,' said Cameron Bell. 'Should I order more champagne?'

'To celebrate your lucky escape? Why not?'

Cameron Bell ordered further champagne. 'To our partnership,' said he, when glasses had been replenished.

'To justice,' said Violet Wond, and they touched their glasses together. 'Not to biblical nonsense, but to justice alone.'

And then they heard the screams.

Outside the Savoy Grill, folk were howling and crying, running this way and that. A frightful hubbub was suddenly on the go.

'And what of this?' said Cameron Bell. 'Not anarchists, I trust.'

The door to the Savoy Grill burst open and a fellow staggered through it. He was bespattered in greens and reds and had taken a pounding to the head.

'Flee!' cried this fellow. 'The world ends today! Frogs rain from the sky.'

42

rogs that fall from an empty sky aren't easy to explain. They frighten those they fall upon and baffle all and sundry.

Miss Violet Wond told Cameron Bell that she had no time for frogs, bade him farewell, raised her parasol and strode in a purposeful fashion from the Savoy Grill.

Cameron Bell stood at the window and watched as she marched away. 'What a most remarkable woman,' said the detective.

Cardinal Cox and his catamite watched the remarkable sight.

'What breed of frogs do you think they are?' enquired the catamite.

'*Biblical*,' said the cardinal. 'And I'll wager that if you were to take one down to the Natural History Museum, it would be identified as *Amietophrynus kassasii*, or the Nile Delta Toad.'

'So not a frog at all,' said the catamite, enjoying the spectacle of Londoners fleeing the terrible downpour.

'The ancient Egyptians did not make the distinction. They included in their great pantheon of deities a frog god

Heqet. It was her duty to assist with forming children in the womb. She shared a temple with Osiris as Mistress of the Two Lands.'

'You are the very personification of wisdom,' said the catamite.

Cardinal Cox patted his special servant on the head. 'Ha, look at the state of that bobby,' he cried. 'That toad knocked him right off his penny-farthing.'

Another bobby fell from his bike in the middle of the Mall.

'What an extraordinary business,' said Lord Brentford.

He, Leah and Darwin sat in a hansom cab. The driver had fled for cover. The horse took it all in his stride.

'Signs and portents in the Heavens,' said the beautiful Venusian. 'I warned you, Berty. Bad things are to come.'

'Let us not be gloomy, my dear. I am sure there must be a logical explanation, but for the life of me, I cannot think of one.'

Darwin could think of several, but he honoured his vow of silence and watched as horrid things came pouring down.

Ernest Rutherford and the Lords Babbage and Tesla had their opinions. As they sheltered beneath the awning of the Victoria Palace Theatre observing the remarkable phenomenon, each fashioned a theory fitting to their beliefs.

'Pan-Spermia,' said Ernest Rutherford, 'in that the seeds of life drift for ever across the infinity of space, occasionally falling onto a planet which offers a fertile soil to take the seed. Here we observe an interesting example. Had this occurred when the Earth was young, then perhaps we would all now be descended from frogs.'

'An interesting proposition,' said Lord Babbage, 'but incorrect. Here we are observing, as it were, the bigger picture.

Recall, as well we all recall, the matter of the recurring chicken. Here we have an example on a greatly magnified scale. Some temporal anomaly of the cosmic persuasion has occurred – these creatures are of trans-dimensional origin.'

'An educated guess,' said Lord Tesla. 'I, however, was brought up as a Catholic and I know the End Times when I see them. The Thames has already turned to blood and this is the Second Plague of the Apocalypse. Let us make peace with our Maker before the Terrible Darkness falls. And—'

But Lord Tesla now found himself all alone, as Ernest Rutherford and Lord Babbage, both sadly shaking their heads, had returned to their work on the *Marie Lloyd*.

'After all my hard work!' shouted Chief Inspector Case, pacing before the window of his office. 'After solving the Crime of the Century and engaging in a life-and-death struggle with a criminal mastermind high up on Tower Bridge – *this*!' He gestured hopelessly towards the outré goings on beyond his office window. 'Frogs falling on London. Hundreds and thousands of flipping frogs. The papers will be full of this. They will forget all about me.'

Constable Reekie watched in awe as the froggy/toady things came streaking down. 'They won't forget you, sir,' he said. 'Have no fear of that.'

'Very nice of you to say so,' said Chief Inspector Case.

'Not if your wife has anything to do with it, sir. She's just served you a summons at the front desk. Means to have her day in court. Well, her week in court . . . or perhaps her month. She told me personally that she knows about all manner of things that you have got up to here at the Yard.'

'What?' cried the chief inspector. '*What?*'

'Apparently you talk in your sleep, sir.'

Chief Inspector Case made growling sounds. 'Where is my crown and my kiwi cloak?' he asked.

'Would you like to see a wonderful thing?' Lord Brentford asked of Darwin.

Darwin nodded cautiously and hoped that it would not involve him being turned into a frog.

'It is at the palace,' said Lord Brentford. 'At Buckingham Palace, up ahead. It is why we have come here today and you are going to see it.'

Darwin made a hopeful face and wondered what this wonderful thing might be.

'You will be the first monkey ever to see it,' said Lord Brentford, shifting his good arm out of the way of rapidly falling froggery. 'And you'll get to meet the Queen again and that monkey maid Emily you took such a shine to, eh?'

A big wide smile appeared on the face of Darwin.

'Ah, you like that, don't you, boy?'

Darwin nodded with much enthusiasm.

'Then hop up onto the driver's seat and steer us towards the palace.'

Cameron Bell returned to his seat, ordered brandy and a cigar and pondered upon his lot. With Lady Raygun on his side, the odds were more favourable when it came to dealing with Lavinia Dharkstorrm. Clearly Miss Violet Wond had some score to settle with her. Mr Bell might well have pondered upon what a fortuitous coincidence this was, but he felt it inappropriate to do so and thus put it down to a case of 'it's a small world' and let it lie. But there was still the matter of where Miss Dharkstorrm lurked. There was no doubt in Cameron's mind that the fall of frogs was the second of the End Times plagues, which meant that matters were now growing ever more urgent. The countdown to the Apocalypse had begun, and if not brought to an early halt, it would culminate at the final midnight of the year.

Which was, frankly, no way to celebrate the dawn of a new century.

Mr Bell tasted brandy and sucked upon his cigar. Things had gone well for him last night. His scheme, although perhaps over-elaborate, had borne fruit and Lady Raygun was now his ally, whether she cared for him or not. Surely in the light of this success he could come up with some other cunning plan designed to ensnare Lavinia Dharkstorrm.

At which point a thought entered the head of Cameron Bell. And as before this thought expanded almost instantaneously into a supposition and thence to a proposition, which encompassed a plan of campaign and brought much joy to Mr Cameron Bell.

'I think I can arrange the very thing,' said he.

And Mr Bell smiled. 'I really love it when a plan comes together,'* he said.

'Please come together and follow me.' A gentleman in a most wonderful costume, all braids and tassels and toggles and woggles, with patent-leather thigh-boots and hat with a high cockade, bowed before Lord Brentford, his monkey butler and the intriguing Venusian ecclesiastic. 'Her Majesty awaits you in the throne-room.'

'And the package has arrived?' Lord Brentford enquired.

'An hour ago,' said the gentleman, affecting a curious high-kneed gait as he walked. 'Her Majesty is eager for it to be opened.'

* *Apparently not a breach of copyright.*

Darwin looked up at Lord Brentford and then all around and about.

They walked through the Blue Gallery, the work of the famous architect Albenoni Dalbatto. The walls were bedecked with turquoise and silver wrought into the most amazing tableaux. Here were scenes of ancient myth. Aboreus defeating the Great Land Snail of Epecus. The storming of Krestica by the Papalations. Feletious declaring his love to the Queen of the Meminites. Even Laneaus of Cronica proving his manhood to the ten thousand sirens of Urethra.

'Pretty pictures,' Lord Brentford remarked. 'Read the Classics at Oxford, you know. Remember that one well enough.' And he gestured to a vast and intricate representation of Polyphagia consuming the Harlot of Palsy, that he might win the heart of Princess Phallicema.

'Never really got the joke of any of them, though,' said Lord Brentford as he followed the gentleman with the high cockade. The plaster casts were now off the legs of Lord Brentford and he walked with a cane and the slightest of limps and no complaint at all.

Queen Victoria's throne-room was not to be entered into easily, for there was considerable security. Soldiers of the Queen's Own Household Standers to Attention stood to attention before the door, fearsome modern weaponry a-bristling. One in considerable armour stepped forward to examine Lord Brentford's papers.

'I only have a *Daily Sketch*.' His lordship brought this out for close inspection.

The armoured soldier laughed uproariously at Lord Brentford's unintended funny, explained where the misapprehension lay and then told his lordship to hand over the correct papers or be shot down where he stood.

Lord Brentford parted with his papers. The armoured

soldier looked long and hard at the nobleman's Monkey Butler Authorisation Certificate and held the sepia identity photo-representation of Darwin close by the monkey's face.

The armoured soldier then looked hard at Leah. The Venusian regarded him with her dazzling golden eyes.

'Go through,' said the soldier, and the three went through.

Soldiers lined each wall of the golden throne-room. Some had ray guns, some had swords and some had bommy-knockers.*

What Darwin could see of the throne-room had him most impressed. It was gold and it was gold and yet more gold.

A hymn of gold, it seemed, to the awestruck ape.

The ceiling was rococo, strewn with golden cherubim.
Columns of Corinthia adorned with golden leaf.
Golden statues too arose
In many a heroic pose
With golden hairs upon their arms, but no hairs underneath.

Darwin had never entertained any particular fondness for hymns about gold, and as he looked upon it all, the splendour, the opulence, the goldenness, it all began to make him feel just a little bit sick.

The wealthy simply had too much wealth.

The poor had too much poverty.

Darwin was suddenly torn between rival emotions. Something instinctively told him that this was all wrong! That so much wealth should be enjoyed by so few. That it was immoral when so many went without. That it was, simply, wrong.

* A form of mace with a bulbous spike-covered headpiece, suitable for striking down ballybots.

But here indeed lay a problem, because Darwin had become an ape who enjoyed luxury, who revelled in good food, fine wines, well-cut suits and things of a similar nature. He found privilege amenable.

Darwin the monkey butler shook his head. Once he'd had ideals. Once he had experienced strong feelings about Man's inhumanity to Monkey. Once he had felt that, as the world's only talking ape, it was his duty to do something about it.

But what had he done?

Nothing, that was what.

He had *not* buckled down to fight for justice with Mr Cameron Bell. And when Lord Brentford came back to reclaim Syon House as his own, Darwin had taken the easiest option and returned to being a monkey butler, because in spite of certain downsides (although the hated bedpan was now happily a thing of the past), the benefits outweighed them.

Not that he had enjoyed getting covered in falling frog and having to leave the majority of his clothes in the hansom cab.

But—

'Hurry along now, Darwin,' said Lord Brentford. 'You are dreaming again.'

Queen Victoria sat upon her throne. Her costume was a triumph in this year's black, which was black. She wore her jaunty crown, a sash bedecked with glittering broaches of office, rather dear little monogrammed slippers and a grumpy face. To one side, on a Persian pouffe, sat Emily her monkey maid, and on the other wheeled Caruthers her augmented kiwi bird.

'Get a move on, Brentford,' called Her Majesty. 'You are late and one does not have all day.'

'My apologies, ma'am.' Lord Brentford put speed to his

stride. 'Slight hold-up in the Mall. Unexpected rain of frogs. Causing frightful chaos.'

'No interest in frogs,' said the Empress of both India and Mars. 'One wants to see one's present.'

Lord Brentford looked towards Leah who shook her head and said nothing.

'Not *strictly* a present, ma'am,' said Lord Brentford. 'More a lendsies, really.'

'A *lendsies*?' queried the Queen.

'You know, when you are lent something, ma'am.'

'When one is lent something, one *keeps* it,' said Her Majesty the Queen. 'That is what being a Queen is all about.'

'Quite so, ma'am,' said Lord Brentford.

'Well, open it, do,' said the Queen.

Queen Victoria's Crowbar-Carrier-in-Residence handed Lord Brentford the royal crowbar and the nobleman set about the packing case with vigour.

It was a large packing case, perhaps eight feet in height and four feet to a side. The words THIS WAY UP were largely printed, so it was the right way up.

Lord Brentford strained with the royal crowbar. Sections of timber toppled away to reveal waddings of wood-shaved packing.

Leah stepped forward, drew in breath then blew away all these packings.

Wood-shavings swirled and something wondrous was revealed. Something truly wondrous.

Hovering three feet above the floor was what at first appeared to be a sphere of glass.

But no such thing was this. Rather, what was to be seen was—

Nothingness.
Absolute nothingness.
A sphere of total
colourless, textureless,
spaceless, timeless
nothing.

All in the royal throne-room stared in awe.
But only one amongst them understood.

43

'We are most amused.' Queen Victoria stepped from her throne and approached the Sphere of Nothingness. She stretched forth a royal hand to touch it.

'Oh, Your Majesty, please do *not*.' Leah the Venusian barred the monarch's way.

'One does *not* say *not* to one's monarch,' said the Queen.

'But, ma'am.' The Venusian smiled upon the Queen. 'Were you to touch it, you would be drawn into it, into the absolute void, never ever to return.'

Queen Victoria's hand withdrew. 'One would not want *that*,' said she. 'But you may leave us now.'

'Leave now, ma'am?' asked Lord Brentford. 'There are some matters to discuss.'

'Later, later, Brentford. I find this item entrancing. I wish to gain scientific opinion regarding this.'

'Let no one touch it,' counselled Leah.

'You are dismissed,' said Her Majesty the Queen. 'The sphere will be safe enough here.'

'I am in agreement with that, ma'am,' said Lord Brentford, bowing politely. 'I wished it to be brought here because I am aware of Mr Churchill's fears for Your Majesty's safety. I know this room to be the safest place in all of the Empire in which to keep it.'

'Quite,' said Queen Victoria. 'Even the Masked Shadow, of evil memory, would not have dared to enter here.'

'Then we will take our leave, Your Majesty, safe in the knowledge that this great treasure will remain under your protection until the end of December, when it will take its place in the Venusian Hall of the Grand Exposition.'

'One is looking forward to that,' said the Queen. 'Farewell.'

They walked from the palace to the Mall. The going was uncertain, for although the rain of frogs was over, many many many were the frogs around and about.

They clogged up the gutters, hung impaled upon railings, cluttered flower beds, smothered the Mall. 'Twas not the prettiest sight.

Stepping carefully, his lordship led Leah and Darwin, who stepped also most carefully, gingerly and fearfully, to the area where now arose the Exposition's halls.

'Coming on a treat, doncha think?' Lord Brentford fished a cigar from his pocket, popped it into his mouth and lit it with a lucifer. 'Much of the framework up already. Need to sweep those frogs out, though, before the glass goes in.'

Darwin looked up at the acres and acres of ironwork. This building was larger than anything he could possibly have imagined. Darwin's little heart raced at the sheer spectacle, and thoughts came and went inside his head in the way that thoughts will do.

They can create wonders, these humans, Darwin thought.

Wonders sometimes fearsome to behold.

Folk were venturing once more onto the Mall, folk who

stepped with daintiness, prodding at fallen frogs with sticks and parasols.

'Berty,' said Leah, 'I would like to go now, if you please.'

'Certainly, my dear. Just wanted you to see how splendidly everything is coming along. Although all the bods who should be working on the building appear to have sloped off. Taken shelter from the rain of froggies, I suppose.'

Darwin tugged at Lord Brentford's trouser and pointed towards two fellows who were approaching. They walked in that way that can only be described as 'purposeful', with chins firmly set and hands made into fists. They wore black bowler hats, black ulster coats and black boots and each of them carried a black leather case and each of them looked stern.

'Surveyors, I expect,' said his lordship. 'Watch me give 'em a telling-off for something, Darwin.'

Darwin prepared himself to be amused.

'Lord Brentford?' said a fellow in a black bowler hat.

'I am he,' his lordship said. 'So speak, if you will, with respect.'

'Mr Gilbert,' said one fellow in a bowler hat.

'Mr George,' said the other, 'of Gilbert and George Solicitors.'

'Can't say I have heard of you,' said his lordship.

'We hold a royal charter,' said Mr George.

'We represent the gentry,' Mr Gilbert said.

'Well, jolly good show,' said his lordship. 'You haven't by chance seen anything of my workers?'

'Indeed we have,' said Mr George, rummaging about in his black leather case. 'We have dismissed them from the site.'

'*YOU HAVE WHAT?*' Lord Brentford roared. 'Then you shall know my wrath.' And he raised his cane.

'We strongly advise against violence,' said Mr George. 'You would not wish it added to the charges.'

'*Charges? WHAT CHARGES?*'

'We would hope that there will be no charges,' said Mr Gilbert. 'should you choose to settle your account without any further delay—'

'My . . . account?' said Lord Brentford most slowly. 'Ah, indeed, my account.'

'What is this of which the gentleman speaks?' asked Leah.

Mr George now gaily flourished papers. 'Lord Brentford is somewhat behind on his payments,' said he. 'In fact, he has failed to honour any of them.'

Lord Brentford made the bitterest of faces.

Leah gazed at him.

'One million, five hundred and sixty-seven thousand, three hundred and ninety-five pounds, seventeen and sixpence,' said Mr George. 'A not inconsiderable sum. If his lordship would care to write out a cheque, we will settle matters here and now.'

'Don't have my chequebook with me,' said Lord Brentford. 'But surely the costs might be defrayed. After the New Year, millions will flock to see the Grand Exposition. All that I owe for the construction costs can easily be paid then.'

Mr Gilbert shook his head. Mr George did likewise.

'At the present rate of interest,' said Mr Gilbert, 'your owings will have doubled before the Exposition even opens. We have not yet factored in the cost of the glass, or the interior fixtures and fittings.'

Leah the Venusian said, 'What would the overall cost of construction be? Including everything.'

Mr George consulted his papers. 'A little under three million pounds,' said he.

Leah looked towards her Berty. 'And how much do you have in the bank?' she asked.

'That is not the kind of thing a gentleman speaks of in public.' Lord Brentford hefted his walking stick and prepared himself to do these fellows harm.

Leah fixed these fellows with her golden eyes. 'There must be some solution,' she said, her voice once more like that of some echoing Heavenly choir.

'You have the most dulcet tones, madam,' said Mr Gilbert, 'and I felt almost impelled to tear up these summonses. However, business is business, as they say. If the debts are not cleared, *in full*, before next weekend, the project will be cancelled and the existing structure torn down for the value of the scrap metal. Farewell.'

And so saying, he pressed his papers into the hand of Lord Brentford, turned with his partner on his heel and smartly strode away. Being careful, however, not to tread on any frogs.

Darwin the monkey watched them go and Darwin the monkey worried.

The long ride back to Syon House was not one filled with joy. Lord Brentford looked pale and stared straight ahead. Leah clutched his arm. Darwin peeped from the hansom cab and worried for what might occur.

At Syon House, his lordship ordered Darwin to fetch him a bottle of Scotch. Darwin went mournfully about this duty.

His lordship entered the Garden Room and dropped into a chair.

Leah took herself to the window and gazed out at the gardens lying beyond.

Presently, Darwin brought the Scotch and poured his lordship a glass.

'Thank you, boy,' said Lord Brentford. 'Looks as if you might have to find yourself a new master, as I may shortly be serving time in debtors' prison.'

Darwin had brought a second glass and helped himself to Scotch.

'Doomed,' said his lordship. 'All gone. My great scheme. My plan for peace. Too much of a dream, I think.'

'It was a pure dream,' said Leah. 'A true dream. The Grand Exposition must go ahead. We must find a solution.'

'Can't ask the Queen,' said Lord Brentford, swallowing Scotch. 'Know she won't cough up a penny.'

'The British Government?' Leah asked. 'It is a matter of national pride, I would have thought.'

'Churchill has it in for me,' his lordship said. 'He'd put the poison in quickly enough, I'm thinking.'

'There must be a solution,' said Leah.

'I'd sell the old ancestral pile,' said his lordship, 'but it's mortgaged three times over. I can think of only one solution.'

There was a certain stillness in the air.

'I feared that this day would come,' said Lord Brentford, 'so I took a certain precaution. Put all I had into a life-insurance policy. Got a very good deal, in fact. I'm afraid I have no option but to load up the trusty shotgun, go out onto the terrace and take the gentleman's way out.'

'Oh no,' cried Leah. 'There must be another way.'

'Touched by your concern, my dear, but it is all I have. I am responsible and I must act like a man. Do the right thing, doncha know.'

Tears rolled from Leah's golden eyes.

'The Grand Exposition will be my memorial,' said Lord Brentford, swallowing further Scotch. 'Perhaps you might see to it that a bronze bust of meself be put in the entrance hall. I'd like that, I would.'

Leah now sobbed fearfully.

And great big tears welled up in Darwin's eyes.

'I'd like to be alone now, if the two of you don't mind. Need to sort my will out. Tie up loose ends and whatnots. The insurance policy is in the envelope there on the mantelpiece.'

Darwin's lip was all a-quiver. Leah took the monkey by the hand.

'Just before you go,' said his lordship, 'I want to thank you both. Darwin, I know I've treated you badly at times. Sorry about all the business with the bedpans. But I've always cared about you, my boy. Never blessed with children. Thought of you sometimes as the son I never had.'

Darwin buried his face in his hands and wept.

'And, Leah, my dear. I have never loved a woman as I have loved you. Know there's never been any hanky-panky. Wouldn't have considered it until we were married, if such a thing was even possible. But sadly cannot think of it now. I am sorry.'

Leah hugged Darwin and the two wept piteously.

'Stiff upper lips,' said Lord Brentford. 'Must be brave and do what must be done. Darwin, stop blubbering, boy, and go and fetch my gun.'

Darwin looked towards his master and sniffed away his tears.

'There will be no guns,' said Darwin, 'for *I* have another solution.'

44

'n the name of Heaven!' cried Lord Brentford. 'He speaks! How can this wonder really be?'

Darwin shrugged. The game was up. There was no other way.

'I was taught,' said he, 'by a gentleman known as Herr Döktor. I spent a great deal of the money you left me in your will. I can read and write also, as it happens.'

'But why didn't you tell me, boy?' Lord Brentford was up on his feet. 'Why hide away a marvellous gift like that?'

'Because,' said Darwin, 'in truth it makes me neither one thing nor the other. I can speak, but I am not a man. I am a monkey, yet I can speak. To be one of a kind in a world such as this is not the best thing to be.'

Lord Brentford looked both long and hard at Darwin.

'Come over here and give me a hug,' he said.

Darwin scampered across the floor and leapt up into his lordship's arms.

'Might I have a hug, too?' asked Leah, wiping tears from her golden eyes.

'Hugs all round,' said his lordship, and there were indeed hugs all round.

'What an amazing circumstance.' Lord Brentford smiled as he said this. 'But sadly it is a little too late. I still must have my gun.'

'No,' said Darwin, climbing down. 'You fail to understand.'

'A talking ape is a wonder of the world,' said Lord Brentford. 'Please do exhibit yourself at the Grand Exposition. Say something nice about me, if you would.'

Darwin shook his little hairy head. 'You fail to understand,' he said once more. 'I know of a solution to the problem.'

'Is there treasure buried somewhere in the grounds?' Lord Brentford asked.

Darwin shook his head and said, 'Now you are just being silly.'

Lord Brentford actually laughed at this. 'Priceless,' he said. 'Here I am, moments from death, and a talking ape is being impertinent to me.'

'Please listen,' said Darwin. 'I really do have a solution.'

The three sat down in the Garden Room and his lordship poured Scotches all round. As Darwin outlined his personal plan, the silence was profound.

'Several years ago,' the ape began, 'I found myself aboard a spaceship carrying a band of Jovian hunters to Venus on a most illegal hunting trip.'

Leah's golden eyes widened.

Darwin continued his tale. 'I travelled in the company of Colonel Katterfelto, a very brave man and a dear friend. He wished to avail himself of *Magonium*, the gold of Venus, to activate a Mechanical Messiah that he had fashioned.'

Lord Brentford's eyes widened at this.

Darwin continued once more. 'There were diamonds aplenty lying all over the soil of Venus and many of the hunters filled their pockets. However, when the remaining members of the party returned to Earth, these precious gems turned into sugar.'

'The Glamour,' said Leah.

'Precisely,' said Darwin. 'The Glamour of Fairyland, where one thing can appear to be another. Or indeed nothing at all. You performed a magical experiment upon me where you made me invisible, did you not?'

Both Leah and Lord Brentford nodded.

'Then,' said Darwin, 'it is my proposal that in order to pay off the owings for the Grand Exposition, we employ a little magical subterfuge.'

'Go on,' said Lord Brentford. 'I am most intrigued.'

'If the Venusian ecclesiastic is willing, I propose we gather together a great deal of base metal and transmute it into gold – which is to say, give it the outward appearance of being gold – then pay off all the debts and all the rest to ensure that the Grand Exposition goes ahead.'

Lord Brentford's mouth had fallen widely open. 'Could that actually work?' said he.

'If the ecclesiastic is willing,' said Darwin, 'I certainly believe that she is capable of such a thing.'

'Leah?' Lord Brentford said.

'It could be done,' said Leah. 'But bear in mind it will not last – whatever we change will change back.'

'In a vault in the Bank of England,' said Darwin. 'Where it will no longer be our concern.'

'By God, he's got it,' cried Lord Brentford. 'I think he's got it.'

Leah's eyes had a far-away look.

'What is it, my dear?' Lord Brentford asked.

'If we were to be discovered,' said Leah, 'it would not go well for me.'

'If we are discovered,' said Lord Brentford, '*I* will take full responsibility. Your name will not be mentioned. All will rest upon my shoulders. All.'

Darwin smiled up at his lordship. 'Did I make a good plan?' he asked.

'Yes, you did,' his lordship said. 'A very fine plan indeed.'

The scent of bananas wafted into the Garden Room upon a gentle breeze and there was a sense of serenity, a sense of peace and also one of joy.

There was little joy to be found on the streets of London. Streets heaped high with piles of rotting frogs. Within two days the stench was appalling and a grim miasma made the Empire's capital a place to be avoided.

The only upside to all this terrible downness was that *The Times* newspaper's Political Columnist had at least found the solution to the mystery.

> 'The frogs were undoubtedly dropped
> upon London from airships under the
> control of anarchists. That none were
> witnessed in the clear blue sky offers
> a posthumous and grudging tribute to
> the ingenuity and cunning of that most
> evil of men, the Masked Shadow, who
> must surely have planned this outrage
> months before he met his fitting end.
> The airships flew very high indeed,
> their underbellies painted sky blue.'

Cameron Bell read of this as he sipped his tea aboard the *Brighton Belle*. It was *an* explanation, that was for certain, but he doubted whether it was *the* explanation. And he noted, ruefully, that the third and fourth of the biblical plagues had come hard on the second.

The rotting frog corpses had soon bred an infestation of lice and of bluebottles.

If there was any encouragement to be felt, it was that Mr Winston Churchill had mobilised the Army and had sworn to have the frogs all cleared by the end of the week.

'Good old Mr Churchill,' said Cameron Bell, toasting with his teacup.

He was dressed today in a sober grey morning suit, with matching topper and gloves. He swung his slim malacca cane that sheathed a slender blade and whistled as he alighted from the Brighton train and went upon his way.

The cabman drove Cameron Bell through the elegant Regency streets of Brighton, all around Hove and Hangleton. At length, Mr Bell tired of the sly detours and announced that Brighton was well known to him and if he did not reach his destination at Roedean in five minutes he would shoot the cabman dead.

The cabman, who had been considering going via Shoreham, stirred up his horse and took the cliff road towards Roedean.

Cameron Bell recalled his holidays in Brighton.

Happy days in much more innocent times.

With less than a minute to spare, the cabman dropped Mr Bell before the gates of the famous school for young ladies and departed grumbling for his lack of a tip.

Mr Bell trudged up the very long drive and presented his card at the door. Presently he was led to the office of the headmistress, which he knocked upon before politely entering.

A lady in tweeds with a fox-fur stole and hair of turquoise

blue sat behind a magnificent desk inlaid with many tropical woods, smoking a short cheroot.

She examined the card that Mr Bell presented and waved him into a chair.

'Well, *Mr Pickwick*,' she said, reading aloud from the card, 'when you wrote to ask for an interview, I did not know whether I was to be the subject of some elaborate hoax, but my eyes do not deceive me and I can see most clearly that you are who you represent yourself to be.'

'At your service, madam,' said Cameron Bell. 'I am, as I told you in my letter, presently in the employ of the eminent author Mr Charles Dickens.'

The headmistress made a somewhat wistful face. 'A fine and most handsome fellow,' said she.

'And one, it would appear, most anxious to make your acquaintance.'

Mr Bell had never fully understood just what it was about Mr Dickens that women found so appealing. But as his present piece of deception relied upon it, he was pleased to see that the mention of the author's name had the required effect.

'Mr Dickens has heard of *me*?' asked the headmistress, colouring slightly at the cheeks before dragging *very* deeply upon her cheroot.

'I think it must be one of the major reasons why he wishes to write the book – *Roedean: A History of the World's Most Notable Academy for Young Ladies*. Would you consent to having your photograph taken with Mr Dickens, for the flyleaf?'

'Oh yes, most certainly.' The headmistress all but swooned.

'He would be thrilled,' said Cameron Bell.

'Would you care for tea?' asked the headmistress.

Cameron Bell said that he would.

A bell was duly rung and tea was duly brought.

Then poured.

Then drunk.

The headmistress dunked a ginger biscuit in hers. 'So what exactly would you like me to tell you?' she asked. 'Your letter spoke of "essential research".'

'Matters of a confidential nature,' said Mr Bell. 'Matters regarding a certain headmistress and a certain pupil.'

'Nothing was ever proved,' cried the headmistress. 'I was found innocent of all charges.'

'Naturally,' said Mr Bell. 'Of course, I do not allude to your good self, but rather to a former headmistress who was dismissed for "unspeakable cruelty" and a student with whom she still associates.'

'Black sheep,' said the headmistress. 'I know of whom you speak.'

'Mr Dickens asked whether you might supply me with the details, in order that he may "rework" them in a fashion that would not reflect badly on the school. It has to be "warts and all", I'm afraid, but the warts can be made over with rouge.'

'I understand,' said the headmistress. 'It is a sorry tale. I can speak in complete confidence to you, can I not?'

'Absolutely,' said Cameron Bell, a-crossing of his heart. 'I am Mr Dickens's man. I have his trust and that is no small thing.'

'Very well. She should never have been made head-mistress, not with her reputation. The best thing they ever did was to shuffle her off to Mars, where she can do no harm.'

'And she calls herself Madam Glory,' said Cameron Bell.

'Not there, she doesn't. There she calls herself by her true name.'

'Which is?' asked Mr Bell, taking out a notebook and a pencil.

'Princess Pamela,' said the headmistress. 'Twin sister to Her Majesty. But you cannot print *that*, of course.'

'Of course,' said Cameron Bell, maintaining the most expressionless of faces whilst trying to control the turmoil within.

Princess Pamela was Madam Glory!

The Evil Mistress to Lavinia Dharkstorrm.

'And the student,' said Mr Bell, in a calm and measured tone. 'This—' and he made a pretence of studying his notes '—this Miss Lavinia Dharkstorrm?'

'A bad one indeed,' said the headmistress. 'So curious, though, as her sister was such a nice girl.'

'Ah,' said Cameron Bell. 'There was a sister.'

'The one to whom the terrible thing occurred. The business with the face. Quite horrible.'

Cameron Bell looked up at the headmistress. 'This sister,' said he. 'Her name would not, by any chance, be Violet?'

45

'iolet,' said the headmistress. 'What a lovely peaceable girl was Violet.'

'The nature of the accident?' Cameron asked.

'It was no accident,' said the headmistress. 'But must we dwell on such awful matters? The Upper Fifth's hockey team beat the girls of Hove High last week, with only two hospitalised.'

'Would you by any chance have a class photograph showing the Dharkstorrm sisters?' asked Mr Bell.

'Possibly in the main hall. That would be the class of eighty-seven, I believe. So tell me please, Mr Pickwick, what is Mr Dickens *really* like?'

'I have heard him described as *delicate*,' said Cameron Bell, surreptitiously perusing his pocket watch.

'Delicate, as in his health?'

'As in his disposition, if you will.' Cameron Bell raised a knowing eyebrow. The headmistress discerned the knowingness of it.

'You mean . . . ?' said she.

Cameron Bell tapped his nose. 'In popular parlance,' said he, 'Mr Dickens bowls from the gasworks end.'

'No!' cried the headmistress. 'Outrageous.'

'It is between you and me.' Mr Bell now winked lewdly. 'We wouldn't want dear Charlie to end up in Reading Gaol like that Willy-Woofter Wilde did, would we?'

'This interview is over!' cried the headmistress. 'Kindly leave my office at once.'

'But, madam.' Cameron rose to his feet and bowed to the lady in tweed. 'I hope this will not influence you regarding the book.'

'I do not wish to have the school associated with such a matter. Please be gone, I want to be alone.'

'As you wish.' Cameron Bell bowed smartly once more, then took his leave of the office.

When the door had closed upon him, the headmistress took up the earpiece of the brass candlestick telephone and spoke into its mouthparts.

'Operator,' she said, 'get me Waxlow two-nine-double-one.'

There was a pause, then a voice spoke at the ear of the headmistress.

'Ah, dear,' said the tweedy body, 'I felt that I should give you a call. It might be nothing, or perhaps it might be everything. I have had a fellow here representing himself as Mr Pickwick and asking questions.'

Words came to her along the telephone line.

'Yes, I recall. You said to inform you if anybody of this description ever paid me a visit. Well, he has.'

Further words passed into the lady's ear.

'Yes, I answered all of his questions as you instructed me to. His interests lay with you and Madam Glory.'

A few further words.

And then . . .

'I understand, mistress,' said the headmistress, replacing the telephonic earpiece in its cradle.

In the corridor, Mr Cameron Bell removed his ear from the door and pencilled the telephone number Waxlow two–nine–double-one into his little notebook.

'An excellent morning's work,' he whispered, slipping away to the hall.

'A Mr Gilbert and a Mr George are waiting in the hall, your lordship,' said the boy whose name was Jack. 'Should I ask them to come through?' And then the boy whose name was Jack cried out, 'Lord love a duck!' when he spied what lay beyond the chair in which Lord Brentford sat.

'Fetch the blighters in, Jack,' said his lordship. 'And don't feel obliged to be polite to them.'

Jack saluted and marched away, soon to return in the company of Mr Gilbert and Mr George.

'What an atrociously mannered young hobbledehoy,' said Mr George. 'You would not believe what he just called us.'

And then he and Mr Gilbert were heard to say, 'Lord love a duck.'

For they too had spied out that certain something.

It rose like the hoard of Montezuma, a glittering golden heap of this and that, the other, too, and many things besides.

'My goodness me,' said Mr George.

Mr Gilbert nodded and said, 'Heavens.'

Lord Brentford rose languidly from his chair. 'Thought I'd have a bit of a clear-out of the loft,' said he. 'See if any of the old solid-gold family heirlooms were still boxed up in there.' He made expansive gestures towards the ample pile, which rose to almost touch the ornate ceiling. 'Surprising what you don't throw away,' said his lordship, making now a careless gesture. 'What would you say is the current market price of gold?'

Mr George drew from his black leather case a brass Babbage, one of those ingenious little gadgets useful for adding up and taking away and multiplying and so forth.

He tapped tiny buttons and said, 'Nine pounds, four and seven pence an ounce.'

'Must be a ton here, at least,' said his lordship. 'That should more than cover all the costs of the Grand Exposition's halls, I am thinking. What say you to this?'

'I say,' said Mr Gilbert, 'that these items must be assayed, to see if they are in fact *real* gold.'

'Please be my guest,' said his lordship. 'I'll just sit here and read the morning's paper, if you don't mind.'

Mr Gilbert brought out a brass contrivance of his own, this one the invention of Mr Rutherford. He gaped at the great golden pile, then selected an item at random.

'I have never seen a solid-gold bedpan before,' said he.

Behind his newspaper Lord Brentford grinned like a wolf.

Cameron Bell had long since ceased to grin. He had been grinning when he left Roedean, a school group photograph rolled up in his pocket. He had been grinning as he strode down the long drive and was still grinning faintly half a mile up the road where he still had failed to find himself a cab.

By the time he reached Brighton Station, he had a fine sweat on and had worn a hole in his left shoe.

He was still grinning inwardly, though.

The journey back to London was enlivened by champagne. At Victoria, the great detective took a hansom cab.

And once more in the garret that he presently called

home, he took off his gloves and took off his hat and took off his coat as well.

And applied himself to the *Greater London Telephone Directory*.

Waxlow he knew to be the Chelsea district, but it would be a painstaking trawl to find the address that went with the number.

When he did find it he almost kicked himself.

THE PALACE OF MAGIC
13 EATON PLACE
CHELSEA

'Where else!' said Cameron Bell to himself. 'Where else would a witch hide herself away but London's most notorious Temple of the Black Arts?'

And indeed the Palace of Magic was just that. It had been a Masonic temple and later a meeting place for the Hermetic Order of the Golden Sprout and was now, to Mr Bell's certain knowledge, under the control of the infamous black magician Mr Aleister Crowley.

Mr Bell knew Aleister Crowley of old. They had been students together at Oxford and had experienced an on-off relationship ever since. Mr Bell recalled that the last time he had seen Mr Crowley, he had been compelled to shoot the black magician in the foot.

'I hope there will be no hard feelings,' said Mr Bell. 'Now I must send a telegram and attend to one or two other matters of importance, then supper and the music hall, I think.'

'I would offer you supper,' said Lord Brentford, 'but I do not wish to interfere with your work. How is all that assaying coming along?'

Mr Gilbert, jacket off and sleeves rolled up, was sweating rather freely. 'I am almost done,' said he.

'And all of the purest gold?' Lord Brentford asked.

'The purest gold that I have ever seen.' Mr Gilbert huffed and puffed. 'What puzzles me,' he said between these huffs and puffs, 'is why your forebears would choose to have had such apparently random and, in all honesty, *inartistic* items fashioned from gold. This small pair of trousers here, for instance, with the snood affair on the back—'

'Eccentric fellows, the British aristocracy,' said Lord Brentford, and he picked up an item of solid gold and feigned a deep, profound perusal. 'A solid-gold banana,' he said.

'I've counted more than one hundred of them,' said Mr Gilbert, 'worth five hundred pounds apiece.'

'There's no accounting for taste, I suppose.' Lord Brentford was struggling against hilarity. 'Personally I wouldn't give the things houseroom, would you?'

At a little after seven of the evening clock, a telegram was delivered to a house in Pimlico, addressed to a certain Violet Wond. The veiled lady took it and hurried to her room.

TELEGRAM
- - - - - - - - -

OUR QUARRY IS TO BE FOUND AT THE PALACE
OF MAGIC EATON PLACE CHELSEA STOP WILL MEET
YOU THERE TO CONCLUDE OUR DEALINGS MIDNIGHT
TOMORROW NIGHT STOP

Miss Violet Wond flung the telegram onto her bed.

Knelt down and drew from beneath this bed a leather-bound portmanteau.

She lifted the lid to display the exotic attire of Lady Raygun: the boots, the brass corset, the leather-sectioned skirt. She drew from silken coverings a shining silver hand weapon with the words *The Lady* inlaid in ivory upon its stock.

'I have saved this gun to use upon you, my sister,' said Violet Dharkstorrm. And viewing once more the telegram added –

'Lady Raygun only works alone.'

46

eon tubings lit the Electric Alhambra, the finest music hall in all the land. Mr Bell had booked the royal box and was pleased when he reached it to find that the champagne he had also ordered was awaiting him in an electrically cooled *buckette glacé*.

Mr Bell looked very smart indeed in his evening suit, with white shirt, white tie, white waistcoat and white socks.

He settled into a plush velvet chair and waited.

Hustling, bustling, laughing, joking, the crowds below filled up the auditorium. Sammy 'the Screw-Scriver' Scrivener was topping the bill tonight – always a big draw and a crowd-pleaser. 'A swagger, a stagger and a saucy song about a screwdriver' – how could it get better than that?

Mr Bell perused his pocket watch, uncorked the champagne, poured two glasses. Waited a little longer.

Any minute now.

The door to the royal box swung open.

Aleister Crowley entered.

The self-styled Beast of the Apocalypse beheld the detective.

The detective beheld the Beast.

'Well, well, well,' said Aleister Crowley. 'I really should have guessed.'

'Guessed?' asked Cameron Bell, a-feigning ignorance.

'A street urchin knocks upon my door whilst I am conducting a magical experiment with two East End slosh-pots and presents me with this ticket.' The Beast flourished same. 'A ticket for the royal box at the Electric Alhambra, where I would meet, the urchin informed me in a confidential manner, "with a lady of great beauty and high social standing".'

'Did the trick, though, didn't it?' said Cameron Bell, gesturing towards both chair and champagne. 'I did not feel that you would have attended had you known that *I* sent you the ticket.'

Aleister Crowley flung himself into the vacant chair and took the champagne that was offered to him.

'I should not be speaking with you,' he said. 'The last time we met you shot me in the foot.'

'You stole from me,' said Cameron Bell. 'Be grateful that I did not shoot you in a more personal place.'

Aleister Crowley crossed his legs. 'Quite so,' he said as he sipped champagne.

'Sammy "the Screw-Scriver" Scrivener is topping the bill,' said Cameron Bell.

'I do not believe that you tricked me here to listen to a man singing a suggestive song about a screwdriver. More champagne, if you will.'

Cameron Bell supplied the Beast with more champagne.

'I am Crowley,' said Crowley. 'Finest Thinker of the Age. Logos of the Aeon. Laird of Boleskine. I am one Hell of a Holy Guru.'

'And enjoying salubrious accommodations at present, I

gather,' said Mr Bell. 'Did another aunt die and leave you a share of her fortune?'

Aleister Crowley made a surly face. 'There are those who will pay to learn the Ultimate Truths,' said he. 'Although these Truths are naturally beyond price.'

'Still charming the ladies of the court, then.' Cameron Bell toasted Aleister Crowley. 'I am sorry to have disappointed you tonight, when you had hoped to meet another willing customer.'

'Say whatever you have to say, and quickly,' said Aleister Crowley. 'I tire of your banal conversation. I have important matters to attend to.'

'As indeed do I.' Mr Bell toasted Crowley once again. Crowley downed further champagne.

'I understand,' said Cameron Bell, 'that you presently have a lodger.'

'My house is always a haven for seekers after truth.'

'I will not mince words,' said Cameron Bell. 'I have every reason to believe that you are harbouring a notorious wanted criminal by the name of Lavinia Dharkstorrm!'

'*Not so loud!*' The Beast did flappings of the hands, spilling much champagne all over his shirtfront.

Cameron Bell replenished his glass.

'The question is,' said Mr Bell, 'has she joined your gang, or have you joined hers?'

Aleister Crowley opened his mouth to lie.

'Ah,' said Cameron Bell. 'Neither. Her circle would consist exclusively of women, I suppose.'

'As does mine,' said Aleister Crowley.

Cameron smiled. 'Miss Dharkstorrm is beyond your powers to charm,' he said.

'The woman is a harridan,' said Aleister Crowley. 'She

moved herself in with that fat tub of lard and chucked out all my women and my servants.'

'By "fat tub of lard", I presume that you are referring to Madam Glory?'

Aleister Crowley nodded. Gloomily. 'They eat my food and drink my drink and when I suggested that the three of us sport amongst the pillows—'

'They did not take it kindly,' said Cameron Bell.

'They did not take it *at all*!' said Aleister Crowley.

'So there you are, fetching and carrying for these women—'

'Well, I would not put it quite like *that*.'

'No,' said Cameron Bell. 'Of course you would not. But let us speak no more of such matters for now. What say we become nostalgic, Crowley? Recall when we were up at Oxford together? What fun then we had on nights out at the music hall.'

Crowley made a thoughtful face, then shrugged his manly shoulders. 'It would keep me out of the house for a while,' he said.

The evening passed in a most enjoyable fashion as the finest turns in London performed on the floodlit stage. There was even an unexpected guest appearance by the lovely Alice Lovell and her performing kiwi birds. Cameron Bell's heart fluttered when he saw Alice, for she had once been the only true love of his life.

The performances reached their climax with the topmost of the bill. Sammy 'the Screw-Scriver' Scrivener swaggered onto the stage (which was the swaggering part of his performance), did a little crowd-pleasing stagger (the staggering part) and then launched into the famous suggestive screwdriver song that had made his name famous –

THE OLD SCREW-SCRIVER

– with which the crowd sang along. Making sure to lay a heavy emphasis upon any word that could possibly be considered suggestive.

> Now I've known many kinds of *tool*,
> But not in the biblical sense.
> They've helped with my *erection*
> Of my grandmother's fence.
>
> I've worn my wrist out *doing it*,
> I tell you I'm no skiver.
> For a nail will fail
> What a *screw* can do
> When you *do it* with your old *screw-scriver*.
>
> *Chorus:*
> I did it with my old screw-scriver
> Did it with my old screw-scriver
> You hold it in your fist
> Do it with your wrist
> It goes in straight
> Or it will go in p★★sed.
> I didn't drown
> When the ship went down,
> I was the sole survivor.
> For I'm not daft
> I built myself a raft
> And I did it with my old screw-scriver.

The applause was truly deafening and numerous young ladies carried away upon the moment tossed their bloomers onto the stage. Sammy 'the Screw-Scriver' Scrivener had once again made it another night to remember.

Cameron Bell upended the champagne bottle.

'Another dead soldier,' he said. 'What a most pleasurable evening.'

Aleister Crowley hiccupped loudly, for he was far-gone with the drink.

'Bit squiffy?' asked Cameron Bell, still surprisingly chipper.

'Drink is never the master of me,' slurred the Beast, sliding sideways on his chair. 'We should go on to a club.'

'We should,' agreed Mr Bell, and he brought from his waistcoat pocket a pillbox.

'What have you there?' asked Crowley, viewing several pillboxes.

'A rather splendid pick-me-up my pharmacist put together for me, part laudanum, part heroin, part—'

'Share them out,' called Crowley. 'I want two.'

'They are *very* strong.'

'I have slipped things down my throat that you would not believe,' said Aleister Crowley.

Cameron Bell added no comment to *that*.

But generously offered Mr Crowley a pill.

'Give me *two*,' said Crowley.

Cameron gave him two.

'Now let us go down and hail a cab,' said Mr Bell. 'First my club and then yours – we will make a night of it.'

'We will,' said Aleister Crowley, rising, tumbling back, then rising once again. Cameron Bell helped up the Beast, who put his arm about the detective's shoulders.

'You are my friend,' mumbled Aleister Crowley. 'My bestest friend.'

'Of course I am,' said Cameron Bell, aiding the stumbling Beast. 'Of course I am.'

By the time any transport could be found, Mr Crowley was no longer able to stand. Nor indeed open his eyes. Cameron Bell and the driver bundled the unconscious Logos of the Aeon into the hansom cab.

'You want I should drop him home, then, guv'nor?' enquired the driver.

'No,' said Cameron Bell. 'Take him please to Saint Pancras Station and put him on the night train to Edinburgh. Here is his ticket. And here a guinea for your trouble. I doubt if he can be woken, but treat him very gently nonetheless.'

'Certainly, guv'nor,' said the driver. 'And might I say that this young chap here should be grateful to have such a caring friend as you.'

'I am more of a friend to him than he knows,' said Mr Cameron Bell.

The hansom departed with Crowley aboard.

Mr Bell perused his pocket watch.

He was still extremely chipper. For after all, he had consumed but a single glass of champagne.

'One down and one to go,' said Cameron Bell. 'And unless I am very much mistaken – and I do *not* believe myself to be so – the fun will begin at the Palace of Magic upon the stroke of midnight.'

ing's Road, driver,' said Cameron Bell. 'And smartly, if you will.'

The driver of the electric-wheeler, whom Mr Bell had engaged for the evening and who had been looking on in puzzlement as his fare helped load an unconscious fellow into a hansom cab, said, 'Certainly, sir.'

The driver climbed into his cockpit and Mr Bell settled down onto the purple leather seating within. He really *did* love it when a plan came together, and he had worked hard upon this particular one. He had successfully lured Aleister Crowley to the Electric Alhambra and gleaned from him the required information that the only people within the Palace of Magic were Lavinia Dharkstorrm and her mistress Princess Pamela, aka Madam Glory. Then administered sufficient champagne and sleeping pills to Mr Crowley to render him unconscious and dispatched him as far away as possible so that he might come to no harm in the ensuing holocaust.

A holocaust he felt confident would shortly be brought into being by Lady Raygun. Mr Bell had reasoned that if he informed the vengeful woman where Lavinia Dharkstorrm lurked and arranged to meet her there the following even-ing, she would surely ignore the proposed arrangement and attack Miss Dharkstorrm on this very night.

'Or at least I certainly *hope* she will,' said Cameron Bell.

'Did you ask me something, guv'nor?' asked the driver of the electric-wheeler.

'No,' said Cameron Bell.

'Only if there's anythink you wants to know, I's be happy to be supplying you with answers.'

'I just need to get to the corner of Eaton Place before midnight,' said Cameron Bell.

'And so you shall, guv'nor. What do you make of this 'ere business with falling frogs and likewise?'

'Anarchists,' said Mr Cameron Bell.

'So you don't think we 'as to worry that it is the end of the world?'

Cameron Bell offered nothing in reply.

'Me missus,' said the driver, ''as the 'ole thing figured owt.'

'I am coming more and more to the conclusion,' said Cameron Bell, 'that women are either in charge of, behind or to blame for almost everything.'

'Fierce words, guv'nor,' said the driver, swerving to knock a passing cleric off his bike.

'And why did you do *that*?' asked Cameron Bell.

'Because I 'olds them to blame,' said the driver. 'Clerics and Godmen. Me missus 'as come to the conclusion that the world will end at midnight upon New Year's Eve.'

Cameron Bell shuddered slightly. 'And how has she drawn this dire conclusion?' he asked.

'Numerology,' said the driver. 'It's all very complicated, but I think I 'as the measure of it. First you add the numbers in Queen Victoria's birth date together and—'

Cameron Bell gazed out of the window and dreamed of happier times.

'And you subtract the difference in days since the date of her birth and the very last day of this year, and add the square on the hypotenuse—'

An airship passed across the starry sky.

'Take away the number you first thought of—'

'Ah, we have arrived,' said Cameron Bell.

'Add one for the pot and half a sixpence.' The driver drew the wheeler to a halt. 'And you 'ave nine hundred and ninety nine,' said he, 'and you cannot argue with that.'

'Nor would I wish to,' said Cameron Bell. 'But what would the significance of this number be?'

'It's the Number of the Beast,' said the driver.

'No,' said Cameron Bell, 'the number of the Beast is six hundred and sixty-six.'

'If it were a *man*,' said the driver. 'But you see, it ain't no man – the Beast is a woman, so her number is six-six-six upside down. Nine-nine-nine is the number of the Lady Beast. And she was born on the twenty-fourth of May, eighteen nineteen,' said the driver.

'Ah,' said Cameron Bell. 'Then according to your wife, Queen Victoria is the Antichrist.'

'Not so loud, guv'nor, not even at night. But it all works out on paper. Not that I would dare to suggest such a thing against our glorious monarch. But unless she 'as a twin sister, it looks like she's the one.'

Cameron Bell climbed from the electric-wheeler on the corner of Cadogan Street and told the driver to wait for him there.

Mr Bell then slipped away into a darkened alley.

And there, had he been of an athletic disposition with the double joints of a contortionist, he would have kicked himself repeatedly in the behind. It was all so obvious. It had been staring him in the face all along and he had failed to see it. It was every bit the clichéd old scenario of *the Evil Twin*. So clichéd that surely no one would dare to trot it out once again. And a *female* Antichrist? Well, that one wasn't so obvious. But it *did* all fall into place. This *was* all to do with women. It was Eve who had committed the first sin – why not a woman to commit the final one? And a woman who was the identical twin of the world's most iconic monarch?

It was prophesied that the arrival of the Antichrist would herald the End of Days, and that only those in his – or in this case, *her* – service would remain on Earth, after the good were gathered up to Heaven in the Rapture.

The four reliquaries had been brought into an unhallowed place. The biblical plagues were an announcement that the Antichrist was coming.

And *when* would the Antichrist come?

As the Book of Sayito foretold: on the very last day of this year.

And *how* would the Antichrist manifest?

By usurping the throne of her sister, Queen Victoria!

Cameron Bell had a vision, and a terrible vision it was. He saw the halls of the Grand Exposition and the thousands come to celebrate the Wonders of the Worlds on the final day of the century. He saw the London Symphony Orchestra and the great choir come to perform Beethoven's Ninth. He saw Her Majesty mounting to a throne within the concert hall. He saw fire, he saw brimstone, he saw torment.

And he beheld Madam Glory.

Who upon the final day of the century . . .

Upon the final hour . . .

Would destroy the Good Queen Victoria . . .

And rule instead upon her throne.

Had Cameron Bell not been possessed of a particularly strong stomach, he would certainly have been sick right there and then in the darkened alleyway.

'There is still time,' whispered Cameron Bell. 'There is still time to stop this.'

'Look at him tremble,' said Lavinia Dharkstorrm, 'all alone in the alleyway.' Lavinia wore a gown of mauve that matched her dazzling eyes. Beside her stood a woman all in pink.

'Ee-oop, chuck,' said Princess Pamela. 'Does wee porky lad be givin' us bother?'

They stood within the Palace of Magic, these evil ladies, studying the image of Cameron Bell, which swam in a silver scrying bowl filled to the brim with dark liquid. Lavinia Dharkstorrm passed long fingers over the surface of this liquid and Mr Bell's image dissolved.

'He is dangerous,' she said to her mistress. 'And I remain puzzled as to how he was raised from the zombified stupor I placed him in. But I perceive glimpses of the future and he will not enter this temple tonight.'

'Then 'appen 'e'll just stand there in the dark.' The pinky princess chuckled. 'Where's Crowley? I want me supper.'

'Slunk away to some brothel, I expect.' Lavinia Dharkstorrm sat herself down in Aleister Crowley's loveseat.

The room was as grim as might be reasonably expected, walls, floor and ceiling all painted the blackest of blacks, the walls relieved here and there by flashes of garish colour, these provided by Crowley's fanciful paintings. Most involved copulation in one extreme form or another, although there was a rather fetching still life entitled *Plums Upon a Paisley* hanging above a cabinet containing mummified toads. A human skeleton maintained a lonely vigil in one corner, and a pair of stuffed kiwi birds imaginatively mounted in the position known as 'taking tea with the parson' lurked in another. Instruments of torture hung above the fireplace. Crowley's book collection was piled all around and about.

The walls owned to no windows. Moonlight entered with trepidation through skylights high above.

'Thou'll 'ave t' kill that little baldy man,' said Princess Pamela of Cameron Bell. 'Now 'ee knows of thy whereabouts, 'e'll make a right nuisance, mark my words and trip me over backwards if he d'n't.'

'All in good time,' said Lavinia Dharkstorrm.

'Don't *all in good time* me, my lovely! Thou shouldst hath killed 'im when thou hadst the chance. But thou got all clever with it and put 'im in a trance. Kill 'im now and bring 'im 'ere – we'll cook 'im up for supper.'

Cameron Bell felt hungry. A *very* late supper would have suited him well. He brought out his pocket watch and held it up so street light fell upon it. It was nearing twelve-thirty. Perhaps he had made a mistake. Perhaps Lady Raygun would not appear.

'A most expensive mistake if she does not,' whispered Mr Bell. 'And I do not want to go through all of this again tomorrow night.'

And then he saw her, high in the sky. A glimmer of transparent membrane, rainbow-hued as oil upon water, surrounding the woman with the tightly fitting rubber headpiece and the corset of brass. She swung about and spiralled down, then came to rest in perfect silence upon the roof of the sinister Palace of Magic.

Within the black-walled sitting room, Lavinia Dharkstorrm stirred the liquid in the silver scrying bowl with the leg bone of a child.

'Look-see,' she said to the princess in pink. 'The little man is leaving.'

And indeed Mr Bell was. If he had learned one lesson when encountering Lavinia Dharkstorrm, it was this: when dealing with an adversary who is capable of foretelling what you will do next, it is always better to appear to be doing something other than you actually are. Which was probably far easier to say than to do.

Or otherwise.

Mr Bell returned to the electric-wheeler, awakened the driver, who was having a little nap, and settled himself once more in a passenger seat.

'Home is it, then, guv'nor?' enquired the driver, hope very high in his voice.

Cameron Bell fished out a cigar and lit it. 'Not just yet,' he said. 'And please be ready to depart when I give the word – there may be a little following to do. However, first I would like you to drive to Sloane Square and then turn around and drive back.'

The driver sighed. 'Whatever you say,' said he.

'And off he goes,' said Lavinia Dharkstorrm. 'Home to his cosy bed.'

'Thou knowest what that means?' said Princess Pamela.

Lavinia Dharkstorrm shook her head.

'Means as wee man's gone, thou'll 'ave to cook me some supper.'

'Beans on toast?' asked Lavinia Dharkstorrm.

Then all manner of things occurred in a great and terrible rush.

There came a dazzling flash as of lightning and a dreadful shattering of glass. Then something smashed down into the living room. Furniture tumbled and paintings fell from the wall.

Lavinia Dharkstorrm opened her mouth but found a firm hand clasped across it.

And the feel of cold steel pressing against her left temple.

A voice whispered softly in Miss Dharkstorrm's ear.

'Remember me, sister?' it said.

48

eturning to the corner of Eaton Place, Mr Bell puffed away at his cigar and awaited developments.

He yawned and called up to the driver. 'From where you are sitting, can you see the coach house next to the building that bears the sign that reads "the Palace of Magic"?' he asked.

'I can,' the driver replied.

'Well,' said Mr Bell, 'shortly a black landau drawn by two black horses will issue from there at speed. When it passes us by, I wish you to follow it.'

'It might not come this way, though,' said the driver. 'What if it were to turn left instead of right when it leaves the coach house? It could then take the first right into Eaton Square, or the next left into West Eaton Place, or indeed carry on to the bottom then swing right into Chesham Street.'

For the driver had done the Knowledge.

'The landau will *not* go *that* way,' said Cameron Bell.

'No offence, sir, but you sound very sure of yourself.'

'There is a postbox on the corner of Eaton Square where it meets Eaton Place,' said Cameron Bell.

'I have no doubt that there is, sir,' said the driver.

Cameron Bell removed from his pocket a slim brass contrivance with an extendable metal rod. A slim brass contrivance that was something of a favourite with him.

The boy who had delivered the music hall ticket to Aleister Crowley had also popped a certain package into the postbox.

Mr Bell's thumb hovered above the FIRE button on the contrivance.

Lady Raygun's thumb and fingers pressed very hard at Lavinia Dharkstorrm's face.

'Ooo the 'ell art thou?' roared Princess Pamela.

'Do you not recognise me, headmistress?' Lady Raygun said.

'Take off thy 'orrid mask and let me see.'

Lady Raygun shook her head. 'My *sister* knows who I am.'

'*You!*' Princess Pamela raised a manicured eyebrow. 'Little Violet. We all thought you were dead.'

'How well you lie,' said Lady Raygun. 'You did this evil thing to me, you and my own sister. Had me altered, turned into a weapon – an assassin to destroy your enemies.'

'And well thou art doing, lass. I've read of thy exploits in the penny dreadful. Should've put two 'n' two together, I suppose.'

'Grmmph mmmph,' went Lavinia Dharkstorrm.

'Thou art suffocating my servant,' said Princess Pamela. 'Give 'er air and we'll 'ave a cosy chat.'

Lady Raygun loosened her grip but slightly and said, 'She will die most painfully. As indeed will you.'

Princess Pamela laughed somewhat at this. ''Appen, chuck,' said she, 'that matters might be no' so easy.'

And she turned to take her leave.

The silver hand weapon spat electrical fire across the room.

Princess Pamela waved the flames away.

'Farewell to thee,' she said. 'And dear Lavinia, best be free as a bird.'

There was a ripple in the air. A troubling of the aether.

And Lady Raygun no longer held the head of Lavinia Dharkstorrm. Instead there was an eagle where the evil woman had been.

The eagle was upon her, all beak and ripping talons. The lady fired her ray gun, again and again and again.

Cameron's thumb was on the firing button.

'Doors of the coach house are opening,' said the driver.

Cameron's thumb did hoverings.

'And the landau's coming out—'

The thumb edged closer to the FIRE button.

'And they're turning—'

Thumb-button-thumb-button—

'Wait for it—'

Button-thumb-button-thumb—

'Left!'

Button down and—

Nothing.

Cameron pressed his thumb down again and again.

And was rewarded by . . .

A mighteous explosion.

The postbox erupted. The landau's horses reared. The landau all but overturned.

But did not.

It swung about in the narrow street and plunged towards the King's Road.

★

On high, within the Palace of Magic, Lavinia Dharkstorrm, now in the shape of a lion, leapt at Lady Raygun.

'Here they come, sir,' said the driver of the electric-wheeler, putting the motor into gear. 'And crikey!' he cried as the landau rushed by. 'There's no one driving that thing.'

And indeed there was not.

A princess in pink lazed back amongst cushions, upon her lap an oversized reticule.

'She has the reliquaries!' cried Cameron Bell. 'After her, man. There's a guinea in it for you if you can drive her off the road.'

'It will be my pleasure,' said the driver.

And the chase was on.

The well-to-do of Eaton Place were throwing up their windows.

A house that had once been handy for the postbox was now very much on fire.

And flames were rising too from the Palace of Magic, as terrible growls and awful screams echoed from within.

Cameron Bell had discarded his cigar and replaced his brass contrivance in his pocket. He now took to rolling up his right trouser leg.

'Faster, man, faster,' he called to the driver as he tinkered at his leg.

It was not a weapon he'd actually tested before. It came in several sections that had to be screwed together. Mr Bell had taped these to his legs, as carrying such a *very large ray gun* into the Electric Alhambra would have been frowned upon by the management.

'Those horses are going like the very Devil,' shouted the

driver as he swung the vehicle upon two wheels as it went around Sloane Square. 'But we'll 'ave 'em, sir, you fear not.'

Cameron Bell was now all over the floor. But he struggled to free further parts of his great big weapon.

It was a pleasant, fragrant night with a gorgeous star-filled sky and it put Mr Bell in mind of another bit of following he had done more than a year before. When he had pursued Lavinia Dharkstorrm to that high, narrow house in the little square between the Temple and St Bride's, where she had quite outfoxed him.

That was the night that he had first encountered Lady Raygun.

Within the Palace of Magic, a mighty battle raged. Lavinia Dharkstorrm changed her shape from beast to bird to beastly thing and each was met by a furious force in the shape of Lady Raygun.

The driverless landau raced ahead, negotiating tricky street corners, swerving to avoid oncoming vehicles, striking down the occasional cycling cleric, cracking on at a truly furious pace.

The driver of the electric-wheeler said, 'My motor's overheating.'

'I will buy you a new one.' Cameron Bell was upside down, but the ray gun was nearly assembled.

It was a Ferris Firestorm Nineteen-Hundred Series, the very latest thing for big-game hunting. Although to a degree somewhat impractical for this purpose, as one blast at an elephant would tend to reduce said pachyderm to little more than four umbrella stands and a flywhisk.

'The landau's heading for Chelsea Bridge,' called the

driver informatively. 'They'll 'ave to stop there, so they will.'

'Why so?' asked Cameron Bell, now proudly cradling a gun of such preposterous proportions that it was hard to believe he could possibly have had all the numerous bits and pieces simply strapped to his legs.

'Why so what, sir?' asked the driver.

'Why will they have to stop?' said Cameron Bell.

The wheeler was on two wheels once again. A party of Jovian tourists fled heavily before it.

'There's a big hole in the middle,' said the driver. 'Sorry, pardon, sir,' he called to a wounded Jovian. 'Traction engine fell through it earlier this evening, sir. Very big hole indeed.'

The landau continued its speedy rushing onwards.

Cameron Bell hefted his mighty weapon into view.

'My, that is a big one,' said the driver.

'There might be a bit of recoil,' said Cameron Bell, 'so best hold on tight when I fire it.'

'Have no fear for me, sir.'

Lady Raygun knew no fear at all.

Lavinia Dharkstorrm knew nothing but hatred.

The two, despite all the magic and mayhem, were really quite evenly matched.

The Palace of Magic was now an inferno within.

And without, fire was spreading to several buildings.

Well-to-do folk were out in their nightshirts and nighties.

Fire-engine bells were ringing.

Chaos had come to elegant Chelsea.

Chaos, mayhem, smoke and flames and things of that nature. Generally.

★

Cameron Bell had the landau in his sights and he squeezed down hard on the trigger of the Ferris Firestorm Nineteen-Hundred Series. A bolt of energy tore from the barrel, streaked through the night and struck home in a public house that was called the Lucky Jim.

Late-night drinkers rushed from the building. Several, it appeared, were rather fiercely ablaze.

'Ouch!' declared the driver as they swept past the Lucky Jim. 'Have another shot, though, sir. And I have to admit, there's very little recoil.'

Cameron Bell was flat on his back. The recoil that he had taken full force had nearly torn his right arm from its socket.

'They're on the bridge,' called the driver. 'Typical, isn't it, no warning signs up, someone could come to grief when they get to the middle.'

'Oh, I do hope so,' said Cameron Bell, struggling up to take another potshot.

'Perhaps you should just wait until they pull up by the hole,' called the driver. 'Shame to damage any more of the bridge, don't you think?'

But Cameron Bell had his finger once more upon the trigger.

And this time his aim was well and truly sound.

The blue bolt of energy sang through the air and bore forwards directly towards the rear of the landau that was now mounting the bridge.

The driver watched as he steered and he shouted, 'It's going to . . . it's going to . . . it's going to . . . it's going to—

'It's *not!*'

For the landau was rising up from the bridge.

And the bolt passed harmlessly under.

Under, for the landau was rising higher now, over the yawning hole and up into the sky.

The horses' hooves drummed onto empty air.

And a pink-clad arm rose up from the rear.

And waved farewell to Mr Cameron Bell.

'Well, I'll be damned!' the driver cried. Then, 'Oh my God, the brakes have blown, we're heading for the hole!'

Mr Bell made to leap from the brakeless wheeler.

But found to his horror that, as if by magic, the doors could not be opened.

49

eneath the waters of the Thames, death did not take Mr Cameron Bell. When one is possessed of a very large ray gun, one can extract oneself from a plunging electric-wheeler.* And, as luck will some-times have it, a pod of dolphins swimming upstream from their regu-lar haunts in the Thames Delta† pulled Mr Bell and the driver ashore, gave a brief demonstration of backflips then swam off into the night in search of big fat fishes.

'Well,' said the driver, once more on dry land. 'Do you want to settle up now?'

Drenched, down at heart and now without a penny to his name, Cameron Bell trudged soggily back to his lodgings. There he discarded the ruination that had until so recently been his evening suit, availed himself of hot water, bathed and took to his bed.

Awaking on the morrow with a very runny nose.

---

* *As Marie Lloyd once said to the Bishop of London.*
† *The home of the Blues.*

Miss Violet Wond was not at home to callers. Mr Bell learned from her landlady that, 'There was an attack or some such and Miss Wond is now in the London Hospital.'

Mr Bell hastened there on foot.

At the door to a private room he was met by Ernest Rutherford.

'Mr Bell,' said the chemist. 'What are *you* doing here?'

'Visiting a friend,' said Cameron Bell, the lie springing easily to him. 'And I overheard a nurse mention the name of Violet Wond.'

'And what is your connection to this lady?' Mr Ernest Rutherford was very agitated.

'Mr Rutherford,' said Mr Bell, 'I am aware that Miss Wond made a gift of the *Marie Lloyd* to you.'

Ernest Rutherford nodded curtly. 'This is so,' said he.

'Then might I ask,' enquired Mr Bell, 'the condition of the patient?'

'In truth, not good.' The chemist's hands were shaking. 'She was viciously attacked last night. She is most severely injured.'

'I am so very sorry to hear that.' And Cameron certainly was.

'She is being well cared for. We can only hope and pray.'

'Indeed,' said Cameron Bell. 'Might I enquire what Miss Wond was wearing when she was found?'

'What an impertinent question.'

'Mr Rutherford, I am a detective. I will do anything in my power to bring the perpetrator of this crime to justice.'

'Of course, Bell, of course. Forgive me. She was found upon her bed, in her night attire.'

Thank Heaven for that, thought Mr Bell. 'And might I ask

one other question? And this is a delicate matter. What is the nature of the injuries to her face?'

Ernest Rutherford made an outraged expression.

'Please,' said Cameron Bell. 'I really need to know.'

The chemist's hands were making fists. 'Years ago,' said he, 'she was most cruelly treated. Some demonic surgeon worked evil upon her tender features, twisted them into a mask of absolute horror.'

'As might befit such a fighting machine,' mused Cameron Bell.

'What did you say?' asked Ernest Rutherford.

'Nothing,' said Mr Bell. 'But tell me this – is there nothing the surgeons here can do to restore the lady's beauty?'

'Sadly, no.' The chemist shook his head. 'It is beyond the skills of this present age. But no doubt in some far and distant time—'

'I see,' said Cameron Bell.

'You *do*?' asked Ernest Rutherford.

'It is your intention to convey Miss Wond into the future in your time-ship, where surgeons with skills far advanced beyond our own can right the wrong that was done to her.'

'Such is my dearest wish,' said Ernest Rutherford.

'And it is my duty to see that this comes to pass. Please convey to Miss Wond my fondest regards and best wishes for a speedy recovery. I must now go off about my business, so farewell, Mr Rutherford.'

But Cameron Bell did *not* go off about his business, for he had no business to go off about at all. He would have returned to the Palace of Magic, in hopeful search of Lavinia Dharkstorrm's corpse, but a morning newspaper informed him that the entirety of Eaton Place and several other streets besides had burned to the ground last night.

With no loss of life reported, said the paper.

Mr Bell found some consolation in learning that this outrage, along with the wanton destruction of a public house named the Lucky Jim, had been put down to the work of anarchists.

And of Princess Pamela's whereabouts?

She had flown away into the sky. She could be anywhere.

Mr Bell sighed dismally, then set off on foot towards Scotland Yard in the hope of scrounging some money.

Days passed into weeks passed into months.

And Cameron Bell came up with nothing at all. Late in November, however, he received a call from Chief Inspector Case. It was a rather urgent call. Mr Bell, who was still drawing a considerable salary from the Yard's petty-cash tin, felt honour bound to answer this urgent call.

Chief Inspector Case was in his kiwi cloak and paper crown. Cameron Bell gave him very careful lookings up and down.

'Well, at least,' said he, 'your wife has left the country.'

'Run off to Milan with that Señor Voice.' The chief inspector's voice had much joy in it. 'And good riddance to bad—'

'And why have you called me here?'

'It is a difficult matter,' said the chief inspector, 'and only you can deal with it.'

Cameron Bell rubbed his hands together. A challenge, *any* challenge, he would take to happily. He was resigned now to the fact that the next encounter he would have with Madam Glory, with or without Miss Dharkstorrm, would be on New Year's Eve at the Grand Exposition. He had absolutely no doubt that it would be there that the Lady Beast, the female Antichrist, would seek to usurp the throne of Queen

Victoria. True, it gave him plenty of time to plan, and he had every hope that a plan would be coming together. But in the meantime he just sat and stewed. And drank too much and worried about what might be.

'So,' said Mr Bell, 'what is it that only I can deal with?'

'The Crime of the Century,' said the chief inspector.

'We have already dealt with that.' Mr Bell found the chief inspector's Scotch and helped himself to a glassful. 'You single-handedly defeated the Masked Shadow and saved the Crown Jewels and I am assured your knighthood is awaiting you.'

'Not *that* Crime of the Century,' said the chief inspector. 'There has been another one.'

'*Another* Crime of the Century?'

The chief inspector nodded his crown. 'The Bank of England has been robbed,' he said.

The two men shared a cab to the Bank of England and as the horse trotted before them, Chief Inspector Case, in his street clothes, explained what he felt concerning the situation.

'You can't have *two* Crimes of the Century,' he said. 'It just isn't done.'

The cabbie, a professional hackney carriage driver who had recently moved from Brighton to seek his fortune in the big city, took them by way of the Mall. Mr Bell was most impressed by the shimmering palace of glass that now covered so many many acres of Green Park.

'Are you listening to me, Bell?' asked Chief Inspector Case.

'I am all ears,' said the detective. 'There cannot be two Crimes of the Century, we are both agreed upon *that*.'

'So I want you to solve this one quietly. With absolutely *no* publicity and no fuss. In a manner that involves no explosions whatsoever and no expense at all to Scotland Yard.'

Cameron Bell made a crestfallen face. That didn't sound like much fun.

Eventually they reached the Bank of England, where the Brightonian cabby was most miffed to discover that he would not be paid anything at all for the journey as his vehicle had apparently just been 'commandeered for official police business'.

The Bank of England truly was a fortress. Its vaults had walls some six feet thick and huge steel doors with mighty locks and big armed guards that none would dare to fuss with.

The chief inspector and the consulting detective were led to the vaults by a clerk who bore an uncanny resemblance to Jacob Marley out of Charles Dickens's *A Christmas Carol*.

'It's sometimes more of a blessing than a curse,' he said to Cameron Bell.

'Working at the Bank of England?' the detective asked.

'Looking like one of Mr Dickens's characters. People must mention it all the time that you look like Mr Pickwick.'

'Never, ever,' said Cameron Bell. 'Is this the vault in question?'

The clerk nodded, 'umbly.*

Cameron Bell examined the door. 'No evidence at all of forced entry,' he said. And he raised an eyebrow at the clerk who resembled Jacob Marley.

'Don't look at *me*,' said the fellow. 'I'm not in charge of the keys.'

Chief Inspector Case called to a burly guard. 'Open her up, please, if you will,' he said.

* *As might Uriah Heep.*

The burly guard went about his business in a manner both slow and sedate, dragged upon the enormous door and waved Mr Bell and the chief inspector in.

Chief Inspector Case lit a gas mantle.

Cameron Bell said, 'Oh my dear dead mother.'

'Certainly makes you think, does it not?' said Chief Inspector Case. 'I mean, what kind of criminal mastermind steals three million pounds' worth of gold from the Bank of England *and* replaces it with a pile of old rubbish? I ask you.'

Cameron Bell beheld the pile of old rubbish. For such indeed it was, being comprised of numerous mouldy bananas, a bedpan and other sundry items.

Mr Bell picked up a small pair of trousers with a strange snood affair at the rear.

'Perhaps they tunnelled in somewhere,' said the chief inspector. 'Why are you grinning like *that*, Mr Bell?'

And Mr Bell *was* grinning, for he had come to a most surprising – but wholly accurate – conclusion regarding precisely how this had been done.

'Might I ask,' said he, 'who owned the gold that was taken?'

'The foundries and builders and suchlike who constructed the Grand Exposition. It was all built at Lord Brentford's expense, you know.'

'Bravo, Darwin,' said Mr Cameron Bell.

'What did you say?' asked Chief Inspector Case.

'Nothing,' said Cameron Bell.

'So what do you propose to do now?'

'Nothing,' said Cameron Bell.

'*Nothing?*' asked Chief Inspector Case.

'Nothing at all,' said Cameron Bell. 'For now. We will solve this crime in January next year.'

'But this is the Crime of the Century!' protested the chief inspector.

'And as you so rightly said, you cannot have two Crimes of the Century in the same century, so I propose that we leave this vault and quietly close the door behind us. Then you can take all the credit for solving it *next* year. When it will be the Crime of the Coming Century.'

'Well, blow me down,' said Chief Inspector Case. 'Do you think it will earn me another knighthood?'

'You will probably receive the Order of the Garter.'

Chief Inspector Case was grinning now. 'Let me buy you lunch, Mr Bell,' he said.

Darwin and Lord Brentford stood within the vast and echoing atrium of the Grand Exposition, where the gigantic arched roof of glass dwindled into great distances, an ornate fountain played and five thousand seats were arrayed before the stage of the concert hall.

'It is all complete now,' said Lord Brentford.

Darwin looked up at his lordship, then reached up and clasped him by the hand.

'It is a wonderful thing,' said Darwin. 'A beautiful thing. I hope that it is everything you wished for and that it becomes a symbol of peace between the planets.'

Lord Brentford looked down at his monkey butler. 'This could not have come to pass had it not been for you,' he said. 'I would be in my grave now and this might never have happened.'

'I am very happy I could help,' said Darwin.

Lord Brentford gave the little hand a gentle squeeze. 'Let me take you to lunch,' he said, 'at Patrick's Flaming Chickens.'

'Might I have a chair to sit on this time?' Darwin asked.

'A chair with cushions and a bottle of bubbly to share between just the two of us?'

'I would like that very much,' said Darwin.

50

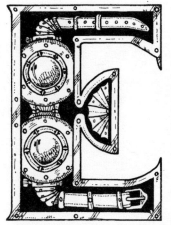very passing day brought news of the Wonders of the Worlds. The papers spoke of very little else. The three glazed halls were now complete and marvels moved by land and sea and air towards the Empire's heart.

Nightly the music halls sounded with songs about the Grand Exposition. The one crooned by 'Topical' Ted McCready was typical of their kind.

WON'T IT BE GRAND AT THE GRAND EXPOSITION?

From India, I hear, there comes an automated elephant
That can carry hunters on a grand shikar.
From China there comes china
And from South of Carolina
A set of clockwork minstrels, most harmonious to hear.

The Czar of all the Russias sends an animated egg
That can walk and talk and dance and sing.

The Rajah of Beirut
Has sent a most surprising suit
That is sewn together from one hundred miles of string.

From Africa, I've heard there comes a diamond
That's easily the size of my old head.
Some umbrellas from Tibet
To keep you dry if it gets wet
Or a handy hat from Harrods, if you fancy that instead.

Soooooooooooooooooooooooo—
Won't it be grand at the Grand Exposition?
Won't there be wonders on view?
With every appliance
A marvel of science
And big bowls of Jovian stew.

Won't there be things to amaze us?
And won't there be plenty to do?
Yes, won't it be grand at the Grand Exposition
If I'm going there with you.

Darwin and Lord Brentford now attended daily, with his lordship directing the setting up and installation of all the marvellous things.

On a morning in late December, Darwin watched in considerable awe and trepidation as an airship spanning a goodly portion of London sky arrived with a Martian spacecraft slung beneath it. A rather spiffing spacecraft, this, all polished enamel and burnished new chrome. A spacecraft that was named the *Marie Lloyd*.

Darwin shivered, for he knew that one day he would die aboard this spacecraft.

'Mr Rutherford's time-ship,' said Lord Brentford to his ape. 'The very symbol of England's scientific prowess. How fitting that a ship of war should become a ship of peace. Assuming that it works, of course. But that's another matter.'

Darwin looked on as roof sections slid aside upon hidden hydraulics and the *Marie Lloyd* was lowered into the great glazed building.

'A special treat for you this afternoon, my boy.' Lord Brentford patted Darwin on his little hairy head. 'The orchestra and chorus will be rehearsing Beethoven's Ninth Symphony under the baton of the Italian Master Arturo Toscanini. Small invited audience. You'll have a seat at the front.'

Darwin knew little of classical music. It was mostly beyond his understanding, but much of what he had heard, he liked. And some of what he had heard that he liked had moved him very much.

It was a well-dressed Darwin who at two that afternoon was to be found in the concert hall of the Grand Exposition, standing proudly beside Lord Brentford as the nobleman welcomed the specially invited audience.

Darwin was pleasantly surprised by the arrival of his old friends Lord George Fox, his wife Lady Ada and their son, the Honourable Connor. Darwin fell to the shaking of Lord George's hand and did not mind overmuch when young Connor gave his tail a hearty tug.

Darwin now saw many familiar faces and he recalled most ruefully where he had seen them before. They had all been guests at Lord Brentford's soirée on that fateful night when the older Darwin had crashed the *Marie Lloyd* into the Bananary.

When all were seated and coughings concluded, Arturo

Toscanini, in velvet tailcoat, white tie, waistcoat and mittens (for it *was* December and there were some problems with the heating), mounted the conductor's rostrum and addressed the audience.

'Good people,' said he, in those Italian tones that set a fair lady's heart all a-flutter, 'it is my deepest pleasure that we perform for you this afternoon – the Glorious Ninth.'

The orchestra numbered one hundred and twenty, the choir two hundred more, and as the great conductor took up the baton and brought the orchestra into the first movement, Darwin found *his* little heart a-fluttering.

Such music he had never heard, nor had such music ever played in such a setting.

The *allegro ma non troppo* of the first movement, in sonata form and played *pianissimo* above string tremolos, curled in orchestrated waves throughout the mighty building, swirling towards the low bassoon that brought it to its close.

The tears were already in Darwin's eyes and he clutched the hand of Lord Brentford.

An hour and a half later, folk drifted from the concert hall, mounted into their carriages and were driven away up the Mall. Lord Brentford and Darwin emerged and Lord Brentford said, 'Words are not really sufficient to express it, are they, Darwin, my boy?'

The monkey butler shook his head. 'I had no idea that such beauty could exist,' he replied.

'Just wait until you hear it again in a couple of weeks, when it opens the Grand Exposition.'

'A couple of weeks?' said Darwin wistfully. 'I had not realised that it was quite so soon.'

And yet it was. And as the two looked off along the Mall in the direction of Buckingham Palace, they could see the arrival of high-sided Jovian cheese wagons bearing their pungent cargoes towards the Hall of Jupiter where jolly men from this swollen world were setting up their stalls.

'Still much to be done,' said Lord Brentford, 'and much more yet to arrive. We will leave the installation of the Venusian exhibit until the very last minute. Don't want any accidents, or anything going wrong.'

Darwin nodded his hairy little head and trembled just a little. It would be a while before he got over the Ninth, if indeed ever he did.

'Cold, boy?' asked Lord Brentford. 'It is rather nippy. Come up here inside me coat, it's nice and warm in there.'

Cameron Bell had attended the concert, though Darwin had not seen him. The detective had hidden himself away at the back of the hall and tried to picture how things would be upon the opening night. A special royal box had been raised to the rear of the concert hall and Mr Bell sat beneath this. There was much ado in the papers about Mr Churchill's 'Ring of Steel' that would protect the royal person, the concert-goers and indeed the entire building from the un-welcome attentions of the anarchists. Mr Churchill's vigil-ance was nonpareil, the papers said, and nothing whatsoever of evil intent would ever slip by him.

Cameron Bell offered up a sigh to this statement. As he had managed to enter the concert hall this afternoon without so much as showing his ticket.

Mr Bell studied a plan of the Grand Exposition and hoped against hope that he would be able to resolve matters with-out the employment of dynamite.

Miss Violet Wond had not attended the concert, although Darwin had sent out an invitation to 'Mr Rutherford and guest'. The veiled lady was engaged in a vigorous exercise regime to re-tone muscles made lax by her hospital stay. To the vast dismay of the broken-nosed and brutish, she lifted weights in a Whitechapel Boxing Club and took on all-comers for sport.

Lavinia Dharkstorrm had suffered considerable damage. She had lost an ear, shot from her head by Lady Raygun whilst she was taking the fearsome shape of a lion. And she had lost too a great deal of hair, burned away in the conflagration at the Palace of Magic. Repeated blows to the chin had fractured her jawbone and her sister had stamped very hard on her foot, breaking three of her toes.

Lavinia Dharkstorrm fumed away in a very secret place and vowed to take terrible revenge.

Leah the Venusian had, to Lord Brentford's deep sorrow, declined his invitation to attend the Ninth's rehearsal. She had things to do, she told the noble lord.

In a gown that was as wisps of frozen smoke, she stood before a council of senior ecclesiastics within the Venusian Embassy.

'Leah d'relh, of Northern Rimmer, Magonia, you come before us with a strange request.' A gaunt and graceful being with pinnacles of snow-white hair addressed the beautiful creature. 'It is your request that you be permitted to marry an Earther.'

Rumblings and mumblings met with this disclosure.

A lofty Venusian muttered, 'Blasphemy.'

'I do this for love,' said Leah, 'and love should know no worldly barriers.'

'You are young,' said the gaunt and graceful one, 'and

have no true understanding of love. Nor do you fully comprehend the gravity of your proposal.'

'Then I would be grateful to receive such knowledge,' said Leah.

'Please understand,' said the senior ecclesiastic, 'that we Venusians are of the First Race. We are racially pure. Our world is as Eden because we have maintained our purity. The people of Earth are warlike and crass. They are little more than barbarians. We tolerate them for now, but should they ever threaten our people, we would have no compunction in destroying them all.'

'In fact,' said another, 'our tolerance may very soon be at an end. There are signs and portents in the Heavens. The Thames has run with blood and frogs have fallen from the sky. Our seers tell us that great evil is poised to strike upon this beastly world. Should this occur, we will have no choice but to erase this planet from the solar system.'

'That you must not do!' cried Leah. 'That is surely evil.'

'To protect what is pure and unsullied can never be classed as evil. Should we have to destroy every being in this family of planets that is impure, so must it be.'

'The Jovians, too?' asked Leah.

'Gourmands and crapulous fools.'

'They are a merry people,' said Leah, 'to be sure.'

Another ecclesiastic spoke. 'Soon,' this being said, 'at the stroke of midnight upon the final day of this planet's current century, there will be a great planetary alignment such as will never again be known for many thousands of years. It is predicted that the great evil, in the form of Pestilence and Terrible Darkness, the Death of the First-Born and the rise of the Christian Antichrist, will occur at this moment. If this happens as predicted, we will purge the other planets from above by the power of Venusian magic, and our race will remain alone in this solar system. So shall it be.'

Tears rose into the golden eyes of Leah the Venusian. Her plans for a January wedding would probably have to be shelved.

The Lady Beast and female Antichrist, Princess Pamela, also known as Madam Glory, lay upon velvet cushions, filling her face with chocolate.

She inhabited a comfortable room with a view in a fashionable hotel. This hotel stood upon the seashore. The shore of the Sea of Tranquillity. This hotel stood on the Moon. The view from the window was of Earth.

'I shall redecorate *that*,' said Princess Pamela, pointing with a languid hand towards the planet. 'When I am in total control, all things will be different. And I'll get rid of all that boyish blue and colour the whole thing pink.'

Planet Earth rolled on through space.

Difficult times lay ahead.

51

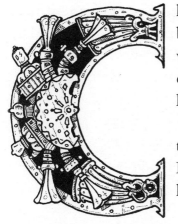hristmas came and Christmas went, but not without its magic. Darwin woke early on Christmas morning, eager to see what Santa Claus had left inside his stocking.

Three bananas, a bottle of Château Doveston and two of Lord Brentford's finest cigars, the monkey butler was pleased to see.

Pleased too was he when, upon reaching his bedroom window, he found himself looking at Fairyland beyond. Snow had fallen in the night, clothing the banana plantations with white and bringing that special enchantment only snow can bring.

Lord Brentford was out upon business for the Grand Exposition. The boy named Jack and the cook raised by kiwi birds had gone home to their respective mothers. But for Darwin, only the maid both spare and kempt remained to enjoy the day.

They dined together in the kitchen, pulled crackers and put on paper hats.

'Why is it that you never speak?' asked Darwin.

The maid got up and brought the Christmas pudding.

Then she tuned in the brand-new Tesla wireless set and together they listened to Queen Victoria's speech.

The Queen, it appeared, was really rather jolly. She wished her subjects greetings of the season, then spoke of how she was looking forward to the great Grand Exposition, and how the British Empire would face the coming century with hope in its heart, fire in its belly and love for its fellow beings, no matter what planet they hailed from. She talked a little about what she referred to as 'hard love' and how you sometimes had to be cruel to be kind and how, if needs must, love and kindness sometimes had to be enforced by men-at-arms.

Then a choir at the palace sang 'Jerusalem' and that was the end of the broadcast for the day.

Darwin smoked a Christmas cigar, was only a little bit sick and then had an early night.

As New Year's Eve dawned upon Albion, there were great goings-on in Syon House.

'Help me do up me tie,' said Lord Brentford to Darwin, 'then put me cufflinks in for me, if you will.'

There would be several changes of clothes today for Lord Brentford: the morning suit, the afternoon 'smart' and the evening formal with the tails. The maid both spare and kempt was dressed for the outing, as were the chef and the boy named Jack, for Lord Brentford felt that his servants should not miss a bit of the day.

As Darwin slotted a cufflink with a Masonic motif into his lordship's celluloid cuff, he worried for the day ahead. There were so many things that might go wrong, when they should go wonderfully right.

The snow was still thick upon the ground and they were

all wrapped up in their warmest of coats as they climbed into an electric landau and were driven off to the palace.

Crowds were milling up and down the Mall. The Grand Exposition halls sparkled, lit by more than one million neon tubes, diamond-hung and crystal-webbed with snow. From the Mall the crowds caught tantalising glimpses of the wonders that awaited them within. The burnished brass of mighty engines. Marvellous artworks gathered from around the globe. Delicious and enchanting smells drifted from the Jovian food hall, but a single hall remained unlit and empty.

Lord Brentford helped the maid both spare and kempt down from the landau. The boy named Jack looked up at Buckingham Palace. 'Well, toast my todger,' he said to Darwin. 'Are we truly going to meet the Queen?'

Darwin nodded and took Jack by the arm. 'She's rather plump and silly,' he said, 'but she does have a lovely monkey maid called Emily.'

Queen Victoria offered Lord Brentford her gloved hand to be kissed. Lord Brentford did as a gentleman should and kissed it. Jack was prepared to give that a go, but Queen Victoria did not acknowledge someone else's servants. She petted Caruthers, her augmented kiwi bird.

'We have so enjoyed the nothingness,' she told the noble lord. 'The more one looks, the more one sees. We never knew there was so much to nothing.'

Lord Brentford bowed towards his monarch. 'So pleased that it amused you, ma'am,' said he, 'but now it must be taken over the road to the Hall of Venus.

'But one can have it back afterwards, can't one?'

Lord Brentford grinned through his teeth at this and

offered something that might have been construed as a kind of a nod.

'Your lady from Venus is playing with one's monkey,' said Queen Victoria, and she clapped her hands. 'Come, Emily,' she called.

Darwin looked on eagerly, straightened his shoulders, thrust out his chest and tried most hard to look noble.

Emily appeared in the company of Leah the Venusian.

Lord Brentford gazed longingly at Leah.

Darwin smiled towards Emily.

Leah, in her gown like frozen smoke, her high-heeled shoes of sanctity click-clacking on the tiled floor, smiled warmly on Lord Brentford and gave little Darwin a wave. Emily fluttered her eyelashes.

Darwin felt the day was going well so far.

'We must take the Sphere of Nothingness to the Venusian Hall,' Lord Brentford said to Leah, 'if you would be so kind.'

'I will.' Leah approached the sphere of nothing at all. 'Those who wish to, follow me.'

Her long fingers wove strange patterns in the air and the Sphere of Nothingness moved weightlessly before her.

Cameron Bell had moved from his lodgings. He had become wary, lest those he sought to attack might first attack him. He had put into place during the final few weeks of the year a number of 'set pieces' in the hope that every eventuality might be catered for when the Final Conflict occurred, but he was far from confident that he had covered everything.

That no further plagues had struck at London puzzled Mr Bell. He had expected at the very least the Pestilence. There should have been animals, too – rats, perhaps. But whatever the case, he felt certain that a Terrible Darkness would precipitate the Death of the First-Born. The latter being something that he intended to avert.

He had resolved that his strongest strategy lay in the defence of the monarch. Princess Pamela, the Lady Beast, would certainly seek to destroy her in order to take her throne.

So Her Majesty must live at all costs.

Cameron Bell had met with Winston Churchill, but the young, ambitious gentleman was having none of Mr Bell's talk of a coming Apocalypse. He dealt in straightforward matters, he told the detective in no uncertain terms. Anarchists were the number-one threat and he had stratagems of his own to prevent them from attacking the Queen.

Cameron Bell sought elsewhere for allies.

And found them in a most unlikely place.

The Sphere of Nothingness hung in place within the Hall of Venus.

The hall itself was otherwise empty, the vast space adding to the drama of the single exhibit. A mosaic floor had, however, been patterned with swirling pathways that those who came to view the wonder might follow.

Darwin and Emily, frolicking together upon the high gantries that ran along the inside of the great arched roof, did not recognise these pathway patterns to be the thing they were – a representation of the lines on the Nazca Plains, which some claimed to be the fingerprint of God.

Leah's hand reached out to touch that of Lord Brentford. 'I am afeared,' she said to him, 'that a terrible evil will shortly come upon this world.'

'Feel just a tad uneasy myself,' said his lordship. 'Probably just first-night nerves, though. All will be well, have no fear of that.'

Leah turned her golden eyes towards the man she loved. A man born upon Earth, a man whom the laws of Venus forbade her even so much as to touch. 'If all is well,' she said, 'if we survive—'

'Survive, my dear? We will survive, I assure you.'

'Then if we do, I would ask—' Leah paused.

Lord Brentford smiled upon her. 'I was waiting for a special moment,' said he, 'to ask *you* something. And this moment feels rather special to me. Just the two of us, alone, amongst all of this nothing.'

Lord Brentford dug into a pocket. Brought out a little red box. 'It was my mother's,' he said. 'My father gave it to her.' He opened the box to display a golden ring with an intricate setting that held a large and sparkling solitary diamond.

Lord Brentford went down upon one knee. 'Will you marry me, Leah?' he asked.

On high two monkeys engaged in monkey business.

Below, Leah said, 'I will.'

Mr Ernest Rutherford had been looking for an opportunity to pop the all-important question to Miss Violet Wond, but of late Miss Wond had been a most elusive creature. There had been long and unexplained absences and periods of silence while they dined together. The chemist felt perhaps his cause was lost.

He had been invited to the concert and official opening of the Grand Exposition that would follow it and Miss Wond had agreed to accompany him. But the veiled lady had not been the same since the night when she had been attacked. And Mr Rutherford felt a great unease.

Her Majesty the Queen was rarely given to unease. A monarch's life did not include such feelings. A monarch had things done for them, was flattered, pampered, praised and shown every kindness. That was the way it should be, for a monarch.

Shortly before three of the afternoon clock, the royal state coach, with all its rococo golden cherubic adornments, drew up outside Buckingham Palace to receive the royal personage and transport her halfway down the Mall to the entrance of the Grand Exposition.

Because if one is the monarch and one has allowed the biggest exhibition hall ever to be built in the history of the world to be erected in one's own front garden of Green Park, then one should get the first look around it when it's finished.

And if there is anything in there that one *really really* wants . . .

Then one should be given it, without any question at all.

Mr Winston Churchill watched through field glasses as the royal state coach left the grounds of Buckingham Palace. He watched from an airship high above, from which he was directing operations. Before the front façade of the Grand Exposition, soldiers of the Queen stood to attention, shoulder to shoulder the very length of the Mall. A regiment of cavalry were quartered to the rear of the great building. Thirty Mark 5 Juggernaut Tanks stood in Trafalgar Square, snipers rested on rooftops, and well dug-in and all around and about anti-airship gunners employing the very latest in back-engineered Martian death-ray technology aimed the snouts of the terror weapons towards the skies above.

Skies of blue without a cloud in sight.

Planet Earth bulged big and blue in a sky of forever night. Upon the Moon in her hotel room, Princess Pamela's personal primper pampered the Lady Beast.

'Lavinia!' called the princess. 'Where art thou, lass?'

Lavinia Dharkstorrm entered the room in a black silk gown, with a black silk hat and a black silk corset, too.

'Thou art pretty as a picture,' quoth the Lady Beast. 'All dressed up for a coronation, yes?'

Lavinia Dharkstorrm nodded and attended to details of dress.

'Art thou strong with spells today?' the princess asked of her.

Lavinia Dharkstorrm nodded once again.

Princess Pamela glanced towards the ormolu mantel clock. 'Our transportation will be 'ere shortly,' she said.

'Private space yacht?' asked Lavinia Dharkstorrm.

Princess Pamela laughed at this. 'Somewhat more than *that*. A new Queen 'as to make a royal entrance. But 'appen,' she said, and she pointed to the window, ' 'ere comes transport now.'

From out of the darkness of the sky something large appeared. Something more than large, indeed, for now as it approached the Moon it threw the planet Earth into eclipse.

Down it drifted, huge and untoward and very pink.

Princess Pamela clapped her hands as onto the Sea of Tranquillity settled her floating palace from Mars.

52

ueen Victoria thought it grand to be at the Grand Exposition and was most amused by almost everything she saw. She greatly admired the animated elephant and the Czar of Russia's automated egg. She considered the clockwork minstrels particularly harmonious and the hardy hat from Harrods a worthy thing indeed.

When it came to the diamond from Russia that was easily the size of a music hall entertainer's head, she all but squealed with delight. She was not, however, at all taken with the suit sewn from one hundred miles of string. This left her singularly unamused.

Lord Brentford drew her attention to Mr Rutherford's time-ship, which stood with its ports wide open to display its inner gubbinry.

'Ma'am,' said he, bowing low to the monarch. 'This craft bears testimony to the genius of your subjects and it is hoped will bring everlasting peace between the planets. For, I am sure you will agree, the Empire that is the master of time must surely become the master of all.'

Leah was not present to hear this remark, but Lord Brentford had phrased it in such a way purely to please the Queen.

'What is it that one sniffs?' enquired Her Majesty. 'Does one smell Jovian hotpot?'

The party processed to the Jovian food hall for tea.

All over London, in swank hotels and the houses of the wealthy, folk were preparing themselves. Folk of substance. Off-world princes. Senior ecclesiastics of the Venusian high elite. Burghers and barons of Jupiter. Lords and ladies of the British Empire. Members of Parliament. Famous writers and musicians, artists and actors. The great and the good. The high and the mighty. The Laird of Dunoon and some of the clergy, too.

Never before had so many high-born and influential people gathered together in a single place. There would be at least five hundred Venusians attending the opening concert, plus as many Jovians and some two thousand humans.

The owners of the banking houses of all worlds would be present. Admirals and generals and the wing commander of the Aerial Armed Forces. Representatives of every royal household. The cream of high society. The very pride of the planets.

The hoi polloi could wait until the morrow.

Tonight, the Grand Exposition belonged to the favoured few.

At six o'clock, Queen Victoria, sagging somewhat from a surfeit of Jovian cuisine, was returned to her royal state coach and in that to the palace.

'Time marches on,' said Lord Brentford to Darwin. 'I think we should take an early supper and return at eight to welcome in the guests.'

Darwin nodded in agreement to this.

'So you will now have to stop doing what you have been doing all afternoon to that lady monkey.'

Darwin nodded once again. But now with far less enthusiasm.

Arturo Toscanini was never less than enthusiastic, and as he bathed in the large marble bathtub in his swanky room at the Ritz, in the company of two lady viola players, he felt convinced that tonight would be the triumph of his career. It certainly had to be a triumph of split-second timing, that was indisputable, because he had been told in no uncertain terms by no lesser personage than the Prime Minister of England that the symphony must conclude upon the very stroke of midnight, when every church bell in every tower in the land would chime in the coming century.

But he could do that. For after all, was he not the greatest conductor in the world? Indeed, in this world *and* the others! He would conduct some of the finest music ever composed before an audience the like of which had never before been brought together.

The musicians were ready. He was ready. Tonight would be a truly religious experience.

Chapter Thirteen, verse one of the Book of Revelation speaks of the Beast that will rise up from the sea, having seven heads and ten horns, and upon the horns ten crowns, and upon the heads the name of blasphemy. What much of that means is naturally open to interpretation, but what is definitely certain is that there *is* a Beast and it *does* rise up from the sea.

As Princess Pamela's palace rose from the Sea of Tranquillity, it did at least fulfil this particular piece of biblical prophecy.

'Set a course for Earth, Mister Mate,' said the princess in pink, upon high in the wheelhouse. 'Take us to t' Grand Exposition.'

'Aye aye, Cap'n,' replied Mister Mate. 'We'll have you there before the stroke of midnight.'

Lavinia Dharkstorrm paced about the bridge.

'Be still, lass,' said the Lady Beast. 'Thou drivest me to the foot of our stairs. Whatever the 'eck that meaneth.'

'I am eager that we be done with them all,' said Lavinia Dharkstorrm. 'My sister, that detective, all of them.'

'Not too keen on me *own* sister.' Princess Pamela made a sour face. 'Mark my words, I'll 'ave 'er 'ead upon a platter by morning.'

Mister Mate said, 'Madam, might I speak?'

'As thou wish,' said the princess.

'I just have a question regarding my status,' said Mister Mate.

Princess Pamela shrugged. 'Go on,' said she.

'As a "Mister Mate", would I be regarded as a minion rather than a henchman?'

'I carest nowt,' said the princess in pink. 'What of it?'

'You see Herbert here?' Mister Mate gestured towards Herbert, who fluttered his fingers at Princess Pamela and Lavinia Dharkstorrm. 'Herbert is the cabin boy. So lowly a fellow, in fact, that had I not drawn your attention to his presence, you probably would not even have noticed him.'

''Appen not,' said Princess Pamela. Lavinia Dharkstorrm shrugged.

'But I am several places up from him in the pecking order,' said Mister Mate. 'I have a special Mister Mate's Certificate.'

'Wouldn't 'ave 'ired thee otherwise.' Princess Pamela folded her arms.

'So I think I should be classified as a henchman.'

Lavinia Dharkstorrm shook her head. 'Your duties are not those of a henchman,' she said. 'Have you ever engaged in cold-blooded murder, the propagation of mayhem, the defilement of the innocent—'

'The needless slaughter of small woodland creatures,' Princess Pamela suggested.

'Never,' said Mister Mate. 'But I am anxious to give my all in such evil endeavours.'

'If I might interject,' said Herbert, 'the *Oxford English Dictionary* defines a henchman as a faithful attendant or supporter. I suspect that you hanker more towards becoming a recidivist or scapegrace. Or indeed a tergiversant or malefactor.'

'If I kill the cabin boy now and serve him up for dinner,' said Mister Mate, 'can I be raised in status to henchman?'

'I'll give thee the loan o' me axe,' said the princess. 'And if thou doest well, I'll make thee Prime Minister of England tomorrow.'

The present Prime Minister was having words with Mr Churchill. Snow was falling heavily down upon Old London Town. The two men stood together in the atrium of the Grand Exposition, watching as the white flakes slid from the arched roof high above to settle upon the ranks of soldiers standing stiffly to attention far below.

'I require your assurance, Mr Churchill,' said the Prime Minister, accepting an offered cigar, 'that everything will go precisely as planned and that Her Majesty is in no danger from these fearful anarchists.'

Winston Churchill lit the Prime Minister's cigar. 'My Lord,' said he, 'you have my word. It would take Lucifer himself to puncture my ring of steel.'

The Prime Minister sucked hard upon Mr Churchill's cigar.

'As long as your ring goes unpunctured,' he said, 'we will all sleep well in our beds.'

Lord Brentford had his own bedroom at Claridge's and he had booked a table for three in the restaurant.

At this table sat his lordship, with Leah to the left of him and Darwin to the right.

'My boy,' said Lord Brentford to his monkey butler as a waiter danced champagne into glasses, 'Leah and I have something to tell you.'

Leah smiled rather coyly. Darwin scratched at his head.

'We are to be married,' said Lord Brentford.

Darwin raised a mighty smile. 'I am so happy for you,' said his lordship's ape.

'And there is something that we would like to ask you.'

Darwin tucked a napkin into his wing-collared shirt and prepared to make an assault upon a crusty roll.

'We would like you to be our best man,' said Lord Brentford. 'Or in your case, best monkey-man.'

Darwin's eyes grew wonderfully wide. 'Ai, ai, ai. Oh, what an honour,' he said.

'Might have to be something of a private affair,' said Lord Brentford, passing out the champagne. 'Leah's family not too keen on the idea. Might have to slip away somewhere. We thought perhaps Jupiter. They have a gambling city there where you can get married by a chap dressed up as Enrico Caruso. They even throw in something called a stretch-landau to take you to the ceremony.'

'All sounds rather fun,' said Darwin. 'Do pardon me while I behave badly with this roll.'

'You've been behaving badly all afternoon,' observed

430

Lord Brentford. 'Will you be doing the right and proper thing with that monkey maid?'

'Alas, no,' said Darwin, crunching messily and noisily upon his crusty roll. 'We were but ships that passed in the night, never destined to share moorings in the harbour of love.'

Lord Brentford raised an eyebrow.

'I could have put it differently,' said Darwin, 'but there *is* a lady present.'

Lord Brentford raised his champagne glass in toast. 'To you, Leah, my love,' said he. 'And to Darwin, loyal servant and friend. No man is there more blessed than I to share such company.'

Champagne glasses touched one to another and, within that candlelit room, Darwin felt both warm and happy. Perhaps, indeed, more happy than he had ever felt before. Because, after all, he *had* saved the Great Exposition, he *had* made love to a most attractive ape this afternoon, he *was* to be Lord Brentford's best monkey-man, he *was* enjoying a champagne dinner at Claridge's and *would soon be* going on to delight in the most lavish performance of Beethoven's Ninth ever staged.

Things had not worked out too badly at all for Darwin.

The monkey butler grinned and drank champagne.

A champagne reception awaited the favoured few thousand who would attend the concert and official opening of the Grand Exposition, and by eight o'clock the Mall began to fill with their conveyances.

There was a busyness of broughams and buckboards and britzkas,
A gathering of gharries and growlers and gigs,
A cavalcade of carriages and curricles and carioles,

Horse cabs and hansom cabs,
Landaus and landaulettes,
Four-in-hands and phaetons
And two enormous pigs.*

As the Poetry Columnist of *The Times* so pleasantly put it. Before hurrying off to the warmth of an alehouse as he had not been granted a concert ticket.

And so they came, these well-tailored men with their well-tended wives. These princes and potentates. These captains of industry. These builders of Empire. Lord Babbage and Lord Tesla were to be seen, and Ernest Rutherford, too, smiling hugely in the company of a veiled lady all in black. Flash pans flared with phosphorous as photographers of the nation's press sought to capture this moment of moments for posterity.

A string quartet played within and the fountain gushed champagne. Jovian savouries were freighted around upon silver trays. Polite conversation fluttered as ladies peeped modestly from behind their winter fans. A monkey butler shared a joke with another of his kind. Neon lights illuminated a palace of wonders.

Lord Brentford greeted each and every guest.

The snow drifted down without.

And within, all appeared just as it should be with the noble British Empire.

---

* *Harnessed to the coach of Cardinal Cox, the controversial cleric.*

53

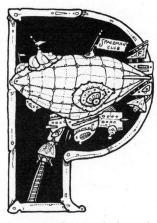rincess Pamela dined upon haunch of cabin boy and Mister Mate was elevated to the rank of henchman. There were many henchmen aboard the Lady Beast's pink palace. Many troops, as it were, prepared to fight and die if necessary to protect their royal ruler. They were generally liveried in uniforms of pink, but upon this special occasion they had been informed that the dress code was *pirate*.

For, as the princess knew, as indeed do all women, every man yearns to dress sometimes as a pirate.

Planet Earth filled more and more of the Heavens.

The palace with its pirate crew sailed on.

Time marched on in the palace of glass. Folk dilly-dallied and sauntered about, viewing the wonders, pointing and cooing, ladies svelte with fluttering fans and gentlemen with cigars.

Ernest Rutherford was conducting tours around his timeship. The Jovian ambassador, his wife and large extended family waddled from exhibit to exhibit, chuckling merrily at all they beheld. Aloof effete Venusians talked amongst themselves and feigned uninterest in everything. Leah enjoined in their conversation, which dwelt upon lofty matters, but she was aware that a tension existed as the planets drew into their fateful alignment and the time of the prophesied tribulation drew ever closer.

At ten o'clock an announcement echoed from the brass bells of numerous electric speakers, to the effect that tonight's performance of Beethoven's Ninth Symphony, conducted by Arturo Toscanini, would shortly begin, so would the honoured guests kindly take their seats in the concert hall.

Lord Brentford had undoubtedly had a lot on his plate, with so very much to organise. The numbering of seats in the concert hall and the scrupulous allocation of tickets was something that had simply slipped his mind. This oversight on his part had not, however, gone unnoticed by the three thousand honoured guests who, at the clarion call to the concert hall, pressed forward in a most unruly mob, each determined to grab the finest seats.

There was some unpleasantness.

Order was finally restored when Lord Brentford summonsed the assistance of armed and snow-covered soldiers, who fixed bayonets and prepared to stick them into anyone who exhibited anything less than decorum.

When all were seated peaceably, a new announcement came through the brass-bell speakers that Her Majesty Queen Victoria, Empress of both India and Mars, was about to take her seat in the royal box.

So, would they all stand up again?

Her Majesty tonight wore the very latest in blacks, the very chicest frock of black stuff and that jaunty crown. The crown, however, rested somewhat heavily upon the royal brow as it had most recently received the extra adornment of a diamond, from Africa, that was easily the size of a music hall performer's head.

Her Majesty was accompanied by her monkey maid Emily, her augmented kiwi bird Caruthers, the designer of the royal frocks – Lady Elsie Grover – and a big-game-hunting friend of the royal household – Major Thadeus Tinker.

Respectful applause rippled up from the auditorium. Lord Brentford proposed three cheers for the regal lady and these in turn echoed about within the great concert hall.

Queen Victoria waved to the assembly, sat herself down, ordered champagne and petted her kiwi bird. All others present took their seats and whispered words of greatest expectation.

Upon the stage before them, the virtuoso musicians of the London Philharmonic Orchestra, in formal dress of white tie and tails, filed to their places and bowed their heads to the rapturous applause they received.

Then came the choir, two hundred strong, ladies in angelic white, gentlemen in black. The soloists took their special bows, then the heads of all upon the stage swung to the left to acknowledge the world-famous conductor Arturo Toscanini as he made his entrance. In truth, he looked a little tired, as if he had perhaps been overexerting himself during the afternoon. But he smiled warmly as the audience clapped their hands and rattled their jewellery and he did look very smart indeed.

He bowed to the audience, turned and bowed to the orchestra and choir, then raised his baton high and the Ninth began.

The music, swelling from the great glass-covered hall beneath, reached faintly to the ears of Winston Churchill. He stood upon the foredeck of the airship that swung in great arcs to and fro above the Grand Exposition, a cigar aglow between his teeth, an army greatcoat muffling his slender body from the cold winter's night. Snow fluttered freely around and about and Mr Churchill's mittened hands brought his field glasses once more to his eyes.

His youthful adjutant Pooley brought Mr Churchill a nice hot cup of cocoa.

'This will keep the cold out, sir,' said he. 'Nothing like a nice hot cuppa to blow away the chills.'

'You are a buffoon,' said Mr Churchill, but he accepted the cuppa nonetheless.

'Do you really think we'll be in for trouble tonight, sir?' Pooley asked. 'I'd rather be in the pub, if truth be told.'

'If there be anarchists,' said Mr Churchill, sipping cocoa, 'we will fight them in the pubs, and in the carriage parks, and in the tea rooms and on the Clapham omnibus. We shall never, ever give in.'

'May I quote you on that, sir?' asked the adjutant.

'I am still working on it,' said Mr Churchill. And then he flicked something from his mitten. 'What is *that*?' he asked.

The adjutant stared in what light there was. 'Looks like a spot of blood,' said he.

'Do you have a nosebleed?' asked Mr Winston Churchill.

'Certainly not, sir. Not allowed on duty.'

'Well, it certainly looks like— Damn me, there's another one.'

Another one there was indeed and then another and another.

'It is the snow,' the adjutant cried. 'The snow is turning red.'

★

436

A cardinal dressed all in red sat to the rear of the concert hall beneath the royal box. He tapped his slippered feet in time to the music and occasionally patted his catamite upon the knee. Cardinal Cox, for it was he, was dressed tonight in his very finest vestments, hand-tailored by his personal Piccadilly fitter and sewn with many extra adornments. High at the collar, broad at the shoulder, pinched in tightly at the waist, he cut the most dapper of dashes. The cardinal drew out his pocket watch. Its face displayed a portrait of the Pope. The watch's hands had been imaginatively fashioned to resemble the arms and hands of the pontiff. At twelve o'clock he raised both hands in benediction, although at half-past six, he appeared to be engaged in something rather rude.

Mostly this watch made the cardinal smile. But he smiled not this evening. 'The time draws near,' he whispered to his catamite. 'Evil comes amongst us.'

Evil now fell into orbit around the planet named Earth. The flying palace, with its many pink turrets and spires, swung through space at a fair rate of knots, sailing high and mightily above the planet of blue that turned below.

'Now what be those?' asked Mister Mate, bedecked as a pirate with tricorn and britches and getting rather into the spirit of it.

'What art what?' replied the pinky princess.

'There be ships a-sailing.' Mister Mate did pointings with his cutlass.

Princess Pamela located a spyglass, bound elegantly in pink flamingo skin, and raised it to her favourite eye. Away into space white forms drifted, ghostlike fluttering forms.

'Venusian aether ships,' said Princess Pamela. 'There art a veritable armada of 'em out there.'

'Should I put a couple of rounds across their bows?' asked Mister Mate.

'No.' The princess shook her head. 'When I take my place on t' throne, they'll bow their silly 'eads same as all t' rest, or blood'll surely flow,' said Princess Pamela.

'Blood! The snow has turned to blood!' Mr Churchill's adjutant began to flap his hands and spin around in small circles.

'Cease your foolishness!' Mr Churchill used his most commanding voice. 'It will be sand from the Sahara or some such. Stay still, lad.' Mr Churchill grabbed the spinning Pooley by the scruff of the neck. 'You will behave yourself, or—'

Mr Churchill paused as the light shining up from the great halls below tinged the adjutant's face a glowing pink. But Mr Churchill saw more than this. Boils were breaking out upon young Pooley's forehead and cheeks. Boils that sprouted where the red snow had touched.

Cries and screams now came to Mr Churchill's ears, rising from the Mall and streets below.

A shout of, ' 'Tis the Pestilence!' was loudly to be heard.

But not within the concert hall of the Grand Exposition, where the red snow touched not and only beauty was to be heard. The audience, enchanted by the glorious music, sighed in their comfortable seatings, their heads bobbing gently, their spirits drifting.

Cameron Bell sat three seats along from the cardinal. He too studied the face of his pocket watch and he too feared for what might lie ahead. The nineteenth century was drawing to a close and although he was here in this wondrous building listening to music that many, including himself, considered to be amongst the highest of human achievements, the great detective felt a chill that pierced him to the bone. She was coming, he knew it, the monster, the Lady Beast. Coming to claim the throne of her sister. Coming to bring ruination to Mankind.

Could he prevent this from happening?

Would those he had urged to help fail him when he needed them the most?

Cameron's head bobbed in time to the marvellous music.

His hand gripped tightly around his pocket watch.

Princess Pamela's hands gripped tightly to the parapet of a curly-whirly tower. The princess wore a lustrous gown awash with sequins all in pink, a cloak with a collar of ermine and a mighty train that spread for many yards.

The flying palace passed into the atmosphere of Earth. Which differed but little from the all-pervading atmosphere of space, but for a smell of smoky chimneys, brass and brickwork and the scent of Man.

The Lady Beast turned up her nose at the rancid stink of Man.

'Picture it pink, lass,' she told Lavinia Dharkstorrm. 'Picture a world run by women, where men do what they art told.'

Lavinia Dharkstorrm pictured such a world. 'It would be pleasing,' she said.

The palace now dropped down towards the clouds that covered London. Clouds from which the bright red snow fell thickly.

'Stay out of the snow, lad.' Mr Churchill dragged the boil-ridden adjutant to the airship's cabin and set him down to rest. 'Call the troops below,' Mr Churchill shouted at the wireless operator. 'Tell them to shield their faces and hands and train their guns upon the sky. I fear that Cameron Bell is right – the danger comes from above.'

Down and ever downwards came the palace of the Lady Beast.

> *And there appeared a great wonder*
> *in Heaven. A woman clothed with*
> *the Sun and the Moon under her*
> *feet.*
>
> Revelation 12:1

> *And there appeared another wonder in*
> *Heaven: and behold a great red*
> *dragon with seven heads and*
> *ten horns.*
>
> Revelation 12:3

And as a great red dragon, the palace descended in silence.

As within the concert hall, the very first movement of Beethoven's Ninth came to its perfect ending.

54

ilence in the concert hall and silence now without.

Arturo Toscanini raised his baton.

Brought it down.

Began the second movement.

A movement in the Heavens drew
the attention of gunners on the
ground, gunners now sheltering
from the deadly snow. Messages
were exchanged. Mr Churchill viewed the descending palace.
Ordered the airship's captain to swing away to starboard.
Ordered the gunners on the ground to open fire upon the
massive structure dropping from on high.

Now blood-red as any dragon, down the palace came.

Bolts of deadly energy tore into the sky, flashed and burned
upon the walls of the falling bloody palace. The flashes and
explosions lit up the sky above the great arched roof of the
Grand Exposition and the concert-goers leaned back in their
seats.

A son et lumière! Fireworks to accompany the great
musical work! How fitting! How absolutely perfect!

Queen Victoria rattled her jewellery, then sipped at her champagne.

Cameron Bell rose up from his seat.

'So it begins,' he whispered.

Mr Churchill had his helmet on. He bawled instructions into the brass mouthpiece of the wireless set. The Mark 5 Juggernaut Tanks lurched into motion in Trafalgar Square, angled up their turret cannons and rolled towards the Mall.

Incendiary shells exploded about Mr Churchill's airship. Mr Churchill hurled invective into his brass mouthpiece.

The bloodstained palace drew to a halt five hundred feet above the halls of the Grand Exposition. In the throne-room on the second floor, Princess Pamela strutted to and fro before a mighty gathering of pirates, her long cloak trailing out behind, a crown upon her head.

'Lads,' cried she. 'I want thee t' go down there and give those soldiers 'ell. Many of thee won't be comin' back, but that don't matter nowt to me as I 'ave bigger things to be going on with. Dost thou all 'ave stuff to throw down?'

'Aye!' went the pirates, as pirates should, and displayed those items they had chosen for throwing down. Pointy objects, heavy things that would hurt if they fell upon your head. Pots of paint, which held to a certain humour. A baby seal and a puppy, which did *not*.

Lavinia Dharkstorrm stood in a towering turret, before her on a pedestal her silver scrying bowl. She passed her hands over the inky liquid, causing ripples and contortions on its surface.

'Let me see you, Mr Bell,' said the evil witch of a woman,

making magical passes and speaking magical words. An image swam into view of a dumpy fellow in pince-nez spectacles, a fellow who bore an uncanny resemblance to Mr Pickwick, standing to the rear of the concert hall. This fellow examined the face of his pocket watch. Examined it once, examined it again.

'Priceless,' said Lavinia, a-fluttering of her fingers. Time within the scrying bowl fled forwards. The solitary image of Cameron Bell just looked at his watch again and again and again.

'You are stuck,' said Lavinia Dharkstorrm. 'Mine to do with as I choose. You will await me there.'

She moved her hands once more over the scrying bowl. 'And where are you, my sister dear?' said she. Images of the concert audience swept across the surface of the liquid. Lavinia Dharkstorrm halted them, diddled with a finger. The face of Ernest Rutherford appeared, a face that wore an intense expression as the chemist immersed himself in the mathematical purity of the music. And beside Mr Ernest Rutherford, a lady all in black with a heavy veil.

'Wait there, little sister,' said the witch. And she poured down magic into the concert hall, securing the lady in the veil to the seat she sat upon.

The pirates poured down sticks and stones upon the troops below.

Sticks and stones and sealing wax and cabbages and kettles.

The troops responded with rifle fire, which struck a pirate here and there, tipping him from his lofty perch and sending him with speed to Jonny Jones.*

* The London-based brother of Davy.

The troll named Jones had not received an invite to the concert. Naturally he concluded that this must have been some clerical error, as one so important as he should surely have been offered a seat with a comfy cushion in the royal box. Mr Rutherford had insisted Jones drive the chemist and Miss Wond to the concert in the elegant pony trap hired specially for the occasion. The two well-dressed humans were now in the concert hall. Jones sat bitterly on the trap, collecting boils as the red snow fell upon him.

He was enjoying the gunfire, though, and he had grown quite excited a moment ago when a pirate plunged down from the sky and splattered in a gory heap a few short yards away.

The pirates on high were now firing flintlocks and muskets. But these made little impression on the convoy of Mark 5 Juggernaut Tanks, which returned fire with a most malevolent force.

Cupolas and turrets exploded, shattered and fell. The palace shook to this assault. Lavinia Dharkstorrm's scrying bowl went tumbling to the floor.

'Enough of this nonsense,' Lavinia cried. 'Men of Earth, you all will know my magic.' She strode from her turret, down spiral steps and into the royal throne-room.

Princess Pamela lazed at her dining table, sucking at the finger meat of the fresh-cooked cabin boy. A violent concussion shuddered the room, hurling a pink-framed portrait from the wall.

'They will have the palace down about our ears!' cried Lavinia Dharkstorrm. 'Let me rain down fire upon their heads.'

''Appen,' said the princess. 'Give 'em a little taste of what's to come.'

Lavinia Dharkstorrm stormed from the royal throne-room, mounted to a battlement, cast aside pirates and flung her arms aloft. Called forth words in a forbidden tongue. Conjured fire from the furnaces of Hades. Hurled it down upon the forces ranged along the Mall.

The concert-goers marvelled as the fire filled the sky. Further jewellery rattled and gentlemen did noddings of the head.

Flames swept down upon the soldiers of the Queen, wreaking terrible death and destruction. Infantrymen were sizzled black and then reduced to ashes. Drivers of Mark 5 Juggernaut Tanks sought escape as metal glowed about them.

A troll named Jones bobbed up and down in glee.

And then was gone to cinders. Just like *that*.

And just like that, Venusians in the concert hall stiffened in their seats. They were sensitive to magic and when it occurred with such force and in such close proximity, they were deeply troubled. Whispers spread amongst them.

Whispers to the effect that they should depart the Earth at once and leave its people to the untender mercies of the Venusian battle fleet that swung in a steady orbit several miles above.

'The evil must end *here*!' cried an ecclesiastic.

Concert-goers shushed at the Venusian.

'I will settle this,' said Leah, rising from her seat.

Concert-goers shushed her, too, and someone called, 'Sit *down*.'

Toscanini flourished his baton. He heard nothing at all but the Glorious Ninth.

Leah the Venusian left the concert hall.

Fire fell once more from high above.

Winston Churchill stared in horror at the massacre below. He shouted into his brazen mouthpiece, but no words were returned to him. He turned his gaze towards the floating palace, saw pirates pouring over the battlements, swarming down lines and rope ladders.

Many alighted onto the high arched roof of the Grand Exposition.

Bringing delight to the audience within.

Beethoven's Ninth *and* pirates? How could it possibly get any better than *that*?

'For better or worse, but for nothing in between.' General Albert Trubshaw rode his chestnut charger up and down before his mounted troops. A dashing chap, was Albert, in his thigh-boots and bearskin, his handlebar whiskers rising to either side of his head as noble antlers and his burnished silver codpiece capable of holding a litre of champagne. As it so often did in the officers' mess where it could not frighten the horses.

'Gentlemen.' General Albert stirred his mount with a riding crop that had reddened the buttocks of many a music hall gal. 'Gentlemen, I have just received orders from Mr Winston Churchill that he wishes us to engage the enemy. Kindly draw your sabres and put on your fiercest faces.' He made a fierce face of his own to demonstrate the look. 'Quite so. Destroy the pirate menace for the honour of the regiment. And *charge*!'

And proudly did the cavalry charge.

Only to draw up rapidly short, upon finding their way barred by dug-in anti-airship guns and a row of fresh latrines.

'And turn! And *charge*!'

To once more draw up short, their way now barred by the rear of the concert hall.

'To the right! Charge!'

To arrive at the Jovian food hall.

'Turn about and charge! And I forbid any fellow to stop!'

It was the way things should be done when it comes to bravery. The horsemen plunged forward, standards flaring out and bugles blowing. The wall of glass before them was that of the Venusian Hall. An empty hall it looked to the valiant lads.

With spurs dug in and battle cries upon their lips, they rode their spirited thoroughbreds through the plate-glass windows and into the empty hall. Horses' hooves raised sparks upon the mosaic floor which might have held the image of the fingerprint of God. They thundered around the Sphere of Nothingness, which was surrounded by a rope barrier as a safety measure to keep the public away. And then through plate-glass windows beyond, a swift left turn and out into the Mall.

The majority survived these brave advances. General Albert Trubshaw plucked a shard of glass from his left eyeball and considered just how extra-dashing and romantic he would look when sporting a black silk eyepatch.

All in black silk, though mauve of eye, the evil witch gazed down upon the destruction she had wrought and found it very pleasing to behold. The last of the pirates cheered her success before thrusting daggers between their teeth and disappearing over the battlements. Princess Pamela came to Lavinia's side.

'Nice work, lass,' said she to the woman in black. 'Ah, see, look at t' horsemen riding out.'

'Should I blast them?' asked Lavinia, raising her hands once more.

'Let pirates battle 'em. Always a guilty pleasure, watching pirates.'

Lavinia Dharkstorrm magicked up champagne.

Princess Pamela took a glass and toasted the witch with it. 'Thou art full of it tonight, lass,' said she. 'We'll 'ave a glass or two of this, then pop down and sort me sister out.'

Princess Pamela broadly grinned as glasses clinked together.

'Darwin,' whispered Lord Brentford. 'I think I heard the sound of breaking glass.'

Darwin shrugged. He really didn't care.

'Be a good boy,' said his lordship. 'Pop down towards the Venusian Hall and see if all's hunky-dunky.'

'Hunky-dunky?' queried Darwin.

'Ssssh!' went a concert-goer.

Sssssh and whoosh and wsssh and chop and slice went flashing sabres. The dashing chargers swept against the pirates. The red snow had finally eased, which meant at least that none of the riders' looks got sullied by boils.

The pirates put up a spirited fight, employing all those underhand tactics for which they are universally despised. Heads and hands were sliced from bodies, horses bommy-knockered to the ground. General Albert leapt from his mount and hacked away with vigour. Gentlemen riders cried, 'Huzzah!' at the pirates.

Pirates 'arrrhed' and 'arr-harrhed' in reply.

The hacking was horrid and the hewing hideous.

And as the second movement of Beethoven's Ninth came to a triumphal conclusion, the final combatant sank to the ground. And no one moved upon the Mall, for everyone lay dead.

55

arwin marched from the concert hall, then loped along the gallery beyond. Darwin was a rather angry ape. He did not want to be out here checking for broken windowpanes. Was there not some caretaker to deal with that kind of business? He wanted to be at the concert listening to the wonderful music.

The Hall of British Industry and All Things Empire was dimly lit and Darwin felt suddenly most vulnerable. He crept past Mr Rutherford's time-ship, which set the hairs a-rising on the back of his little neck, and slunk past the automated elephant.

Behind him the dramatic beginning to the third movement struck up. Ahead there was a curious silence. Darwin cocked his head upon one side. Electric street lamps cast light in from the Mall, but it had an unearthly red hue to it. A nasty smell came to the simian's sensitive nose. It was the smell of human blood. Darwin's eyes grew wide.

Beyond was the entrance to the Hall of Venus. The air was growing colder as the monkey butler moved upon his way.

Then a voice called, 'Darwin,' and the monkey butler all but soiled his trousers.

'Darwin – here.' The voice was that of an angel.

'Leah?' said Darwin. 'Leah, is that you?'

The Venusian lady stepped from the shadows. 'Come to me, Darwin,' she called, and she held out her hand to the ape.

'London, 'ere we come,' said Princess Pamela. 'Mister Mate, where art thou?'

'I'm here, ma'am. Ah-harr-harr-harr.' Mister Mate flourished his cutlass. Princess Pamela clipped him round the ear.

'Take us down!' she said to him. 'Land me palace *there*.'

'*There*, ma'am?' Mister Mate pointed with his cutlass. 'But there's something already there. We could land in the park.'

'*There!*' the princess said with such fierceness that it would even have put the wind up General Albert Trubshaw, now deceased. '*There!*' she shouted, very loudly. 'Land it right there on top of Buckingham Palace!'

Darwin and Leah looked out from the palace of glass. Looked out towards the Mall and viewed the carnage that lay beyond the glazed walls of the Grand Exposition. The broken bodies of horses and horsemen, charred and twisted corpses, too, and all, it very much appeared, afloat in a sea of blood. It was truly a vision of Hell right there in the heart of London.

Darwin turned his face away and Leah held him close. 'You must aid me, Darwin,' said she. 'Great evil is amongst us and if it is not destroyed, all will be lost. My people will cleanse this planet of all upon it.'

Darwin looked up at the beautiful creature. 'I am only a monkey,' he said. 'What can a monkey do?'

'*Do it!*' shouted Princess Pamela. 'Do it *now*, Mister Mate!'

Mister Mate swung the steering wheel and then released the handbrake.

> *And the dragon was wrath with*
> *the woman and went to make*
> *war with the remnant of her seed.*
> Revelation 12:17

The flying palace passed over the halls of the Grand Exposition, swung past Mr Churchill's airship and, as that man looked helplessly on, settled down amidst sickening crunches right upon Buckingham Palace.

The walls of Queen Victoria's London abode buckled outwards and windows exploded as priceless artworks and artefacts within were crushed into flattened ruination. Servants sipping cocoa in the pantry fled as the stuccoed ceilings fell. The throne-room buckled and the throne itself became splintered fragments of gold. The turquoise and silver frescoes depicting supposedly mythical tales, which few found even vaguely humorous, were mangled into oblivion. And like some bloated mother hen settling onto its nest, Princess Pamela's palace came to rest upon the soil of Albion.

As sole surviving minion, Mister Mate offered up three cheers for the Lady Beast.

Princess Pamela smiled upon him. 'Now, lass,' she said to Lavinia Dharkstorrm, 'what say thou and I take a stroll t' me throne.'

One might naturally have assumed that the mangling of Buckingham Palace would certainly have been heard within the concert hall. But if one had naturally assumed it, one would have been *most* wrong.

Toscanini conducted the lyrical third movement, with its subtle variations of rhythm and melody, as if his baton touched the precious skin of the one he loved. Or, perhaps more prosaically, stroked the inner thigh of a lady who played the viola.

The crowd, enraptured as ever, hung upon every note.

Princess Pamela hung Mister Mate upon a hook in her pantry. 'Changed me mind about thee bein' Prime Minister,' she said. 'Lavinia,' she called, 'art thou ready, lass?'

Lavinia Dharkstorrm was loading the four reliquaries into her oversized reticule. Their importance upon this night had not been forgotten by *her*, for she alone knew what had to be done with them. They must stand in an unhallowed place as the planets drew into alignment, and she must perform the blasphemous ceremony that would usher the Lady Beast to power as the new millennium dawned. You had to attend to the *details* if you wanted the *all* to occur. And Lavinia Dharkstorrm wanted the *all* to occur.

She hefted the reticule over her shoulder. 'I am ready,' she called.

Cameron Bell did not look very ready. He studied his pocket watch once, then twice, and then again and again.

The grand main entrance to the princess's palace had been barred to Cameron Bell upon Mars, where he had entered by the door reserved for tradesmen. A splendid drawbridge now dropped before the grand main entrance. A slightly more splendid portcullis arose. And splendid to the highest degrees were the doors that swung within to reveal the Lady Beast and the witch named Lavinia Dharkstorrm.

Princess Pamela sniffed at the air. 'I love the smell of Man blood in the evening,' she said. 'Smells like victory, wouldst thou not agree?'

Lavinia Dharkstorrm nodded her head and gazed at the world beyond.

'All nicely pink, don't you think, lass?' said the princess.

Pink it was, the world without. The lamp posts and the trees all pinkly stained, the burned and battered bodies, the carriages, the melted tanks, the fallen horses, all.

They strolled towards the gates of Buckingham Palace.

The princess said, 'I think I'll 'ave these painted pink.'

Within the concert hall, the third movement entered its final variation, interrupted by those episodes where loud fanfares for full orchestra are answered by octaves played by the first violins.

Cameron Bell's head bobbed up and down but his eyes remained upon his pocket watch.

At the gates of Buckingham Palace, Princess Pamela paused.

'Now is my time,' she said.

Cameron's eyes were focused on his pocket watch. The great detective appeared to be enchanted by the time.

However.

Had someone peeped over his shoulder, they might just have seen that the face of Mr Bell's pocket watch displayed neither numbers nor hands. Rather there was only a mirror where the face should be. A mirror that reflected a certain image.

Through other mirrors cunningly set out someways

above, Mr Bell could clearly see the palace of Princess Pamela and the Lady Beast herself in the company of her witchly associate as they paused before the gates of old Buck House.

Cameron Bell now whispered to himself, 'I know it is not a new trick,' he whispered, 'and there are some who might well criticise me on the grounds of unoriginality, but then—' And he drew from his pocket that slim brass contrivance, extended its aerial parts and positioned his thumb upon the button marked FIRE. 'I *do* like a really big bang.'

And he pressed down hard on the button.

The sentry boxes to either side of Buckingham Palace's gates had been loaded well with dynamite. Mr Bell had perhaps been overgenerous and dynamite *was* expensive. But. If a job is worth doing, it really, truly *is* worth doing *well*.

The twin explosions lit up much of the sky and rattled many a pane of glass in the halls of the Grand Exposition. Concert-goers felt their seats shifting under them and Toscanini wobbled on his rostrum. But the great conductor did not miss a single beat and the orchestra continued with its magic.

A great deal of debris rained down on the Jovian food hall.

Though thankfully little fell into the stew.

Tongues of fire barrelled upwards in a suitably apocalyptic fashion. Turrets toppled from Princess Pamela's palace.

Within the concert hall, Cameron Bell had his fingers very firmly crossed. His mirrored watch face caught the reflections of flames and of smoke and of rolling dust and debris.

★

'That was probably Mr Bell,' said Darwin. 'He really loves to blow things up whenever he gets the chance.'

He and Leah peeped towards the chaos, but numerous street lamps no longer cast light and a terrible darkness shrouded the end of the Mall.

Leah gazed into the darkness, her long fingers weaving patterns in the air. Street lights closer at hand now dimmed to nothing. Darkness stalked its way along the Mall. And this no ordinary darkness of night. This was almost a liquid thing. It flowed forwards, engulfing the corpses and wreckage, smothering all that lay before it.

'Away from here,' cried Leah. 'Back into the hall.'

In the concert hall, Cameron Bell adjusted his pocket watch. All was utterly black upon its mirrored face.

'The explosion must have shifted one of the mirrors,' he whispered. 'But it was a fine explosion nonetheless.' And he prepared to tuck away the watch.

But then he caught a glint of movement, a shimmer held within the mirror's glass. Cameron Bell's mouth opened and his eyes grew terribly wide. For from the watch the face of Lavinia Dharkstorrm glared at him with hatred.

Lavinia Dharkstorrm dusted down her gown of night-black silk. The Lady Beast did dustings at her cloak.

'That was loud,' said the princess. 'And also right hot.'

'And might have been deadly, too,' Miss Dharkstorrm said, 'had I not taken the precaution of protecting us with magic. One might criticise Mr Bell on the grounds of un-originality, methinks.'

Princess Pamela laughed. 'What d'ye think o' me dark-ness, chuck?' she asked.

'Very very black,' said Lavinia Dharkstorrm.

'So,' said the female Antichrist, 'no 'arm done. Shall we away t' ball, as t'were?'

Lavinia Dharkstorrm linked arms with her mistress.

'Away to the ball indeed,' said she as the two stepped into the darkness.

Toscanini flourished his baton once more and brought it down on the final note of the symphony's third movement.

Cameron Bell moved with unease and felt his thumbs a-pricking. Something evil was coming his way and he had used the last of his dynamite.

56

t was twenty-four minutes to midnight as
Arturo Toscanini raised his baton high and
plunged it into the strong variations that
would lead to the famous choral finale of
Beethoven's Ninth.

Cameron Bell slipped quietly away, as
indeed did certain other folk.

Lord Brentford was not amongst them,
however. He was conducting from his
seat. And he honestly gave little thought
at all as to what had become of Darwin.

Leah and the monkey butler stood in the vast and echoing
Venusian Hall.

'I don't know what to do,' said the ape. 'And I am
mightily afraid of magic.'

'When the time comes,' said Leah, 'you will know what
to do.'

'You know what I'm goin' t' do wi' this, lass?' said Princess
Pamela as she and Lavinia approached the big front door of
the Grand Exposition.

'Paint it pink?' asked Lavinia Dharkstorrm.

'No, I'm goin' t' knock it down. It ruins me view to me square.'

'Trafalgar Square?' asked Lavinia Dharkstorrm.

'We'll change t' name,' said the princess. ''Ow's about Dharkstorrm Square? Though with a statue of me on t' column in middle.'

'Naturally,' said the witch.

'Got reliquaries with thee?'

Lavinia Dharkstorrm pointed to the bag upon her shoulder. 'I must perform the ceremony on unhallowed ground to bring you to your powers at the precise moment of midnight. We will hold this ceremony in the atrium. Those who might seek to interrupt, I will destroy without mercy.'

'Sound stuff,' said Princess Pamela. 'Then I shalt truly become Madam Glory. Let's go in and make right nuisances of ourselves.'

And through the door went the horrible twosome and into the atrium.

The sounds of the Ninth's fourth movement swelled through the entrance hall. To the centre the fountain still danced with champagne. Beyond and flanking the entrance to the auditorium, two sweeping flights of stairs led up to a balcony before the galleried seats and the door to the royal box.

Princess Pamela rooted her finger into her ear and said, 'What is that 'orrible music playing there?'

'I believe it is Beethoven's Ninth,' said Lavinia Dharkstorrm.

'Remind me t' ban it once I gets t' throne.'

'That,' came a voice from on high, 'is something you will never do.'

Princess Pamela raised her eyes. 'Do I hear a little baldy man?' she asked.

Lavinia Dharkstorrm rubbed her palms together. 'Your time has come, Mr Bell,' said she. 'Step into sight, if you will.'

A voice behind her said, 'That would not be wise.'

Princess Pamela laughed most merrily. 'I think, Lavinia lass, little baldy man 'as been takin' lessons in t' art o' ventriloquism.'

Mr Bell's head popped up from behind the fountain.

And then ducked down again.

'There.' The princess pointed.

Mr Bell waved from the balcony.

And then was gone.

'No, there!'

Mr Bell said, 'Hello,' right behind them.

Princess Pamela turned to catch a fleeting glimpse of Cameron Bell.

'I truly tire of this,' she said. 'Blast damn place with fire, Lavinia, please.'

Lavinia Dharkstorrm raised her hands. Invoked the terrible forces.

Cameron Bell peeped out from under a staircase.

'Set to it, lass!' demanded Princess Pamela. 'Don't 'ave all night!'

Lavinia Dharkstorrm looked at her fingers, raised her arms once more and shouted words of terrible power.

A wisp of smoke rose up from her hands, stuttered and vanished away.

'And what of *this*?' cried the Lady Beast. 'What of this, Lavinia?'

'He has done something,' said the witch, and she sniffed at the air. 'He has—' A scent of incense reached her nostrils. 'He has had this hall blessed – we stand upon hallowed ground.'

Princess Pamela jumped most nimbly for a lady of her ample proportions. 'Well, *de-*'allow it quickly!' she shouted at the witch. 'Time marches on!'

'I cannot,' cried Lavinia. 'We should *not* have entered here.'

'And thou shouldst have known!' cried the princess. 'Thee with thy powers of seein' t' future.'

'He has magic of his own!' Lavinia's eyes glowed purple. 'He is here and there and there, too. He has employed the Glamour.'

'Will you please just kill 'im?' bawled Princess Pamela.

Cameron Bell stepped out on the balcony. He flourished his rather large ray gun. He pointed it down at the ladies.

'How dare ye point yer oversized weapon at *me*,' said Princess Pamela. 'Twist this dog turd's 'ead upon 'is shoulders, Lavinia.'

Lavinia Dharkstorrm wore a helpless expression. 'My magic cannot flourish here,' she said.

'However,' said Cameron Bell, 'I can vouch for the efficiency of my oversized weapon. Ladies, I regret that I have no other option but to shoot the pair of you dead.'

'No, please,' Lavinia Dharkstorrm pleaded, adopting the voice of a helpless little girl. 'I beg you, kind sir – do not murther a poor defenceless female.'

Cameron Bell shook his baldy head. 'You must die,' said he.

'I can repent,' said Princess Pamela, adopting the voice of a helpless little boy. 'I might join t' Salvation Army and 'elp save fallen women.'

Cameron Bell took aim.

'No, please,' wailed Lavinia Dharkstorrm, in a manner most sincere.

Cameron Bell once more shook his head, then squeezed upon the trigger.

Or *would have done* . . . had the gun not suddenly been torn from his grip. Firm hands fell upon Cameron Bell, casting him aside.

A figure loomed on the balcony.

A most dramatic figure.

'No one kills my sister but me,' came the voice of Lady Raygun.

Cameron Bell did flounderings on the floor.

'Sister!' cried the lady in the black rubber headpiece. 'Sister, it is time for you to die.'

'Sister, dearest sister,' crooned Lavinia Dharkstorrm. 'Let bygones be bygones. My magic can set you to rights.'

'Only *your death* can set *me* to rights,' said Lady Raygun.

Lavinia Dharkstorrm shook her head and rummaged deeply within her reticule. 'I have a present in here for you,' she said.

'And *I* have one for *you*.' Lady Raygun now flourished *her* weapon. It was a ray gun of a respectable size. But nothing on the scale of Cameron Bell's.

She raised it high and said, 'And so you die.'

But Lavinia Dharkstorrm reached a trigger first and a bolt of raw red energy tore from within her reticule, crossed the atrium at something approaching the speed of light and struck Lady Raygun full force in the brass corsetry. The lady fell backwards from the blast. Lavinia Dharkstorrm fled.

She fled in the company of Princess Pamela into the Hall of British Industry.

'I'm not one for runnin', chuck,' puffed the pinky princess. 'And I 'ave an appointment with me sister.'

Lavinia Dharkstorrm urged her mistress onwards. 'We

must seek an unhallowed area to perform the ceremony,' she cried. 'Faster, mistress, faster.'

Within the atrium, Lady Raygun helped Cameron Bell to his feet. 'I am sorry,' she said, 'but I must do it my way.'

'Fair lady,' said Cameron Bell, fearfully aware that his months of planning would certainly now come to nothing. 'I regret that your headstrong ways may be the death of us all.'

'Not while breath remains to me.'

Lady Raygun mounted the parapet of the balcony then flung herself into the air. The curious membrane swirled around her, bearing her aloft. She swept through the doorway in pursuit of her sister.

Cameron Bell picked up his oversized weapon and sighed. 'My plans have now come all apart,' said he.

'Mr Bell,' came a voice. 'Mr Bell, if you please.'

Cameron Bell glanced down to the fountain.

Where stood Cameron Bell!

'Ah, Jonny,' said Cameron Bell. 'Or is it Neville?'

'I'm Neville,' said another Cameron Bell, stepping out from under the stairs.

'And we are quitting,' said Jonny. 'You told us this was a birthday surprise for your mother.'

Cameron Bell made a pained expression. He had indeed said some such thing.

'You also said it would be a harmless practical joke,' said Neville.

Norman, another Mr Bell, said, 'You didn't say anything about women with ray guns.'

The heads of various Cameron Bells nodded up and down.

'I really do need your help now more than ever,' said the detective. 'It really is *very* important. I will double your wages, if needs be.'

'No,' said Jonny, and he shook his baldy head. 'As founder member of both the Charles Dickens Appreciation Society and the Mr Pickwick Look-Alikesters, I wish to inform you that we have a strict policy regarding payment. You can expect our invoice in the post.'

Cameron Bell looked most downcast, for most downcast was he.

'But perhaps you might take some of these.' Jonny now marched up the staircase and pushed a bundle of cards into Cameron's hand. 'We do themed weddings in the gambling city on Jupiter,' he said. 'So if any of your friends might feel inclined to be married by Mr Pickwick—'

'Please leave now,' said Cameron Bell. 'Or I will shoot you dead.'

'Shoot someone dead,' puffed the princess. 'I can't be 'avin' with all this lark. Find anybody and shoot 'im.'

Lavinia Dharkstorrm ran on ahead, rushed through the doorway and into the Hall of Venus.

And here she became no longer Lavinia Dharkstorrm.

She became a panther, springing forward, lips drawn back, claws outstretched, terrible teeth a-gleam.

Princess Pamela reached the doorway and leaned upon the doorpost, wheezing fearfully.

'Ah,' said she, between such fearful wheezings, 'we 'ave reached t' safety of unhallowed ground once more.'

Lavinia became Lavinia again.

She lowered the reticule to the floor and removed the reliquaries. 'We will perform the ceremony here,' she said. 'Once done, and on the hour of midnight, you can do as you please to that sister of yours.'

'And what of thee and thy sister, my petal?'

'On unhallowed ground, she is mine to control.'

' ''Ope thou art right.' Princess Pamela pointed. 'She took thy ear'ole off last time, lass.' Princess Pamela tittered.

'Perhaps, if required, you might offer some assistance,' Lavinia Dharkstorrm said.

The Lady Beast turned up her palms. 'Behold t' darkness lyin' beyond,' she said, 'and don't forget the rain o' frogs and pink snow that 'ad 'em all covered in t' boils.'

Lavinia Dharkstorrm sighed. 'But you have no magic at all that you can contribute here?'

'Thy job for t' present.' Princess Pamela had now caught her breath. 'Thou dost not buy a dog then bark thyself, or so the sayin' goes.'

The reliquaries stood upon the inlaid marble floor. Lavinia Dharkstorrm raised her arms to the heavens.

In space the planets wheeled towards alignment.

And high above Earth the Venusian armada received telepathic orders to go to red alert.

The clock ticked on towards the midnight hour.

Toscanini wielded his baton.

> *Freude, schöner Götterfunken,*
> *Tochter aus Elysium!*

sang the choir. Which was to say:

> *Joy, beautiful spark of the Gods,*
> *Daughter of Elysium!*

Within the Venusian Hall, Lavinia Dharkstorrm called out the barbarous names. Shrieked the words of blasphemy that would herald in the time of the Lady Beast.

And of the four, of the Air and
of the Fire and of the Earth
and of the Water, that they
should be brought together into
an unhallowed place, so shall
the Lord God know that his
people have fallen from his
Grace and he be done with them.

The Book of Sayito

A darkness of Death itself cloaked all without.

A chill wind blew through the ragged holes in the great hall's wounded sides.

Lavinia Dharkstorrm screamed the spell of terrible power.

And things looked rather grim for planet Earth.

57

hunder rolled across the sky. Lightning tore the heavens into shreds.

Within the concert hall, the Ninth was growing steadily towards its climax.

Ihr stürzt nieder, Millionen?
Ahnest du den Schöpfer, Welt?

You bow down, millions?
Can you sense the Creator, world?

Within the Venusian Hall the darkness from without was seeping in across the floor, spreading like an oily flood.

Lavinia's voice echoed, shrill, inhuman, atavistic.

Queer vibrations buzzed and battered at the walls of glass.

Princess Pamela wrung her hands together.

Lavinia Dharkstorrm howled and howled and howled.

And then the great arched roof above buckled inwards, twisted, shattered and fell. Glass cascaded to the floor, bursting with explosive force.

Lavinia Dharkstorrm shielded her face as down with the maelstrom of glass came Lady Raygun.

She grabbed the witch by her raven hair and hurled her from her feet.

'Too late!' cried Lavinia Dharkstorrm. 'The spell is done. The wheels are in motion. Nothing now can stop it.'

'But I can kill *you*, sister dear.' Lady Raygun drew her weapon, aimed it at her sister.

Princess Pamela knocked it from her hand. 'Wilt thou please kill this bl★★dy woman!' she shouted.

'With the greatest pleasure, Madam Glory.'

Rain lashed in through the broken roof. Darkness crept across the floor, far darker than the shadows left by lightning.

Lavinia Dharkstorrm shifted shape, becoming once more a panther.

She sprang towards her sister, but her sister ducked aside.

The panther's claws raised sparks upon the marble floor. Its tail whipped and its growl, deep-throated, was the very sound of Death itself.

Once more it leapt. Lady Raygun snatched up one of the reliquaries and smashed it into the panther's head. The creature lashed out with a claw, tearing flesh from her sister's left shoulder.

Lady Raygun sprang into the air, the curious membrane lifting her beyond the reach of the panther's slashing talons.

The panther prowled beneath, became an eagle, took to flight.

Princess Pamela knotted her fists and called for the witch to kill.

The eagle swelled, became as some terrible dragon.

'Ee-oop,' went Princess Pamela, ' 'appen me powers are arrivin'.'

> *And there was war in Heaven*
> *And the angel did give battle*
> *with the dragon.*
>
> The Book of Sayito

The dragon's claws closed about Lady Raygun. Impregnable this lady might be to bullets, but not so to magic.

'So die, sister!' shrieked the dragon. 'All is lost for you.'

Its claws crushed harder and harder, squeezing life from the lady in the armoured corset, pressing in upon her heart, crushing at her bones.

Lady Raygun's eyes saw nothing but blackness. Darkness wrapped about her as a shroud . . .

And then the dragon squawked. It cried and squawked and fell. Lady Raygun crashed to the floor, rolled over and lay still. The dragon, no longer a dragon, squawked as a chicken should.

'And what of *this*?' howled Princess Pamela.

Leah the Venusian stepped from shadows, Darwin creeping fearfully behind her.

'Who art *thou*?' asked Princess Pamela, very much appalled.

'I am your destroyer,' said Leah. 'You would bring this world to ruination. This I cannot allow.'

'Thou art comely,' said the princess. 'Side with me, thou pretty thing. When all t' world is mine, I'll 'ave thee for my sweetest concubine.'

Leah shuddered somewhat at the thought. And shuddered too for the chill that was growing in the great hall. As the storm raged above, icy rain fell and evil darkness closed from every corner. Leah snatched up the chicken and swiftly wrung its neck.

'*What?*' The princess stared in horror. 'Thou hast killed my acolyte?'

'And so too you must die.' Leah raised her wonderful fingers, weaving magic from them into the troubled air. White light spread from her fingertips, became a dazzling radiant beam that struck out at Princess Pamela.

But the Lady Beast in pink just shook her head. 'No, no, no,' said she, a-waggling a fleshy finger. Then, opening very wide her mouth, she swallowed up the light. 'Only moments now,' said Princess Pamela, belching rather loudly. 'And all shalt kneel before me. But thee first, I'm thinkin'.'

And now a fierce pink light welled out about the princess, focused into a fiery ball and flew at Leah's face.

Leah raised a slender hand. The ball of fire became as ice and fell in dazzling splinters to the floor, mingled with the shattered glass and spreading darkness, faded and was gone.

Leah threw wide her arms. 'You are alone in your evil,' she cried. 'But we of Venus are the First Race and we have remained pure. Your magic is no match for ours.'

'Thou liest, chuck,' said Princess Pamela, pushing back her sleeves. 'Thy people skulk now in space, preparing to toss bombs down on t' Earth. But moments soon, when planets align, I shall cast a ring o' fire to swallow every one.'

Leah opened wide her mouth to sing a spell of death.

Princess Pamela shook her head. 'Thou canst not do it,' she said.

Leah's golden eyes shone from within. Rain lashed down upon her. Lightning etched her features onto blackness. Her fingertips plucked magic from the aether.

A look of doubt appeared upon the face of Princess Pamela.

Icy fingers clutched about her heart.

'Oh no, lass,' she croaked, and staggered backwards. 'Is this the power of thy people – that thou wouldst give up thine own life to destroy mine?'

'Gladly,' cried Leah. 'To save the people of this world and my own, too, from you.'

Princess Pamela made her fiercest face. 'If thou desirest death,' she shouted, 'then thou shalt 'ave it now!'

For the princess had seen what Leah had not. That a single flea had dropped from the chicken when Leah wrung its neck. A single flea that now swelled into the shape of Lavinia Dharkstorrm. The evil witch sprang forwards and took Leah by the throat.

Princess Pamela cocked her head on one side. 'Oh dear,' she crowed. 'Thou art lost for words, my pretty. Dear Lavinia, kill 'er, if thou wilt.'

Her left hand gripping Leah by the throat, Lavinia Dharkstorrm laughed, and as the storm thrashed now within the Hall of Venus, she raised her left hand to the sky and a weapon of death appeared in it, a magical athame.

'It takes powerful magic to kill one of powerful magic,' she cried. 'I put my force in this so you might die.'

Lightning flashed within the great hall, showered sparks from the tip of the magical blade, shone upon the women's faces.

Upon Princess Pamela, bloated, vile, the twin of the noble monarch, yet a monster in human form.

Upon the beautiful Leah, helpless to speak words of magic, golden-eyed as Athena, virgin Goddess sprung from mighty Zeus.

Upon Lavinia Dharkstorrm, evil incarnate, mauve of eye and black of heart. The worst and most deadly of women.

And now upon something more. Something terrific and awful to behold. A hand snatched the magical blade from Lavinia's grip. Another spun her about on her heels to stare at the face of Death.

The face of a demon glared upon the witch. A face of foul, malignant distortion. The eyes those of a basilisk, a lipless mouth displaying jagged sharpened teeth. Rain spattered, as of blood upon scaled flesh, ran down from the naked scalp, dropped from the pointed chin.

Lavinia Dharkstorrm gaped in horror at the monstrous face. And then the blade went in. Again and again it plunged into her heart. Again once more and again.

Lavinia Dharkstorrm's eyes became glazed. And perhaps for that fleeting moment some humanity returned to her.

'Sister,' she whispered. 'Dear sister, please forgive me.'

Lady Raygun cast the lifeless corpse aside. ''Tis done now,' said she, 'and done with a magical blade.'

She wiped this blade upon her leather-sectioned skirt and advanced upon the princess all in pink.

Lightning rent the heavens with its fury.

Rain gushed in.

A fierce wind blew.

'Of fire,' cried Lady Raygun, 'and of water and of air. And you shall know the earth.'

'And what knowest thou of *this*?' howled Princess Pamela.

'You crafted me a demon's face. But I know well my scriptures,' said the Mistress of Mystery, her terrible mouth curled in a hideous grin. 'You have spent your magic upon the Venusian. You have no more to hurl at me.'

'Too late.' And at that moment there was nothing to be heard. The sound of the storm ceased its awful cries. The raindrops appeared to hover in the frozen air. The darkness closed on all beneath and drew down from above.

Yet moving, somehow, with the slowest of motions. As if viewed through the slot of zoetrope, Lady Raygun threw herself forwards at the Lady Beast, struck her from her feet and flung her into the terrible darkness.

The Lady Beast rose up and swung a fist and knocked the lady down. And all about the great hall, the two figures wrestled, locked together in titanic conflict.

To the centre of this hall, the Sphere of Nothingness

glowed from within, as above the seconds closed towards midnight and the planets fell into alignment.

The Lady Beast snatched up one of the heavy posts that held the ropes shielding the Sphere of Nothingness. She raised it high above her head and brought it down with force on Lady Raygun.

The lady buckled beneath the monstrous blow. The Lady Beast stepped forwards and stood astride her. 'Now is *my* time!' she cried. She lifted high once more the heavy post. Prepared to bring it down a final time.

Lady Raygun looked up at the Lady Beast that loomed above her. The Lady Beast that would take Victoria's throne, lay waste to the people of the Empire and indeed kill the one she loved so dearly. Lavinia Dharkstorrm, the evil sister, was dead. Leah lay unconscious in the ever-rising darkness. Only she remained to slay the Lady Beast. And she, it appeared, would very shortly die.

The Lady Beast held high that heavy post. 'Mine, all mine!' she shouted.

Then—

'Get off me! Ouch!' she bellowed, swinging around and flailing at herself. Something was attached to the buttocks of the Lady Beast.

That something was Darwin the monkey.

The simian's teeth were well dug in to the flesh of a beastly buttock. The Lady Beast danced squawking to and fro.

And all, it appeared in this twilight moment of time, slowed down to almost nothing at all.

Lady Raygun arose as the Angel of Death. Her high boot-heels left the terrible darkness and the magical membrane bore her smoothly aloft. She swung in an acrobatic loop a foot, striking home in a jowl of the Lady Beast.

Princess Pamela, Madam Glory, Lady Beast and all toppled backwards.

Darwin loosened his teeth and skittered away.

And flailing at the frozen air, unable to maintain her balance, back she fell.

Backwards. Backwards.

Into the Sphere of Nothing whatever at all.

A flash of light.

A clash of cymbals.

> *Be embraced, millions!*
> *This kiss for the whole world!*
> *Brothers, above the starry canopy*
> *Must a loving Father dwell*

Arturo Toscanini brought down his baton to close the fourth movement. He mouthed a single word to his orchestra and chorus. The single word, 'Bravo.'

The audience erupted into cheers.

The thunder and the lightning ceased.

And all throughout the British Empire . . .

Church bells hailed the coming century.

58

he audience in the concert hall rose to a standing ovation.

The choir bowed, the orchestra bowed and Arturo Toscanini blew out kisses to the ladies.

'Wasn't that just the most wonderful thing?' called Ernest Rutherford, up on his feet, to the seated Violet Wond.

The lady in the veil said nothing at all.

'Are you all right, my dearest?' Ernest Rutherford touched her shoulder. The veil and clothes fell in upon themselves. For there was no one inside them.

'Now however did you do *that*?' wondered Ernest Rutherford.

But that was something he would never know.

Lady Raygun drew her rubber headpiece down across her terrible features. Darwin stroked the head of Leah. The Venusian opened her golden eyes and smiled upon the ape.

'Did you do what you had to do?' she asked.

Darwin nodded. 'I did.'

Leah clutched his hand and said, 'And now all will be well.'

Two men stood in the doorway that separated the Hall of British Industry from the Venusian Hall. One was a controversial cleric. The other looked very much like Mr Pickwick.

The Pickwickian fellow lit up a fine cigar.

'You could have helped,' said Cardinal Cox. For it indeed was he.

'You, too,' said Cameron Bell, exhaling smoke. 'You were all prepared to speak the words of the exorcism.'

'True,' agreed the cardinal. 'But you are the one with the dirty great ray gun.'

Cameron Bell shouldered the dirty great ray gun. 'And I would have used it,' said he. 'Perhaps. If it had been absolutely necessary. But if there is one thing that this long and troubled case has taught me, it is not to get involved with wilful women, if you can possibly avoid it.'

Cardinal Cox nodded his head.

'Two women started it all,' said Cameron Bell, 'and another two women finished it.'

'Two ladies,' agreed the cardinal. 'And there was some monkey involvement.'

'Ah, yes,' said Mr Bell. 'Darwin,' he called out to the ape. 'Are you all right there, my old ex-partner?'

Darwin raised a thumb to the detective. 'Hello, Mr Bell,' he said. 'And thank you so much for not blowing all of us up.'

'We are going for some champagne,' said Cameron Bell. 'Would you care to join us?'

'And the ladies?' Darwin asked.

'Indeed,' said Cameron Bell. 'Those two ladies certainly deserve the best champagne.'

There were of course many questions that had to be answered regarding what precisely had actually occurred in London on New Year's Eve, and at times the answers appeared to fall a little short of the mark. The newspapers came to a consensus, however, which held to the opinion that the hero of the day was Mr Winston Churchill.

His selfless tactics had brought an end to the anarchists' reign of terror. For the anarchists, in the garb of pirates, all lay dead in the Mall.

The newspapers were also in agreement regarding the matter of the vast pink turreted castle which stood four-square upon ground once occupied by Buckingham Palace.

It was all the work of that fashionable fellow Señor David Voice, the London-tram-driver-turned-architect whose famous bagnio was well attended by members of the press.

The pink palace had been erected overnight as a gift from a grateful nation to their much-beloved Queen to celebrate the dawning of the twentieth century.

And when corpses were cleared and red snow washed away, the Grand Exposition, with its Venusian Hall temporarily closed for repair work, opened to the general public.

Mr Rutherford's time-ship proved a most popular exhibit, but soon had to be withdrawn from display.

It just prompted too many questions.

Chief amongst these was this. Why, folk wanted to know, if the British Empire now possessed a time machine, why did it not dispatch soldiers of the Queen in the company of modern back-engineered weaponry to destroy all the

Martians in eighteen eighty-five, *before* they attacked this world?

And many other such questions.

Many involving the anarchists.

There were no anarchists present upon February the fourteenth when Lord Brentford married Leah the Venusian.

The wedding did not occur in secret at a gambling city upon Jupiter, but was a state occasion in the very heart of London. Queen Victoria attended. So too did many of the senior ecclesiastics of Venus.

Their telepathic powers had enabled them to know the part Leah had played in the destruction of the Lady Beast, and as she had every intention of marrying Lord Brentford anyway, no matter what they thought, they deemed it diplomatically best to give the wedding their blessing.

Darwin proudly fulfilled his role as best monkey-man, even making a speech at the reception, which greatly amused Queen Victoria.

Lord and Lady Brentford were flown to Jupiter at Her Majesty's expense to enjoy a week's honeymoon at the gambling city.

And one month later, in the company of others, they gathered at the Victoria Palace Theatre. They did not come to enjoy the pleasures of the music hall, but to say their fond farewells.

To Darwin and Cameron Bell.

Mr Bell looked very chipper and was particularly well dressed. He had recently received great accolades and even greater financial remuneration for restoring the stolen reliquaries to their rightful owners. Princess Pamela's he had hurled into the sea, that the four could never be reunited.

He had declined, however, the entreaties from the newly knighted Chief Inspector Case to aid him in solving the Crime of the New Century. The one involving the three million pounds' worth of gold looted mysteriously from the Bank of England and replaced with a pile of old junk.

He said his farewells to Chief Inspector Case and shook the policeman by the hand. He knew that their paths would never cross again.

Ernest Rutherford's time-ship, the *Marie Lloyd*, stood in the auditorium of the theatre, its entrance port open, gubbinry glowing within.

It was late in the evening now and the Large Hadron Collider that passed for the Circle Line was in full operation doing what it did and slowing time.

Mr Rutherford stood before the time-ship with the heavily veiled Miss Violet Wond.

Darwin was dressed in the uniform of Space Admiral of the Fleet.

Ernest Rutherford approached the ape of time. He handed Darwin the operating manual and the letter addressed to Mr Rutherford that Darwin would deliver to the chemist nine months into the past. 'You know what has to be done,' he said to Darwin.

'I do,' said Darwin, sadly. 'I must travel back in time and deliver this letter to Mr Bell at Lord Brentford's soirée. And on that night, Lord Brentford will shoot me dead.'

'Very sorry about that,' said his lordship. 'Bit of a misunderstanding. Thought you were an anarchist, or a Martian suicide pilot.'

Darwin shook his lordship's hand. 'It was not your fault,' said he.

Lord Brentford wiped away a manly tear. 'A few things I wanted to say to you, my boy,' said he. 'I have thanked you many times for what you achieved regarding the Grand Exposition. Without you it could not have gone ahead.'

'I simply did what I could do,' said Darwin. 'It felt like the right thing, and if it is the right thing, I think you should do it if you can. I have wondered hard about Man and Monkey, about justice, about the rich and poor, but I have drawn no conclusions. I really do not know what it is all about. Or what, indeed, any of it means.'

'Let me tell you something,' said Lord Brentford. 'Something that my father told to me. Everyone wonders at times, you see, about what it all means. Whether there *is* a meaning to life. My father thought he had an answer, and it was this. If, when finally you leave this world behind, you can do so knowing that you did your best to make it just a little better than it was when you entered it, then your life has had a meaning.'

'And *that* is the meaning of life?' said Darwin.

'I think so,' said Lord Brentford. 'Not all of us can be big famous people with the potential to do great good. But even the most humble amongst us can help make the world a little bit better, rather than a little bit worse.'

'I shall remember that,' said Darwin. 'Although for something of a brief period, I believe. But I will bear it in mind when my end comes. I hope I have made this world a slightly better place by being here.'

'You have, my boy, you have.' Lord Brentford now gave Darwin a very manly hug.

'And you have to come with me, Mr Bell,' said Darwin, 'at least for part of the journey. I know you got to meet your future self upon Mars.'

'I did indeed,' said Cameron Bell, 'and the encounter set me to thinking. Recall, if you will, that the you that crashed the time-ship into the Bananary was a *very old* you.'

'A *very old* me,' said Darwin.

'Well,' said Mr Bell, 'the me I met upon Mars was rather old, too. Looked very much the same, of course – portly men with baldy heads appear to age rather well.'

'So how old were you?' asked Darwin.

'Eighty-seven,' said Cameron Bell. 'You see, my little partner, it would appear that you and I will go on to have many adventures aboard the *Marie Lloyd* and live to be very old before you meet your fated end. There are many wonderful things and times we might visit. You missed the end of the Ninth Symphony. I think we should travel back and see Beethoven himself conduct it. What do you say to this?'

'Ah,' said Darwin. 'How absolutely splendid.'

'Just one thing,' said Mr Rutherford. 'Before the two of you depart. If you will pardon us.'

He led Violet Wond into the time-ship and the entrance port closed upon them.

There came from within a whirling and grinding of engines. The time-ship flickered – then vanished – then all of an instant returned.

The port swung down and Mr Rutherford stepped from the time-ship. He now wore a very dashing silver suit with flaring shoulders and trouser bottoms and a pair of shoes with platform soles.

Upon his arm was a lady in a sparkling silver gown that hugged her slender body. A lady with a beautiful radiant face. She had grey-green eyes and the sweetest nose that might be imagined and her smile fairly lit up the great auditorium.

'I can recommend the future,' said Mr Rutherford.

Miss Violet Wond leaned forward and kissed Darwin on the cheek.

And as it should be, at the end of a great performance, there was not a dry eye in the house.

Cameron Bell, the great detective, and Darwin the educated ape bade their farewells and walked into the time-ship hand in hand.

The port swung shut.
The engines whirled
And then the
ship was

GONE

EPILOGUE

Lop Lop, God of all the Birds,
looked down from the Heavens
and spoke with the Great Mother Hen

'I just do not know what to make of
Mankind,' said Lop Lop. 'Sometimes I
find it hard to believe that *they* are
descended *from us.*'

The Great Mother Hen snuggled down
upon her vast galactic nest.
'I rather liked the monkey, though,'
said she.

AUTHOR'S AFTERWORD

During the opening years of the Second World War, my father, serving as a fireman, was stationed in Lily Road, Fulham. As someone who had always loved the circus, this gave him many opportunities to visit the one permanently showing at Olympia.

There were many sideshows there and my father became friendly with several folk who displayed themselves before the public. He recalled a giant who could pass a copper penny through the ring he wore on his little finger and an albino from the Congo with white hair twenty-four inches in length. One sideshow particularly fascinated him. It was only there for a week, but he went to see it several times. It featured a talking monkey that could answer questions put to it by the crowd. My father said his first thoughts were that this was some kind of ventriloquist act. But after several viewings he became utterly convinced that the monkey could actually reason and speak. He could not recall the showman's name, only that he bore an uncanny resemblance to Mr Pickwick. He remembered the monkey's name, however, as it made him smile to think of it. The monkey's name was Darwin and I'm very glad he made my father smile.

THE END